Cameo Courtships

Published by Barbour Books, an imprint of Barbour Publishing, Inc., 1810 Barbour Drive, Uhrichsville, Ohio 44683, www.barbourbooks.com

Our mission is to inspire the world with the life-changing message of the Bible.

Member of the
Evangelical Christian
Publishers Association

Printed in Canada.

Cameo Courtships

4 *Stories of Women Whose Lives Are*
Touched by a Legendary Gift

Susanne Dietze
Debra E. Marvin
Jennifer Uhlarik
Kathleen Y'Barbo

BARBOUR BOOKS
An Imprint of Barbour Publishing, Inc.

Prologue

by Susanne Dietze

DEDICATION

For Suzanne Wagner,
woman of prayer, dearest of friends.

ACKNOWLEDGMENTS

Thank you, Deb, Jen, and Kathleen for
your hard work, brainstorms, feedback,
and friendship. I'm grateful for you ladies!

Trust in the Lord with all thine heart;
and lean not unto thine own understanding.
In all thy ways acknowledge him,
and he shall direct thy paths.
PROVERBS 3:5–6

*D*on't touch anything, Letitia." Aunt Felicity's harsh whisper prickled like a coarse horsehair brush. "We don't yet know why Her Majesty summoned you here. If it was to scold you in person, you will worsen matters if she were to enter the room to see you touching her things."

Stifling a sigh, Letitia Newton released the edge of the drapery. Aunt Felicity meant well, wishing Letitia to make as fine an impression on Queen Victoria as possible. But Letitia was six and thirty, no child in need of a reprimand.

Even if a rebuke was what Aunt Felicity feared she would receive. Why else would Queen Victoria have summoned Letitia to Buckingham Palace with all haste, immediately after Letitia sent her a gift?

Letitia glimpsed in one of the gilt-framed mirrors on the pale blue papered walls, patting a wayward tendril of her dark hair and centering the simple but elegant gold pendant hanging about her throat. "Perhaps

7

she *liked* the gift, Aunt Felicity. After all, Newton Glassworks produces the finest flint glass in America. And the cameos Edgar encrusted in the vases—"

"Were presumptuous. Brash," Aunt Felicity interrupted. "Perhaps Her Majesty found it forward of your brother to place her and the prince consort's faces on flower jugs."

"I thought the *vases* honoring, and quite well done." Masterful, in fact. Her brother Edgar's ability to inscribe cameos on glass—on knobs, tumblers, and vases, as he'd done for Queen Victoria—had gained his glassworks a reputation for quality and beauty.

But not yet in Europe, which was why Letitia had come to England. Although she and Edgar had been born and still resided in the States, their father was English and had not forgotten his family, including his older sister, Aunt Felicity, who'd married a baron.

Though she was accustomed to associating with royalty, Aunt Felicity stood rooted on the scarlet rug of the 1844 Room in Buckingham Palace, her prominent chin trembling as if she feared for her own reputation, not just Letitia's.

Hoping to set her aunt at ease, Letitia smiled. "Thank you for accompanying me here. Your support means a great deal."

"I couldn't allow you to come unchaperoned, could I?"

No. Letitia was not married. She could not go anywhere without a chaperone. Certainly not to meet the Queen of England.

Behind her, the door latch clicked, and Letitia spun around. A servant held the door for a diminutive woman with dark hair and blue eyes. *The queen!* Aunt Felicity dropped into a deep curtsy, and Letitia followed suit, holding the full skirt of her best rose silk gown just so.

"Lady Stourbridge, how do you do."

Aunt Felicity rose. "How do you do, Your Majesty. May I present my niece, Miss Letitia Newton?"

"Miss Newton." The queen inclined her head. "Welcome to London."

"Thank you, Your Majesty. I am honored to be here."

It was true. Despite her English heritage and her aunt's marriage to

Lord Stourbridge, Letitia was not the sort of person who could ever expect an audience with Queen Victoria. She was the daughter of an artisan and businessman—a wealthy one, true—but an American.

The queen folded her hands at the waist of her pale blue gown. Pinned beneath her collarbone was a striking cameo: a woman's profile carved on an unusually deep blue agate—a rich color fit for a queen, surrounded by small pearls and set in gold. Her Majesty's blue eyes flashed. "You are wondering why we requested your presence."

"Yes, ma'am." A skitter of nerves traversed Letitia's spine. Was Aunt Felicity correct? Had she offended the queen?

"The vases you gave us on your brother's behalf. . .We have not seen anything quite like them." She paused so long Letitia thought her heart would explode. Then the queen smiled. "Convey our thanks to him for his beautiful gift."

Letitia couldn't restrain a relieved smile. "I shall, ma'am. Thank you."

"Cameos engraved into the glass, and with such accuracy," the queen continued. "How was such a thing accomplished?"

"A sulphide process, Your Majesty." Edgar was the only American proficient in cameo incrustation, and in Letitia's somewhat biased opinion, his work was finer than any in Europe. "My brother saw to the likenesses personally."

"He captured His Highness with exquisite detail." The queen's expression went soft at the mention of her beloved Prince Albert. "And I am so fond of cameos."

Letitia smiled as the queen's fingers brushed the cameo she wore. "I am delighted to hear it, ma'am."

Hopefully, since the queen was pleased with the gift, she would tell others, who would in turn seek out Newton Glassworks for their needs. The Newton name and craftsmanship would be known in Europe as well as America.

"Your brother will be pleased to see you when you return," the queen said. "He must be grateful for your assistance in his work."

"She is a maiden, so she has ample time at her disposal." Aunt Felicity cast the queen a conspiratorial look. "Her traversing hither and yon will cease once she weds, of course."

"You are betrothed? Many congratulations, Miss Newton." Queen Victoria smiled.

Letitia's stomach lurched. "No, ma'am. My aunt is hopeful, but I have not yet met the right gentleman."

"Ah." The queen nodded. "I understand."

At least someone did. Letitia had been considered "on the shelf" for more than ten years, but she'd declined the suits of several men for one reason or another. Her family thought her too selective, but she'd not yet met a gentleman who would be her best friend. One who cared for her and not just her dowry. One whose smile robbed her of breath.

The queen spun at the clacking of paws against the hardwood floor in the hall. A long-eared, coffee-brown dog trotted into the chamber on short legs. "Ah, Deckel."

Letitia clasped her hands in delight. "What a fine one he is. May I pet him?" Recalling too late Aunt Felicity's stern warning not to touch anything, Letitia bit her lip, but the queen's nod set her at ease.

"Deckel is a dear one," she said. "Six years we've had him."

His short hair was silky to Letitia's touch, and warm brown eyes gazed up at her while she stroked his squat, sturdy back. "I'm not familiar with his breed."

"Dachsund. He's excellent company, as this has been, ladies, but we are to leave for the Crystal Palace."

"Oh?" Letitia started to rise, but Deckel pawed her leg as if urging her to continue petting him. Adorable little thing!

"The official opening of the Great Exhibition is tomorrow, and— Deckel, down!"

Deckel's head bumped Letitia's chin, and his paw batted her chest. Not at all painful, but her head twisted back, and her torso did not move with it. Something tugged at her neck like a leash and then gave way. Deckel scampered back to the queen.

Letitia's necklace pooled on the red rug in a heap, the chain broken.

Deckel's paw must have caught on it.

"Your necklace, Miss Newton. I am sorry."

Regret panged in Letitia's stomach, but it would be well. "It may be repaired with ease, ma'am. 'Tis no matter." She gathered the necklace, rose, and smiled to prove the point.

"I disagree. You cannot go out without a bauble. Here." The queen reached to her collarbone. A tug, and then she held out the cameo in her tiny hand. "Take it."

A gift? "I could not."

"This cameo is accompanied by a story, Miss Newton. It has seen its wearers experience adventure, even love. I received it one week before my husband arrived to court me."

Letitia felt her brows rise to her bonnet brim. "A memento to treasure, then—"

"I have other mementos. Many. And when it was given to me, I was told that one never *owns* a cameo. One wears and enjoys it, but one is its custodian, preserving and protecting it for those who come after. The woman who gave it to me insisted she knew I was the one to receive it, and she urged me to pass it along when I had a similar feeling as to who the next recipient should be. I believe it is you, Miss Newton. Now do not argue, I pray, for we are already late."

"Thank you, ma'am." The words were inadequate, but her breathlessness seemed to convey all the gratitude the queen needed to hear.

She pressed the cameo into Letitia's hand. "Perhaps you too will find an adventure soon, or meet your husband, as I did when I received this."

Aunt Felicity stifled a snort, covering it as a cough. But there was no time to say another word, for the queen took her leave. Letitia's fingers trembled as she strode to the mirror with the cameo. 'Twas stunning, and exquisitely crafted. Now that she held it in hand, she could see a gold loop at the top, should she wish to wear it as a pendant on a chain.

But not today. Letitia pinned the cameo to her bodice. *I have met the Queen of England, and she gave me a cameo. Who would have imagined such a thing?*

"Ladies?" A servant ushered them out into the hallway.

Aunt Felicity's brows arched, a sure indication she had a great deal to comment on once they were alone. For the moment, however, there were too many others about, servants and courtiers and ladies-in-waiting. Muffled conversations grew louder as Letitia and her aunt approached the hall where they'd first entered the palace.

Several gentlemen lingered there clustered in small groups. One tall fellow with streaks of gray lightening his dark blond curls stood in their path. He bowed. "Ladies, how do you do?"

"How do you do, Mr. Hollingsworth?" Aunt Felicity's tone was bright. "Letitia, allow me to introduce you to Mr. Peter Hollingsworth, my neighbor's nephew. He is on the prime minister's staff. Mr. Hollingsworth, my niece, Miss Newton."

"A pleasure, Miss Newton." Blue eyes twinkling, Mr. Hollingsworth bent over her hand. His was the sort of bright and vibrant smile that made the sun seem weak in comparison.

For the first time in her thirty-six years, a gentleman's smile robbed Letitia of her breath.

Pinned Above Her Heart

by Susanne Dietze

❧ *Chapter 1* ❧

Pittsburgh, Pennsylvania
July 1851

*H*er green hem dusted in ash, Clara Newton stepped as close as she dared to the burned-out shell. "Thank God no one was inside."

"Don't go any farther, poppet." Papa's tone brooked no argument. "Just because there is still a roof on it doesn't mean the place is stable."

"I won't." The burned building *wasn't* safe—she knew that—but Clara had to see for herself. She needed every detail impressed on her brain for later on, when she had paper and ink.

A few remaining members of the fire brigade remained on the scene, sloshing pails of water onto smoking piles of debris or carrying crates of salvageable goods. Those crates seemed to be all that was left of Purl Textiles, the business situated just yards away from Papa's Newton Glassworks along the banks of the Monongahela River. The glassworks stood whole and proud, its sturdy brick walls undamaged by the arsonist's blaze.

Unlike Mr. Purl's building. But if the wind had shifted during the fire—

Clara's stomach knotted. The blaze could have overtaken her family's glassworks—their livelihood and heritage, and the source of employment for several craftsmen.

Upon learning the news of the fire over breakfast—arson, at that—Clara and her family had come to the scene at once. It had taken two carriages to bring them all here: Clara and her parents; her elder brother, Wallace; Aunt Letitia, Papa's younger sister, who lived with them; and Peter Hollingsworth, the affable fiancé Aunt Letitia brought home from England. They stood clustered together on the street gazing at the remnants of Purl's once-thriving business.

Clara returned to them, joining in their silence. They'd all been too shocked to say much. The fire was bad enough. Knowing it was arson was even worse.

But what unfolded before them now? It was beyond belief.

A constable and some well-dressed men gathered around the middle-aged, wild-haired Mr. Purl, not in support, but as if they expected him to flee.

"That's Sylvester Vanacore." Papa gestured at a well-built fellow, their newest neighbor. "I should've guessed he'd be here, along with other representatives of the mayor's policing committee."

Clara looked away. "I thought we'd be comforting Mr. Purl over his loss, not witnessing his arrest."

Mama shook her head. "I cannot believe an upstanding gentleman like Mr. Purl is engaged in suspect dealings."

"'Tis sad." Clara clutched her parasol.

"Perhaps it's a misunderstanding." Wallace, a man of average height like Papa, fiddled with his chestnut-brown mustache, a sure sign he was upset over the turn of events.

Papa's chortle was scoffing. "Doubtful, Son. Purl's up to his bushy eyebrows in whatever this is."

Wallace turned his head away, and a twinge twisted Clara's abdomen.

Whenever Papa disagreed with Wallace, it seemed to aggravate her brother like a poke to an old wound.

Her mouth opened, but what could she say that she hadn't already? Nothing she'd done or said came close to bridging the gap that had been growing between Wallace and the rest of the family for a few years now. She could try again to restore relations with her brother, and would, but it wouldn't be appropriate to air her grievances, as Mama would say, in front of others.

The constable gripped Mr. Purl's arm and hauled him to a waiting carriage.

Aunt Letitia turned toward her Mr. Hollingsworth. "America has not been boring for you, has it, Peter?"

"I am never bored when I'm with you," he said.

Despite the gravity of the scene, Clara couldn't help but smile. Aunt Letitia had found love. Would Clara? Perhaps someday, but it did not seem to be God's current plan.

Aunt Letitia caught Clara's smile and reached for her hand. The morning sun caught on her jewelry: her new blue cameo and the large sapphire engagement ring Aunt Letitia wore with pride.

Clara looked into her aunt's eyes. "This is not the start to the festive day we planned, is it, Auntie? I am sorry."

"Nonsense." Aunt Letitia squeezed her fingers. "This is important. We don't mind, do we, Peter?"

"On the contrary," he said, his crisp British accent cheerful. "I'm happy to roll up my sleeves and assist the volunteers with clean-up, if needed."

Papa chuckled. "What would the prime minister say?"

"I hope he'd lend a hand as well." Mr. Hollingsworth grinned.

Clara grinned back at him. "Oh, I like your fiancé, Aunt Letitia."

"I do too." She winked, and perhaps it was the effect of the lingering smoke, but Mr. Hollingsworth's cheeks pinked a touch.

"Generous as your offer is, Mr. Hollingsworth," Mama said with a smile, "I do not think there is anything we can do here today. I suppose we should return home to continue preparations for your engagement party tonight."

Clara fidgeted. She couldn't leave now, not that she wished to explain her reasons to her family.

"Let's go then." Wallace's shoulder lifted a trace to avoid brushing against Papa as he offered an arm to Mama. Aunt Letitia released Clara's hand to take Mr. Hollingsworth's arm.

"Not me." Papa backed up a step. "I wish to speak to Vanacore, find out what's going on."

This was Clara's chance. "I'll return in the second carriage with Papa."

"There's room for you with us." Mama frowned.

Papa offered an indulgent smile. "She won't be long, Anne. I'll have her home within the hour."

Clara nodded. That was plenty of time.

After waving farewell to her family, Clara peered up at Papa. Though she was short like Mama, she looked more like Papa than she did blond Mama, having inherited his dark brown hair and hazel eyes. She'd also received his direct nature. "I didn't wish to tell Mama, not yet, but I think this might be a good topic for my article. I'd like to go around back for a look. I promise I shall give the rubble wide berth."

"Oh, I suspected you had ulterior motives, but I thought you wanted to chat with Vanacore there. He's a handsome fellow, eh?"

She'd met their neighbor a few times, and he was fair of face and form, true, but he made her uncomfortable. He hadn't done anything untoward, but he seemed almost *too* amiable. Then again, he was running for political office, and he doubtless was affable with everyone.

She shook her head. "I prefer to focus on my article, Papa."

"What a resourceful poppet you are." His cheeks rounded with the sort of pride he seldom lavished on Wallace. "Shall I accompany you?"

"No, I'll be fine."

Leaving Papa, she strode around the building's footprint, lifting the hem of her green-plaid walking dress above grass still wet from the fire brigade's efforts. As she drew closer to the river, a gentle breeze stirred off the water, sending shivers down her spine.

Or perhaps the shivers had more to do with the fact that she stood mere feet from an empty space where the back wall of a building stood last night. This was the scene of a crime.

A *vacant* scene, she must remember, and the villain long gone. She was three and twenty, after all, no schoolroom miss to be set aquiver at the slightest occurrence.

She peered into the building.

From her position, she could not see much. But if she stepped closer—just a little?

"Darling, what are you doing?"

Clara jumped, hand to her chest, and probably yelped too, but her heart was pounding so loud in her ears she wasn't certain. "Auntie, I thought you'd left."

"And I thought you were staying behind to speak to Mr. Vanacore. He is an attractive one, with that golden hair. I thought you'd formed an attachment to him."

"What? Of course not," Clara sputtered.

"Well, he is speaking to your mother right now, if you wish to catch him."

"I don't."

"She's invited him to the party tonight."

"Auntie, remember the article I told you about? The assignment to find something newsworthy and unique?" Her hands made grand gestures. "The news of this fire will be everywhere by noon, but not everyone will know it was arson. We only know because it was Papa's night watchman who spied the culprit in the act and alerted the fire brigade. That gives me exclusive information, and if I am first to report it, the editor will have to take my story. But I must make haste."

Aunt Letitia's mouth formed a soft O. Then she sighed. "Do your parents know?"

"Papa does."

"Your father no doubt thinks it marvelous. He admires initiative."

Which was probably why Papa got so irritated with Wallace, who had yet to show much interest in handling the family glassworks accounts. Or anything else, for that matter.

"I'll tell Mama. Later." Just in case the notion of her daughter traipsing around a burned building gave her apoplexy. "I must make haste. You of all people should understand how much I need this. You have an occupation."

"My single state allowed me to travel and represent the glassworks, true." Aunt Letitia's unfocused gaze looked out over the river, as if she were seeing things inside rather than out. "But things will change now that I am to wed."

Ah, that someday a fine gentleman would look at Clara the way Peter Hollingsworth looked at Aunt Letitia. Like he appreciated her mind as much as her face. . .or her dowry.

But thus far the prospect of love had eluded Clara. She was like the steamships down on the river, paddling alone toward an unknown destination—but it was a path of God's choosing, and Clara had every confidence He'd see her to the end of it.

She straightened her shoulders. "Your calling has changed, Auntie. But mine is the same as it was six months ago. I believe God wishes me to write. This—here, investigating the ruins for evidence of arson—is what I must do to succeed."

Aunt Letitia shook her head, grinning. "Then go ahead and investigate, but do be careful."

Clara threw her arms around her aunt for a brief embrace. "Thank you."

"Before I go, I have something for you." She unpinned her cameo from its spot on her lapel. "Here."

"What are you doing?"

"Aren't cameos your favorites?"

"Always." Papa first began encrusting cameos into some of his glass pieces, like the vases he crafted for Queen Victoria, because of Clara's preference for them.

"Then take it."

Take? As in *keep*? Clara's hands remained at her sides. "I cannot accept this. I know quite well who gave it to you."

"Her Majesty made it clear that I was to give it away. She said, 'One never owns a cameo. Other jewelry, yes, but one wears a cameo and enjoys it, but as a custodian for its next owner.'"

"She said that?"

"Words to that extent. I wrote it down in my diary, and I will jot it down for you, because you'll wish to get it right when you pass the cameo on to another someday." Aunt Letitia noted Clara's lowered hands and, grinning, pinned the cameo onto Clara's deep green jacket.

It seemed she now owned a cameo with a history.

"When should I give it away?"

"That is between you and the Lord. The queen said she had been waiting to give it to the right person, and she believed it was me. And now I believe you're to have it." Aunt Letitia eyed her handiwork, frowned, and fiddled with the cameo. "Straighten, will you? So, Clara dear, the queen also said she received the cameo right before Prince Albert arrived to court her, and wouldn't you know, I wore it, and within five minutes—*five!*—I met Peter. The greatest adventure of a lifetime was thrust upon me. You're of age, and I sense you're about to embark on an adventure too."

"A German prince will come courting?" Clara teased.

Aunt Letitia chuckled. "Consider this gift a symbol that you are now your own woman, and I support and love you."

Clara hugged her. "Oh Auntie."

Aunt Letitia kissed her cheek. "I will see you at home."

"Thank you. For everything." Auntie was a gem, dearer than any cameo. Later she'd reflect on Aunt Letitia's words and the kindness of her gift, but for now time was short.

There might be evidence of arson left among the rubble.

Using the tip of her parasol, she poked into the debris and ash at her feet.

Blackened nails. A penny. And oh—a paper. Well, a scrap of it, the sides singed and pierced by a few burned-out holes, but the remaining writing on it was still legible.

A gentle footfall sounding behind her drew her upright. A young man in a long brown coat and brown-and-green-checked trousers stepped in her direction, but he hadn't spied her yet. His face turned upward toward what was left of the roof, revealing his square-jawed profile to her.

A once-familiar profile.

"Byron?"

She didn't think she'd said it aloud, but his head turned. Light brown brows rose, and then he favored her with one of his lopsided smiles.

"Clara?"

"Hello, Byron." She should have been more formal and called him Mr. Breaux. It had been four years, after all.

Four years of wondering what had become of him after he'd vanished from her life.

"What are you doing in this mess, Clara? You're covered in ash." The words were out of Byron's mouth before he could unscramble his tangled thoughts. Here she was in front of him after all this time, and he'd blurted out something without thinking.

"So are you." A faint dimple manifested at one side of her chin. "Your sleeve."

He brushed it, but the fine ash clung to his coat. "We're both a sight, I expect."

She tilted her head to gaze at him. He'd always been at least a head taller than her, even though they were the same age. She'd never caught up to him.

She hadn't changed. Same small stature. Same smile. Same chestnut-hued hair too, but most of it was tucked beneath a straw bonnet. There was something about her that had drawn him from the start, something he'd always liked. Friendship between them had been easy.

But they weren't friends anymore.

"How are you?" He didn't ask the other question burning the tip of his tongue.

Have you thought of me at all?

"Quite well. You? And the children?"

It pleased him that she'd asked about his siblings. "We're in good health. Pascal is almost as tall as I am now."

She laughed. "Giants, you Breaux boys. Are the girls tall too?"

"Of course." He glanced up at the roof again, marveling that it hadn't yet collapsed. "I shall tell them I saw you in an unusual place."

"When we heard the news, the entire family came to see the extent of the damage. We wanted to make sure the glassworks was safe." She gestured to the sturdy brick building several yards distant. "And you're here because—are you with the insurance company?"

"I write for the *Gazette*." Something he'd worked hard to achieve. "Still not a full-time hire. I'm paid by the piece. I'm hoping to remedy that, however, and an article on this fire could give me an advantage for an opening at the paper for a salaried position. I've learned this was an arson fire set as retribution for Purl's terminating an agreement with someone over stolen goods here—"

"You know it's arson?" Her jaw went slack.

He nodded. "Everyone does."

Her shoulders slumped. "They do?"

"Well, perhaps not everyone, but enough that it's making the rounds among the fire brigade."

"Stolen goods, you say? So that's why Mr. Purl was arrested. What's this about an agreement? With whom?"

"He claims not to know. They used a middleman." Byron stopped at the look of utter despair on her face. "I see I've upset you. I'm sorry."

"I'm distraught over this, of course. But I confess to being disappointed too. I thought to write an article on the fire myself. For the *Gazette*." She bit her lip.

There were no female journalists at the *Gazette*. None anywhere else he could think of either. Clara had always been an excellent writer though, and up to anything she wished to do.

But this article? He could not give it up so readily. "You're suggesting I bow out?"

She looked up at him with large hazel eyes. "Would you mind? It's so kind of you to offer."

"I'm not offering." Not even when she batted her eyes like that.

"It's important, Byron. You see, I am on the cusp of—well, it might sound trivial to you. I'm about to realize my dream."

"It's not trivial." He had no idea what her dream had to do with being at the site of a fire, but nothing she said or did had ever been trivial to him.

She fidgeted with the ebony handle of her ash-dusty parasol. "These past few years I've written numerous devotionals and essays on spiritual disciplines. Several people have found them helpful, so I showed them to the reverend, and he told me they might make a good column in a magazine. So I contacted the editor of *A Woman's Home Companion*. He is willing to publish my pieces."

"That's wonderful."

"It is, but I should say, he *will be* willing, after I've worked with a newspaper." Her tone sounded dismal. "He says I require more experience and tutelage, and he's far too busy at the moment to help. That's why he wants me to work with a newspaper editor first. I was disappointed and angry—well, I still am angry—but I realized he is correct. If I write about trust, faith, growth, and submitting to spiritual discipline, how can I not expect to be subject to discipline as well? I must remain teachable."

Admirable, but he wasn't sure he understood. "So you are trying to get on as a journalist with the *Gazette*?"

"Oh, I have no desire to be a journalist, but I must gain experience, as I said. Unfortunately, the *Gazette* was not interested in my usual fare on faith, so I must find something more 'newsworthy' to write about." She met his gaze. "And this is it."

"Do your parents know?"

"Papa does." She looked away. "He knows I'm here. I haven't long though. So, will you cede the story to me? There will be another story for you, I'm sure."

Would there be? Byron scrubbed his jaw. Much as he understood Clara's plight, he needed this. "I've been waiting for months for something like this. I can't wait any longer."

"What do you mean?" She looked skeptical.

"As I mentioned, there's going to be an opening for a salaried journalist at the paper. This story could help me clinch the promotion. It will come with more clout and more money."

"You didn't used to care about money."

"I am raising three siblings, Clara."

"Oh, I didn't think of that. But of course, you're all they have now." Her fingers fluttered in a nervous gesture, and a paper slipped from her fingers.

He bent to retrieve it, not intending to read it, but its singed edges and holes made evident that this was a remnant of the fire. "What's this?"

"Rubbish, blown in on the wind from the glassworks. At least, that's my guess." She leaned in to point, and her lavender fragrance enveloped him despite the strong smells of smoke and charred wood surrounding them. "It mentions blue glass and vessels, fine leaf decoration. But the rest of it appears to be Latin. Perhaps Papa has an order for someone in Italy."

The words scrawled on the paper did indeed look like a list of things made in the glassworks. But the other words did not. *Pugio. Gladius.*

Latin indeed.

"Ho there," a man's voice shouted, accusatory in tone. Byron had been too occupied looking at the paper to notice Clara's brother approaching.

Clara spun around. "Wallace."

Scowling, Wallace marched closer. He hadn't changed much in four years, other than the mustache. He still bore a frustrated expression, and something like envy flashed in his eyes. "Byron Breaux, as I live and breathe. The woodsman's boy."

Byron felt shame at many things in his life: that his memories of his parents were growing foggier with time; that, as yet, he'd not been able to provide for his three siblings in the manner that he wished; that it was easier to be numb than to let himself feel anything after aching for so long.

But he would never, ever, be ashamed that his father had been a humble woodsman.

But humble didn't mean ill-mannered. He'd not stoop to Wallace Newton's level.

He extended his hand. "Good to see you again, Wallace."

"Er, yes." Wallace clasped his hand for a quick shake, the minimum response to Byron's gesture he could make. Then his gaze swiveled between Byron and Clara. "What on earth are you doing with my sister?"

Chapter 2

$\mathcal{C}$lara's jaw clenched so hard it hurt her molars. What abominable behavior from her brother! "Byron is investigating the fire, Wallace. He's a journalist."

Wallace tipped his head. "Not in the family business of chopping trees then?"

Byron's brow quirked. "I'm still more than adequate with an ax, if that's what you're asking."

Clara bit back a smile. "And a whittling knife, I hope. I still have the mouse you made for me."

"Do you?" Byron's face softened.

"How could I not? It's a masterpiece." Not just because of the craftsmanship, but because he'd made it for her. The little mouse sat on her bureau, a reminder of simpler times. Of who she and Byron used to be.

Wallace lifted a hand. "If we're finished talking about Clara's trinkets,

I'm still unclear why you're here, Byron."

"Clara?" Papa's voice called from behind her. "Ready to go?"

Before she could answer, Byron brushed past her, sending a faint waft of his soap around her. It was fresh and light compared to the smoke, and the fragrance took her back to Sunday school with him. And other times, like when she leaned back in the circle of his arms the May she was seventeen—

"Byron Breaux, sir." He extended his hand. "Not sure if you'll remember me."

"Of course I do." He seemed pleased, but Clara couldn't help but wonder, as she had several times over the years, if her family had said or done something to discourage Byron from seeing Clara because he was poorer than they were, or some such rot. Back when Byron's visits diminished, Clara expressed her sadness to Mama and Aunt Letitia. Auntie said that friendships grew and receded. It was the way life worked.

Mama had agreed, suggesting Clara turn her attention to "eligible young men." And Papa had come into the room then, echoing Mama's sentiments. *"You're nineteen,"* he'd said. *"Time for a change."*

Her life had changed, for certain. Byron wasn't part of it anymore. She'd asked her parents if they'd said anything to discourage Byron. They'd denied it, of course, but she remained confused. All she knew was that about the time Byron's parents died of scarlet fever, Byron stopped visiting. She'd understood he had new responsibilities with his siblings, two of whom had also been stricken with the fever but survived. She'd offered to help, but he declined, and then he'd started attending a different church service. After that, he faded from her life.

So she'd chosen to believe her parents, which left the lone alternative: Byron hadn't wanted to see her anymore. He'd no longer wanted to be her friend.

Papa gestured toward the glassworks. "Let's talk in my office." He took Byron along with him, leaving her and Wallace to follow behind them.

"I have much to say to you later, Wallace," she whispered through gritted teeth.

"And I to you. What are you thinking, lurking in such a dangerous place?"

"I was at a safe distance. What were you doing there?"

"Looking for you."

"I thought you'd left with Mama."

He flushed. "I decided to stay. Like you."

"How rude you were to Byron." Her brother might be older than she, but only by eleven months. He should well remember what close friends she and Byron had been once upon a time. Wallace hadn't always been like this, judgmental and hostile, but he'd changed a few years ago into someone she still didn't recognize. Nevertheless, she wouldn't stand for his attitude toward Byron.

With the jingling of keys, Papa unlocked the glassworks and ushered them inside. Stepping into the blue-papered antechamber, Clara wiped her damp boots on a small, utilitarian rug set near the door for such a purpose, so as not to soil the vine-patterned carpet. Papa led them past oak cabinets displaying samples of products produced at the glassworks: sugar bowls, flasks, vials, salt bowls, and pieces with cameos encrusted into them, from drawer knobs to vases, like the ones he'd made for Queen Victoria.

"I'll show you around first, if you like." Papa looked eager, as he always did at the prospect of showing off his business. Byron nodded, his brow lifting in what looked to be genuine curiosity. As far as Clara knew, he'd never been in the glassworks.

Papa led them into a tidy workroom with a table, tools, molds, and a six-pot furnace. When the men were working, the place was hot, but the windows facing the river allowed cooling breezes in. Clara stopped by the stool where she sat when she watched the craftsmen at work blowing glass.

"Fascinating." Byron bent to examine the tools.

"My father started Newton Glassworks in a shed not thirty feet square. Now we have this entire building, plus two sheds for raw materials and another for crates awaiting shipping. We ship out every Monday unless there is a special order, as we have today. Come." He led them through other offices. Wallace stiffened when they passed his empty desk.

Poor Wallace had no aptitude or enthusiasm for accounts. Was there nothing else he could do at the glassworks to please Papa?

Clara wished, yet again, something could change as they walked to the shipping room, with its wide door leading to the back. A few dozen crates waited, ready to be loaded onto wagons and taken to destinations beyond.

Byron peered at a few. "San Francisco, New York, Harrisburg."

Clara tapped one of the crates bound for England. "Aunt Letitia visited London and gave Queen Victoria a gift of vases. Since then, there have been orders from Britain."

Byron's eyes widened. "Extraordinary."

"This is the shipment that must go out today. I wonder why the crates are not in the outer shed for the deliveryman. Wallace, see to it."

"Yes, sir."

Papa beckoned. "You two, come to my office so we can talk." He led back the way they'd come and opened his door. "Have a seat."

The room was decorated in rich browns, well-enough illuminated by the summer morning light streaming through the east-facing window that no lamp was needed. Clara adjusted her bell skirt and perched on the plush sofa of chestnut velvet with Papa. Byron removed his hat, revealing waves the light reddish-brown shade of unstained cherry wood, and took a chair facing them.

"Interesting to see you after so long." Papa came straight to the point. "This was a happenstance meeting?"

As if Clara made a habit of scheduling meetings with gentlemen? "Of course, Papa."

"We have not seen one another in years, sir. We are no longer acquainted."

It was true, but Byron's matter-of-fact statement nipped at Clara anyway.

"I see." Papa's face revealed no emotion. "You were saying as we walked over from Purl's that you write for the *Gazette*? Well done. I admire a young person who has such direction and enthusiasm for work."

Wallace entered at that moment, and he took a seat. A muscle clenched in his cheek. No doubt he wished to hear such praise from Papa. "Sir, the wagon is here. No need to transfer the cargo to the shed for them, as they are taking it out of the shipping room instead."

"Very well. Now, you are writing an article?" He looked to Byron.

"It appears both Clara and I were searching for evidence of arson." Byron glanced at her.

Wallace sat a little straighter. "Did you find anything interesting?"

Nothing but that piece of paper. Which Byron must have slipped into his pocket. No matter. It hadn't meant anything. "The night watchman's testimony is enough."

Byron shifted. "There remains the question of the article. The gentlemanly thing to do is to allow you to write about the arson, Clara. I mean, Miss Newton."

Clara blinked. Why the quick turnabout? Moments ago he'd said he needed to write the story himself to get a promotion. What made him change his mind? "That's kind of you, By—Mr. Breaux. Are you certain?"

"As you said, something else will come along."

The same could be said for her. "But—"

Papa burst into laughter. "This is like the tomahawk argument all over again."

"It is nothing like the tomahawk argument." Clara nudged her father's arm with her shoulder.

"You wanted something from him, pleaded for it, and he said no a hundred times."

"But he's saying yes now."

"I said yes then too," Byron interjected. "Eventually."

"This is precisely the same." Papa lifted a finger. "Back then he said yes, and then you *still* argued with him about whether or not he was sure. I had to step in and stop you two from arguing. Although I couldn't blame

Byron for his concern for your reputation."

Clara smoothed her skirt over her knee, prim as could be. "Throwing tomahawks at a tree stump is not at all scandalous."

Wallace snorted. "It's not ordinary though, is it?"

Byron's lips twitched. "Your sister has never been the least bit ordinary."

Clara fixed her gaze on her hands. Byron had meant it as a compliment, and it was true that she was not like the other girls. She never had been. Back when she and Byron were friends, she hadn't cared about teas or needlepoint like the other lasses in school. She'd wanted to do all the fun things he did, like whittle (though she never mastered the skill), run free through the woods, and yes, throw a tomahawk. The old stump behind her house had seemed the perfect target.

And she hit it, after several attempts. Unlike her attempts with throwing a knife at a fence when she was seventeen.

But by then, her interests had also grown to include domestic pursuits, as Mama called them. Watercolors became more enjoyable. Needlepoint had its blessings too, and she'd received satisfaction the first time she donated linens she'd labored over to the church. And she'd learned the joy of writing, something Byron had always loved.

Little wonder he'd become a journalist, although she'd always seen him doing a different sort of writing, something that revealed more of his heart.

She couldn't read his heart right now though, not the way she used to. Something shrouded his emotion from his eyes as his gaze bored into her. "I insist you take the article."

"Thank you." She meant it. She'd start writing at once. Her prospects of publication with it were high, she could sense it.

Then Byron's gaze turned toward Papa. "I've realized there are two stories here, and I shall cover an aspect separate from the arson. Perhaps I might ask you a question in its regard, Mr. Newton."

Clara's stomach tightened. She might be writing the article and be one step closer to achieving her dream, but it all felt secondary to her curiosity about what Byron was about to ask her father—and with such a serious look on his face too.

Newton nodded, and Byron continued. "I must clarify, sir, this is for the newspaper. I'm obliged to tell you I may use your words in print."

Newton waved his hand. "Go on."

"A short time ago, you were speaking with an importer by the name of Sylvester Vanacore?"

"Our neighbor. On one of the city committees. Plans on running for Congress. He's coming tonight, by the way, Clara." The way Newton glanced at her, it was clear Vanacore had an eye for Clara.

The thought did not sit well on Byron's stomach.

Not your business, man. "You are aware that Vanacore was burglarized recently?"

"Yes, poor fellow. The entire household staff was at church, as was he. A burglar took advantage and cleaned out Vanacore's entire collection of Roman antiquities."

"I never saw them," Clara said, "but Papa told me what an impressive collection he had. Coins and figurines and pottery."

Wallace shifted in his seat. "Any leads on who took them?"

"Not that I am aware of, no. Neither do I know if Vanacore hired an investigator." The number of persons employed by the city to enforce law and order could be counted on two hands, sometimes one, depending on available funds. Byron viewed his role as a journalist as more than reporting on facts. He wanted to help set things right.

Drawing others' attention to issues was one way he could do that. And if he could help the local constables solve a case? Well, he'd do that too.

That was why he'd decided to yield the article on the arson to Clara. God had given him another story to tell.

"I've only one more question for you, Mr. Newton, if you don't mind."

Newton glanced at his pocket watch, a fine timepiece far grander than anyone in Byron's family had ever owned. "Not at all, but the one question must be it. My sister's engagement party is this evening."

"Letitia?" His eyes locked with Clara's. "Please offer my congratulations."

"I shall." Clara smiled, that old familiar way she had where her cheeks rounded like young apples. Byron had always been fond of that smile. And Clara's Aunt Letitia. He was happy for her.

He'd not be marrying anytime soon, if at all. He had other matters to tend to, like the promotion—and with God's help, this new article might just help him achieve it. He returned his focus to Newton. "Do you think last night's fire was related to the fact that some of Vanacore's stolen artifacts were shipped out in secret through Purl's business, masked as textile orders?"

Clara gasped. Wallace muttered. But Byron's gaze didn't break from their father.

"That's why Purl was taken by the constable? He had Vanacore's things?"

"Someone packed a crate for shipment as if it were a textile order, but instead of fabrics the box contained a phial of blue glass, some coins, and the remains of a *pugio,* an ancient Roman dagger. And the blade of a *gladius*—a sword used by Roman foot soldiers. This crate's bottom was damaged in the fire. When it was moved, it fell apart, revealing its contents. Purl was confronted with the evidence and admitted his guilt, but insisted he is no more than a component in a larger machine. He knows not the others' identities except for a fellow named Axel."

"Others? 'Tis a regular crime ring." Newton looked uncomfortable. So did Wallace, but who wouldn't? Learning one's acquaintance was involved in criminal activity was enough to make a man ill.

Byron pushed to his feet. "I lack evidence, but I believe a burglar was hired to steal Vanacore's Roman artifacts for someone else, and this person's lackey hired or blackmailed Purl. Whether the intention is to keep or sell the artifacts, I don't know."

"Regardless, 'tis a most illegal scheme." Clara's tone demanded his full attention.

Byron met her hazel gaze. "Agreed."

"How do you know any of this? You didn't arrive until after we did." Clara's probing tone hadn't changed in its insistence. She *would* make a fine addition to the *Gazette*, were it her desire.

"Oh, did I not mention that?" Byron smiled. "I am part of the fire brigade. I am the person who found the artifacts."

❧ Chapter 3 ❧

$\mathcal{O}$nce home, tending to final party preparations, Clara related the morning's news to Mama and Aunt Letitia. She'd been right—Mama didn't quite approve of her nosing around an arson scene—but the news that Byron had reappeared in her life turned the conversation away from one awkward topic onto another. Clara was peppered with questions about him. *Where does he live? What did he think of seeing you again? Is he married?*

Clara answered all of them by shrugging and saying, "I don't know, Mama."

Mama and Aunt Letitia exchanged glances they thought outside of Clara's view and at last returned the discussion to Mr. Purl.

"I wonder who stole the artifacts from Mr. Vanacore." Mama shook her head as she arranged a bouquet of roses for the evening's party.

Aunt Letitia counted the roses in her vase. "This Axel fellow?"

"Perhaps." Clara shoved one last waxy stalk of greenery into her arrangement—there, it looked fuller now. "Makes me wonder if he was the one who wrote the items on that paper I found. The one that said blue glass and *pugio* and *gladius*, and I thought had to do with the glassworks. It was a packing list for a criminal. I wonder if that's how Byron got the idea for his article. He recognized the items on it as those he'd seen in the shipping crate."

"And said nothing to you?" Aunt Letitia's brow furrowed.

"He might have intended to, had Wallace not found us then." Clara hoped, at least. "I should go upstairs to write the article, I suppose. I've summoned a courier to pick it up tonight."

"Go on, dear." Mama blew her a kiss.

The article should have been easy, but several hours later, still sitting at her bedroom escritoire, Clara dipped her pen and slashed ink across the last paragraph. *Lord, I need your help. This is terrible.*

Or maybe it was just that she was so anxious about this opportunity to submit an article on a publishable topic, she was second-guessing everything she wrote.

"Clara, are—oh you're still writing." Mama's entrance drew Clara around.

"I'm not writing, Mama. I'm massacring the English language."

"Whatever you're doing, you're in danger of staining your new sleeves with ink." Mama rushed into Clara's bedchamber, a flurry of rustling orange silk. "If your sleeve brushes the page, you'll have to change clothes, and there isn't time. The party is about to start."

Clara had been careful to avoid dunking, brushing, or otherwise slathering the white lace weepers she wore beneath her pale blue pagoda sleeves in ink. But Mama had a point. She mustn't be tardy for Aunt Letitia and Mr. Hollingsworth's engagement party.

With one last, longing look at the page, Clara joined her mother, sending her wide, flounced skirt swirling about her ankles. "I'm not certain how to end the article, and the courier will be here soon."

Mama scrutinized her appearance. "Why aren't you wearing the cameo? Your gown would set it off to perfection."

"I forgot jewelry in my haste to dress."

"Where is it? Ah." Mama caught sight of where Clara had placed it, on her bureau beside the little carved mouse Byron had whittled for her so long ago. They looked mismatched—a stunning blue agate and pearl cameo next to a pine figurine carved by a boy learning to whittle—but in Clara's mind, they were tethered, bound by the day's events.

The day she received the cameo was the day she encountered Byron again.

Mama scooped up the cameo and beckoned Clara to the looking glass. "I'll pin it to your bodice for you, dear. Oh, the color is striking."

With Mama blocking her view, Clara couldn't see the cameo, but she could see the reflection of her own face. Byron had seen it today for the first time in four years. Had she changed to him?

He had to her, somewhat. In other ways, not at all. But seeing him reminded her how much she missed him when he stopped being her friend.

Mama stepped back. "There. Now, leave the article to sit. You know how you are. You write something, step away, and realize how to improve it. I imagine you'll have an idea within half an hour. Come greet guests, and then slip back upstairs to finish it."

"Thank you, Mama."

Mama led her into the hallway, toward the staircase. "Promise not to be overlong though. 'Tis our duty to care for our guests."

"I shan't. One last paragraph is all."

"Here they are," Papa called from the bottom of the stairs. "What a fetching sight you two make."

As did the rest of the family. Papa, Wallace, and Mr. Hollingsworth looked dashing in their evening finery, and Aunt Letitia—well, there was no word to describe her but radiant. Dressed in a creamy embroidered gown, with her dark hair arranged in elaborate curls, she was lovely, but her glowing smile eclipsed her physical appearance.

She had the look of a bride.

"Congratulations, both of you." Clara embraced Aunt Letitia and smiled at Mr. Hollingsworth, who bowed in response.

"The cameo looks well on you, dear." Aunt Letitia nodded her approval.

Within moments guests arrived, filling the rooms with chatter, laughter, and the clinking of crystal cups. Clara milled among the guests, including Papa and Aunt Letitia's sister, Mary, and Mary's daughter, young Alice. When her aunt and cousin wandered off, giving Clara a moment free from conversation, her brain became occupied with the article. How to end it?

With an arsonist loose on the streets of our fair city, is any structure safe from his blazing inclinations?

No, too melodramatic.

Will the arsonist execute his fiery craft again?

Perhaps she shouldn't end the article on a question. . . .

A familiar thrill shot up Clara's spine. She knew what she'd do. Rather than leave the article on a note that drew more attention to the arsonist, she'd finish with praise for the fire brigade and investigators.

Five minutes was all she'd need. She slipped through the crowded parlor into the hall, almost colliding with Aunt Letitia and a gold-haired gentleman.

"Miss Newton." The man grinned, revealing even white teeth. When he kissed her hand, the strength of his bay rum scent made her stomach queasy. "How stunning you look in blue."

"Doesn't she though? And the cameo is from Queen Victoria herself." Aunt Letitia's tone teased in a way only Clara could recognize.

"Amazing," he gushed. "Such connections your family has. As I was saying to my friend, Mayor Guthrie, connections are crucial when it comes to running for Congress, which, as you know, I'm humbled to be doing."

"We do." Clara nodded, although she wasn't sure about the *humble* part.

"Public safety is of vital importance to me, here in town and in our fair state. It is something I plan to improve when I am elected."

Aunt Letitia made a sympathetic noise. "And you, so recently a victim of burglary. Of course the matter is close to your heart."

His lips turned down. "Yes, tragic. Of course, I'm pleased some of the items were discovered today. Horrid business. But that is not a topic fit for feminine ears."

Clara and Aunt Letitia exchanged a glance. "Oh?"

"Far better to speak of more genteel matters. On such a note, the mayor was saying I have every characteristic required to be a successful politician, except, of course, a wife and family." His eyebrows twitched—no, was he wiggling his eyebrows—at Clara?

Oh dear, he *was* wiggling them. Her stomach flopped. While her neighbor was a nice-enough fellow, she had no interest in him that way.

She must change the subject at once. And she had good reason. The courier would be here for her article soon. "Pardon me, but I've an urgent matter I must see to. If you will excuse me."

Mr. Vanacore opened his mouth in protest but nodded. Slipping through the guests, Clara returned to her room. Careful with her sleeves, she scrawled a new closing paragraph, blotted the page, secured the article in an envelope, and hurried down the back stairs, leaving instruction with a servant to deliver it to the courier.

Done. The *Gazette* would publish her article, and then. . .then perhaps this bit of experience would be enough for the magazine editor to contract her devotional pieces. She would realize her dream. Returning to the party, her thoughts flickered to Byron. She would have to send him a thank-you letter for the opportunity he allowed her to write the article—

If only she knew his address.

Would she ever see Byron again?

She made her way to the foyer, a grand entrance room just inside the front doors of their Greek revival–style home. The chamber was two stories in height, matching the two-story porch outside. She'd always liked this room because it echoed, and she always sounded like a better singer in here.

Once she'd stood in the center of this room and sung with Byron, a folk tune about a frog courting a mouse. She and Byron had liked how the humming parts of the song reverberated off the high ceilings.

The hair at her nape stood at attention. Turning about, she locked gazes with a new arrival. Not a guest though. Aunt Letitia wouldn't have known to invite him.

Byron.

It was difficult to breathe when he walked toward her across the room.

"Good evening." He bowed, giving her a chance to admire his wavy hair. He wore what was probably his finest suit, a dark ensemble that was not quite formal enough for the occasion. It fit his broad shoulders to perfection, but the cuffs showed signs of wear. Perhaps it had been purchased for his parents' joint funeral four years ago.

His lips lifted in a sheepish smile. "I knew you were having a party, and I'm sorry I barged in like this, uninvited, but I had to see you."

"You're most welcome here. But is something wrong?"

"I—um. Yes." His gaze raked her pinned-up hair. "You look lovely."

"So do you." Oh! She should not have said that aloud. "That is, thank you. What were you saying was wrong?"

"Wrong?"

"You said so. I think."

He brushed the fringe from his forehead. "Oh yes. I'm sorry, but—"

"Breaux, this is a private party." Wallace appeared at Clara's elbow.

Clara's chin lifted. "He is my guest." As of this moment.

Behind Wallace, Aunt Letitia swooped in with a rustle of fabric. "Young Mr. Breaux. I was so jealous to learn I'd missed seeing you today."

"Miss Newton." He kissed her hand, a far more chaste and polite gesture than what Clara had received from Mr. Vanacore. "Congratulations on your upcoming nuptials."

"Two weeks from today, here at eleven. You must come. Bring your wife."

"I'm not married."

"A sweetheart then?"

His head shook. "Too busy, I'm afraid."

"A pity." Aunt Letitia glanced at Clara with a look that said it wasn't a pity at all.

Oh dear. Aunt Letitia had the wrong idea about why Byron had come tonight. Now that Auntie was betrothed, it seemed she was eager for Clara to wed too. Sure enough, she patted Byron's forearm. "I see a friend I must speak to. Come, Wallace, I wish to introduce you."

It sounded like a blatant ploy to leave them alone, but Clara didn't mind. In fact, she was thankful. The moment her relatives glided off, she met Byron's gaze. "What's wrong?"

"May we speak somewhere quieter? The terrace, perhaps?"

No one stopped them as they adjourned through the french doors into the dark evening. Two of Auntie's friends sat at a small table enjoying the cool air, and a couple leaned against the railing overlooking the back garden. Byron took Clara's elbow, leading her to another section of the railing. Someone looking on them might judge this to be a romantic assignation, but the look on Byron's face was not the least bit amorous.

"It's your article. I'm sorry, but it won't be published."

She flinched as if she'd been splashed with ice water. "How can you know that? I just finished it."

"Another freelance reporter submitted an article a few hours ago. The editor chose it."

All of that work, trying to be first. "I was too slow."

"It's not your fault." He took hold of her chin, gently forcing her to look up at him. "These things happen."

Her chin was cold when he let go. "I have to trust something else will present itself."

"I've found it. But I think it would be best if we wrote the article together."

"What do you mean?"

"You know I planned to write about Purl dealing in stolen artifacts. I think we should collaborate and write the article together."

It was a newsworthy topic, with the added benefit that Byron might be able to help her in areas where her writing was unschooled or lacking. However, the advantage seemed all hers. "Why would you share this with me? You could do this well enough on your own. I can add little—or nothing—to help you."

"Looking around the glassworks today, when we paused beside the outgoing shipments? I noticed one destined for Harrisburg. It didn't strike me until later, but the name and address on it were the same as those listed on the crate I found at Purl's. The one containing Vanacore's stolen goods."

Her blood iced. "You think Papa is shipping out stolen goods, just like Mr. Purl."

"Of course not. I hope not," he amended. "But someone at his glassworks seems to be complicit in the scheme. Why else would there be a crate addressed to the same name and address, John Smith of Harrisburg?"

"There might be two John Smiths there. 'Tis a common enough name."

His brow quirked. "Too common, if you ask me, and it's too great a coincidence that two men with the same name in the same town would come to our attention the same day, especially when one is the recipient of the stolen goods. No, they're the same person. And if a crate addressed to Mr. Smith from Purl's contained contraband, it stands to reason—"

"The one at the glassworks does too?" Clara couldn't accept it. "Let's examine that crate at Papa's."

"We cannot. The crates are gone. Your father oversaw their shipment this afternoon, remember?"

Now that he mentioned it, of course she did. She took a step back toward the party. "Let's find Papa then, and ask him about it."

"Clara." He took hold of her elbow. "I'd rather not. Not yet."

"Why ever not? You said you don't think Papa is involved."

"I don't. But we must be discreet." He glanced at the others on the terrace, who didn't appear to be paying the least bit of attention to them. "I'd like to find out as much as we can before we tell him, so as not to warn off the offender. Does that make sense?"

"Of course, Byron. I desire discretion above all else, because if stolen goods are being smuggled out of the glassworks, the news of it will harm Papa's reputation. Newton Glassworks is his life."

"I fear the news will come out, one way or another. I'd rather be the one who does it, with care and honesty, before someone else reports it. Or something bad happens."

"Like another arson fire?" She chewed her lip.

"Purl was targeted, undoubtedly because of his involvement with the smuggler. It could happen again to others who are tangled in the scheme, in one way or another." Byron stepped closer. "I could tell this story without you, but your assistance—your partnership—would benefit us both. You have access to the glassworks. I can make inquiries with the constables and question Purl at the jail. Let's find out who dares use the glassworks for such ill deeds. And get my promotion and your newspaper experience while we're at it." His hand remained between them. "You trusted me once. Will you again, and work with me now?"

Not for the sake of her goal of publishing for the *Gazette*, although yes, this could help. No, if she did this, it would be for Papa. To protect him and the glassworks.

She took Byron's hand and shook it.

Byron hadn't touched Clara's hand since he taught her how to throw an eight-inch knife, so long ago he couldn't remember how long ago it was. He'd forgotten how small her hands were, how delicate the fingers.

She let go. "So what do we do first?"

"Research, and we can start right now." He gestured that she should precede him back inside the house. "Does your father keep paperwork here at home? Financials or a client list that might contain the name John Smith of Harrisburg?"

"Mama says accounts give him indigestion, so she's forbidden them in the house." Her lips twitched. "But he does keep a copy of the client list here, for writing letters and such. However, John Smith won't be on the list. I'm sure of it, since I've handled much of Papa's correspondence.

Come, the office is this way."

Her lavender fragrance swirled around him, distracting him from keeping focused on the article. What was happening to him? Just seeing her in her evening finery had rendered him idiotic earlier, hadn't it? Byron rolled his eyes at himself. It was as if he'd never noticed she was female before tonight.

Well, he'd noticed now, not that it changed anything. He must focus on his goals rather than how beautiful she was.

"Miss Newton." A broad-shouldered man of thirty or so stepped into their path, boasting a gleaming smile, slicked blond hair, and an expensive coat that must have been drenched in cologne, the way its odor carried. Sylvester Vanacore, congressional candidate. Byron didn't miss the possessive look the fellow cast at Clara. He didn't care much for it either.

"Mr. Vanacore." Clara offered a polite smile. "Are you acquainted with Mr. Breaux? He writes for the *Gazette*."

Vanacore pumped Byron's hand. "Journalist, eh?"

"Indeed. In fact, I'm curious about your stolen antiquities."

"Aren't we all, Mr. Brothers, aren't we all?"

"Breaux," Byron corrected.

"In fact, Mr. Breaux was the one to discover your things at Mr. Purl's," Clara noted. "You two didn't meet?"

Vanacore's features twisted as if he was dismayed at himself for not remembering a potential constituent. "Quite a bit of chaos after the fire, of course."

"Indeed," Byron agreed. "You came to the scene as a member of the policing committee, as I recall. You must have been shocked when we discovered a crate, full of your stolen artifacts."

"Astonished. If you care to quote that, please refer to me as congressional candidate Sylvester Vanacore."

"May I ask you a few more questions then? Perhaps Monday, at your office?"

Vanacore's already large chest puffed out. "I was hoping Miss Newton and her mother would accompany me to luncheon on Monday."

"Luncheon?" The word came out sounding strangled.

Say no, and let's look at that client list.

"Your mother has already assented." Vanacore's grin grew.

Something in Byron's gut gnawed like a hungry beast. It grew worse when Clara nodded. "Then yes, of course."

Enough was enough. Byron rushed to change the subject. "Our interview? Shall I visit your office before lunch Monday?"

"Fine, Mr. Broom."

"Breaux." Not that Vanacore was paying attention. He couldn't tear his beady-eyed gaze off of Clara.

"The restaurant's French chef is magnificent." Vanacore moved too close to Clara for propriety. "Wait until you taste the *coq au vin.*"

At this rate, they wouldn't be able to look at that list tonight, but Byron had to admit that wasn't what tied his insides into a knot.

It was jealousy. Pure and simple.

How ridiculous. He didn't know Clara anymore, and he'd always known they were different classes of people, on different paths. He had no right to feel jealous over something he didn't even want, did he? Something he'd never receive?

Byron was, as Wallace reminded him earlier today, the son of a woodsman, raised close to nature. He grew up helping his father fell trees, chop firewood, and mill planks, whittling scraps into figurines and building shelves and chairs.

He wasn't that lad anymore though. He wanted to be someone far different than a woodsman's son. Not someone like Vanacore, with his priceless collection of Roman antiquities and political aspirations—Byron didn't want that sort of money. But he yearned to be established enough as a journalist that he could receive respect, to send his brother, Pascal, to university, and give the girls a solid start in whatever they wished in life. He wanted a house more like this than the one he'd grown up in.

But to achieve it, he needed the permanent position at the paper, not distractions. And if he wasn't careful, these new feelings for Clara would be precisely that.

He'd best banish those sorts of thoughts of her now, for good. The gnawing in his stomach spilled into his arms, filling him with the need to swing an ax, a remnant from his past that still worked out his frustration and anxiety.

"Pardon me." He interrupted Vanacore's rambling soliloquy. "I've work yet to finish tonight. Elsewhere." He executed an exaggerated bow and left them.

"Byron?" Clara called after him, but he didn't turn back.

❧ Chapter 4 ❧

ou're gems, both of you, coming with me." A prick of guilt needled Clara's chest. Circles of fatigue rimmed Aunt Letitia and Mr. Hollingsworth's eyes this morning, and after last night's party, she couldn't blame them for being weary. She'd hardly slept either. But once she'd explained to them how she'd parted with Byron, they'd been willing to forgo the later church service the family preferred and come with her to the first service.

The one Byron attended.

"We don't mind at all." Mr. Hollingsworth's cheerfulness belied his lack of sleep, and he rocked on his heels as they stood on the walk outside the church, awaiting Byron. "Every time of day is a good time to praise the Lord."

Aunt Letitia grinned. "I do like how you set me on the better path, Peter."

That was what a marriage was, wasn't it? Setting one another on the better path and walking it together.

Byron had always set her on the better path. He'd encouraged her, challenged her, and made her feel valued. But that was a long time ago.

And last night she'd offended him somehow.

"Don't worry, pet." Aunt Letitia squeezed Clara's arm. "He'll listen to you."

"I hope so, Auntie."

"I say." Mr. Hollingsworth smiled. "There he is now, if I'm not mistaken."

He wasn't. Striding up the street came a party of four, Byron and three children. The boy, Pascal, was fifteen and almost as tall as Byron, with similar hair and the gangly look of an adolescent boy. The two dark-haired girls in matching yellow skirts, Genevie and Adele, were indeed tall for their ages, thirteen and nine, respectively.

Clara stepped forward as they approached. "Good morning."

Byron's face fell. Pascal's broke into a smile. "Miss Newton?"

"Yes. You remember." She greeted him and the girls.

The church bell rang, announcing five minutes' warning. Byron placed his hands on the girls' shoulders. "We'd best find our seats."

"First, may I have a word, Byron? In private."

His reluctant nod at his siblings didn't give Clara much confidence, but at least he'd agreed.

The younger Breauxs filed into church. Aunt Letitia and Mr. Hollingsworth remained outside as discreet chaperones, stepping away to allow them privacy.

"What is it?" A muscle clenched in Byron's jaw.

Clara fingered the cameo at her neck. It had been worn by women of strength and dignity. She must show those traits now. "Last night. You left. We were going to look for Papa's client list."

"I thought so as well, but you were otherwise occupied."

With Vanacore? "I couldn't well dash off. He was a guest."

"Unlike me."

This was going horribly wrong. "No, Byron, I meant I had to be polite."

His shoulders deflated. "Which I'm not doing. I'm sorry. I'm behaving like a boor."

"And I'm sorry for not better including you in the conversation with him. It was rude to discuss a restaurant when you weren't invited, and. . ." She'd been so flabbergasted by Mr. Vanacore's public invitation that she hadn't been considerate of Byron. Clara met his gaze. "You should know, I wanted to look for the client list last night, and again this morning, but the office was occupied both times, door closed. Papa was busy, I suppose."

"We will try again."

His use of "we" brightened her spirits. "Friends again?"

The corners of his mouth lifted in a lazy, handsome grin. "We never stopped."

Hadn't they though? For four long years.

Clara caught Auntie's discreet nod. "Church is about to begin, but we hoped you'd join us for a picnic at the house. Aunt Letitia invited a few friends, at noon. Bring your siblings."

"They're attending a birthday luncheon for a friend."

"Then come alone." Oh my, that sounded rather forward. Her cheeks heated. "Perhaps you and I can look for the list."

"I shall then. Thank you."

"Oh, and Mr. Vanacore is not invited," she said over her shoulder as she turned to join her family.

She didn't miss the tiny smile that lifted the corners of his mouth.

As the clock hands neared twelve, Clara perched at her bedroom window overlooking the street. Her hands, damp from anxiety, cradled the little carved mouse Byron had fashioned for her so long ago out of a pine scrap. It fit just right in her palm, and when she brushed her fingers just so over its long nose, the carved whiskers soothed her. One day she might rub those whiskers into nothingness, but for now the motion and sensation helped calm her nerves.

Lord, help me. I don't want to be hurt again, but my heart is as open to him as it was four years ago. That's why I'm watching for him, isn't it?

She should return the mouse to the bureau and go downstairs. Byron would come when he came. Her watchfulness wouldn't speed him along. But her eye caught on Mr. Vanacore, striding past the house with another man. Or trying to escape him, the way he was walking with long strides while the other man jogged to catch up. The unknown man glanced up at her house, revealing a snub nose and jowls, like a pug dog.

Whoever the man was, Mr. Vanacore didn't slow for him. Until he stopped and faced him, his features hard and almost frightening. The fellow dashed back the direction from which he'd come.

Curious. But now another man was treading up the street, flowers in hand. She'd recognize his broad-shouldered form and long-legged stride in a heartbeat. She returned the mouse carving to her bureau and hurried downstairs as the clock struck noon.

She was waiting when he entered the foyer. First he greeted Mama with a posy of white and yellow daisies, and then he offered another small bouquet to Aunt Letitia. One remained in his hands. For her?

"These are beautiful." Mama caressed a petal. "Thank you, dear." So tender was her expression, it was clear she was happy to see Byron again. Clara hadn't thought that her family might have missed him too. He'd been a part of the life of the household for several years before he vanished from their sphere.

She couldn't have helped it though. She hadn't been as important to him as he'd been to her.

"For you." Byron's voice was soft when he held out the flowers. "I hope you don't mind daisies."

"They're perfect."

"Are you certain? You look like something's wrong."

It showed? "Nothing. Just thinking about the past."

"How long ago in the past? Yesterday? Or when Father Abraham walked the earth?"

She laughed. "Not quite so distant. Four years."

His smile fell. "Clara—"

The gong rang for lunch. At least it had saved him from saying something awkward, like he'd noticed her affection for him back then and couldn't bear it anymore. Clara forced a wide smile. "Come. We're showing Mr. Hollingsworth a real American-style picnic. Roast chicken, potatoes scalloped with ham, pickled oysters, corn relish, and strawberry flummery."

"The groom will have good memories of our food to take back to England with him, that's for certain."

"Oh, but they're staying here in Pittsburgh. Mr. Hollingsworth has always wanted to settle in America." Following the other guests, Clara led him outside to the lush lawn behind the house, where a long table of sumptuous fare had been laid out near small dining tables and blankets spread on the grass. Already Aunt Letitia and her fiancé helped themselves to the dishes, and a short line formed behind them. Clara and Byron joined the end of the line. "His work for the prime minister has finished, and he's pursuing other interests. We couldn't be happier we get to keep Auntie close, and now that we know Mr. Hollingsworth, we're glad to keep him too."

Although Wallace didn't look it. A few folks ahead of them in line, he frowned down at his empty plate.

Byron caught her gaze. "Wallace has changed."

"Yes." Wallace was close to her and Byron's age, but during childhood he'd been keener to run about with older boys. Still, he should have been happy to see Byron again after all this time—but he'd been nothing but rude, as sullen as he'd been the past several months.

Allowing Byron to take her full plate and lead her to a vacant cloth spread on the grass, she sighed. "It isn't you, Byron. The past few years have been. . .difficult. He's avoided church, been cross, and, well, it's taken longer for Wallace to get his bearings than Papa would like."

"How do you mean?"

"Papa wants Wallace to take over the accounts for the glassworks, but he doesn't have the enthusiasm for it. In fact, he has no interest in the glassworks at all."

"What does interest him?"

"That's part of the problem. He isn't sure."

"Let's ask him to join us, shall we?"

How kind. "Thank you, Byron."

Abandoning the picnic blanket for the moment, they walked side by side toward her brother. Wallace stood straighter as they approached. Clara gestured to the blanket. "Sit with us."

"Of course." He followed them back to the blanket, and they settled with their plates. Gathering his fork and knife, he looked side-eyed at Byron. "A journalist, eh?"

Byron nodded, poking his fork into his potatoes. "I am."

"I always expected you to follow in your father's footsteps. Work at a sawmill or some such."

Not this again. "Wallace."

"Sons are oft expected to do what their fathers do. Papa insists on it, although he's lenient with you. I know most women are encouraged to wed and keep house, but Papa lets you do whatever you wish."

She couldn't argue that. "I'm sorry, Wallace."

He shrugged. Was there anything she could say to ease the lines of tension around his mouth? *God, Wallace so wants Papa's approval. How can I help?*

All she could do was pray.

And perhaps try to do a better job at letting her brother know she cared for him. "Maybe there's something else at the glassworks that might be of more interest to you than the accounts. You're good at many things."

"Such as?" He swigged his mint punch.

Byron stretched out his long legs. "I always admired your power of observation, Wallace. You notice things others miss."

It was true. Without being nosy, Wallace had always been able to discern people's moods, relationships, and motives, often without appearing to pay keen attention. Even now Wallace was attentive, but his glances flickered to the others. Especially Papa, whom Wallace always monitored hoping for a scrap of praise.

Clara could have kissed Byron's cheek for complimenting Wallace— but that would embarrass them both. Clearing her throat, she returned her gaze to Wallace. "Byron's right. You understand people well, Wallace."

"That's one thing." He offered a halfhearted chuckle.

"There's more. You're a wonderful singer." She said the first thing that popped into her head.

This time his laugh was genuine. "I doubt Papa would approve of me taking to the stage."

At least they were finding humor in things now. *Thank You for helping cheer him, Lord.* "Let's see. . . You're a smart dresser. You can fall asleep anywhere in under a minute. And animals love you."

"There's something else." Byron's smile remained, but his gaze was serious. "The violin."

"Oh, do play for us all this afternoon." Clara folded her hands under her chin.

Wallace rolled his eyes. "Are you in league with Aunt Letitia? She asked me to play in the parlor after lunch."

Clara clapped. "Wonderful."

"I look forward to it." Byron lifted his punch in a toast.

Perhaps it was Clara's imagination, but Wallace seemed a tad less tense now. "She also said one of her friends is a plant expert and wishes to see the conservatory, and another is hoping to view the Shakespeare collection, so I am not to be the afternoon's sole entertainment. Nevertheless, I should exercise these stiff fingers." He dabbed his lips with his napkin. "See you inside."

Clara smiled at Byron as Wallace strode toward the house. "Thank you for encouraging him."

"We all require encouragement now and again." He brushed his shirt-front free of crumbs and held out his hand. "Shall we go inside?"

His long fingers wrapped around hers, and he helped her stand. As soon as she was upright, however, he let go.

What would it have been like had he held on longer and we strolled across the grass like Aunt Letitia and Mr. Hollingsworth did, hand in hand?

She shook off the thought. "Should we look in Papa's office for his client list?"

"There will be time for that later. I don't wish to be a moment late for Wallace's concert. He seems like he could use a friend."

Yes, he did. And she'd clearly failed her brother in that way, for he was miserable.

Byron rested an elbow on the carved marble mantelpiece at the far side of the parlor, allowing other guests to take advantage of the chairs. Besides, this way he had an excellent view of Wallace, who tuned his violin.

While Byron hadn't heard Wallace play violin in years, he was already impressed. Clara's brother had no sheets of music at the ready. He'd memorized whatever he was to play.

"Wallace, darling," Letitia said from her chair in the front row. "What will you play?"

"A surprise." Wallace set his rosined bow to a string. The first strains carried through the room, slow and melodious. He paused for a beat, two, then quickened the pace into an energetic tune, perhaps Irish in origin. Clara, seated beside her aunt, nodded her head to the beat.

Mrs. Newton followed suit. Beside her, Mr. Newton looked on, his features inscrutable.

Would it kill the man to show his son a smidgeon of approval?

At least Byron had held his parents' affections when they died. He didn't have to guess how they felt about him or earn their love.

Perhaps if he had, though, mourning them might not have been so difficult. Their loss was so hard to bear, he'd decided it might not be smart to love with such vulnerability again. Not even his siblings, or he'd be devastated if he had to lose them too.

Oh, he cared for their needs. Fed and clothed them. Took them to church. Planned for their futures so they would fit into this class of society with greater ease than he did. But he'd walled off a part of himself from them to protect himself.

And them too, so they wouldn't hurt so much if something happened to him.

They knew he loved them, though, didn't they?

Byron sat with his uncomfortable thoughts for several minutes while Wallace played British folk songs that Peter Hollingsworth well knew, if the grin on his face was anything to judge by. Then Wallace transitioned to a slower, familiar tune.

Nettleton, the setting for a hymn they sang sometimes in church, "Come, Thou Fount of Ev'ry Blessing."

Byron knew the words by heart, and they echoed in his being along with the strains of the violin.

> *Come, Thou Fount of ev'ry blessing,*
> *Tune my heart to sing Thy grace;*
> *Streams of mercy, never ceasing,*
> *Call for songs of loudest praise.*

A fitting call to worship, but the story of the hymn might make a fine devotional for Clara to write, were she so inclined. As he recalled, the author had led a life of self-indulgence before coming to the Lord and becoming a pastor.

> *Jesus sought me when a stranger,*
> *Wandering from the fold of God;*
> *He, to rescue me from danger,*
> *Bought me with His precious blood.*

Byron shifted his weight from one foot to the other, his heart pierced by the words. Clara's lips moved a quiver, not as if she were singing along, but as if she too were well-aware of the the lyrics, recalling her own journey of faith.

Prone to wander, Lord, I feel it,
Prone to leave the God I love;
Take my heart, O take and seal it;
Seal it for Thy courts above.

The final strains of the violin echoed through his being. *Have I wandered from You, Lord?*

Of course he had. Daily he made choices that were not in line with God's will. In closing off his heart to his siblings and friends, had he also closed parts of himself to God?

Byron knew God waited for him to initiate a frank talk, man and Creator.

Wallace's eyes glimmered bright. Perhaps he was thinking something similar.

The small party's applause reached the ceiling, and Wallace received it with a small bow. Clara was on her feet, inciting the others to a standing ovation.

"Well done," Byron told Wallace once the others had offered their praise.

Wallace's smile made him look younger, freer. "Thank you."

"Now, everyone"—Letitia raised her voice—"there are refreshments on the terrace, or you're most welcome to join Mr. Sheldon in the library for Shakespeare or Mrs. Mulroney in the conservatory to view orchids."

A murmur of conversations hummed through the room. Byron wove his way to Clara's side. "Now might be a good time for our search."

Would it, though? A pang of guilt riddled his stomach. This might be an opportune time for their search, but he hadn't been thinking of propriety. A lady sneaking away with a gentleman to an empty room, unchaperoned, was simply not done. Not that Byron had untoward intent, of course, but he knew the rules of society. Clara, however, did not seem the least bit concerned. No doubt, she believed that the sooner she proved there was no one named John Smith on her father's client list, the better. "Let's go."

As they exited to the hallway, he kept watch to see if anyone noticed their direction. They turned a corner, and satisfied they were alone, he followed her into her father's office.

"Oh," she said.

Piles of paper spread over the desk. Files stacked on chairs. The office was a disaster.

"I don't know where to begin." She sounded overwhelmed. "He normally keeps the list in a file, but it appears he's sorting through things."

Byron headed for the piles on the chairs. "You search the desk. But if you see anything at all naming John Smith—"

"I'll tell you, fear not."

They hadn't much time, but Byron made quick work of skimming through files and notes, designs of vases, and correspondence—none with John Smith.

Byron looked up. "No client list here."

"Or here." Her voice cracked. "But I did find this in the drawer."

She held out something small, like a copper-green button.

No. A coin.

Her chin trembled. "I think it's Roman."

It had that appearance, but Byron was no expert. "That doesn't mean it's Vanacore's."

Her nod looked unconvincing. In fact, it looked downright sad.

"Clara, there's nothing incriminating here to tell us your father knew stolen goods were shipped out of the glassworks."

She stared at the coin. "Unless he—"

"That little coin is not proof. It may be a curiosity he's picked up along the way. Let's tuck it in the back of our minds for now, shall we? Revisit it later?"

Her nod was reluctant.

"I think it's time I looked into John Smith of Harrisburg."

"How?" She replaced the coin in the open drawer in front of her and slid it closed.

I'll travel there after I interview Vanacore tomorrow, right before your lunch with him."

"Could you not telegraph someone in Harrisburg to investigate him for you?"

"I could, but my editor suggested I visit the capital to research other articles anyway."

"But this John Smith is a criminal. What if your poking about turns dangerous?"

"It's more probable things will be boring." His words didn't ease the furrow between her brows. "Let's meet again to look through the glass-works. It's closed Saturday, isn't it?"

"It is." Many factories and employers kept their workers busy six days a week, but Papa allowed his personnel both Saturday and Sunday off.

"I'll be back from Harrisburg by then. Could you get us in so we can look at crates, that sort of thing?"

"Aunt Letitia and I have dress fittings in the afternoon, so we'll be out and about anyway. She'll not mind if we meet you, but I'll have to tell her what we're doing."

"Of course. I trust her discretion."

"Noon?"

He nodded. "In the meantime, perhaps you and I can begin writing the article. I'll start on the John Smith aspect if you wish to describe Vanacore's stolen antiquities. Perhaps you can inquire more about them at your lunch."

"A fair division of labor," she said, ignoring the slight barb in his tone when he mentioned her lunch with Mr. Vanacore. "And I shall keep my eyes open for the client list."

They'd been in here too long. Being caught wouldn't do for her reputation. Byron gestured toward the door. "Let's rejoin the others now."

By mutual agreement, they parted to join different groups. Within half an hour or so, however, the guests began to disperse. In the foyer, Byron retrieved his hat, thanked Clara's parents and aunt, and stopped to bid farewell to Clara.

Something was bothering her—her fidgeting fingers gave her away.

Was it that Roman coin she'd found? Or her brother, perhaps?

She didn't meet his gaze. "Godspeed on your trip, Byron. Do promise you'll be safe."

So that was what worried her? Him? Something shifted in his chest, like a cog in a long-dormant machine had been prodded to life.

And the last thing he wanted to do right now was leave her.

But he had to go, and he wanted to leave her smiling. "Thank you, Clara. I promise to take care. And enjoy the *coq au vin* tomorrow."

Her snort was most inelegant, and absolutely charming.

Byron walked home on light feet. Trouble or not, he couldn't deny it any longer. His feelings for Clara Newton had definitely begun to change.

❧ *Chapter 5* ❧

*C*lara had plenty to occupy her over the following days. She'd been enlisted to assist Aunt Letitia with wedding-related correspondence, and Mama sought her help with the reception menu. Throughout the week, Clara had been diligent in her household duties but also jotted down devotional pieces as well as composing the antiquities aspect of her article with Byron.

At least she was doing her best to write it, but to her utter vexation, Mr. Vanacore hadn't wanted to talk about his prized collection during their luncheon. She'd inquired three times, but he was more interested in discussing his political plans and introducing her and Mama to the influential friends he encountered in the restaurant.

Had Byron fared better in his quest to glean information on his trip east? She'd thought about him more than she wanted to all week, using her thoughts as a discipline to pray for his safety. At last the week was over, and she'd see him in a few hours, hale and hearty.

She hoped.

"Clara?" Mama entered Clara's bedroom. "You're going out?"

Clara tied the wide blue ribbon of her bonnet under her chin. "Aunt Letitia and I have our final dress fittings, Mama."

"I'd hoped to go over the reception menu one final time, but I suppose I am overthinking." Mama wandered to Clara's bureau. "Weddings are a great deal of work. Not that I mind, of course. When you marry, do not for a moment fret about the amount of effort involved. It is a pleasure to do it." Mama fiddled with the little mouse figurine on Clara's bureau beside the cameo. "Mr. Vanacore seems interested in courting, doesn't he?"

"I don't know, Mama. He never asks me much of anything." She reached past her mother to retrieve the cameo, pinning it to her blue jacket. "Why don't you put your feet up whilst Aunt Letitia and I are out and about?"

"Why are you so spirited this morning?" Mama scrutinized Clara's face. "Normally a dress fitting bores you."

Was she animated this morning? If so, it had more to do with meeting Byron in half an hour than with a dress fitting. Pausing to pat the mouse figurine on the head, she kissed her mother's cheek. "See you soon, Mama."

Downstairs she saw movement at the door, but it wasn't Aunt Letitia awaiting her. Wallace stood in the threshold speaking to a snub-nosed, jowl-cheeked man she'd seen before. Oh yes. He'd been in the street with Mr. Vanacore.

"Not here, understand?" Wallace's tone was rough.

The man said something Clara couldn't hear, but before she could cross the foyer, Wallace had shut the door.

"Who was that?"

"No one." His face was ashen.

"You said, 'Not here,' though. You know him?"

"He's a—salesman. Should've called at the glassworks."

"I saw him with Mr. Vanacore on Sunday. Perhaps he came to the wrong address."

"That must be it." But Wallace seemed more upset about it than he should have been over a sales call at the house or wrong address. Perhaps he was upset about something else. Had he exchanged tense words with Papa? Recalling her determination to be a better friend to her brother, she patted his arm. "How are you, Wallace? I've not seen much of you this week."

His smile wasn't convincing. "I'm well. Trying to stay out of the wedding business. Hollingsworth and I went fishing while you ladies had that tea Wednesday."

Clara hadn't fished in ages, but at once she thought of Byron, who excelled at fly fishing—there wasn't much out of doors he could not do well.

"Ready, darling?" Aunt Letitia almost floated into the foyer.

"Happy dress fitting," Wallace said.

"Thank you, dear." Aunt Letitia shared a conspiratorial smile with Clara. In the carriage, she rubbed her hands together. "This is so exciting."

"The dress fitting?" Clara teased.

Aunt Letitia rolled her eyes. "Meeting Byron at the glassworks."

"Thank you for accompanying me."

"You must have a chaperone. But this is also quite fun. Not that burglaries and arson are fun—I have bungled this."

"I knew what you intended." Clara gave her aunt's arm a fond squeeze. "I wonder what Byron gleaned on his trip to Harrisburg."

"That's been fun too—you and Byron together again." Aunt Letitia wiggled her brows.

"There is nothing between us, Auntie."

"There is *something*. Unlike you and Sylvester Vanacore."

"Byron and I are working on an article together—that is all."

Aunt Letitia nodded, but her amused smile didn't falter.

As today was Saturday, the glassworks was empty, and the street had the vacant feel of an abandoned city. It was so quiet, Clara could hear the lapping of the Monongahela River against the banks behind the building.

Aunt Letitia took a bracing breath. "The weather is magnificent. I hope it's this fine next Saturday."

"Rain or shine, your wedding day will be glorious."

"Look." Aunt Letitia gestured toward the steamboats chugging along the blue-green river.

It was a day to savor, indeed. To thank God for. *I haven't thanked You much of late, Lord, yet look at all You have provided. My dear aunt and family. A calling to write. This world around me.*

Byron's footsteps against the brick walk drew her around. She grinned. "You're in one piece. I was concerned."

"And I was bored, as expected." He bowed to Aunt Letitia. "Hello, ma'am."

"Byron, you've had our girl worried that the made-up John Smith and his thugs would harm you."

"Alas, I did not meet John Smith. The address I found on the crates is a warehouse. Locked tight, of course, and none of the workers in the neighboring buildings recall meeting a Mr. Smith, although they've seen one or two fellows at work in the nighttime hours."

Clara listened, although it was difficult to think of much beyond the fact that Byron was here, safe and sound. She resisted the urge to touch his cheek. "Is John Smith even a real person?"

"Public records show the warehouse belongs to a John Smith, and while a real man owns it, I am convinced the name is false and the warehouse is a front for illicit dealings. And now that I've made inquiries, I suspect our Mr. Smith will hear of it and disappear."

Aunt Letitia hummed. "This will make a fascinating article."

"To that end, shall we begin?" Clara withdrew the heavy key from her embroidered reticule. "Kent, our driver, will wait for us, but it wouldn't do to be here overlong."

"Indeed not," Aunt Letitia agreed as they entered the office. "Byron, what are we looking for, precisely?"

"Crates addressed to John Smith of Harrisburg. Paperwork indicating he is a client, that sort of thing."

"I'll look in Edgar's office." Aunt Letitia slipped inside, leaving Clara and Byron to hasten to the shipment room. Crates were piled in neat stacks awaiting Monday morning's shipment, and a manifest sat on the simple desk.

"Perhaps the client list is here." Clara hurried to the desk.

Byron pulled down the higher crates, restacking them as he finished reading the addresses. "Nothing to Harrisburg at all, but this one's for California. That's quite a ways."

"What a journey it will have, down around the bottom of the world."

He glanced at her. "So, you were really worried about me?"

"Of course. If that warehouse had been full of criminals, they could have hurt you."

"You do know not all criminals are thuggish brutes, don't you? I once heard of an eighty-year-old woman in Massachusetts who ran a smuggling ring."

"Nonsense."

"It's true."

"I don't believe it." She set aside the manifest, not finding a single Smith among the lot. Nor did she find a client list, so she joined him at the crates.

"One thing I know from reporting for a newspaper: criminals look like everyone else."

"Not in stories. Villains are always ugly," she teased, perusing a few addresses. "But that isn't real life. Our hearts are sometimes far uglier than our outward appearances."

Aunt Letitia strode into the room, dusting off her hands. "Nothing. I found the client list, and there's nothing in Harrisburg with a Smith in it."

"We aren't faring any better." Clara scrutinized another crate. "This one is to a Mrs. Petra Hill. I'm not familiar with that Christian name."

"Petra?" Aunt Letitia peered over her shoulder. "It's a feminization of my new favorite name, Peter."

Clara let the name sit on her tongue for a moment. "It's beautiful."

"I think so too." Byron smiled before turning back to move another stack of crates.

They'd almost finished when Clara snapped her fingers. "I recall hearing Papa say a shipment was going out today by special courier. It would be in the shed out back. The courier knows a key is hidden beneath the slab under the downspout."

Aunt Letitia grimaced. "What an unsavory place for it."

"I'll brave the slime." Byron looked at Clara. "Show me where it is?"

"Go on." Aunt Letitia waved them off.

Clara unbarred the back door and led Byron outside. The building abutted the river, and out here the air was sweet compared to the stuffiness of the shipment room. "This way."

"I hope we find nothing, Clara."

She did too, but a thrill of fear skittered her spine. Someone had dared use Papa's glassworks for illicit business. Justice must be served. *If there's anything to find, Lord, show it to us.*

Byron bent to lift the small mud-soaked slab beneath the downspout and withdrew a key.

As Byron held up the key for Clara, his eye caught on the pretty blue cameo pinned to her jacket. She'd worn it before, but he hadn't given it much thought. "Striking cameo."

"It has a history of accompanying adventure, and I guess it's true for me too."

"A history?" He twisted the key in the lock.

"Yes. I received it from Aunt Letitia, who received it from Queen Victoria."

"*The* Queen Victoria?"

She burst into laughter and then preceded him into the minuscule shed, which smelled of damp wood and rot. Three crates waited for the courier, stacked one atop the other.

They were quite large. He'd have to pull the top one down just to read its address. Thankfully, there was sufficient light from the open door to read by.

"How did your aunt come by the queen's cameo?"

Clara shared the story while he heaved down the heavy crate and set it at his feet. It was addressed to someone in New York. He didn't need to move the one beneath it to read its destination: a mercantile in Philadelphia.

Clara frowned. "One crate left."

"You should write an article about the cameo. Not for the newspaper. For the magazine, when you're contracted." *Oof.* This crate to Philadelphia was even heavier than the first.

"I shall. The cameo is a treasure, but I'm more touched by the generosity of it than the item itself, if that makes sense. The cameo reminds me of my aunt and her words of support when she gifted it to me."

He set down the crate to get a better grip. "That is why things become heirlooms. Like a mother's wedding ring. The financial value may not be great, but the value of the memory is precious."

"That right there sounds more like how you used to write. Narratives, I mean. Not about cameos and wedding rings, but other things."

"Narratives are— Well, journalism pays bills. Pa and Ma died within two days of one another, you recall. There were debts. The children and I moved to a smaller house, but it was better, all things considered. Closer to town and work."

"You were busy. I understood." She took a deep breath. "But I stopped seeing you at church."

"Attending the early service seemed best. Changing our routines so as not to be bombarded by memories of our parents at every turn." He prepared to lift the crate again.

"Your siblings must still miss your parents though."

"Probably." He lowered the crate atop the first one. "We don't talk about that sort of thing. Better to focus on the future and how I can help them achieve their goals so they can have lives of a gentleman and young ladies here in the city, not like where we came from." It was all far easier than talking about emotions with them, reliving the pain.

She flinched. "What's wrong with living where you came from? It was beautiful."

He stared at the address on the bottom crate. "Clara."

She went still. "John Smith. Harrisburg. Oh Byron."

He should be glad they'd found evidence. Instead, his gut ached for Clara. For her family and what this might mean.

Tools lined the back wall. Byron found a clawed cat's paw and a hammer and set about removing the nails. Clara clasped her hands beneath her chin as if she were praying.

He should do that too. *God, whatever this is here, help us do the right thing.*

He tugged off the lid and looked up at Clara. "Do you want to leave?"

"No. I want to see."

The blanket of packing straw prickled Byron's palms as he brushed it aside, revealing a box. Within it was a glass vase.

"One of ours. But it's inferior. See here?" Clara's finger traced a variation in the glass. "Papa would never send it out."

Byron retrieved more boxes from the crate. The next one was a vase as well, but not glass. A brown, glazed urn with figures painted on it, depicting a scene of ancient life. Roman life.

Clara's hand went to her mouth. "What do we do?"

"We don't allow it to ship out." Byron stood and returned the two vases to the crate. Hammering the lid back in place, he looked up at her. "Can you have the carriage driver take it to your house?"

"Yes." Her voice was small.

"Clara." He took her elbows in his hands. "Don't fret. One of your father's employees is about a dangerous game here, and we will put a stop to it."

She nodded, but her breath came in small, uneven pants.

He pulled her to him as if she were one of his sisters. But with her bonnet tucked under his chin and her lavender scent filling his senses, it didn't feel like he held a sister in his arms. "Shhh, Clara. All will be well."

In response, her arms wrapped around him.

The shed stank, and they stood beside stolen goods, but Byron relaxed into the moment, savoring the feel of her in his arms.

But only for a moment. He released her before he did something stupid, like continue to hug her until Letitia came looking for them. "I'll carry the crate. You lock the door, and I'll come back to hide the key under the slab. No need for you to get your hands dirty."

She pushed open the door, and he hauled the crate into his arms. It weighed far less than the crate headed to Philadelphia, but it was no light burden as he started hauling it to the main building. Behind him, the scrape of the key in the lock sounded. "Got it locked then?"

"Byron." Her voice was strange. Strangled.

He turned. A man shielded himself with Clara's body, one arm wrapped around her neck, the other holding a stubby blade to her ribs.

"All's I want is the gems and cash." The man's voice shook. "Quick-like and no one gets hurt."

His hands cold and vision swimming in red, Byron set the crate down in a slow, gentle motion.

"That's right," the thief said while Byron was still bent down with the crate. "Toss your purse this way." Then his hand—his filthy hand—snaked to grip the cameo pinned on Clara's dress.

Byron's hand reached into the back of his left boot and unsheathed a knife. He sent it sailing through the air before the thief could take another breath.

Chapter 6

*T*hwack.

Clara heard the knife hit the shed wall before she'd realized Byron had thrown it. It missed the brigand who held her, but his grip on her throat slackened.

She shoved the key over her shoulder where her captor's foul breath had wafted onto her cheek into what she hoped was their face. A yowl confirmed she'd hit something, and she kicked backward, hard, and broke free, running toward Byron.

Byron tugged another knife from his right boot. "I missed on purpose the first time, but I won't again."

The would-be thief dashed around the building. Clara gave chase, but Byron was faster, and he lunged past her, dropping his knife and catching the fellow around the knees. They tumbled to the grassy ground in full view of Kent, the carriage driver, who'd climbed down to stretch his legs.

Clara beckoned. "This man attacked us, Kent."

Kent ran toward them as Byron gripped the thief's wrists behind his back. "Rope, Kent?"

Aunt Letitia appeared from the back of the building. Upon seeing them, she stopped cold. "Clara?"

Clara offered a hasty explanation while Kent jogged back to the carriage and searched through the boot. He returned with a length of rope, and he and Byron tied the man's wrists behind his back.

"That isn't all." Clara gripped her aunt's arm. "We found something. A crate addressed to John Smith."

Her aunt's lips parted. "What was inside?"

"I'll show you." Clara led her aunt around the glassworks. They rounded the corner to the back.

Nothing awaited them between the building and the riverbank, however, but damp vegetation, flattened in the area where Byron had set down the crate. "But—I promise, Auntie, it was here. Where is it?"

Despair welled in Clara's chest. She ran around the other side of the building but saw nothing, no one.

Byron had joined Aunt Letitia by the time she returned. "It's gone, Byron."

"Someone took it whilst we dealt with that cutpurse. Perhaps it was chance, or perhaps they were working together and set up the attempted robbery as a distraction."

Tears began to spill. She took the handkerchief Aunt Letitia offered. "We lost the evidence."

"But we saw it. We know it exists." Byron dabbed a stray tear from her cheek with his thumb. "We will solve this puzzle yet."

"Alas, not today." Aunt Letitia dabbed moisture from her eyes too. "Shallow as it seems at the moment, darling, we have a dress fitting."

Clara almost groaned, but she had no desire to ruin anything for Aunt Letitia. This final fitting was important. Sniffing away the last of her tears, she nodded.

"Remain here a moment and compose yourself, dear. Byron, stay with her. I'll tell Kent we're almost ready, and perhaps we'll find someone to run to a watch house and fetch a constable, if any can be found there in daylight hours." Aunt Letitia's expression was grim, but Clara shared her aunt's frustration that the city watchmen were paid only to work at night. "Otherwise, we'll have to somehow transport that cutpurse ourselves to Mount Airy."

Clara smiled at Aunt Letitia's use of the nickname for the jail on Grant's Hill.

Once she left, Byron dug in his pocket. "Do you need another hand-kerchief? That one looks soggy."

It was, but her tears had stopped. "No, I'm all right now."

He strode toward the shed. With a tug, the knife he'd sent into the wall was free. He returned it to its hiding place in his left boot. He caught Clara watching and shrugged. "No matter how hard I try, the woodsman is still in me, I guess."

"I hope you stop trying to hide him. I loved that boy."

She froze, still as stone. She had *not* just said that. Had she?

Oh yes, she had. Byron was staring at her like she'd grown new ears.

Stomach shrinking, she grasped for words. "I meant, cared for. Liked very much. Loved as my *friend*."

He smiled. "You were kind not to judge me by what my father did or where I lived when so many thought his work beneath their notice."

She snorted, relieved he didn't press about her slip of the tongue. "Then they were fools. Without your father, many of them would have suffered cold winters without firewood, wouldn't they?"

"Perhaps."

"And your father was a kind man. You know, none of us are our occupations."

Byron looked out at the river. "Maybe for some, but those sailors there on the steamboats, most of them are men of the water. It's in their blood."

She'd once thought wood flowed through Byron's veins too. Like sap.

"I suppose. But we are more than what we do."

"I agree." He offered her his arm. "I don't wish you to be late for your dress fitting."

"I'd rather search for that crate."

Aunt Letitia rounded the corner, hand to her chest. "He's gone. The cutpurse."

First the crate, now this? Clara lifted her hem and jogged in a most unladylike fashion, circling the glassworks to behold the driver slumped against one of the large yellow carriage wheels. "Kent?"

"He's just now come to." Aunt Letitia knelt at the carriage driver's side, as did Byron.

Kent pushed himself upward. "I can stand, sir."

"Careful, man." Byron assisted him. "That's a brutal knot on your head."

"I kept my eyes on him, sir, honest, but the horses were edgy, and all I did was see to 'em. Next thing I know I'm on the ground with Miss Newton callin' my name. I don't know how he knocked me out with his hands tied behind his back, but he found a way."

"That brute." Clara shuddered.

"My spare knife is missing too." Byron's gaze searched the lawn. "I dropped it before I tackled him so I wouldn't hurt either of us. Looks like he went back for it."

"Was it your father's?"

"Yes. A bone-handled five-inch. . . Never mind. I'm far more concerned about Kent."

"I'm fine, sir." But Kent winced when he rubbed his head.

"Are you able to drive?"

"I am. My head is thicker than brick."

"Then I suggest you all go on, but see a doctor if needed, Kent. As for me, I shall find a constable or someone on the police committee."

"And the crate?" Clara hesitated while Kent assisted Aunt Letitia into the carriage.

"I'll inform the committee of that as well." Then he smiled, as if everything in the world was well. "Pray too. And have fun with your aunt. I'll speak to you soon."

She wanted to ask when, but Byron stepped away. There was naught left for her to do but pray and watch him walk away.

It was difficult to think of much beyond the cutpurse, the crate, and Byron—had she really said she'd *loved* him?—but Clara did her best to be attentive during the fitting and through the rest of the afternoon. The night was restless too, so she gave up on sleep before dawn, lit the lamp at her desk, and started to write.

First, she wrote a page for the article she and Byron were writing, then a page for her own eyes about the cameo, on how it came to her and how she wondered where it would go someday. Last, she penned a devotional piece on gifts, inspired by the cameo, and how she felt loved by Letitia and God to have received it—and how the fact that it was to be given again made her more mindful of His role in it. What a blessing it was to be the giver of a gift rather than the recipient.

Her fingers cramped by half past seven when she dressed for church. After writing the piece—and perhaps after having a knife in her ribs yesterday—she was awash in gratitude. She hurried downstairs to break her fast, kissing each member of her family good morning.

Wallace eyed her askance. "What's gotten into you?"

Papa set aside his newspaper. "Can't you be cheerful for once, Son?"

Wallace's face turned an odd shade of pink. "I'm fine."

"You've been foul of face since returning home yesterday afternoon. What were you doing, anyway? Gallivanting in town?"

"Nothing." Wallace scowled.

"Not nothing. You were gone three hours."

"Business."

"What sort of business?"

"I'm not ready to say yet. I'm wanting to surprise you." For the first time, Wallace's expression turned hopeful as he stared at Papa.

Papa grunted. "From your mood yesterday, I'd say your business isn't faring well."

Wallace's jaw set in an angry line.

Do something. Clara lifted the porcelain coffeepot. "More, Wallace?"

"No, thank you." Wallace excused himself.

She couldn't blame him for being hurt by Papa. She would have been too.

Mama reached her hand across the table toward Papa. "Perhaps it *is* business this time."

"What sort? And on a Saturday too. He's gambling, I'm sure of it."

The mood was grim the entire carriage ride to church. No one uttered a sound until the carriage pulled to a stop, and then Clara gasped. "Byron and the children."

Aunt Letitia widened her eyes as if to say *I told you there's something between you two.*

Clara wished she didn't hope her aunt was right, but she did. Not that she could explore her complicated feelings about Byron now.

Byron and the children met the carriage, and he greeted her parents, Auntie and Mr. Hollingsworth, and then her and Wallace.

"You've come to the later service," Clara said, stating the obvious, hoping for an explanation.

"Yes." Adele, the youngest girl, bounced on her toes. "The Sunday school picnic is after this service."

Of course—how foolish of Clara to have hoped this had something to do with her. "Those are such fun. That's how I first became friends with your brother. We were tied together in a three-legged race."

Genevie's smile was just like Byron's. "There's a Bible quiz too, and a prize."

"Which I'm certain you'll win, the way you've been studying," Byron noted with pride.

"Good for you," Papa said. "I always like to hear of a young person excelling in worthy pursuits."

"Byron." Pascal's voice was raspy, as if it pained him to talk. "I can't swallow."

Clara stepped closer. "Pascal?"

He stared at Byron, eyes wide with fear. "'Tis worse."

White lines formed around Byron's mouth. "Does anything else hurt? Never mind, do not speak, lad. I can see. Things have changed since we set out this morning."

Pascal's cheeks were flushed, but Clara had assumed it was from the exertion of walking to church. Now, with his weary-looking, watery eyes and cracked lips, she suspected fever. Paired with an aching throat, so bad he couldn't swallow. . .

Her ears and limbs tingled. *Scarlet fever?* She mouthed the words to Byron.

The thing that took his parents. Their declines began with sore throats and fevers.

Byron didn't need to nod. The fear in his eyes spoke enough.

He bolstered Pascal with an arm about the shoulders. "Pardon me. We must return home at once."

Pascal collapsed, unconscious. Papa rushed forward to ease the burden of the boy's weight. "Look here, Breaux, the boy must be examined by a physician."

"Agreed. But 'tis Sunday."

Adele started to cry. Clara wrapped the child in her arms.

Wallace, who'd been quiet since breakfast, cleared his throat. "Mercy Hospital. On Penn Street."

"That's it," Papa agreed. "Well done, Wallace. Come, we'll take him in the carriage."

Byron's face was pale as ash. "But you'll need the carriage. And the girls—"

"We do not mind walking home from services," Mama insisted.

"And I'll stay for the picnic with the girls." Clara would not tolerate him arguing with her. "I'll see them home and stay with them. Now go."

So upset was he that he didn't even look back. Genevie was crying now too. Clara offered her handkerchief and swallowed back the lump in her throat. "Have courage, girls. They have him in hand."

Mama made a sympathetic sound. "We will pray. Shall we all sit inside together?"

They did, but the girls didn't cheer much through the service. Neither did Clara. She was not surprised when Adele announced she wasn't interested in staying for the picnic.

"Me neither," Genevie agreed.

Clara couldn't blame them. "Let's go home then."

Mama chucked Clara's cheek and inquired as to the address. "I shall send a carriage for you at four. If Byron is not home by then, all three of you come for supper, understood? And bring night things, girls, just in case."

"Thank you, Mama." Clara gave her a quick hug before setting off with her charges.

Genevie folded her arms tight about her chest as they walked. "Is it what our parents had?"

Clara wished she could reassure her. "I don't know for sure." Although it seemed so. Sore throat, painful swallowing, and fever without congestion or other symptoms did often lead to scarlet fever. One never knew until the scarlet rash, rough as sandpaper, popped out on the skin. *Please God, do not let it be so.*

She walked between the girls to a neighborhood far different from the one on the wooded edge of town where Byron had been raised. This neighborhood was far more central for Byron's work, but this two-story, narrow townhouse of red brick before her seemed almost suffocating compared to the life the Breauxs must have lived in the woods.

He'd wanted to escape being a woodsman's son. By the looks of it, he'd achieved it.

Genevie let them inside the house, one room wide. They passed a staircase she guessed must lead to the bedrooms and found a parlor, a dining area that also doubled as a workspace, and a small kitchen at the back. It was cozy and tidy, but dark, with few windows.

Clara found leftover roast in the icebox, the family's intended supper. Well, they'd dine at Clara's house tonight, so eating it now wouldn't matter. While she set out the food, she noted a tin of sugar and an herbal tincture in the pantry.

"Girls, may I use this?"

"Are you sick too?" Adele's chin quivered.

"Of course not. I thought we might make lozenges for Pascal's sore throat after lunch."

When they'd forced down a few bites, they tidied their plates, and Clara gathered ingredients. "Adele, fetch a thimble."

The girl looked at her as if she was daft, but complied.

Clara showed them how to combine the sugar, tincture, and water until it formed a stiff paste. Then she used a rolling pin to flatten it. "Punch out rounds with your thimble."

The girls took turns at the task, and Clara found a roasting pan. "Here, lay them out on this. We'll dry them in the oven."

"They look like candy," Genevie noted.

Adele pulled her finger from her mouth. "Taste like candy too."

They all giggled.

While the lozenges dried, Clara and the girls settled into the parlor with books. Clara attempted to read but spent the time praying and looking out the lone window onto the street. After a while, she stood. "I'll check on those lozenges."

They weren't quite dry, but she'd needed to stretch her legs. With slow steps, she made her way back to the parlor, pausing in the dining area and workroom.

Here she found all of the intimate, normal signs of family life: the girls' sewing kits, school primers, chalk and slates, a store of ink, and reams of paper. Atop a shelf, she found even more paper, but these sheaves were filled with Byron's familiar handwriting.

She shouldn't—but she couldn't help herself.

. . .that this region, known in the Seneca tongue as "Di-
ondegâ" was explored by the British and French. When
first the eyes of the European voyagers alighted on the lobed

leaves of the poplar, one of the largest of all hardwood trees
in our fair land, did they yet know of its use? Soon enough,
they hollowed the trunks for canoes, that they might
navigate the local waterways. The poplar also. . .

Poplars? Clara read on as Byron described their historical and current value. Was this some sort of report?

Following the hard-won War of Independence in 1783, the
little village of settlers outside Fort Pitt grew. Many of its
first rudimentary structures and log cabins were built of
eastern hemlock. The tree grows slowly, but lives long. . .

Trees. Byron was writing about the history of the Pittsburgh area, yes, but woven through each account, he also wrote about trees, the very thing he'd known best as a boy. She flipped through the pages, finding the beginning—she assumed, since it was an account of the Iroquois Confederacy's hunting ground, to stories of the Shawnee and Lenape tribes, to where she'd started to read. Byron described the people and the land, especially the trees.

From the beauty of the white and pink bracts of a blooming dogwood in spring, to the way white spruce needles feel rolling between one's fingers, Byron described them as he knew them, with vivid detail and with affection.

This was no article. It was a narrative, like he used to write. A chronicle of Western Pennsylvania's history and a description of the land.

"The trees are a greater part of you than you even know." Clara couldn't help but smile.

"Clara?" Genevie called from the front room. "Byron's coming up the walk. He's alone."

Clara returned Byron's narrative to the shelf. "Alone?" Where was Pascal?

She hurried to meet him at the door, fearing the worst.

Three pairs of concerned female eyes met Byron at the front door. Smiling, he raised his hands. "The physician is confident Pascal does not have the beginnings of scarlet fever. He lacks certain indicative symptoms, but they wished to keep him overnight for observation."

Clara slumped against the hall wall. "Praise the Lord."

"I was so frightened." Genevie sniffed.

"I was too, the way he fainted." Adele hugged herself.

Relief coursing through him, Byron pulled his sisters into his arms. "The Sisters of Mercy are taking good care of him. He'll be fine."

But Byron couldn't say the same of himself.

He'd worked so hard to guard himself against feeling this sort of fear again. Then he'd thought Pascal would succumb to the same thing that took his parents, and the fear toppled his wall like an earthquake.

His sisters squirmed to be released from his arms. Unsurprising. He hadn't hugged them like this in a long time.

"We made lozenges," Genevie announced.

"They're delicious." Adele added.

"And they're for Pascal," Clara said. "I hoped they might help ease his throat."

"You look tired." Dark pouches beneath her eyes disagreed with the way she shook her head. "Your father awaits you in the carriage."

"He stayed with you?" Clara pushed off from the wall.

"His presence was a comfort." And a surprise. Byron had long assumed Newton thought him beneath their family, although he never said as much. Byron had misjudged the man.

"Well, let's all go join him. Girls, fetch your coats."

"Join him?"

"You're all welcome for supper. Mama is expecting us, and there is little left for you here anyway. We ate part of your roast."

Tempting, but Byron held up a hand. "We cannot impose any longer."

"I insist." When he didn't relent, she smiled. "Please?"

He was tired, his emotions wrung out like wet laundry. And truth be told, he didn't want to be without her right now. He nodded.

They piled into the carriage. If Mr. Newton minded all of them coming home with him for Sunday supper, he did not show it. In fact, his attention was all for the girls. "Who won the Bible quiz?"

"We don't know, sir." Genevie smoothed her skirt over her knees in a ladylike gesture. "We were not up to attending."

Adele nodded. "We made candy for Pascal instead. I mean lozenges."

"Clara's lozenges? They're quite good, aren't they?" Newton winked.

Adele giggled.

Byron sat across from Clara, their knees brushing in the close confines of the carriage. She didn't look at him, but at his sisters, her expression weary but content. She liked them, didn't she? They seemed to like her too.

Their families had never intertwined like this. He'd run free at her house as a lad, and she'd played with his siblings at Sunday school picnics and such, but today felt different, with her parents involved. It didn't feel like charity, or even like hospitality for him and his sisters in their crisis. This felt more like what he remembered about being with family.

His knees burned where they met Clara's.

Soon enough they were in the Newton's elegant foyer, receiving warm greetings from Mrs. Newton, Letitia, and Mr. Hollingsworth and concerned inquiries about Pascal. The scents of supper—ham, perhaps—reached Byron, making his stomach squeeze. He hadn't eaten since breakfast, and that had been a simple bowl of porridge. *Thank You, Lord, for a place to land tonight. That I can be with Clara. I don't know why I so crave her company now, but—*

Wallace bustled into the foyer, followed by a familiar, barrel-chested figure.

Mrs. Newton gestured. "Mr. Vanacore stopped in, so I invited him to dine with us."

Byron's hand was grasped by Vanacore's and given a vigorous pumping. "Terrible news about your brother, Mr. er—"

"Breaux. And thank you, but he will recover."

"Good." Vanacore clapped his shoulder and then left him for Clara.

Byron's stomach tightened, and no longer from hunger.

Clara did not appear delighted by Vanacore's attention during the simple but hearty meal of baked ham, steamed potatoes, and creamy parsnips that tasted far richer and more delicious than Byron ever remembered a parsnip tasting. Perhaps it was his empty stomach, or his relief over Pascal's diagnosis, but he asked for seconds.

"Clara's recipe," Mrs. Newton said.

She cooked? His surprise must have shown, because Clara laughed. "I'm known to frequent the kitchen."

"Her lozenges are her most delicious recipe, though," Adele added.

Vanacore shifted in his seat. "One of the finest meals I've eaten was in Harrisburg. As I was saying to the mayor about my congressional plans. . ."

Clara smiled at Byron while Vanacore droned on.

When the peach pie had been consumed and everyone adjourned to the parlor, Clara approached Byron. "I'd like some air, wouldn't you?"

He glanced at the french doors to the terrace then back at her family. "Would they mind?"

"I don't think so."

"Vanacore might."

Rolling her eyes, she led him outside. "I notice you did not inform Mr. Vanacore about his vase in the missing crate."

"The captain of the watch thought it best to further investigate before raising Vanacore's hopes."

A cool evening breeze tousled a few loose strands of her hair. He tucked a wayward tendril behind her ear.

"Thank you. I must be a mess." Before he could argue she was perfect, she smiled. "I'm glad about Pascal."

"When I thought it could be scarlet fever, it opened some wounds I thought long-healed. But they weren't. I'd just ignored them. Just as I have the children, in a way."

"You haven't ignored them. Look at the girls." She tipped her chin toward the parlor, where his sisters curled on the floor with a game. "They know you love them."

"Today was the first time I've embraced them like that in. . .I don't know how long."

"You used to be so affectionate with them."

"Affection leads to pain when someone dies, Clara." He shook his head. "I thought if I held back my emotions, loss wouldn't affect me so deeply the next time."

Admitting this both ached and soothed. In his mind, he heard the old hymn again that Wallace had played on the violin: *Prone to wander, Lord, I feel it, prone to leave the God I love.* How he'd wandered by refusing God access to his heart.

"Love brings risk of loss, yes. But it also brings joy. Your siblings are wonderful, and, look there at Auntie and Mr. Hollingsworth." The couple shared an affectionate glance inside the house.

"Your aunt and her fiancé seem well matched. As do your parents, but your father's love for his children comes with conditions. Much to Wallace's unhappiness." He scrubbed his face with his hand. "Clara, I'm sorry. My fatigue has gotten the best of me, I'm afraid. I didn't mean that."

"Yes you did." She stiffened. "And you're right. I think Papa believes he's pushing us to success with his comments, but they haven't helped. He loves us unconditionally, but there are conditions to his praise. I wasn't aware until you helped me see it, but observing what it's done to Wallace has opened my eyes to my failure to be his friend."

"I haven't been a friend to my siblings either."

"You've been too busy being their father."

"I've provided, yes, but today, when I might have lost Pascal? My choice to close off my heart to him didn't protect me from fear or pain at the prospect of losing him. All it's done these past few years is put distance between us."

Her warm hand slipped over his. Her touch was gentle, but the connection was so strong it felt as if she tethered him to earth. "These past four years have been difficult for you. You've given up so much."

"Some, but with the promotion at the *Gazette*, I should be able to afford more for them. And a larger house."

"With trees, I hope? Not in the center of the city?" She looked at her toes. "I saw your writings today. The narrative on Western Pennsylvania. I'm sorry I snooped."

Embarrassment flooded hot in his chest. "Ramblings, that's all."

"Do not dare diminish it. I found it quite compelling. And enlightening."

"The history?"

"Interesting, yes, but I meant your words about the trees. The woods are still such a part of you. What I read today was how you used to write, free and unencumbered. I could smell the green of the fields you described and feel the fir needles rolling between my fingers. You should seek its publication, Byron."

"For what purpose? I'm a journalist now."

"A journalist and a historian and a man who knows the land. A loving brother. A fierce provider. A gentleman."

"I was not born a gentleman like your father."

"*Gentleman* refers to character, not to birth. And you are a gentleman, Byron."

Their hands were still touching, even as she shifted to stand in front of him. So close he could kiss her.

He wanted to. His lips burned. Just one little tug on her hand, pulling her closer. Her head was already tipped up toward him, like a flower to the morning sun.

Voices carried from the garden below. Angry voices.

Clara pulled back and peered over the banister. "Wallace?"

Sure enough, Wallace strode away from the house with another man. Their conversation, while too hushed to make out, carried angry tones.

The other fellow's stub nose wrinkled in anger. Byron squinted to see in the darkness. "Who is that?"

"A salesman, according to Wallace. But I saw him with Mr. Vanacore too." Gasping, she turned back to face Byron. "I don't think he's a salesman."

Byron's stomach dropped. "I think you're right."

The french door scraped against the terrace floor. "I beg pardon for intruding," Mr. Newton said.

Byron dropped Clara's hand. How stupid he'd been, forgetting they were in plain view of everyone. Holding her hand and thinking of kissing her? If he'd harmed Clara's reputation in any way, he'd kick himself.

Mr. Newton's chin lifted. "Does this mean I am to expect a conversation with you, Breaux?"

Any idiot would know what Newton meant by "a conversation." Byron's silk necktie felt as if he'd knotted it too tightly.

But he nodded. "Yes, sir. We should speak. Now. In private. With Clara."

⚘ Chapter 7 ⚘

*T*here is no need for a *conversation*." Clara's spine straightened stiff as a yardstick. "We were talking, Papa. That was all."

"So I could see."

Clara couldn't meet Papa's gaze, but judging by his tone, he could read her embarrassment.

She and Byron might only have been talking, but she'd certainly wanted more to happen. She had since she was seventeen and Byron had pulled her against his chest when he taught her how to throw a knife. In that moment, which hadn't been intended to be romantic in any way, she'd realized how much she cared for him.

And she never stopped.

Shaking off her traitorous thoughts, she folded her arms. "It won't happen again."

"You don't plan to talk to me ever again?" Byron's lips twitched.

This was insufferable. He knew what she meant!

Unaffected by her glare, Byron tipped his head. "Let's join your father."

With a huff, Clara stomped past Byron and Papa into the house, marching straight to Papa's office. If she was to receive a scolding about holding hands with Byron on the terrace, fine. But there was no reason for it. There was nothing romantic between them. They were working on an article—

Oh. Byron intended to inform Papa about the article. He'd wanted to wait, but now he felt he had no choice but to tell Papa to explain their being together so often.

She sat down on one of the chairs that had recently been piled with papers. Despite herself, her gaze flittered to Papa's desk, where she'd found that copper coin. She should ask him about it when she had opportunity.

"Sir." Byron took the seat Papa offered. "Clara and I are working together on an article."

"Oh?" He looked amused. "Do tell me about it."

Byron crossed his ankle over his knee. "First, I apologize for taking such liberties with Clara, holding her hand. She was comforting me about Pascal. But as to the article, you'll recall my inquiry about Purl and Vanacore's stolen antiquities."

Papa looked disappointed. "I do."

"I couldn't write it without Clara. She and I are partners, investigating the illegal dealings surrounding Vanacore's stolen antiquities, which, I am sad to say, have continued."

"What do you mean?" Papa stiffened. Then his gaze broke away as the door opened behind Clara.

Wallace lingered in the threshold. "Sorry for disturbing you. I . . . need a pencil."

Who had he been talking to outside? She'd ask him the moment they were finished with Papa.

Papa beckoned Wallace into the office. "Did you know Clara has been writing an article with Byron about Vanacore's stolen goods? Seems they're still being shipped out. Not sure how, though, since Purl is in jail."

"I hadn't heard." Wallace strode to the desk and retrieved a pencil from the top drawer. Did he see the little coin in the drawer? "Sounds dangerous."

Byron faced Papa. "It was, I'm afraid, and I take full responsibility for the cutpurse taking a knife to Clara's ribs."

Papa bolted from his chair, his face flushing scarlet. "What is this? Someone had a knife to your ribs?"

Oh dear. She offered a smile to calm him. "Byron protected me. I am fine. And Aunt Letitia was chaperone." It seemed important to mention that, since Papa had seen her and Byron holding hands.

Papa's nostrils flared. "You could have been killed."

"I said I'm fine, Papa. I scarcely felt that knife at all. What's more important is Mr. Purl was not the only one to ship out Mr. Vanacore's stolen items. Byron and I believe—oh Papa—someone is using the glassworks to do the same. I'm so sorry."

His nostrils flared again, but he returned to his seat. "You've proof?"

Byron nodded. "We lost it, but yes." He gave a brief recount of the name he first saw at Purl's, John Smith, and of seeing it on a crate at the glassworks, as well as all that led to yesterday's occurrence and their decision to speak to the captain of the watch. "Unless an outside person had access to your discarded vases, the culprit must be someone who has right of entry to the glassworks, sir."

"I'm most disappointed someone betrayed me by using my business for such a thing." Papa rubbed the bridge of his nose, still visibly upset, but at least he wasn't quite as bright a shade of red anymore. "Be assured, Byron, Clara, there will be no more illegal shipments from the glassworks, if I must inspect every outgoing crate personally."

Byron glanced at Clara. "So we may finish the article, sir? We will not dishonor your name or the glassworks."

"I don't care about that, so long as you are safe. No more knives to her ribs, you understand." He cast a meaningful look at Byron.

"I do, and again, sir, I apologize."

Papa exhaled a long breath, glancing at Wallace before returning his gaze to Byron. "You understand too you might never know the identity of the lawbreaker I've the misfortune to employ. Men come in and out of the glassworks, working a few weeks and then hopping a steamboat for a new place. Some of the most talented in this craft prefer transience and hard drink to stability. One of my employees left Friday, in fact."

"Maybe that's the fellow who did all of this." Wallace broke his silence. Until now he'd stood, tense shouldered and wide-eyed, by the desk.

"Hopefully we—or the watch—will identify the culprit and return Vanacore's possessions, if any more are left to be found." Clara sighed. That would be the most satisfying end to the article and the situation, at any rate.

"Either way, the story sounds big enough for you to get your newspaper experience so you can write your devotionals for the magazine, poppet." He glanced at his son. "Any other thoughts, Wallace?"

Wallace's brows rose. "If the culprit has not left the glassworks, but he is not able to ship out stolen items anymore, the arsonist might strike again, as he did at Purl's. The fire was retribution for Purl stopping the arrangement, wasn't it?"

"He has said so, yes." Byron's eyes narrowed. "But I didn't know that was common knowledge yet. It was said in my hearing the morning of the fire, but the only others around were the constables and Vanacore."

"That must be how I heard it." Wallace shrugged.

Papa rose and strode to his desk. "I'll hire another night watchman for the glassworks, and a day watchman too." He jotted a note to himself. When he opened the drawer to return the pencil to its tray, Clara remembered the coin.

"Papa, yesterday I noticed something in that drawer. A little coin. Roman, maybe."

Papa held it up. "Is this what you're talking about? I found it outside the glassworks. Is it Vanacore's? The thief must have dropped it. I'll return it to him." Papa pocketed it as his gaze flickered to Clara. "Other than returning this to Vanacore, I assume I am to remain discreet about the other matters we discussed? I shan't tell anyone but your mama. Speaking of whom, she'll have the coffee waiting. We should rejoin the others before it's cold."

Clara didn't want to go yet. The conversation felt unfinished. All of tonight's conversations felt unfinished. The one on the terrace, this one—and who was Wallace arguing with in the back garden anyway?

Something about Wallace's expression disturbed her. It was stiff, like a mask. As if—

A wave of dizziness washed over her.

Papa and Wallace led the way from the office. She fell back, gripping Byron's sleeve, keeping him in place for a moment. "Wallace is involved, isn't he? Shipping out the stolen items? I don't know why, or if he stole Mr. Vanacore's things or how he fits into what happened at Mr. Purl's, but I think he's part of this."

His fingers covered hers over his arm, in comfort. And agreement, because he couldn't answer, not with Wallace turning back to look at them.

"Coming, you two?"

Byron lowered his hand, and it felt as if she'd lost more than the tender pressure of his fingers.

It felt like the world was falling apart.

"No coffee, thank you, ma'am." Now that he believed Wallace was shipping stolen goods out through the glassworks, Byron's churning stomach wouldn't tolerate anything, but he couldn't say that to Mrs. Newton. "The girls have school tomorrow, and I wish to be at Mercy Hospital in the morning."

Newton tugged the parlor bellpull. "I'll call for the carriage."

Adele trudged toward Byron in a comic display. "May I stay home from school to welcome Pascal?"

"Recall your manners, now." Byron could, however, relate to her vexation. He'd rather do anything than function like an adult tomorrow. *God, what are Clara and I to do now?*

90

Adele spun to the Newtons, casting her charming smile on them. "Thank you for supper."

"Yes, thank you," Genevie chimed in. "It was delicious."

"Our pleasure." Mrs. Newton hugged the girls. "I'll send soup for Pascal's supper tomorrow, if I may."

"Thank you." Byron tried to make his smile reach his eyes. He was grateful, but his heart was heavy.

Wallace—what have you done?

He and Clara lacked proof as yet, but they knew in their bones her brother was guilty. Now they faced a choice: continue the investigation and prove her brother dealt in stolen goods, or ignore Wallace's actions and spare Clara's family the shame.

Could Byron live with himself if he kept mum about Wallace's crimes or stopped searching for proof?

There was, of course, a lesser issue, but if he didn't write this article— or something else worthy of his editor's attention—his editor would not promote him to steady work and would give the position to someone else. Byron would be forced to wait until another senior journalist left the *Gazette*, however long that would be.

You must keep searching for proof and write the article for the sake of justice. And for the children, who deserve better provision than you offer now.

But what will it do to Clara? The truth exposed will devastate her family.

No one in the room could guess at the war waging in his chest. Vanacore pocketed the coin Mr. Newton returned to him without showing any surprise or relief at seeing it again, choosing instead to blather on about his commitment to improving law and order once he was a congressman. Meanwhile Byron's sisters commandeered the attention of everyone else.

"Thank you for inviting us to your wedding," Genevie said to Letitia. "We've never been to one."

Clara's overbright smile didn't fool Byron a whit. "Never? Not a one?"

Adele shook her head. "But I know a song about a wedding: 'Frog Went A-Courtin'."

"I used to sing that. With your brother." Clara glanced at him.

She remembered that too?

Mr. Hollingsworth's brows lifted. "I know it from my nursery days, a thousand years ago, but I always thought it was about Mary of Guise and the French Prince Louis. *Frog*, you see. . ."

"Not now, dear." Letitia nudged him. "Girls, sing it, do."

Adele's sweet, somewhat flat voice started the tune. "Frog went a-courtin', and he did ride, mm-hmm."

Genevie joined in. Soon the adults added their voices. "Took Missie Mouse upon his knee. Mm-hmm. Took Missie Mouse upon his knee, said, 'Missie Mouse, will you marry me?' Mm-hmm."

It was a regular choir when Clara slipped away and sidled beside Byron. "Am I correct? About Wallace?"

"I think so, yes."

Watching him tonight while they informed him and Newton about the smuggling, he'd seemed frozen, silent until he encouraged casting the blame on the transient worker at the glassworks. Not once did he grow angry like his father, or even confused. He'd been as still and silent as a sculpture. In fact, he'd seemed to Byron like he knew about the situation and didn't want to reveal a thing.

"He couldn't have been the one to steal the artifacts though. They were stolen on a Sunday morning. Wallace was in church with us."

"One thing Purl said was that there was a man in the middle, betwixt him and the person in charge of the scheme. That means this middleman might well be the thief, delivering them to Purl and now perhaps to Wallace. Could he be that man outside tonight? You said you saw him with Vanacore though too."

"I did, but it makes no sense."

Nothing did. "It's the work of a journalist to make sense of these facts, Clara."

"But I don't want to be a journalist. I don't want to do this anymore."

Pain speared Byron's gut, like he'd been kicked. "You don't want to pursue the story now." He could read it on her face, which she'd turned away from the rest of the group, as if she looked out onto the terrace.

"If we do, what will it do to my family?"

"And if we do not, what about justice? We would let criminals steal and burn and go free?"

Her fingers crumpled fistfuls of her skirt. "I know, Byron. I know. Allow me time to think. To pray."

Byron turned his gaze away, toward the others. His sisters seemed so happy, entertaining the others while they awaited the carriage.

This was the sort of house he wanted for them. Not this grand, of course, but a safe home in a respectable neighborhood, flush with the advantages that came from having money. At least a little money.

His dream of the promotion crumbled this moment, like dry bread left on the counter too long.

But that didn't mean he'd abandon his scruples.

"I won't write the article we'd intended, Clara. But I will see justice done another way."

Clara spun around. "But—"

"You've monopolized Miss Newton long enough." Vanacore approached, smiling as if he joked, but his eyes were tight.

"The carriage is here," Newton called.

"I leave her at your disposal, Vanacore. Good night, Clara." Byron offered a crisp nod.

"Wait," Clara called. "When will I see you next? I—I want to hear how Pascal is doing."

"We will send word."

With that, Byron gathered the girls and left the house. He didn't look back.

Maybe Clara understood what he hadn't been able to say, that he wasn't just walking away from the story. He was walking away from her too.

She was shocked, as he was, over their suspicion Wallace was in such trouble. But right had to win out. Justice had to prevail.

Even at the cost of parting ways with Clara.

❧ *Chapter 8* ❧

*H*ow had Clara managed to sleep that night? Or any night since Byron left with the girls six days ago? Every evening, she'd clutched the little mouse Byron whittled for her years ago and prayed for help, guidance, forgiveness, and for Byron. Then she'd set the mouse beside the cameo and tried to sleep.

She yearned to talk through the dilemma, come to a solution about what to do with their suspicions—

But the only contact between his home and hers this week was a note to her parents thanking them for their help and hospitality, saying Pascal was much improved. Byron hadn't mentioned whether he was still coming to Aunt Letitia's wedding today.

Perhaps he'd intended his silence as a message for Clara. She took as deep a breath as she could manage in her close-fitting rose maid-of-honor gown and gazed out the window of Aunt Letitia's bedroom.

"Things will never be the same again."

"I'm not going far." Aunt Letitia, resplendent in her simple yet elegant wedding gown, kissed Clara's cheek. "But yes, things are changing. Except for how I feel about you."

Clara laughed and teared up at the same time. "Oh Auntie."

Aunt Letitia withdrew a handkerchief from the top drawer of her bedroom dresser. "No more tears. I am marrying Peter today."

"And I'm happier than you can know."

"You haven't seemed it this week." She chucked Clara's chin. "But I suspect it has more to do with Byron than me."

"It's everything," Clara admitted. Watching Byron walk out into the summer night on Sunday ached. It wasn't as if a maiden lady like her could call on him at home, or write a note begging him to visit. Aunt Letitia and Mama needed her help with the wedding anyway, so she'd run their errands and crafted decorations, and in the evenings, she wrote. She'd even submitted a few things to the newspaper, well-knowing they weren't "newsworthy" enough for the editor, but she'd tried anyway.

Aunt Letitia patted her arm. "You're worried about Wallace too, of course."

She'd told Aunt Letitia everything that had transpired Sunday night. They'd stayed up late that night to talk, in this very room.

"Wallace has been gone most days, out late at night. And Papa has been busy too, although he told Mama he spoke to an investigator about the smuggled goods going through the glassworks, so I know the constables are involved."

"Your brother and papa have avoided me too, but I've been praying."

"Me too. And. . .I think Byron is right. We cannot allow crime to continue."

"I agree."

"Here I am, blathering about crime on your wedding day. What nonsense." Clara tucked the hanky in her sleeve. "Shall we go?"

"You're not ready yet. You're not wearing the cameo."

She hadn't worn it all week. It reminded her too much of Byron, which was silly, because it had nothing to do with him.

Clara slipped out to her room, took the cameo from its spot by the carved mouse on the dresser, and returned to Aunt Letitia's room. "Where shall I pin it?"

"Above your heart. Allow me." Aunt Letitia affixed the cameo to Clara's rosy bodice. "I told you this cameo might accompany adventure. It has, but I do not think your adventure is finished. It's just beginning. Every day new adventure awaits. I know the cameo did not bring me love, of course. But the gift of it coincided with the arrival of love, both for the queen and for me, and I still hope it will bring the same to you."

Clara squashed her aunt in an embrace. "I love you."

"And I you. Things are changing, yes, but not everything. I will always be your aunt. More than that, your friend."

A sob sounded from the doorway. Mama swiped her eyes and joined them, wrapping her arms around both of them. "I'm so proud of you both."

"For what, Mama?" Clara smoothed the rumpled fabric of Auntie's gown.

"For loving one another." She took a fortifying breath. "I came to tell you it is time. The guests are in the parlor, Reverend Brown waits, and Peter looks as if he might faint. I suggest we hurry."

"Indeed." Clara handed her aunt the bouquet of pink roses that had been waiting on the bureau. "Mr. Hollingsworth should swoon when he sees you, not before."

Papa met them in the hall and took Aunt Letitia's arm. "You're a beautiful bride. And you're a beautiful bridesmaid, poppet."

"Thank you, Papa."

Clara knew her job. She descended the staircase and strolled to the parlor, where a few dozen guests waited. Relatives sat among friends and neighbors, with Mr. Vanacore seated beside Wallace. And oh, she'd know the caramel swirl of Byron's hair anywhere.

He came. The girls and Pascal too, his cheeks rosy and eyes bright.

Byron smiled at her. A tiny one, but a smile nonetheless.

She took her spot near the hearth, which had been filled with flowers for the occasion. On the far side of Reverend Brown, Mr. Hollingsworth stood at attention. The moment Aunt Letitia entered the room on Papa's arm, he grinned. There was no disputing his affection for her.

Thank You, Lord. For this wedding and marriage. For Aunt Letitia's love and prayers for me. For Byron being here. Please allow us an opportunity to speak.

And for Wallace's heart, Lord, please. . .

She didn't know what else to pray. She'd have to trust the Lord with her brother.

Within short minutes, the service was over, and Mr. Hollingsworth kissed Aunt Letitia.

Clara embraced them both. "Congratulations, Aunt Letitia, *Uncle* Peter."

"I like the sound of that," he said before he kissed her cheek.

They adjourned to a luncheon reception set up in the shady garden. Surrounded by bright green shrubs, herbs, and fragrant rosebushes, the scene was the picture of summer. It was as if the brightness and blossoms of the day heralded the start of Letitia and Peter's marriage, promising a bright future.

After the speeches, the happy couple cut into a sugar-frosted fruit-cake rich in nuts and dried cherries. Free to mingle, Clara rose from her chair. She'd been waiting to speak to Byron—and Wallace, for that matter—and now that her duties as maid of honor were executed, she didn't wish to wait another minute.

Mr. Vanacore's broad form blocked her path, preventing her from taking more than a few steps. "You're a vision, my dear."

"Thank you, but I am not your dear."

He didn't seem to have heard her. "Tonight, let's ride through the park."

"I am committed to family, Mr. Vanacore."

"Are you? Or do you have plans with that Mr. Brick fellow?" He glared at Byron.

"Mr. *Breaux*. You've met him several times. He interviewed you for the newspaper, and the article made the third page."

"It was a favor I did, allowing him to interview me when he's a nobody. Paid by the piece, did you know that? Not even salaried."

"He's the finest writer I've ever encountered, and I take umbrage with your slur. He did you a favor, interviewing you, yet you are most ungrateful."

His small eyes narrowed. "Are you two courting?"

"No." Not that it was his business. "I am courting no one, and I do not see that changing in the foreseeable future."

His lips worked a moment. "Perhaps you've forgotten, but I'm to be a congressman."

"I have not forgotten. Enjoy the party, Mr. Vanacore."

His face turned hard, just as it had when she noticed him outside her window when he spoke to the jowl-cheeked man with whom Wallace had spoken. How could she have forgotten to ask Vanacore about it? But now it was too late, for he marched away, shaking his head.

Meanwhile, there were others to speak to. Where was Wallace? Or Byron? She didn't even see his siblings. Perhaps they'd gone inside. In the foyer, one of the manservants they'd hired for the occasion caught her eye. He held an envelope.

"This arrived for you, miss."

"Thank you." She carried the envelope to the conservatory. Taking a seat in the empty room beside a potted palm, she tore open the envelope with her thumb.

"Good news?"

Byron lingered in the threshold. She stood, so overcome with relief that he was speaking to her, she couldn't form words. She held out the letter.

"May I?" He hesitated before taking it from her hand.

"Please." There, she found her voice at last.

As he read, she thought about the contents of the letter, which was from the editor of the *Gazette*. She'd submitted a few stories to the editor earlier this week, and he liked the one on the Sisters of Mercy and their work at the hospital. It wasn't breaking news, but he'd found it worthy of publication. Some editing was required, and would she mind making changes? He would be happy to teach her in some areas where she was deficient.

Byron grinned. "You'll have newspaper experience. Congratulations."

"Thank you. I've not forgotten our joint endeavor to publish, however. In fact, there's not much else I've thought about all week. Papa and Wallace have avoided me, and I don't know any new facts." She swallowed hard. "I have nothing to tell you in regard to that story, but so, so much else to tell you, Byron."

But would he stay long enough to listen?

The last time Byron walked out of this house, he didn't think he'd ever return. He'd understood Clara's hesitation to write the article. Would he have wanted to write it if it meant Pascal would go to prison?

Of course not. But his conscience couldn't let him go on as if he knew nothing about the truth. He and Clara differed on this ethical question, and it would ever be insurmountable in their friendship.

He'd forgotten about Letitia's wedding, but the children reminded him. Adele had been singing the Frog and Missie Mouse courting song all week. They were so eager to come, he couldn't disappoint them.

So they'd attended the wedding, but he had no intention of renewing his relationship with Clara. Seeing her tested his resolve, however. The moment she entered the parlor and captured his gaze—he'd been lost to everything else.

She was his friend. His. . .Clara. He could not break off their relationship as easily as he'd thought.

"I'm here, Clara." He stood in front of her, gazing into her sad eyes. "I'm listening."

Even though she probably wanted to dissuade him from writing the article. He would listen to her, because he cared so much for her.

"This is harder than I expected." She looked down.

Maybe it would help if he spoke first. "Then should I tell you what I have learned this week?"

At her nod, he met her gaze and held it. "The man who tried to rob us at the glassworks was caught attempting a robbery with my bone-handled knife. According to the captain of the watch, he is an everyday sort of thief they've encountered before, who claimed to know nothing about the stolen goods. They believe him, as do I."

"Did you get your knife back?"

In answer, he patted his right boot. There, that coaxed a smile from her.

"The captain of the watch believes Vanacore's goods were shipped through the glassworks by an employee who quit without notice the day before, as your father suggested. However, this fellow never worked at Purl's. Nor, I discerned, could he read or write. I do not believe that man guilty. I still believe Wallace is involved, along with that other fellow he's been talking to." He grieved the fact that his words brought her pain.

Her throat worked as she processed the information. "Then we must move forward. I'm not certain how to investigate the matter, unless Papa finds more crates for John Smith, but I somehow doubt he will. All I know is we cannot stay silent. Even if Wallace is guilty."

How much had the words cost her? "This conclusion can't have been easy for you."

"It's been miserable." A trembling smile didn't hide her sadness. "Especially with Wallace avoiding the house all week, and Papa not available to talk through it with me. I've prayed, and while I have little comfort in this, I know that pursuing the investigation is the right thing to do. Wallace has changed, Byron. I regret that I have not been his friend as I should have been. I regret that I sought Papa's favor over God's at times, well-knowing Wallace could not seem to get Papa's approval for anything."

"It's not your fault."

"But I didn't do a thing to change it, to help Wallace see himself in

God's eyes rather than Papa's. Or to show Papa what his actions were doing. Now it's too late."

Byron lifted her chin with his forefinger so she was forced to look up at him. "It's never too late."

Not for Wallace or Newton or Clara. In fact, it wasn't too late for Byron either.

He lost breath, didn't need it, looking down into her eyes. They'd solved their ethical quandary. They were on the same side. He need never walk away from her—

A soft rap of knuckles against the open door sounded behind him. His hand fell.

"Wallace?" Clara's cheeks pinked.

"You're needed, Sis. Bridal duty. Aunt Letitia wishes to change her ensemble or something."

She nodded. "Before I go, Wallace, I must talk to you. Today."

"We'll talk. I promise. But right now you have a duty, and I wish to speak to Byron. Alone."

Did he? Byron clapped him on the shoulder. "Let's talk then."

He exchanged a meaningful look with Clara as she left them. He could tell her prayer was the same as his now. *Lord, this is in Your hands.*

"And then he said he wanted to talk to Byron alone." Upstairs in Aunt Letitia's room, Clara unfastened the tiny buttons on the back of Aunt Letitia's gown and helped her shimmy out of it.

Aunt Letitia reached for her going-away gown of pale yellow silk while Clara laid the wedding gown on the bed. "I doubt they'll finish their talk before Peter and I leave. You must write me the minute you have more information, darling."

"You'll be on a ship to England."

"Address it to Hollingsworth House. Maybe it will arrive when I do." She turned her back so Clara could fasten the gown. "I'll want to know everything that happens this summer. By fall when we return, this will all be settled, but in the meanwhile, Peter and I will be praying."

"Thank you." She patted her aunt's shoulder, to say, *Finished.*

Aunt Letitia turned. "I'm praying for you too, and your heart." She tapped the cameo. "Wear it knowing that I love you. I believe in you. Your life is a gift and an adventure. Trust God to know what He has in store for you next, even when you cannot see."

That was the true gift of the cameo, wasn't it? To wear it as a reminder that she was loved and supported while she trod the path of God's choosing.

Even when the path was difficult.

"I shall miss you, Auntie."

Many kisses, hugs, and congratulations were exchanged as they rejoined the group of well-wishers in the foyer. Even Byron and Wallace were there, but when the new Mr. and Mrs. Hollingsworth left on their English honeymoon, Byron, Wallace, and the younger Breauxs had gone.

"I didn't say goodbye to the children." Clara sat beside Mama in the now vacant parlor.

"No? I wonder how you missed them. They were quite charming. I sent them home with extra cake."

"You like them, don't you?" Clara wiggled her toes within her shoes. Oh, how she longed to remove them.

"It's fun having children here again. And Byron." Mama laughed at her expression. "I see you do not wish to discuss it. Very well."

"Where are Papa and Wallace?"

"Your papa ran an errand, and Wallace left with Byron and the children. Said he'd be home for supper. I told him it would be as informal a meal as possible. I am utterly spent."

"Why do you not lie down for an hour then?" Clara kissed her cheek. "I wish to put on slippers."

"Excellent notion, dear."

So, no Papa. No Wallace. Up in her room, Clara unpinned the cameo from her gown, weighing it in her palm. *I am loved and supported while I journey this path, even when I can't see where I am to go.*

Thank You, Lord, for never leaving me.

With trust—and a little trepidation about the future—she changed into a simple gown and curled atop her bed to read. Next thing she knew, she jolted upright. Late afternoon sunlight slanted through the window. She'd slept? With all the turmoil roiling in her chest?

Yawning, Clara tidied her appearance, slipped on comfortable shoes, and padded downstairs.

After the activity earlier, the house was oddly silent. The servants they'd hired for the occasion had restored the furniture in the parlor and gone, and no one was about.

Papa's voice carried from the dining room, followed by Mama's. Perhaps they'd all begun eating without her. She turned into the room. "Sorry, all. I nodded off."

Her parents weren't eating. In fact, there was no food on the table, and they weren't alone. Wallace and Byron stood at the table's head, still dressed for the wedding. Before them, a large wooden crate sat on the mahogany expanse, its contents unpacked.

The Roman antiquities.

"Good, you've awakened." Wallace's cheerful words didn't match the grave set of his mouth.

Mama reached for Clara's hand, pulling it so Clara would sit beside her. Mama's eyes were red and damp.

Clara squeezed hard. "What's happening?"

❧ *Chapter 9* ❧

*N*o one answered Clara. The silence was interminable while Wallace stuck a finger into his collar, loosening it, before clearing his throat. "I was about to tell our parents how I came to acquire these objects."

"Sylvester Vanacore's stolen collection, if I'm not mistaken." Papa's voice was tight with tension.

"His things, yes. As for stolen?" Wallace glanced at Byron, who nodded encouragement. "A few months ago, Vanacore approached me with an investment opportunity. New rail line. The money I'd recoup would be impressive and I—I was frustrated about my place at the glassworks. Weary of disappointing you, Papa. So I thought if I made a tidy sum, you might approve. I borrowed funds from a questionable person."

"Son." Mama's voice was strangled, but Papa didn't speak.

Wallace looked down. "Needless to say, Vanacore's scheme was not legitimate. He needed money for his congressional bid. Meanwhile, I was indebted to the wrong sort of fellow. I thought gambling the answer."

"It's never the answer," Papa all but growled.

Mama's soft sob drew every eye. Clara clutched her mother's hand harder. The pain of this conversation wouldn't easily soothe, but enduring it was necessary. They must remain strong enough to hear Wallace's story.

"At the gaming tables, I met a fellow named Axel. He could see I was in dire straits. He knew I had access to the glassworks, and he said I could make a decent sum by secretly shipping goods out with the glass. I figured it was contraband of some sort, but I was desperate, and I knew not to ask questions. I agreed." Wallace smoothed his mustache. "Axel met me behind the glassworks with a wagon. He had a list of items he consulted, and he gave me small boxes. I didn't look at the contents. I packed them under castoff glass and sealed the crate. Addressed it to John Smith in Harrisburg." His voice caught, and he broke off.

Clara began to pray for Wallace. This could not be easy for him.

Wallace cleared his throat again. "I knew Purl was doing the same as I—I saw Axel talking to him the day before the fire. But I didn't know until Byron found the crate at Purl's that it was Vanacore's collection I was shipping out. When I confronted Axel later, he told me Purl wanted out, so he'd set the fire to warn him to be quiet, but it was also a threat to me. If I protested, quit, or talked, the glassworks would be next. He came to the house to press his point."

Byron nodded. "Clara and I saw you with him."

He nodded. "His threats were—well, convincing."

Clara's heart ached. "What an intolerable burden that must have been."

"One that you didn't have to bear in the first place." Papa's voice was tight with unexpressed fury. "You should have come to me."

"I didn't want to disappoint you."

"But you wouldn't have been a criminal." Papa looked away.

"You're right, Papa. I made poor choice after poor choice."

"Wait a moment." Clara sat taller. "That man—Axel—I also saw him with Mr. Vanacore."

For the first time, Wallace's face relaxed. "That's because Vanacore was responsible for his collection being stolen in the first place."

Papa gaped. "How is that possible?"

"He instructed Axel how and when to steal his collection. He and the staff were at church, so Axel wouldn't encounter any resistance. Or witnesses."

Clara's hand went to her stomach. This story was worse than she'd imagined. "I knew you couldn't have stolen those things, Wallace. You too were in church. But I'm struggling to understand. Why would Mr. Vanacore pretend to have been robbed and arrange for this Axel fellow to ship out his collection to John Smith?"

"Brilliant scheme, actually. Vanacore received sympathy for having been robbed, which gave him some notoriety to advance that platform against crime he's always talking about."

"Who is John Smith?" Mama asked.

"The false name used by an influential man in Harrisburg, ma'am." Byron withdrew a paper from his pocket. "This afternoon I received a telegram from a contact I've enlisted to help identify the fellow. In exchange for the artifacts, this so-called gentleman promised political support to Vanacore."

Clara peered at Wallace. "So who took the crate Byron and I found? You or Axel?"

"I'm sorry, Clara. I'd gone to the glassworks to ensure the courier picked up the crates and, well, there it was, out in the open, lying on the ground, with no one around."

"We were in front of the glassworks, dealing with the cutpurse," Byron added.

"The what?" Mama demanded.

"I shall tell you later," Clara said. She hadn't yet told Mama about that.

"You absconded with the crate." Papa returned them to the story.

"And hid it in the cellar while I struggled with what I'd done, who I'd become. At the picnic with Byron and Clara, I felt more like myself than I had in a long while. Then at Aunt Letitia's request, I played violin. I hadn't intended to play the hymn, but the tune burned my heart in a way I've never known before. I can't describe it. So I played it."

"The words affected you also," Byron said.

"They did. 'Prone to wander, Lord, I feel it, prone to leave the God I love.' I'd wandered far. But I wanted to come home."

Eyes damp with unshed tears, Mama disentangled her hand from Clara's, rose, and took Wallace into her arms.

"So what will you do?" Papa rose too, calmly pushing his chair under the table.

"Byron will escort me to the captain of the watch. I'm ready to make a statement about my involvement, no matter the consequences. I'm sorry how this will reflect on the family."

Mama sobbed in earnest now. "I don't care about that. My son!"

Papa pulled his hand through his hair. "I've been doing my own investigation this week. Since one of the employees quit and disappeared, the law presumed him guilty. But I knew it was you, Wallace. I saw it on your face when Clara mentioned the coin I'd found. I didn't know why, or about that snake Vanacore, but I knew you were responsible, my son. And I wanted to find proof to help you." To Clara's surprise, Papa enveloped his wife and son in his arms.

"I'm sorry I failed you, Papa."

"I failed you, Wallace." Papa pulled back. "I thought if I pushed you to be more active in the glassworks, you'd find motivation to move forward. I thought if I withheld praise, you'd work for it. I was wrong. I see that now."

Wallace pulled away from their parents, his gaze fixed on Clara. "Before I go, I must tell you one more thing. One last confession. I'm the one who sabotaged your friendship with Byron four years ago."

Byron stiffened. "That's not true, Wallace."

Clara's head snapped back. "I don't understand."

Wallace's smile was sad. "I was jealous of your confidence. Your deep friendship with Byron. After his parents died, I told him some rot about how I was amazed by his dedication to his family and how hard he'd have to work to support them. I even told him you had plans for a party one night, and it was a pity he couldn't go because of the burden of caring for his siblings, but your lives were headed different directions now. Then I wished him well. Except I didn't at all." He looked at Byron. "I planted seeds to get you away from Clara. You can't tell me it didn't work."

Byron rubbed his head, as if trying to remember. "I already knew it was time to grow up. No more strolls with Clara or throwing tomahawks at tree stumps. But yes, it was then I realized it was time to focus on bettering myself. Distancing myself. Sparing us all more pain."

Clara couldn't swallow past the aching lump in her throat.

Byron clasped Wallace's hand. "I forgive you, Wallace."

"So do I," Clara said before reaching to hug him.

Nevertheless, that didn't mean she didn't ache. Forgiveness was not always easy or painless, she realized.

But she also knew God would help and heal her. He would help and heal them all.

For Clara the next few days passed in a flurry. Papa and a lawyer friend of his joined Byron in ushering Wallace to the captain of the watch. Wallace was held in the jail on Grant's Hill. Sylvester Vanacore was likewise incarcerated there, along with his accomplice, the jowl-cheeked Mr. Axel. No one yet knew what would happen, but Clara did her best to have faith.

Sitting in her bedroom scrawling a letter to Aunt Letitia, she reached for the cameo pinned to her blouse, a tangible reminder that life was an adventure. Not always a pleasant one, but an adventure nonetheless, with God by her side.

But it didn't mean she didn't wonder what Byron had been doing these past few days. She rose and crossed to the bureau, taking up the little mouse he'd made for her. "Where is he, little one?"

"Clara?" Mama called up the stairs. "You've a visitor."

She hurried downstairs to the parlor, where Mama waited with—oh, the sight of Byron made her heart flutter. He looked almost shy, smiling at her, clutching a brown folder at his side.

"Byron."

"Good morning. I just told your mother that Wallace will be released tomorrow."

It couldn't be true. "How?"

"He's worked out an arrangement with the authorities. He will testify against Vanacore and Axel and, in exchange, receive a reduced sentence."

She clutched her hands to her chest, realizing after something hard hit her collarbone that she still held the mouse. "That's wonderful. Oh, where are my manners? Will you be seated?"

"Not I." Mama sounded more cheerful than she had since Wallace left. "I'm in the midst of a. . .grocery list." A tiny smile tugging her lips, she shut the door behind her.

Clara's eyes narrowed. What was Mama doing, shutting the door on her unmarried daughter and a gentleman?

"This way we can talk freely. About the article," Byron said, holding out the folder. "The editor has seen the draft and says he'll publish it. And he's offered me a salaried position."

She took the folder. "That's wonderful. Congratulations, Byron."

"This is not the piece we started to write though. I've made changes. It's about Vanacore's downfall and your brother's redemption. Don't worry, Wallace gave me his permission. I was with him an hour ago. Your father is there now too. But as for the article, if you have additions or alterations, be sure to let me know soon. Your name will go on it too."

"That's generous, and unnecessary."

"I couldn't have done this without you."

"I'll read it soon." Clara sat on the sofa and set the article and the mouse on the coffee table.

"Is that the mouse I gave you?" He dropped beside her and laughed. "I was a horrid whittler back then."

"She's beautiful, but I'll ignore your slander of her because I'm so grateful for all you've done for us, Byron."

"I didn't do anything. Wallace made the decision to take responsibility."

"I wish I'd known he interfered in our. . .friendship. I knew you were busy, but I thought—well, when you stopped coming by and began attending the earlier church service, I thought you didn't like me anymore."

"That wasn't it at all, but I should have offered you more of an explanation. I received Wallace's words as unintended advice, however. That I wasn't good enough for you."

"Never." Which made all of this even sadder. "Yet you have been his friend. You stood with him through this."

"And I will continue to do so."

"So, we'll see more of you then?" She couldn't look at him.

"I hope so." He cleared his throat. "I decided you were right about my writing. I'll finish the narrative you found when you were snooping. I'm calling it *Pittsburgh and the Wilds Beyond: A Narrative Natural History of Western Pennsylvania.*"

"I wasn't snooping." She feigned insult. "And I'm glad you're finishing it. It was very good."

"Good or not good, it's me." He stared at his hands. "I tried for four years to close off my heart to protect myself from pain. I wanted to remake myself into a different sort of man. One who would be taken seriously by fops like Vanacore. I used to look at your house and want it. One like it, large enough for all of us, that signified that I could give the children the advantages that come from money. But I was wrong."

He shifted closer so their knees were touching. "I'd focused on the security of a house, not the people within it. A family. Aunts and uncles and weddings and support when one of us is sick. You reminded me that my siblings don't need me to be a successful journalist who earns enough to buy them a grand home. My siblings need me."

"And you need them."

"I do." He twisted closer. "I don't want a house like this anymore."

It was hard to think with his knee touching hers. "What do you want?"

"A home in the trees, with enough land that a body can walk and think. A room in which to write. With two desks."

"So the children have a place to study?"

He shook his head. "One for you."

"Me?"

"You'll need a place to write your devotional articles. By a window, I think, so you can see the weather change outside. Leaves falling in autumn, the first snowfall." His hands were on hers now, warm, strong.

"Daffodils popping up in spring," she said.

"Plums in summer."

"There's to be a plum tree then?"

"There is. And a stump for our children to use when they learn to throw a tomahawk. If you'll have me." Byron's head lowered so his forehead rested against hers. "I can't offer you a house like this. All I have is my pen and three siblings and my love. But I missed you so these past four years."

"I missed you too. I loved you when you taught me to throw the knife when we were seventeen. I still loved you when you left."

"Can you love me again?"

"I never stopped."

His lips descended on hers, soft at first, then more insistent. The kiss went on, outside of time, until Clara was breathless and tingling from the top of her head to the soles of her feet.

He pulled back, digging into his coat pocket. "I forgot. I have something for you."

A ring? Oh, nothing of the sort. Pine-gold and the size of a boiled egg, its sanded smoothness fit in her palm. "A whittled frog? Is this like the fairy tale? I'm to kiss it and it will turn into a prince? Or are you suggesting you're a frog?"

Shaking his head, he laughed. "The girls were singing that wedding song for days; I couldn't get it out of my head. You know the one, about the frog and the mouse. I thought, since you kept the whittled mouse I made you—"

"On my bureau!"

He glanced at the mouse she'd set on the table. "I thought she might like a friend."

The little frog had a ring carved on the palm of its hand—or whatever a frog appendage was called. How on earth had Byron accomplished that? It must have taken him days. She smiled shyly. "She would."

"Remember the song?"

She nodded as he tugged her closer so his lips were almost on hers. He sang, "Took Missie Mouse upon his knee. Mm-hmm. Took Missie Mouse upon his knee, said, 'Missie Mouse, will you marry me?' Mm-hmm."

"Mm-hmm," she hummed with him at the end.

"Your father gave his blessing. So did your mother and brother. Marry me, darling Clara?"

"Yes, Byron. I will."

He kissed her again. She wished he'd never stop.

❧ *Chapter 10* ❧

Late autumn

*M*ost of her friends' weddings were held in parlors, true, but Clara and Byron decided they wanted their wedding to be held in the place where they'd first met—in church.

Clara caught her reflection in the church door window, spying the cameo pinned to the bodice of her wedding gown.

"One never owns a cameo. . . . One wears a cameo and enjoys it, but as a custodian for its next owner."

Queen Victoria had deemed Letitia fit to be its next caretaker. Letitia passed it on to Clara, and sure enough, it had come with adventure. And even love.

What had Auntie said?

"I know the cameo did not bring me love, of course. But the gift of it coincided with the arrival of love, both for the queen and for me, and I hope it will bring the same to you."

And it had. A warm blush spread up her neck. To think Byron was inside the church where they met, waiting to marry her.

She mustn't keep him waiting any longer.

"Ready, Clara?" Genevie fussed with Clara's sleeve. Clara couldn't have asked for two better bridesmaids than Genevie and Adele.

"I am."

"Then let us see you married." Papa offered his arm.

Every eye turned back to watch the girls process, and then there were wide smiles as Clara walked up the aisle. Byron stood beside his grooms-men, Pascal and Wallace. How good it was to see her brother, who had served his reduced sentence in exchange for his testimony in the trial against Sylvester Vanacore. So changed was Wallace that he was not only learning more about God, but a new career too, one related to law and order. Mama couldn't be happier to have her family back together. Neither could Clara. And Papa, well, he had been a tremendous support to Wallace, serving as a source of encouragement and praise. Their reconciliation was nothing short of a blessing.

So much good had happened these past few months, and she'd even learned she'd received a contract to publish her devotionals in the ladies' magazine. It was a dream come true, but this, here, was an even greater dream. Here in this church was everyone she loved.

Would God want her to give the cameo to someone here? Clara didn't know, but she would tend it until the Lord directed her to pass it along. Perhaps Clara would only care for the cameo for a few months, or maybe she would keep it until her own daughter was grown and ready.

Her daughter! Hers and Byron's.

Byron met her at the front of the church.

"I love you," he whispered.

"I love you too." Taking his hand, she was ready for whatever God had in store for their future.

Susanne Dietze began writing love stories in high school, casting her friends in the starring roles. Today she is the award-winning author of a dozen new and upcoming historical romances who has seen her work on the ECPA and Publisher's Weekly bestseller lists for inspirational fiction. Married to a pastor and the mom of two, Susanne lives in California and enjoys fancy-schmancy tea parties, the beach, and curling up on the couch with a costume drama and a plate of nachos. You can visit her online at www.susannedietze.com and subscribe to her newsletters at http://eepurl .com/bieza5.

Taming Petra

by Jennifer Uhlarik

Chapter 1

Cambria Springs, Colorado Territory
Late summer 1875

*B*uckskin Pete Hollingsworth!"

The gruff voice froze Pete's tracks. People all around the crowded street stopped, and tension climbed. Was someone wishing to start a gunfight? If so, the voice wasn't familiar, but such details were hardly important to those cocksure young bucks who fancied themselves gunfighters. They'd look for anyone with a bigger reputation than their own and call them out, all to garner fame.

In the last two years, the name of Buckskin Pete *had* become known about those parts—though *not* as a gunfighter.

Gripping the rifle in one hand, Pete blew out a breath and turned. "Who's askin'?"

"I am." A man of about eighteen stepped into the street from outside the Wells Fargo office. "Been lookin' for you for a month."

What on earth for? "State your business."

"We got a couple packages for a Petra Jayne Breaux. That's you, ain't it?"

At the mention of her proper legal name, a chuckle rippled through the crowd, and folks along the street shifted anxious glances between her and the gent.

Heat and ire flashed through her. He'd exposed her true identity over *packages?* Just how had he figured it out, anyway? Only two other people in Cambria Springs knew her real name. Lucinda Braddock, the dime novelist who'd dubbed her Buckskin Pete after her successes at the Founders' Day wood-chopping competition that started her rise to notoriety, and the town postmaster. Had one of them shared the information? Lu and her husband, Marshal Rion Braddock, were two of her few real friends in the area. She could trust Lu with that secret. Tamping down her unwelcome emotions, Pete stopped in front of the brash man.

"Petra. Pete. One and the same. Now what about those packages?"

The fella waved her toward the Wells Fargo office.

"Lemme get the door for you, Pete." Tibby, a stately old gentleman despite his unkempt white mutton chops and threadbare clothes, stepped from the crowd to turn the knob. He pulled the door open and, with a flourish of his hand, bowed.

"Get out the way, old man," the Wells Fargo fella barked.

She turned. "Shut your mouth. A proper gentleman opens doors for a lady."

He gave her a contemptuous glance, eyes lingering on her buckskin trousers, then swept to the Colt Peacemaker and the Indian tomahawk on her belt, and finally stalled on her short-cropped hair. "You ain't nothin' close to a lady."

She put on a placid smile. "You don't say?"

"Think I just did."

Pete shrugged. "You're entitled to your opinion." As she turned again to Tibby, he swung the door wider and stepped out of her way.

"Thank you, kind sir." Pete tucked her right foot behind the left and, rifle in hand, executed a perfect curtsy. As she straightened, she drove the butt of her rifle into the Wells Fargo fella's gut.

He went to a knee with a loud *oof*. Some in the crowd guffawed and applauded, though several pretentious ladies turned up their noses, harrumphed, and scurried away. Without missing a beat, she looked to her whiskered friend.

"Tibby, is Mrs. Milroy well today?"

"Ain't rightly sure. Been gone a couple days. I'm headin' her way now."

A twinge of guilt struck her. She should've gotten by the Milroy place earlier. "Please tell her I'll be by tomorrow."

At his gentlemanly nod, she stepped in, and he shut the door, causing the bell to jingle.

"Be right there," someone hollered from a back room as she paced toward the counter.

"Take your time." Pete faced the front door.

On the street, Tibby whistled "Oh! Susanna" and tipped his hat to a few of the ladies as he moved along. She grinned. That man had been a godsend, drifting into the area when he did.

"Forgive me," the same voice called from a back room, approaching footsteps accompanying the call.

At the same moment, the young man from the street limped into the room, glowering and holding his belly.

Pete turned to the counter, senses primed for trouble.

"How can I help you?" The man behind the counter wiped his hands on a rag.

"This yahoo work for you?" She jerked her thumb over her shoulder.

"Yes. Why?"

She shrugged. "You might ought to teach him some manners. Ain't wise ta insult your customers." Pete played up her colloquial speech—far from the proper English she'd learned in Pittsburgh. If her family could only hear her now.

The fella's jaw muscles popped as he looked at the younger man. "I see. I'll be sure to remind him of that." His expression softened as he turned to her. "Please, how may I help you?"

"I understand you've got a couple packages for Petra Jayne Breaux. That's me."

"Ah yes, we do." The gent smiled. "You've had us flummoxed, ma'am. We've been trying to find Miss Breaux so she could take delivery."

"Mystery solved, although I'll thank you to keep that other name to yourself. I'm known around these parts as Pete Hollingsworth, and I'd like ta keep it that way." As if she could keep her real name from spreading, now that the thoughtless oaf had shouted it on the street.

"Of course." He fetched two small wooden boxes from a safe, then returned and flipped through a ledger book. Pointing to a particular line, he turned the book to face her. "You'll need to sign for them."

Pete scratched her signature, and the gent slid the smaller box toward her. "This one came maybe a month ago." He turned to a later page and indicated another line, then slid the slightly larger box over. "This one came yesterday."

Homesickness swept over her. Even without cracking the lids, she knew their origin. Pittsburgh. Her family. The addressee was Petra Breaux, after all. In the two years since she'd adopted the name Buckskin Pete, she'd not had the courage to tell her mother about her unconventional life. It would only break Mama's heart and cause Papa no end to his worry.

"Thanks for doing business with Wells Fargo, Miss *Hollingsworth*."

"Pleasure." She stashed the smallest box in her coat pocket and tucked the larger one under her right arm. Rifle gripped firmly in her left hand, she turned to leave.

The other fella stood between her and the door, eyes smoldering. As she brushed past him, he caught her just above the right elbow. Pete's heart raced as he hauled her close, the box clattering to the floor.

"You best watch yourself," he hissed. His breath stank of liquor.

"Bice!" his boss barked. "Unhand the lady and get out. You're fired."

When Bice didn't release her, she jammed her rifle barrel under his jaw and braced the stock against her left thigh. One-handed, she cocked the hammer and shifted her finger toward the trigger guard.

"You heard the man. Let me go." Blast it all. Her voice—along with the rest of her—shook.

Bice stiffened, eyes rounding, and he loosened his grip.

Petra jerked free, took a big step backward, and trained the gun on his chest. "Pick up the box."

He did, slowly, as if he was still feeling her rifle butt in his belly.

"Now hand it to your friend and back away."

The other gent rounded the counter to receive the item.

"I don't know what your problem is, mister, but I want no truck with you. Steer clear of my path, and I'll steer clear of yours. Understood?"

"Ain't natural—a woman dressed as a man," Bice sneered.

She laughed. "That's why you're so flustered? Mister, I'm a scout, a hunter, I ride and traipse through these mountains. Those things don't lend themselves to frills and lace. Not that it's any of your concern. Now back up."

With Bice on the far side of the room, the other gent handed her the box.

"Thank you kindly." She never took her eyes from her nemesis.

"Yes, ma'am."

Pete backed toward the door and, uncocking the hammer, slipped outside and hurried along the boardwalk. When she was a safe distance away, she shifted her mental focus to the boxes.

Typically Mama and Papa sent letters—nothing larger. In her sporadic writings to them, she didn't ask for a thing. And she *never* mentioned her unconventional attire—a detail that would send her mother, an author of devotionals as well as fashion and domestic style articles, into heart palpitations. She also kept details of her unladylike job preferences and her snug mountain cabin, small enough to fit inside any one room of Mama and Papa's very comfortable Pittsburgh home, a secret. Papa was a wonderful provider. It would break their hearts to know the seeming lack she'd chosen to live in. Already they asked in nearly every correspondence for her to return home soon.

One day—but not yet. Even two years later, her grief was too overwhelming. She wasn't ready to leave, nor was she strong enough to go home.

Pete ducked onto a cross street and wandered toward the livery. She was anxious to know what Mama and Papa had sent, but she wouldn't open the boxes in plain view. Instead, she entered the stable and headed toward her sorrel's stall.

Before she reached it, two young voices called out. "Buckskin Pete."

She turned to find a boy and a girl, maybe twelve and ten respectively. "Yes?"

The little girl bashfully stepped forward, extending a stack of dime novels with Pete's picture. "Will you autograph these for me, please?"

Despite being asked many times, the request for her signature always left her speechless. She smiled and gave the requested signatures, taking just a moment to talk to the children before sending them on their way. They ran off, chattering in excitement.

At her sorrel's stall, she gave Falco some attention, then squatted in the corner.

Balancing a box on each knee, she studied the smaller box first. Noting that the seam between the top and bottom halves had a tiny bead of sealing wax, Pete drew her knife and ran its tip along the line. With some prying, the seal popped, and a folded paper tumbled out. Biting her lower lip, she removed the velvet pouch contained within.

Inside the bag was a lone key. To. . . ? She unfolded the note.

> *Dearest Petra,*
> *Keep this safe. It will unlock a special birthday gift I am sending soon.*
>
> *Love,*
> *Mama*

Her birthday. It was. . .*today*. Her twenty-second. Oh goodness. How had she forgotten?

Stunned, she turned to the second box. This one contained no sign of sealing wax, just a small keyhole in which the key fit perfectly. Holding her breath, she turned it and opened the lid to find another velvet pouch and paper. Petra unfolded the note first.

> *My dearest girl,*
>
> *Happy twenty-second birthday. I had intended to give this to you on your twenty-first, but I held on, hoping I could watch you open it in person. Since you haven't returned, I'm sending it to you for this year's celebration. Surely you'll remember the stories. It is time, my daughter. Wear it proudly, and when the time comes, you'll know which person you should pass it to.*
>
> *All my love for your birthday,*
> *Mama*

Oh goodness. It wasn't. . . Was it? Perspiration dampening her forehead, Petra steeled herself and opened the velvet bag. Ever so gently, she shook it, and out slid the cameo that once belonged to Queen Victoria. The rich and unusual blue agate was set in gold, with half-pearls adorning the setting's edge. It had both a bail and a pin to wear as a pendant or brooch. Absolutely breathtaking. Given the stone's rarity and the fact it once adorned the clothing of royalty, it was priceless.

"Mama, no." She stared at the beautiful jewel, mind awash in memories. This little lovely had been pinned to Mama's chest all throughout Petra's life. She and her brothers had heard how it was given to Great Aunt Letitia by the queen, and as she'd worn it, she'd fallen in love with and married her handsome suitor, Peter Hollingsworth, for whom Petra was named. And Aunt Letitia had passed the cameo to Mama, who reacquainted herself with Papa, a childhood friend from Sunday school, and rekindled their young love.

"Why would you do this, Mama?" She was the *last* person who should possess such a treasure. She, Buckskin Pete, didn't deserve such beauty.

Not her, and not out here. She'd return it first thing tomorrow. It would break Mama's heart all over again, but this was too valuable an heirloom for *her* to be entrusted with.

Hands shaking, she attempted to slide the cameo into its pouch, though before she could, footsteps shuffled near, and the stall door opened. A breathless, sweaty boy of about nine backed inside and eased the door closed, peeked over its top, then ducked down.

"Mickey." She jabbed the boy's shoulder.

Mickey Milroy spun to face her, causing Falco to whinny and prance. "Hey, Pete." The boy's face turned the color of beets.

Cameo and pouch tightly in hand, she rose to calm the horse, and Mickey also stood to avoid the horse's hooves.

"Shhh, Falco. Nothing to be afraid of." She gave the big animal a vigorous rub, and once he settled, she turned on the boy again. "What're you doin'?"

A handsome stranger rounded the corner and stopped near the stall, peering around as if lost.

At the sight, Pete pinned the boy with a hard look. "What've you done, Mickey?"

The gentleman—tall, muscular, with dark hair peeking from under a dark Stetson hat—turned her way. "Pardon, ma'am, has a boy about eight or ten years old come this way?"

She latched onto Mickey's upper arm and pushed the door wide.

"Is this the one you're looking for?"

Dustin Owens gaped. Had the firm, motherly voice he'd heard inside the stall come from the slim, buckskin-clad beauty? She held the boy with a vice grip, her vibrant green eyes pinning first him, then the boy.

"Will one of you please tell me what's going on?" Sweeping the tattered slouch hat from her short-cropped blond head, she dropped it on the floor and tossed something into it. "Has Mickey done something?"

Was this the boy's mother? She was hardly old enough. Perhaps a big sister. "Yes, ma'am." He cleared his throat, hoping that would clear his thoughts too. "He stole apples from outside the mercantile."

The woman dropped to a knee and tugged the hem of Mickey's coat, as if to get his attention. "Did you do what he said?"

The red flash of a ripe apple streaked from the bottom of his jacket, hit the boy's foot, and landed near her hat. After watching it come to rest, the gal grabbed the boy's other arm and gave him a gentle shake.

"How many did you take?"

The mortified boy shrugged, and a second and third apple dropped to freedom.

The woman's shoulders slumped. "Hand 'em over. All of 'em."

As Mickey produced the contraband, Dustin retrieved the three escaped apples.

"Why'd you do this?" she hissed, her tone reflecting more hurt than accusation.

The boy leaned close. "We ain't had nothin' ta eat in three days." He handed her several apples. "I was tryin' to get somethin' ta tide the littles over till you came."

Dustin's heart lurched. Three days without food? *Lord, I assumed he was stealing for the thrill, not out of a real need.*

"Hasn't Addie been hunting like I taught her?"

The child shook his head. "She's been gone. She finally came home yesterday and said she got a job in town somewhere. Me, Sarah, and Carrie have been trying to hunt until we ran outta bullets."

The woman rubbed her forehead with the back of one apple-filled fist. "Next time you have this kind of trouble, come find me. I'll help you. Understand?"

"Yes, ma'am." He hung his head. "Sorry, Pete."

Pete? An odd name for a woman—although this one seemed anything but usual. Despite her peculiarities, she showed an admirable concern for the boy.

"Are you two related?"

Her eyes flashed. "Is that any of your business?"

Scolded like a misbehaving child. "Probably not, though if I can be of help—"

"Mickey and I are friends. I assist his ma from time to time." She turned an apologetic smile on the boy. "Guess it's been a little too long since I checked in on 'em."

One hand full of apples, Dustin grabbed her hat and dropped them inside. But a flash of blue, gold, and—pearls?—caught him, and he snatched the apples back. Inside the hat lay a costly looking cameo brooch, its delicate gold setting rimmed with pearls. What an unexpected contradiction. A rough-around-the-edges gal possessing such a feminine bauble. He grinned.

"I don't know what you're lookin' at, mister, but stop nosin' in other people's affairs." She grabbed her hat, depositing apples inside, then fished out the cameo and tucked it within her coat.

Scolded again. "Forgive me, Pete, was it?"

She arched her brow.

Mickey grinned. "She's Buckskin Pete Hollingsworth, mister. She's got dime novels written about her. And I'm her friend, Mickey Milroy."

The boy was busting buttons over his association with his *famous* friend. But *Buckskin Pete*? She was far too pretty for such a moniker.

"Nice to meet you, Mickey Milroy." He shook the boy's hand, then turned and nodded. "And you, Miss Hollingsworth."

Hat in hand, her eyebrows arched, and her eyes sparkled with sass.

Dustin pressed on. "I wasn't trying to intrude. I was rounding up the apples. To help."

"And you are. . . ?" She held the hat out to Mickey so he could add his fruit.

"Oh." He laughed. "That's needed information, isn't it?"

She cocked her head. "Generally speaking, it is."

Heat flooded him. "I'm Dustin. Owens." He held out the apples he'd collected. "My sister, Josephine, and I are new here. We're starting a church." He smiled. "Hope you both might consider coming."

The saucy demeanor melted. "You're a preacher?"

"*Reverend* Dustin Owens, ma'am." He nodded. "If I can be of any assistance, I'd b—"

"You've helped enough, thank you." Cradling the hat, she reached for a rifle leaning against the wall, then looked at young Mickey. "Let's go. We'd better get to that mercantile before it closes."

Chapter 2

$\mathscr{S}$tanding in the darkness of a putrid-smelling alleyway, Pete ran her thumb over the cameo's face. What a *glorious* birthday. The run-in with Bice at Wells Fargo, the homesickness Mama's unwelcome gift produced, the discovery of the Milroy family's dire circumstances, and both she and the Milroy family being cut off at the mercantile until they'd paid their bills. Could things get any worse? Oh wait. They did the moment that nosy, if handsome, preacher butted into her business.

Why did a preacher coming to Cambria Springs bother her so? Just because a church opened didn't mean she must attend. Nor did she have to be friends with the reverend.

"Forget the minister and the church, Pete." Right now, the most important thing was paying down those mercantile bills. Pete and Tibby could provide Agnes Milroy and her eight children meat for their table. The older girls, Addie, Sarah, and Carrie, had planted a small vegetable garden to augment their stores. But flour, sugar, ammunition—those things came from the mercantile.

She shook her head. So many needs, including her own. She was low on just about everything as well.

The only way she knew to get the money she needed quickly was to gamble for it, which was why she stood in the alley beside the Gold Spur Saloon. Pete puffed out a breath and dug deep for her courage. She'd need it.

"Get to it and go home. Then forget this day."

She tucked the cameo into its pouch and stashed it in her coat's interior pocket. Rounding the corner, she slipped into the crowded room. The stuffy interior stank of sweat, whiskey, cigar smoke, and sawdust. Laughter and murmuring permeated the smoky air. Men lined the bar along the right wall, nursing their whiskeys. The small, square tables scattered throughout the room were more than half full. Several scantily dressed women circulated, some delivering drinks, others seated with the men.

One such girl, maybe all of sixteen, headed straight for her. "You shouldn't be here," she hissed quietly. She gripped Pete's arm and attempted to push her through the door. "Find another saloon."

Pete balked. "Why?"

"Edna?" a voice boomed.

Ashen, the girl faced the corner. "Yes, Mr. Roy?"

A portly fella in a suit looked their way, a bottle of whiskey and a half-full glass his only companions. "Hope you're extending a warm welcome to Buckskin Pete. She's a legend round here."

Her, Petra Jayne Breaux, a legend. She hadn't intended to become part of the local lore. She'd intended to hide, to grieve. Yet the uncouth woman, Pete, had captured the people's fancy.

"Yes, sir," Edna mumbled. "I'm aware."

"Come in, Pete. Clarence Roy, at your service." Mr. Roy stood. "What brings you through my door?"

Pete extracted herself from Edna's grip. The girl whispered, but Pete ignored her and approached the rotund man. "I'm looking for a card game. The Gold Spur is the largest of the three saloons in this town, so I thought—"

"You're in the right place." An oily smile greased the man's lips as he looked her up and down. "Do you prefer faro or poker?"

"Depends." She'd learned both games on her way west. "What're the stakes?"

"There's a faro game going—small stakes." He nodded toward a table in the far corner. "Or, if you're daring, I've a higher-class poker game in the back room."

"I usually prefer poker over faro." The latter game, where players bet on which cards would come up next in the deck, had always seemed too stacked in the dealer's favor. "But high stakes are too rich for me. Guess I'll buck the tiger."

"Help yourself." Mr. Roy motioned to the faro table.

"Thank you kindly."

Pete weaved through the crowd and, reaching the faro table, took one of the last two chairs.

"Howdy, Pete." Bull Simpson, a cowhand she'd spoken to on several previous occasions welcomed her. "Good ta see ya."

"Howdy, Bull." She grinned.

The man between her and Bull looked at the dealer. "Y'all lettin' girls in here now, Percy?"

"No, sir. I'm dealing faro. It's up to Mr. Roy who he lets in. She'll be welcome until he says otherwise."

"You done talkin' about me like I'm not here?" She pinned her neighbor with a glance. "I came to play faro, after all."

Percy dealt the two-card hand, and the fella who'd complained swore bitterly at the outcome.

"Watch your tongue, Aiken," one of the other men called. "There's a lady present."

Pete leaned forward to look at the other fella. "While I appreciate the considera—"

Aiken slammed a hand on the table and, glaring, swore a string of sulfurous words.

When he finished, she smiled. "You done?"

"No woman's gonna hem me in."

"Good to know. You want to keep jawin' about this, or can we play faro?"

His belligerent expression dissolved into confusion. Rattled, he tossed back his whiskey and waved at the dealer. "Keep going, Percy."

Pete traded her last dollar for chips and placed a one-dollar bet. As the dealer prepared to show the next set of cards, she held her breath and nearly offered a silent prayer. But she hadn't prayed since Uncle Peter's passing, and to start now would be ridiculous, particularly since gambling was surely a sin.

Light footsteps creaked behind her, and Pete tensed, hand near her boot knife. The newcomer, another of Mr. Roy's soiled doves, leaned over Pete's shoulder with a glass of whiskey.

"Compliments of the owner," she breathed, barely loud enough to counter the noise in the room.

"Thanks." It wasn't worth mentioning she never drank whiskey and wasn't about to start while gambling. Faro was a fast-moving game that took all her concentration.

As she faced the table again, a slight figure near the back of the room caught her eye. Pete turned, craning her neck, but whoever she'd seen was gone.

The game proceeded, and Pete won her first bet and split the winnings to make two new bets. With the next hand, neither of the bets won, so she let them ride. The third round, she won with one bet and lost the other. And so it went, hand after hand, winning more than she lost.

As her stack of chips grew, she made larger bets. Luck seemed to be with her. Perhaps her birthday *wasn't* all bad.

Bull, losing a particularly big bet, cursed under his breath, then glanced her way. "Sorry, Pete. Just slipped out." He gathered his remaining chips and left the table.

Aiken, long drunk, guffawed at Bull's misfortune.

During a lull, as the dealer reloaded the card box, Pete calculated her winnings. She had nearly enough to pay both mercantile debts, but if she wanted money to last beyond that, she'd have to keep playing.

Pete reached to the back of her chair for her canteen, but then rolled her eyes. Idiot. She'd left it and her guns with Falco in the livery. *Pete, you know better.* Desperate for something wet, she reached for the whiskey. She'd take just enough to wet her tongue.

Drops of liquid fire rolled across her palate, and she willed her eyes not to water.

"Bottoms up, girl." Aiken tipped the glass with his index finger.

Whiskey flooded her nose and mouth and, sputtering, she jerked her boot knife free. The blade flashed as it settled against Aiken's throat.

Eyes wide, his maniacal cackling ceased.

"You *ever* touch me or my things again, Aiken, and it'll be the last thing you do." She spit whiskey and dragged the back of her free hand across her mouth.

"It was a joke," he protested. "Didn't mean nothin' by it."

"Whoa, now," Clarence Roy bellowed. The floor seemed to sway as he pounded across the planks.

"I don't like your sense of humor," she whispered, dragging the blade against his skin until blood sprouted.

Aiken sucked in a breath then cursed her.

"Pete." Mr. Roy barged up next to them. "Put the knife away."

"He just tried to drown me."

"I did no such thing," Aiken groused.

"You're in *my* saloon. Seeing blood spilled is bad for business. Now sheath that blade, and I'll take care of Aiken for you."

With whiskey still stinging her nostrils, her eyesight blurred.

"I meant what I said, Aiken." She withdrew the knife from his throat and sheathed it.

As Aiken's posture relaxed, Roy jerked the man from his chair. "Get him outta here."

"What about my chips?" Aiken faced them again.

"You just forfeited 'em to Buckskin Pete. Now get out of my saloon."

Her limbs trembled. She'd practiced wielding blades with Papa since her childhood, but she'd never held one to a man's throat with the chance she might have to kill him. Again, Pete wiped her nose and mouth, then began to scoop her chips into her hat. Roy caught her arm.

"You're not leaving, are you?"

She rubbed one eye to clear her vision. "Think I'm done for tonight."

"That was a scare. Why don't you take a minute. Freshen up some, then decide."

Her head spinning a little, Pete continued scooping chips, and Roy sat beside her.

"Let me help." The fat man snatched her hat and guided not only her chips, but Aiken's stacks into the hat. "There now." He took her elbow and pulled her to her feet. "This way."

"I. . ." Pete's thoughts swirled, and she was unable to grasp the words. "I. . .I think. . ."

He guided her to a door and, calling to the barkeep, asked for a damp rag. The gent behind the bar squatted out of sight, and when he did, a familiar young face weaved into Pete's view.

"Addie?" She squinted. "Addie Milroy?"

The girl darted a glance between her and the barkeep, who stood again and tossed the asked-for rag to Roy.

"Get yourself cleaned up." Roy shoved the storage room door open and placed her hat on a shelf just inside. "I'll fetch you a bucket of water."

He guided her inside, and as soon as the door clapped shut, Pete brought the rag to her still-stinging lips and nostrils. A strange odor permeated the rag, and weakness overtook her. She grabbed for the nearest shelf, but her knees went completely soft, and she collapsed.

Lord, help!

Sleep eluded Dustin Owens. Whether because of his worry for Mickey Milroy or his ponderings about Buckskin Pete, he couldn't decide.

But *something* had him pacing.

The least he could do was pray for his new mission field.

Thankful for the full moon, Dustin stepped from the cozy house and, after locking up, walked to the end of the lane. He paced the streets, whispering petitions for the town and its residents, speaking a brief prayer over each house he passed.

"Lord, You know I didn't want to come back here." Dustin peered into the darkness of the next road. "I was comfortable in Wyoming." Far from the Colorado Territory, the place he once called home, lousy as it was. "But I'm here, so what're Your plans for Cambria Springs?"

His mind strayed to Miss Hollingsworth, and he shook away the recurring thought. What in heaven's name? She'd come to mind several times, and he'd almost mentioned her to Josephine over supper. However, he hadn't wanted to gossip. Nor did he want to give his sister reason to presume he had a special interest. Jo had a bad habit of pointing out the available young ladies from their church in Wyoming.

"She'll make someone a beautiful wife, Dusty. Why not you?"

He adored Jo, but no sense giving her fodder. There was no marriage in his future.

Dustin moved into the business district, praying over shops and their owners while keeping an eye for a suitable location for a church. Until a property could be found, he'd host services near the pine grove at the edge of town. Its shade would be comfortable enough until the weather turned colder.

He carried on until he neared the saloons and brothels at the far end of town. There yellow lamplight and raucous laughter spilled from the three establishments' doorways and windows. Somewhere a tinny piano sounded.

An unwelcome feeling—a familiar thread of anger—coiled tight around his belly, and a heaviness settled over his heart like a shroud.

"Lord. . ." No further words would come. Memories flooded his mind—memories from a lifetime ago. Things he wished he could erase. *Lord.*

He began to move again, more slowly. The hitching posts were full.

Through windows he caught glimpses of women in revealing attire, some dancing as men ogled them, others sitting intimately close to the customers. Dustin's stomach knotted. These women were somebody's daughters, somebody's sisters, somebody's mothers. Surely their loved ones wouldn't want them living such a life.

Lord Jesus, did You bring me here to throw this in my face?

The unbidden question flowed through his thoughts, and he pushed away a swirl of feelings he thought had long been dealt with.

Forgive me, Lord. I don't know where that came from.

As he drew a shaky breath, words tumbled forth.

"The Spirit of the Lord God is upon me; because the Lord hath anointed me to preach good tidings unto the meek."

With the words of Isaiah sixty-one ringing in his mind and heart, he quickened his pace.

The farther down the street he walked, the tighter and more palpable the heavy shroud became. His footsteps stalled again. A strong and unfamiliar presence pressed in on him. There was something here. Something unseen but real. A chill felt not with the skin, but in his spirit. "He hath sent me to bind up the brokenhearted." Dustin uttered the next portion. "To proclaim liberty to the captives, and the opening of the prison to them that are bound." A warmth swelled in his chest, repelling the darkness.

"To proclaim the acceptable year of the Lord, and the day of vengeance of our God; to comfort all who mour—"

A primal wail halted his words, and instinctively, his right hand strayed to his hip. But he'd not worn a gun belt since he'd left his old life. Good riddance. Heart hammering, he listened. The gut-wrenching sound came again from the alley.

Father God, protect me.

Dustin moved slowly down the rancid alleyway until the sound erupted a third time. Pinpointing its source, he eased around a stack of trash-filled crates and found Buckskin Pete Hollingsworth sitting in the dirt, her face streaked with tears. At his appearance, she hefted a knife at him, arm shaking badly.

Was she drunk? "Miss Hollingsworth?"

Hands splayed, Dustin eased onto one knee and directed the knife away from his face. She made no attempt to stop him. In fact, she appeared to have difficulty just following his movements.

He guided her arm to her side, then pushed a bouncy lock of hair from her eyes. "Do you remember me? From the livery?" She wouldn't look at him, so he tipped her chin his way. "Reverend Dustin Owens. Remember?"

She gave a feeble nod and leaned her head back. But just as quick, she pitched forward and slammed her head into the wall with a sob.

"No." Dustin drew her slim frame against his chest, but the scent of whiskey turned his stomach.

"Are you drunk?" *Lord God, I've had my fill of this type of behavior. Please don't make me do this again.*

She collapsed against him, sobbing silently.

Despite his repulsion, something stirred in him. She was small. Frail. Anything but the sassy, capable woman he'd seen earlier. And her slim frame pressed against him stirred his desire—no, his need—to protect. Reluctantly, Dustin held her.

"Miss Hollingsworth." He rolled a glance heavenward. "Can I help you get home?"

Pete nodded against his chest. As her hands twined into his shirt-front near his shoulders, another scent—faint, but familiar—caught him, and he wrestled her left hand from his shirt. Peeling her fingers open, he brought her palm to his nose.

Ether?

He breathed in again, but due to the smell of whiskey on her mixed with the overpowering rottenness in the alley, he couldn't catch the aroma a second time.

Lord, this doesn't make sense.

"Do you live here in town?"

She finally shook her head.

Outside of town then. She was in no shape to sit in a saddle, much less direct him to her place.

"I'm taking you to my sister, Josephine." They'd figure out the rest after she'd slept.

Dustin pushed to his feet, dragging her up with him.

She clung to him, face buried in his shirt.

"Can you walk, Miss Hollingsworth?"

When she attempted it, her lower half gave way. Dustin hoisted her into his arms.

Lord, if I truly smelled ether. . . He shook his head. *Show me what's going on, please. And let Miss Hollingsworth be all right.*

The little gal wasn't heavy. Not at first. But by the time he carried her several blocks, Dustin's arms were on fire. Outside his house, he lowered her feet to the porch and fumbled for the key in his pocket.

"Dustin?" Josephine called from inside.

"Open the door, Sis."

The key turned, and when Josephine hauled the door open, he once more hoisted Pete into his arms. Her breath stirred against his neck, sending shivers down his spine.

Josephine stared. "Who in heaven's name is this?"

"Buckskin Pete Hollingsworth." Strength waning, he headed toward the settee. "I'll need your help, Sis. She needs attention."

"*She?*"

"Yes. Pete's a woman."

"Is *she* wounded?"

He lowered her to the furniture. "Maybe drunk, or. . ." Dare he tell her? "Could be something else."

Josephine stepped to the settee and gave him a mischievous grin. "Dusty. You brought a woman home. And she's downright pretty."

"Oh for mercy's sake, Jo. Stop." Heat crept up his neck as he left the room to gather rags and water.

Lord, forgive me, but I've been thinking the same thing.

❧ Chapter 3 ❧

*H*ints of daylight peeked through an unfamiliar curtained window. *Whose* window? Pete had never seen this room before. The room was decorated in soft colors—pastels and lace. Frilly and feminine. A nosegay of dried flowers hung beside the door. A small vase of wildflowers—columbine and Indian paintbrush—sat beside the bed. She rolled to her side and tried to sit up, but something akin to a hundred sharp knives pierced her skull, and she sagged into the mattress with a groan.

"Miss?" A dark-haired young woman about Pete's own age hurried through the door and eased into the chair beside the bed. "I'm Josephine Owens. And you're. . .Pete. Is that right?"

"Petra." She snapped her eyes open. Oh for goodness' sake. What was she thinking? She was mush-headed. "But I much prefer Pete."

"Why? Petra's such a beautiful name. Very unusual."

"So my mother tells me." Mama had recounted the story many times of how she'd so loved the name Petra, she'd tucked it away for a future daughter, even before she and Papa married.

Pete gently probed her head to find what caused the intense pressure inside her skull. When she nudged a lump at the back of her scalp, she sucked in a sharp breath.

"You smacked your head pretty hard, miss. Do you remember?"

At the sudden introduction of a man's voice, sleepiness fled. The preacher stood in the doorway, one well-muscled shoulder leaning against the jamb. What was his name? Owen Davids. No. David Owens. Daniel? Oh blast. *Reverend* Owens.

And his younger sister, Josephine. A good eight or so years younger.

"What'd you ask me?"

"Whether you recall smacking your head last night."

"No."

"I found you in the alley alongside the Gold Spur Saloon."

Her heart rate grew erratic as half-formed memories came to mind. She'd been playing cards with. . .Bull Simpson. . .and that loud-mouthed fella. Had she won? Yes, she'd been winning. Then something had gone horribly wrong. What? How'd she end up in the alley? And why had she allowed herself to be brought wherever *here* was?

She glanced around. Oh drat. She was in their house.

"You slammed your head into the wall. Does that ring a bell?"

"No." Why couldn't she remember?

"How much did you drink last night?"

Josephine spun. "Dustin."

Dustin Owens. That was it.

He glared back. "I'm just *asking*, Jo. Not judging."

Sure. A straitlaced preacher like him probably saw her as a scourge on society, a corrupting force to ruin polite company. Well, she might dress eccentrically, and her skills might not be typical for most *proper* women, but she had her standards, and she'd not broken them since leaving Pittsburgh.

"I don't drink." She rolled onto her back and massaged her forehead. "And I only gamble when I need money."

Money. She'd needed money. To pay two mercantile bills. Pete patted her chest through the light quilt, then lifted the covers to find she wore a nightgown. Surely Josephine's.

"Where are my clothes?"

"Your coat and trousers are there." The young woman pointed to a couple wall pegs in the corner. "I washed your shirt and vest." Her cheeks reddened. "You smelled like you'd bathed in whiskey."

How could she have smelled *that* strongly of spirits?

Despite the pressure threatening to explode her skull, Pete tossed off the quilt and, reaching for the brass footboard, she shuffled around the end of the bed into the corner. Snatching her coat, she continued around the bed and seated herself on the far side of the mattress, her back to her hosts. The strong aroma of whiskey *did* permeate the garment.

Oh goodness. What happened?

She held up the coat. A fresh stain slopped down the front. She put the garment to her nose. The comforting scent of leather mixed with the woody and grainy odor of whiskey.

Wait. She *had* taken a sip. But *just* a sip. Then, that loudmouthed fella had dumped it on her, nearly drowning her. She'd pulled her knife on him, and. . .what? She'd begun to feel awkward. Like her limbs were leaden, and her thoughts like molasses. What—

"Oh no." Pete checked the coat's outer pockets. Empty. She thrust her hands into each of the inner pockets. All barren except the last. There, she found the two letters from her mother. Her stomach seized.

No money and *no cameo.*

A soft sob shook the petite woman. Dustin stepped into the room, though Josephine stayed him with a sharp gesture.

"What is it?" His sister sat beside Miss Hollingsworth. "How can we help you?"

"You can't." She shook her head, her hands straying to her temples as she groaned.

Lord, she must be in some fearsome pain. Help us, Father.

"Surely there's something we can do. Tell me what's wrong." God bless her. Josephine's voice never failed to soothe, and he loved her for it.

"I—" Miss Hollingsworth looked at the corner. "I need my shirt and vest, please."

"They're not fully dry. Please, tell me what's happened?"

Miss Hollingsworth ducked past Jo to the corner and plucked her things from the peg. "There's no fixing this. It's my mistake, and it'll cost me dearly."

Jo also stood. "Cost you what?"

"My family. If I can't get the cameo back, they'll never forgive me."

"I'm sure that's not the case," Jo whispered. "It's just a piece of jewelry—"

"It's a brooch once worn by the Queen of England herself," Miss Hollingsworth snapped. "It's irreplaceable, and it's gone."

Dustin stepped further into the room. "The brooch you had yesterday was worn by the queen?" Surely she was joshing. What would Buckskin Pete Hollingsworth know of Queen Victoria's jewelry?

She glared. "Yes, that one. You didn't take it, did you, Reverend?"

The sharp question stung. "Me?"

"To my knowledge, you're the only one in town who knew I had it."

"I knew you had a cameo. But what reason—or opportunity—would I have to steal it? After you and Mickey left the stable, Josephine can attest, I came home to prepare a sermon and stayed until well past dark."

Unsteady, she braced a hand against the wall, calming slightly. "I'm sorry. That was uncalled for. I know you didn't take it."

That was a start. "Do you know who did?"

"I suspect the Gold Spur's owner, Clarence Roy."

"What makes you think so?"

With a hand pressed against her temple, she shook her head, though the tiny movement stopped suddenly. "When I walked in last night, one of the soiled doves tried to warn me to leave. But Mr. Roy welcomed me in, pointed me to the faro table, and even gave me a whiskey on the house."

Ugliness swirled in Dustin's chest, and Josephine darted a haunted look his way. *Lord God, this is all too familiar.*

"You drank it?" *Please say you didn't.*

"I didn't touch it." Her immediate indignation gave way to a haunted expression like Jo's. "Not until hours later." Miss Hollingsworth tottered to the bed again, facing him. "Then I had a sip. Like I said, I don't drink."

Her headache and other symptoms suggested she'd downed a bottle or more. If she truly wasn't a drinker, then there was something else going on. "Tell me what happened."

"I don't know for sure. I was thirsty, so I took a sip. The next thing I remember clearly is waking up here."

"He drugged her, didn't he?" Josephine shook. "Just like—"

"You ladies stay here." Dustin strode toward the bedroom door.

"Dusty, where are you going?"

The raw quaver in Jo's voice stirred his anger even more. "To pay Mr. Roy a visit."

Chapter 4

Sunlight streamed down the same street where, hours before, Dustin had felt a palpable sense of evil. The recollection brought a shiver.

"Roy." He pounded on the Gold Spur's door. At half past ten, it wasn't likely the saloon owner was awake. His ilk typically awakened around noon and lived their lives at night. But surely he'd be inside. If Dustin roused him early, he might catch the man off guard, get him to admit what he'd done to Miss Hollingsworth.

"Clarence Roy." He pounded again on the door. *Lord, wake him up. Please. I've a mouthful of things to say to a man unscrupulous enough to drug a young woman.*

He banged a third time. "Clarence Roy, open up!"

After a brief pause, Dustin cupped his hands around his eyes and peered in the nearest window. Tables were straightened, every chair tucked in. No one stirred. Not unusual for a saloon this early in the day.

In fact, those inside might still be so inebriated they couldn't rouse themselves yet.

Lord, I'm not giving up. This can't happen again.

He stepped into the foul-smelling alley and stalked to where he'd found Miss Hollingsworth. Her knife glinted in the sunlight, and a few feet away, her tattered hat lay abandoned. He could at least return those.

In the livery, she'd dropped the cameo into her hat. Might she have done so last night?

Holding his breath to avoid the stench of decaying refuse, Dustin squatted near the hat. Not inside, nor was it easily visible on the ground. Taking another deep breath, he tipped nearby crates from their places. A large rat scurried out, and Dustin lunged up, startled, as the nasty animal darted away, disappearing into another pile of refuse. Squatting again, he took another hard look.

Not that it mattered. If Roy went to the trouble of drugging her, there was little likelihood she got out of the saloon with the cameo.

Father, does this Roy fella have her brooch, or did she gamble it away?

At the sound of a creaking door, Dustin grabbed Miss Hollingsworth's belongings and hurried to the back corner of the building as a large, shirtless man lumbered into the outhouse. Was that Roy? He hadn't thought to get a description. If it was, it would be easy enough to catch him before he ducked into the saloon. If it wasn't, Dustin would be downright embarrassed.

In the alley, he leaned against the corner of the building.

Minutes ticked by, but when something stirred, it was at the far end of the alley near the street. Miss Hollingsworth rounded the corner and, making eye contact, headed for him. Dustin glanced to the outhouse, then hurried her way.

"Have you found him?"

"What are you doing here?" This was the last place she ought to be, especially if she'd been drugged. Besides, Josephine had said her clothes weren't dry. Yet a bright blue checked fabric peeked from under her coat. His jaw slackened. "Is that my shirt?"

The woman glanced at the material and gave him that same sassy look he'd seen yesterday. "I liked the color."

Surely Jo hadn't allowed her to help herself to his bureau.

"Don't worry, Reverend. I'll return it." Her eyes, rimmed with dark circles, strayed to the knife and hat in his hands. "Oh good. You found 'em. Thank you." She snatched the hat away and tugged it in place, wincing.

When she beckoned for the knife, he held it out of reach. "What do you think you're doing here?"

She stiffened. "Getting my cameo back. What are *you* doing here?"

"Confronting Clarence Roy to discover what happened to you."

Miss Hollingsworth huffed. "I can take care of myself, Preacher." She darted past and attempted to grab the knife as she went.

He tightened his grip, drawing her up short. "You shouldn't be here. You're in no shape."

She offered him a contemptuous glance. "And who appointed you my guardian angel?"

Oh, the insolence. "You seemed pretty thankful when I helped you last night."

Her cheeks flamed. "Thank you for your kindness in my moment of need, but under normal circumstances, I'm more than capable of looking after myself. I don't require a man to take care of me, and certainly not a straitlaced preacher—"

A shrill whistle sounded from the end of the alley, and they both turned to find the shirtless man.

"Shut up. Take your arguing somewhere else. There are people trying to sleep."

Miss Hollingsworth jerked the knife from his grasp and, holding it out of sight behind her leg, marched down the alley toward the man. "What'd you put in that whiskey last night, Roy?"

"Don't know what you're talking about."

"Oh, I'm betting you do." She stepped closer. "I was fine until I took a sip from that glass you brought me. Then everything went cata-wampus. Woke this morning with my head pounding and my valuables gone." She produced the knife and tapped the flat of the blade against his chest. "Did you drug me so you could rob me?"

Eyes flashing, Roy grasped her wrist and twisted the knife away, contorting her small frame in an awkward position. "I didn't rob you, little girl."

"Hey!" Dustin barged toward them.

In an attempt to free herself, Pete smacked Roy in the chest with her free hand.

"If you recall," Roy continued, "Aiken spilled your whiskey, so I kicked him out and gave you his winnings. After you'd cleaned yourself up, you asked to try poker." A humorless grin twitched his lips. "Your mistake. Faro is more your game—"

"Get your hands off her." Dustin slammed into Clarence Roy's generous frame, driving the man into the building.

Roy's grip on Miss Hollingsworth was broken, though she also tumbled into the building, knife clattering to the ground.

Righting herself, she swung to face him. "Back off. I can handle him." Sure she could. She looked like a twig in the hands of a giant.

"Who's this?" Roy jutted his chin at him.

He muscled his way forward. "The name is Dustin Owens, and I'm—"

"Nobody." She shot him a fearsome look, then turned to the saloon owner again. "Now, where is my brooch?"

Roy thrust a hand in his pocket and produced the stunning blue cameo.

Miss Hollingsworth made a grab for it, but Roy drove the heel of his hand into her shoulder. She tottered backward, and Dustin caught her. As soon as she had her feet under her again, she jerked free of his grasp.

"If you didn't want to lose it, you shouldn't have gambled it, woman."

"*I didn't.*" She spat the words.

"What do you want for it?" Most of his money was allocated for the church, but if he could keep her from dealing with his type. . .

Roy looked at him. "I told Pete last night." He turned a leering grin her way. "Remember?"

Miss Hollingsworth stared. "What stakes? How much money will I need to buy into the game?"

A mocking grin spread across the man's lips. "Oh, you can't gamble for it. That's too risky. Come be one of my girls, and you'll get it back. *Eventually.*"

Pain crackled through Petra's skull. Become a soiled dove? *Never.* Queen Victoria's cameo or not, she wouldn't stoop so low.

But—

She gulped, almost unable to breathe. If she didn't, she'd lose the jewel forever. Not only that, but surely her family too.

"You're evil." His fat frame, glistening with a thin sheen of sweat, turned her stomach. "Vile."

Clarence Roy laughed. "Now that we're clear on terms, say the word. You'll be a real crowd-pleaser."

Petra shook her head. "Not on your life."

"Your choice." Hands in his pockets, Roy shrugged and turned toward the door. She grabbed her knife and darted after him, and as Roy stepped through the doorway, she drew back and threw the blade.

A strong hand caught her wrist, causing the knife to fumble, then drop feet in front of her. The door clapped shut, as if sealing her fate.

Pete's ire sparked. "Why'd you—"

"I understand your feelings," Reverend Owens said, "but that man is *not* worth getting your neck stretched."

She glared. "Oh, what do you know about it?" She'd intended to plant her blade right beside his fat head—scare him good. Not hit him.

Pete stashed the knife in her boot and charged down the alley, beelining for the street. Her skull throbbed, but she could ignore the pain if it meant getting away from the nosy preacher.

The full weight of her mistakes settled like a boulder on her chest. The heirloom cameo was gone, and only a miracle would bring it back. Pete huffed. No miracle would come. She'd quit believing in such fantasies the day Uncle Peter died.

"Miss Hollingsworth?"

Pete turned down the nearest street, headed toward the livery.

Reverend Owens trotted up beside her. "I'm sorry. About your losing your jewelry, I mean. I understand it was important to you, but God will reward you for making the right decision. Nothing is worth what that man is asking."

She turned on him. "Are you done?"

Confusion flashed, but he attempted a weak smile. "That depends. Have I infused you with hope?"

What was there to hope for? A repulsive saloon owner had stolen her money and the family heirloom Mama never should have sent her. "Look, *Reverend,* I do appreciate that you and your sister took me in. If I had any money with me, I'd pay you for the trouble I caused."

"We aren't asking anything in return—"

"But I don't want what you're peddling." She rubbed at her temple. "Please leave me alone." She stalked away.

Several quick strides carried her toward the livery and Falco. She'd breathe easier once on horseback. But with a whisper of sound, he was at her side again.

"If I can be honest, ma'am, I'm having a hard time leaving you alone." She hadn't noticed.

Pete stopped. "Pray tell, *why?*"

His brown eyes were full of compassion. "Last night you were in a real bad way, and it's obvious you're still hurting today. You've just suffered a loss of something that's obviously very important to you. And to my knowledge, you've got no one looking out for you. That has me a little worried." He shook his head. "A *lot* worried."

"I can take care of myself. I've been on my own for years now."

"I believe you. You're a very capable woman. But we all have a bad turn now and then, and we all need a friend from time to time." He shrugged. "All I'm *peddling*, Miss Hollingsworth, is my concern and friendship. If you don't want to come to church, that's fine. If, after today, you don't want to talk to me again, that's fine too. But if you'd allow, I'd like to escort you home, just to be sure you're safe."

Petra's jaw went slack. How long had it been since a man offered his genuine concern for her well-being? Not since she'd become Buckskin Pete. She'd so effectively adopted that persona, few men dared. And those who did, she rebuffed. Strongly.

Maybe it was some lingering homesickness, or perhaps whatever Clarence Roy slipped her was still having a strange effect. But with her insides aquiver and her voice a whisper, Petra nodded. "All right."

❧ Chapter 5 ❧

By the time they neared her cabin a few miles outside of town, the throbbing between Pete's temples had abated some, but her awkwardness remained. Since when did being in a man's company draw out her shyness? Getting tongue-tied around a fella was Petra Breaux's trait—one she'd hoped Buckskin Pete Hollingsworth had banished forever.

Reverend Owens patted his strawberry roan's neck. "So why would you lose your family because of a brooch?"

When she met his warm brown eyes, her heart stuttered, and she faced front again. He was a preacher, blast it all. She couldn't forget that. "It once belonged to the queen."

"Yes, you said that. And?"

"And what?"

"Exactly. And what? Certainly, a piece of the queen's jewelry is precious, but will your family become destitute without it?"

Pete guffawed. "Hardly."

"So it's not the monetary value. Aside from the fact it was worn by royalty, what is so special about it that your family would disown you?"

Was he really going to force this conversation? "It was given to my mother's aunt Letitia by the queen, who told her that"—she spoke in a perfect British accent—"One never *owns* a cameo. One wears it, yes. Enjoys it, certainly. But one is merely a custodian of her cameo, preserving and protecting it for those who come after." She sighed. "I *cared for* this heirloom for mere hours before I lost it. To a filthy brothel owner." Shame spiraled through her.

He nodded slowly. "I gather your family relationship is tenuous?"

Drawing Falco to a halt, she stared. "No. What right do you have to ask such a question anyway?"

Reverend Owens also drew up, turning innocently. He exhaled. "Don't you see? It's not as bad as you might think."

"Aunt Letitia and Uncle Peter fell in love after Aunt Letitia received the cameo. When she gifted it to Mama, Mama and Papa fell in love and married. All these years, Mama bided her time, waiting for her only daughter—me—to grow into a responsible young lady so she could pass it along." She attempted to swallow the lump in her throat. "And now it's in the hands of that filth Clarence Roy. Even if I did somehow get it back, I've probably ruined it forever." She urged Falco forward again.

"Do you think your kin are incapable of falling in love without the talisman of the cameo?"

"That's not what I mean."

"Good." He came alongside her. "People have been falling in love for centuries, just by looking deep into each other's eyes and speaking sweet words to each other." He pinned her with a crazy, moon-eyed look. "No cameo needed."

Her cheeks flamed, and she stifled an embarrassed laugh. "Stop that."

The reverend *did* have beautiful eyes. And a strong jaw, now sporting a day's worth of whiskers, which only added to his rugged handsomeness.

"It's the truth."

Pete shook her head. "Before this, the cameo was something pure and beautiful with a rich history. If I get it back, which would take a miracle, it'll forever be tainted."

"Bet that's how the Israelites felt when they got carried off to Babylon."

Israelites? "What on earth are you talking about?"

"In the beginning of the book of Daniel, the nation of Israel got captured by Nebuchadnezzar, the king of Babylon. Along with the people, they carried away all the special pieces made for worship in the temple, and they were locked away in Nebuchadnezzar's vaults."

A cynical laugh boiled out of her. "A history lesson, Reverend?"

"Years later, Belshazzar came to power, and he went into the vault, retrieved those sacred items, and had a party. He took things that were set apart to worship God and used them for getting drunk—and worse."

"I attended Sunday school too. I've heard the story. God wrote on the wall. Belshazzar died, and someone else rose to power."

"Yes, Darius. But do you know what happened to the temple pieces?"

Her mocking response disappeared. "No. What?"

"The book of Ezra says King Cyrus came to power, and God told him to let the Israelites return to Jerusalem to rebuild. When he let them go, he returned all the sacred items to them, and they were prayed over, reconsecrated to God, and put back into service in the temple."

A tendril of hope she was almost too afraid to acknowledge sprouted. "So you're saying it's not permanently tainted."

"More than that. I think God has a plan to bring your cameo back with no ill effects from its current possessor."

Could she allow herself to believe that? She'd always believed God answered prayers until He'd failed her when she'd prayed the hardest. For Uncle Peter.

"My cabin is just ahead." She waved a fidgety hand to the bend in the rutted path, then chided herself for her awkwardness.

Reverend Owens grinned. "Last night I debated whether to take you to your house or bring you to mine. Seeing how far we've come, I think I made the right choice."

The kindness of this brother and sister duo was more than she expected. The more refined side of society deemed her too uncouth to help. The parts of the community that embraced her outlandish attire were plenty accommodating, but they also presumed she was less of a lady than she was. Good thing Dustin and Josephine Owens were the ones who'd taken her in. They'd provided care with no expectations of anything further.

"Why'd you choose to live *here?*"

Rounding the corner, a beautiful meadow opened. Green grass and myriad wildflowers carpeted the area. Bright sunlight glinted on a chuckling stream meandering through the idyllic picture. All around, peaks rose in the background. And her tiny cabin sat in the midst of it all.

She nodded at the majestic scene. "That."

The preacher halted his horse, and he grinned. "I don't know if I've ever seen a place more beautiful."

"I don't think one exists," she whispered, taking a moment to drink in the sight before she urged Falco toward the house.

The reverend caught up. "You live here alone?"

Pete shot him a sideways glance. "That's rather meddlesome, don't you think?"

"Think of it as concerned, not meddlesome."

Before she could answer, the distant notes of "Hard Times Come Again No More" carried on the breeze.

Obviously hearing it too, Reverend Owens motioned her to stay as he eased from the saddle.

"What are you doing?" Did the man intend to protect her from every perceived threat she ever faced?

"Someone's here."

"So I noticed."

"I thought you live alone," Reverend Owens whispered.

"I do, unless you count Falco." She patted the sorrel's shoulder, then pointed in the direction of the sound. "*That* is a neighbor. A white-haired gentleman of about fifty years old named Tibby." The wandering man had come to town a couple months before, then showed up at her home asking for odd jobs in exchange for being allowed to bunk in her barn. While she hadn't needed the help, the Milroy family did. Tibby was the perfect answer for the widow's difficult circumstances. "He's staying about a mile that direction."

The information drew Reverend Owens up short. "Sorry. Guess I'm still on edge after that scene in the alley."

As was she, though she hadn't decided if it was due to the lingering aftereffects of the altercation or the handsome company. "You're forgiven."

She wouldn't dare admit it to him, but it was charming, him wanting to protect her.

Petra nudged Falco forward and scanned the meadow. "Tibby? Where are you?"

The beautiful tenor voice faltered midphrase, and Tibby stood from the foot of Uncle Peter's grave, wiping tears.

"You all right?" She reined Falco toward him, the reverend mounting again to follow.

On his feet, Tibby dug a toe in the ground, looking shamefaced. "Well now. Reckon I just got a little nostalgic is all."

Her own throat knotted. "This tends to be a nostalgic spot, truth be known."

Tibby bobbed his head. "Didn't know you'd already buried a husband, ma'am. I'm real sorry."

Petra's smile faltered, and she dismounted. "Not a husband. An uncle." Her favorite. He'd been bright and funny. At times the perfect gentleman, and yet he was also the one who'd secretly taught her to play poker and faro. "He's the reason I came west. He was British, and he'd always been fascinated with the West. He talked for years about touring the frontier, so a few years ago, he and Aunt Letitia and I set off on a grand adventure to see every corner."

They hadn't told her until they were already well into the journey that Uncle Peter was sick. This was as far as they'd gotten.

And this was where she'd stayed.

"An uncle." Tibby scrubbed a hand across his mouth. "Didn't know you had one of them either."

Petra laughed. "If we're to be accurate, I *haven't* had a husband, but I do have my parents, three younger brothers, several aunts and uncles, and some cousins."

"Where are they?" Her riding companion had also dismounted and was standing off a couple of paces. "If you don't mind another meddlesome question, that is."

She quirked a brow at him. "I'm growing accustomed to your prying," she teased. "My family is from Pittsburgh."

"And who're you, young fella?"

"Reverend Dustin Owens." The preacher stepped forward, hand outstretched.

Tibby narrowed a glance at him, then shook his hand. "Reverend, huh?"

"Yes, sir. My sister and I are new in town, come to build a church in Cambria Springs."

"Every town needs a church. Glad to make your acquaintance, Reverend. I'm Tibby."

"So what brings you this way, Tibby?" she asked. "Did you come to check on me, or. . ." Tibby had gone to work for Mrs. Milroy, but he often rode his mule, Pierrepont, between the two cabins and looked in on her, asked if she needed help, or sometimes just sat to talk awhile.

"No, ma'am. Mrs. Milroy sent me to fetch you."

Alarm gripped her. "Well, why didn't you say so?" She reached for Falco's saddle but caught a glimpse of the reverend's blue-checked shirt peeking from under her coat sleeve. She should at least change so she could return it to him, as promised. "Let me do one thing, and we'll go see Mrs. Milroy."

By the time they turned away from the creek toward the Milroy house, it was afternoon. Dustin should be getting home to Josephine. Not only would she be worried, but he had to finish preparations for his first church service in Cambria Springs, scheduled for the following morning. However, something told him he needed to accompany Miss Hollingsworth on her errand to the neighboring house.

They rode over a hill, and a rambling cabin came into view. The structure looked as if it was built in stages, the original house and later a couple of small additions. The place was run-down but showed signs of some recent repairs. A rickety barn stood to one side, with a patched-up corral out front. A couple of horses in the pen nickered at them as they approached.

"Reverend, be prepared." Tibby chuckled as they dismounted. "The onslaught is about to come." As they walked farther into the yard, children raced from the house and barn, spilling across the yard toward them.

The children swarmed Miss Hollingsworth. She laughed, seeming to enjoy their overwhelming attention. Some hugged her, and all chattered, each one talking over the next. As they surrounded her on all sides, Miss Hollingsworth picked up one of the littlest girls. Tibby lifted another one that looked to be the child's twin.

The crowd was mostly girls. Only two boys. Mickey, and one several years younger. For an instant, Miss Hollingsworth attempted to quiet them but finally resorted to sounding a shrill whistle.

Dustin grinned as the yard went silent.

She looked at the bunch. "Good afternoon."

A chorus of hellos and cries of "Howdy, Pete!" ensued. She commanded the crowd like a schoolmarm perfectly in control of her class. Only this woman didn't look like the grouchy schoolmarms he'd come across.

"Can we practice throwing your tomahawk, Pete?" Mickey blurted.

"Please?" a slightly older girl chimed.

"Maybe before I leave, but I need to speak to your mama first."

"She's been out of sorts today." One of the older girls shook her head. "Had to rest a lot."

Dustin's concern sparked. Was their mother ill?

"Is she sleeping now?" Miss Hollingsworth focused on the child who'd answered.

"She woke again about an hour ago."

"Good."

"Please, Pete. Would ya at least throw your tomahawk once for us?"

The entire group seemed to agree with the request.

With a sigh, she put the little girl down, stepped to the edge of the group, and took the tomahawk from her belt. Dustin shifted to see over the heads of the children, Tibby moving right alongside him. Miss Hollingsworth hoisted the weapon and, exhaling, launched it at a dead tree about thirty feet away. The weapon spun through the air with precision and landed with a heavy *thwack*, its cutting edge buried in the trunk.

The kids erupted in hoots of laughter and applause, a couple of them racing to the tree to collect the weapon.

Tibby whistled in admiration, attention focused on the little girl in his arms. "Did you see what Pete did?"

The little girl ducked her chin with a shy smile.

Dustin grinned, thoughts spinning. This woman—Buckskin Pete Hollingsworth—was the subject of dime novels, could throw a tomahawk better than most any man, but somehow came to possess a cameo once owned by the Queen of England. *Lord, she's a woman of mysteries and layers, isn't she? A woman of contradictions.*

And suddenly, he wanted to discover them all.

Miss Hollingsworth received the tomahawk from one of the girls, stashed it safely on her belt, then picked up the little girl she'd held earlier.

"Before I go talk to your mama, I want you to meet my friend." Miss Hollingsworth beckoned to him.

Friend. A good sign. Perhaps she wouldn't take him up on his offer never to speak to him again—and he could eventually discover her various layers.

Idiot. He scrubbed the stubble on his chin. There were incongruities in his own life, and no woman in her right mind would look past them.

He stepped forward. "This is Reverend Dustin Owens. Preacher, these are the Milroy children." She drew each one forward, apparently in order of age. "This is Sarah and Carrie. You met Mickey yesterday. Then

Bess, Ernie, and the twins, Lily"—she nodded toward the child in Tibby's arms, then bounced the girl on her hip—"and Rose."

Another paradox. She was just as confident with a baby on her hip as throwing her tomahawk. And like Jo said, she was downright pretty.

He swallowed hard. What the blue blazes was he thinking? Dustin tugged at the collar of his shirt. These were *not* the type of thoughts a preacher ought to have, particularly about a woman he'd just met. He pulled his hat brim lower. "Pleasure," he mumbled.

Miss Hollingsworth turned to the older gentleman. "Tibby, would you go see if Mrs. Milroy is prepared for a visit?"

Tibby handed Lily off and stalked away, humming "I Dream of Jeanie with the Light Brown Hair" as he went.

"So where's Addie?" She looked around the group.

"She's been gone all week looking for work." Carrie's voice dripped frustration.

"Remember, Pete? I told ya that yesterday." Mickey turned her way.

"Hasn't helped around here at all lately." Again, Carrie shared.

"She dragged in early this morning," Sarah spoke. "Brought supplies, but then said she's gotta be back to work tonight. She slept some, then left again."

Back to work *tonight*?

Miss Hollingsworth set little Rose down. "Where is she working?"

"Didn't say." Mickey again. "She just said she's washing dishes."

"At night?" Dustin couldn't hold back. He'd walked the town at night. The only places open after dark were the three saloons. All would have dishes to wash.

Miss Hollingsworth's face blanched, and her haunted green eyes turned his way. "This is bad." She stepped from the group and, grasping his hand, started toward the house. "Addie was *there* last night. At the Gold Spur before I—" She shook her head. At that moment, Tibby came to the door and beckoned, so she scurried inside. "Mrs. Milroy?"

Dustin entered and stopped beside Tibby near the door. Across the room, a dark-haired woman, perhaps forty, sat in a rocking chair near the fireplace. At the sight of Miss Hollingsworth, relief flooded one half of her face, though the other drooped. Her right hand lay withered in her lap, and a sturdy cane leaned against the wall close by.

"Mrs. Milroy." Miss Hollingsworth dropped to a knee beside the woman.

"Pete." The widow's half-smile deepened. "Good."

She labored over the simple words.

Miss Hollingsworth turned again to him. "Ma'am, I brought a friend. I hope you don't mind. This is Reverend Dustin Owens. He's building a church in Cambria Springs."

Mrs. Milroy beckoned him with her left hand. "Come."

On leaden feet, Dustin crossed the room and took the hand she offered. She gripped his fingers with unexpected strength. "Mrs. Milroy. It's a pleasure."

She bobbed her head.

"A year and a half ago, Mrs. Milroy's husband passed. Then, eight months ago, she suffered an apoplexy." The younger woman grinned at the elder. "She's worked hard to recover, and she's doing very well. Following all the doctor's orders, aren't you?"

The elder woman attempted to answer, but after a moment of struggle, she huffed, her frustration evident.

"You've made great strides." Miss Hollingsworth laid a hand on her arm, then looked at him again. "I was doing all I could to look after things here. Then, about two months ago, Tibby came by my place in kind of a bad way himself. Needed a job. So I brought him here. He sleeps in the barn in exchange for doing repairs, helping with the children, and whatever else is needed."

Pride swelled in his chest. *Lord, this young woman has quite a heart.*

He turned to their host. "Mrs. Milroy, my sister, Josephine, and I can help as well. I'd be more than willing to assist Tibby with larger projects, or we might be able to provide some supplies, if that would help."

The woman seemed to consider, then reached for his hand again. "Good."

Miss Hollingsworth pressed on. "Did you know Addie got a job in town?"

The widow's eyes clouded, and she grew agitated. Again, the woman tried to form an answer, but words failed her.

"Ma'am, I'm worried about her."

The widow nodded vigorously.

"All right. I'm going to head into town now. I'll find her and bring her home."

"I'll go with you, Pete," Tibby called from nearby.

She shook her head. "I'd feel better if you stayed here, Tibby. I can handle the run to town." She started toward the door.

Dustin hurried after her. "You're not going alone. I hope you know that."

Not after last night.

✤ Chapter 6 ✤

$\mathcal{P}$ete tied her horse to the hitching rail outside the Gold Spur. "You don't have to do this. I can take care of myself."

Reverend Owens looked over the back of his roan. "Anyone who's heard the name Buckskin Pete would say you're capable of handling yourself. But I'm not going to let you walk in there alone. Not after what Roy did to you."

The reverend truly was charming. So charming it flustered her. But. . . "Won't being seen in a place like this harm your standing as a preacher? People might think wrongly of you."

He tied his horse with a disdainful chuckle. "Anyone who knows me has plenty of reasons to think badly of me."

She laughed. "You? You're about as straitlaced as they come."

Sadness clouded his expression. "I mean you no disrespect, but thank you. I'm glad I was able to fool you."

Fool her? What on earth—*him?*

He walked into the saloon, and she darted after, nearly running into his solid frame just inside the door. The room was even more crowded tonight than the previous evening. It was a Saturday, after all.

"Buckskin Pete," Roy called from the corner table.

She turned, and the reverend stood beside her, his back rigid.

"Surprised to see you. After our conversation earlier, I didn't expect you'd return so soon." A mocking grin stained his lips. "Have you re-thought my offer?"

Never. So long as the ransom for the cameo was to debase herself, she'd face the devastating consequences with her family.

Reverend Owens rocked forward, as if about to approach Roy. However, she stepped into his path and walked toward the table. The preacher remained a half-step behind her, though not happily, if his low growl was any indication.

She stopped a foot from the table. "Where is Addie Milroy?"

"Why do you ask?" The fat man's brows arched.

"She's a friend. Her mother asked me to bring her home."

Roy shook his head. "You can't do that."

"Why not?" Reverend Owens spoke, a snarl in his voice. "She's a child who belongs with her family. Not in this lions' den."

"Addie came to me crying about her family needing money. She asked for a job, and I gave her one."

The preacher put two fists on the edge of the table, leaning toward Roy. "Consider this her immediate resignation."

Roy's lips curved in a smug grin. "Are you that girl's daddy or brother? Husband, maybe?"

"No."

He leaned in, nose to nose. "Then you've no right to speak for her. Now, either drink, gamble, or clear out."

She wouldn't clear out. Not without Addie. "You can't hold that girl here, Roy."

Clarence Roy stood and beckoned to someone across the room.

Addie looked their way an instant before she hurried to them, empty tray in hand. A wave of relief flooded Pete at seeing the girl's typical, chaste attire.

"Addie." She charged at the girl, meeting her several feet from Roy's table. "Are you all right?" Pete kept her voice low.

"Are you?" Concern reflected in the girl's dark eyes. "You didn't look very good last night."

Her breath caught, mind sparking with a thousand questions. But she shoved them aside and looked Addie straight in the eye. "Has Mr. Roy touched you?"

"We shook hands when he gave me the job."

Heat wound through her. "I mean. . .anywhere else."

The girl's brow furrowed, and then her eyes widened. "No. He hired me to wash dishes and straighten up at night. Not—" She shook her head fiercely. "I wouldn't do *that*."

Oh, thank God. She grabbed Addie's hand and pulled her toward Roy's table. "Tell him you quit, and let's go."

The girl set her feet and pulled free of Pete's grip. "I can't."

"Why not?" Reverend Owens croaked the question on her mind too.

"Because I paid her." Roy's slippery tone slicked the air. "Handsomely. In advance."

Stomach flopping, Pete turned on Addie. "Give him back the money, and let's go."

"I *can't*. I paid our mercantile bill and bought supplies. The money's gone."

Lord Jesus, no. The uninvited prayer bubbled through her thoughts as she sought. . .what—comfort? Reassurance?—from Reverend Owens's dark eyes.

"How much did he give you?" he asked the girl.

Roy sat and held his whiskey glass up to the light. "Twelve dollars. She'll be washing dishes for months." The man returned the glass to the table and, satisfied, leaned back in his chair, his hands spread across the wooden surface.

Pete grabbed the tomahawk and swung it, the edge shattering the glass and sinking into the tabletop between the man's fat hands. Clarence Roy jerked to his feet, cursing.

She relished the fear that flashed in his eyes. "You touch that girl, and I'll make sure you never touch another thing."

The man stared at his trembling appendages, probably counting digits.

As Pete jerked the tomahawk free, the saloon owner caught her by the neck, and the weapon slipped from her grasp. Panicked, she reached for his wrists.

"You little wench," he hissed. "Don't you dare walk in my saloon and threaten me—"

Wood screeched against wood, and Clarence Roy pitched backwards, releasing her with a sickening grunt. Pete hit the floor.

"Get up!" Addie rushed to her side and all but jerked her to her feet.

Nabbing her tomahawk, Pete scrambled out of the way and slowly backed up, pushing Addie toward the door.

With Roy pinned between the table and the wall, Dustin Owens launched a punch to the saloon owner's jaw. The wicked strike snapped Roy's head sideways, and the fat man sagged.

Hesitating half a breath, the reverend rushed toward them. "Get Addie out of here!"

"Pete!" a man bellowed.

The chilling rack of a shotgun silenced the room and brought her to a halt, Addie with her.

"You and your fella get out and don't come back," the barkeep called. "But the girl stays."

Dustin froze. One of Roy's soiled doves, inches behind Miss Hollingsworth, aimed a derringer at her head.

Lord, help.

The woman nodded toward the door. "You heard the man."

At the woman's husky words, Miss Hollingsworth twitched a glance behind her, then back to him. Something in the way she held herself—the rigidness of her shoulders, perhaps the quickening of her breath—told him she was scared.

He was too.

"Go." Again, the woman bobbed her head toward the doorway.

Dustin reached for Miss Hollingsworth, willing himself not to shake. "C'mon."

Her pretty features stoic, she dragged teary-eyed Addie into a bear hug. "Listen to me." She spoke softly, barely a quaver in her voice. "While you're here, don't you eat or drink anything you didn't make yourself. Understand? And don't let anyone touch you." She pulled away, but she caught Addie's hands. "Expect that they'll try to take advantage. Roy drugged me last night and stole an heirloom cameo I—"

"Enough jawing, Pete." The derringer-toting woman pressed the gun's barrel to Miss Hollingworth's temple.

Addie sobbed.

He turned to the woman with the gun. "Tell Roy I'll bring him his twelve dollars—plus some. When I do, I'll expect Addie to be released from this working arrangement, and she'd better have Miss Hollingsworth's cameo in hand."

"Expect whatever you want. Mr. Roy decides what agreements he makes." She waved the derringer. "Now git."

Dustin took Miss Hollingsworth's hand and pulled her onto the dark boardwalk. The moment they stepped out into the evening, his muscles uncoiled. *Thank You, Lord, for getting us out of there.*

As if nothing had happened, Miss Hollingsworth untied her horse and mounted.

He stepped into his saddle. "Unless you've got a better idea, we can go to my house."

Miss Hollingsworth turned to follow.

He slowed. "Did he hurt you?"

Silence.

As they passed the window near Roy's table, several soiled doves hovered around the unconscious man. An ugly desire to finish what he'd started roiled through him. Dustin clenched his fist, and the raw sting of broken skin and bruises lanced his hand. He fantasized about smashing Roy's smug lips, turning them to a bloody pulp. Of throwing a jab and a cross that, in combination, would crush the man's prominent nose. Of knocking Roy down, straddling him, and launching punch after—

Beside him, Miss Hollingsworth leaned on the saddle horn, shoulders trembling with silent sobs.

"C'mon. Let's get you home." He quickened the pace, and despite her emotion, she kept up.

Shame wrapped icy fingers through him. *Father, I shouldn't have hit him. I promised You. That life is over.*

But that environment—the coarse conversations and drunken ramblings, the smell of whiskey, cigars, and the soiled doves' cheap perfumes—all took him back. And—God forgive him—seeing Roy's stubby fingers wrapped around Miss Hollingsworth's throat ignited a protectiveness that grabbed him unaware.

They reached the house, and Dustin dismounted and tied the roan to the fence.

She didn't move.

"Can I help you down, ma'am?"

At his question, she slid to the ground but stood clutching the saddle horn. He tied the sorrel, then returned to her side, where she fumbled with the buckle of her saddlebags. When she failed to unlatch it, he untied it from behind the saddle.

"Why don't you come inside?" Despite the urge to pull her to him and hold her, he wrapped a protective arm around her and led her to the wide porch.

Same as the previous night, Josephine called out. "Dusty?"

"Yeah, Jo. Open the door."

"Oh, thank goodness." The key turned. The door swung open, and Jo stood in their path. "Where on earth have you been all day—" She stepped back, eyes widening. "Oh. Is everything all right?"

"Rough day, Sis." He guided Miss Hollingsworth to the settee, dropping her saddlebags on the floor beside it. "I bet Miss Hollingsworth would appreciate some tea."

"Of course." Jo disappeared into the kitchen.

Alone with his guest, Dustin brought the lantern nearer. "Miss Hollingsworth, did he hurt you?" he asked in a firmer tone than before.

At the faint shake of her head, he placed the lantern on the small table and dropped to a knee. He removed her hat, then turned her chin first to one side, then the other.

"I'm not injured." Her voice was small.

"Yeah? Well, you're not acting yourself. And excuse me for being blunt, but you don't look so good either."

Not entirely true. She was beautiful but emotional. Distraught. And neither of those qualities was helping him *not* want to hold her.

"How do I explain this to Mrs. Milroy?" she whispered. "I told her I would bring Addie back."

"You will." Dustin sat on the edge of the table, elbows on his knees. "Josephine and I have money set aside—for the church, but I think rescuing an innocent girl from that environment is as much the work of the church as preaching sermons."

"You'd let us borrow the church's money?" Her big green eyes met his. His heart stalled. "No."

"But—" As she pulled back, he caught her hands.

"We're not *lending* the money. We're *giving* it. No one needs to repay it. Not you, and not the Milroy family."

After an instant, she pressed her eyes closed. "Thank you, Reverend."

He squeezed her hands, then released them and sat back. It would be all too easy to overstep his bounds.

Grabbing her saddlebags, Miss Hollingsworth fumbled with the buckle again. Loosening it, she removed a book, returned the bags to the floor, and hugged the tome to her chest.

He arched a questioning brow at her. "You suddenly got an itch to read, did you?"

She shook her head. "My papa is an author. This is one of his books." Placing it flat in her lap, she turned it to face him.

"*Pittsburgh and the Wilds Beyond: A Natural History of Western Pennsylvania* by Bryan B-r-e-a-u-x." He turned a questioning look her way. "*Brew?*"

She traced his name with a still-trembling finger. "*By*-ron. . .*Bro.*" She hugged it to her chest. "Sometimes it helps to keep his book close. Particularly when I'm missing home or having a hard time with something. He can't hold me, so I hold a little piece of him."

The words tugged hard at his heart, and Dustin eased onto the settee beside her. "Sounds like you two are close."

"Very."

Her shoulder pressed into his, and she darted a quick, awkward glance his way, then averted her gaze again.

Oh, for the love of— *Lord, if this is wrong, You're gonna have to forgive me.*

Twisting, Dustin looped his arms around her. After a couple tense heartbeats, she collapsed. Head resting on his chest, she exhaled, and her muscles released, as if the day's anxieties drained out in a flood.

Neither spoke, and he dared not move for fear she'd spook. Instead, he closed his eyes and drank in her nearness.

Lord, this—she—feels good.

Her slender frame fit perfectly at his side, and her reclining against him eased the tightness in his muscles as well. Holding his breath, he sank a little deeper against the settee's back.

Gentle fingers brushed the back of his hand, tracing around the abrasions on his knuckles. "Thank you."

"For?"

"Not leaving me alone today." She burrowed deeper into his grasp. "I needed a friend more than I knew."

Her blond hair glimmered in the lamplight. If he eased his hand up, he could twine his fingers in her silky locks and tilt her head back.

Perhaps she'd let him kiss her.

She brushed a particularly tender spot on his knuckles, and he stiffened, tension flooding his shoulders again.

Idiot. What in heaven's name was he thinking?

"Thank you too for stepping in when Roy grabbed me." She pulled back to look at him. "Who taught you to fight like that?"

The teapot whistled in the kitchen, and Dustin pushed her up.

Miss Hollingsworth straightened, confusion etching her features. "Did I do something wrong?"

He lurched to his feet. "You didn't. I did." He strode toward the window.

"What?" She also stood. "What is it?"

"Miss Hollingsworth, I'm not who—or what—you think I am."

"You're not a preacher?"

"I am, but—"

"I don't understand."

No, she didn't. But he'd make sure she did—so nothing like this would happen again. "You want to know where I learned to fight? Some saloon in Missouri when I was five or six years old. The barkeep and the owner taught me."

"Why were you in a saloon at that age?"

He forced himself to meet her eyes. "Ma'am, mine is not the strait-laced life you seem to think it is. I spent my first twenty years in saloons and brothels. My mother is a harlot who goes by the name Fair Meri, and I've absolutely no idea who my father is."

~ Chapter 7 ~

𝒫etra stared. Reverend Owens—the son of a harlot? Oh, the pain that must have caused him. To not know his father. Her father was her whole world. And to live with the knowledge that his birth wasn't one his mother anticipated, planned for—or even wanted. Had she treated him as a burden, an imposition? Had she cherished him or hated him?

Oh Lord, has this man ever known the love of a family?

"I'm so sorry."

"For what?"

Somewhere down the hall, cupboards opened and teacups rattled. Josephine would return soon.

That didn't matter now. Only he mattered in this moment.

Petra laid the book aside and crossed to him. Peering up, she slipped her arms around him and pressed her cheek to his chest. "I'm sorry for the pain that must have caused you."

His muscles drew taut, and a grunt rumbled in his chest. His hands braced against her hips, holding her apart, but she twisted past them and burrowed closer, resting her forehead in the crook of his neck.

His palms settled at the small of her back.

Oh goodness, it felt right, holding and being held by this man. His touch was like water on parched ground, awakening something she hadn't realized she missed.

His fingers skimmed slowly up her spine, sending goose bumps along her flesh. As he reached the nape of her neck, his thumb brushed her cheek, her earlobe, her hair. He delved his whole hand into her thick locks and, heart pounding, Petra angled her chin upward, her lips close to his.

His breath stirred against her cheek for an interminable moment. Then he gave a tiny shake of his head. "I can't. . ."

She caught him and pressed her lips to his. The reverend froze, and she broke the kiss, her mouth hovering near his. "Yes, you can," she whispered, then timidly kissed him again. When, still, he didn't respond, she drew away enough to meet his beautiful brown eyes. "Please."

The third time she touched his lips, he claimed her mouth soundly. Lightning shot through her, and her muscles turned to warm butter. He pulled her to him, and his kiss deepened, stealing her breath. Firm and experienced and terrifying.

But oh so right.

The rattle of teacups intruded, and the reverend pulled back suddenly, his neck flushed a deep red.

"Tea." Josephine's sweet voice chimed from behind her.

Petra's own face flamed as she gripped the reverend's arms, unable to trust her muscles.

Reverend Owens glowered.

"Oh. I, um. . .forgot spoons." Josephine set down the tray for them and retreated.

Once Josephine was gone, he turned that surly look on her. "Why'd you do that?" He spat the question under his breath. "You don't need to get tangled up with someone like me."

The sharpness of his tone stung, and Petra stared. "Really?"

"Yes, really. Didn't you hear what I told you—what I am?"

"I heard you say you had a difficult start. A bad turn, so to speak. *Someone* told me we each have a bad turn now and then, and in those times, we can use a friend."

"I was being neighborly, making sure you got home safe after a difficult night. That's a far cry from falling into a passionate kiss with someone with my spurious origins."

"*I don't care* what your origins are, Reverend. I care about the man standing before me now. And that man? I rather like him." After that kiss, she *really* liked him. "That man is kind and compassionate. He offers to help widows he's never met, and he fights for little girls who get themselves into bad situations. And he's treated a bigger girl who walked away from a life of affluence to live in the wilds of Colorado, one who throws knives and tomahawks and wears men's britches, with respect and decency. Like she's every bit a proper lady, even when she doesn't act like it."

Heavens, how he made her *want* to act like a lady again.

Petra skimmed her fingertips across his bristly jaw, then settled her palm over his heart. "That's a special man, and despite whatever *spurious origins* he might have, his heart is pure and beautiful."

Before she could slip back into his arms, she paced to the settee and sat down, and gathering Papa's book, she tucked it into her saddlebags.

"Tea?" She drew the tray nearer.

Mute, Reverend Owens stood, a befuddled expression clouding his handsome features.

She poured two cups. What on earth was he thinking? For that matter, what was *she*? They'd only met the afternoon before, and she'd just brazenly kissed the man.

They were still strangers, but in the twenty-four hours they'd spent together, he'd seen through her tough veneer and treated her not as the absurd subject of dime novels and local legend, but as a woman. *A lady.* Someone worthy to be protected, treated gently, with kindness and concern. He'd not shied from her bolder side. It almost seemed he *liked* it.

And at the same time, something about him made her want to be soft and sweet, to be the demure woman Mama always hoped she'd become.

Could she possibly be both?

Reverend Owens approached and dropped uncomfortably onto the settee beside her.

Petra sat back, spine stiff, and folded her hands in her lap.

"We having tea?"

"No spoons."

A tense moment ticked by. "Thank you. For what you said." As quick as he said it, he twisted to see over the settee. "Jo, are we supposed to stir this tea with our fingers, or are you waiting until it's cold?"

Dustin could barely meet Miss Hollingsworth's eyes as he gulped his tea, and he surely wasn't going to meet Jo's. Not when she could barely contain the fool grin ready to bust across her face. No doubt Josephine would take this to mean they'd be getting married. Nothing was further from the truth, no matter how diplomatic Miss Hollingsworth might be.

Laying aside the empty teacup, he rose. "I'll get the money and go after Addie."

Miss Hollingsworth rocked to her feet. "I'll be ready."

"No, ma'am. I'm going alone. Clarence Roy has grabbed you by the throat, and a soiled dove held a derringer to your head. That's enough for one night." For a lifetime. "Stay with my sister, please."

Before she argued, he stalked to his bedroom, lit a lamp, and dug through his sock drawer until he found the stash he'd hidden there. He pocketed twenty-five dollars. The remaining roll of bills was slim. Too slim for comfort. But if God meant for this church to thrive, He would provide the means.

When Dustin stepped into the sitting room, Jo and Miss Hollingsworth's quiet conversation ceased.

"Dusty, please tell me you're taking a gun."

"You know I won't, Sis. I promised God that life was over."

So why had he allowed himself to fantasize about thrashing Clarence Roy within an inch of his life? Because Miss Hollingsworth brought out his protective side, something only Jo had done so strongly.

And he'd killed to protect Josephine.

Miss Hollingsworth stood. "Please let me come. I'll—"

"No." He glared. "Stay here. I'll return with Addie."

Lord, please *let me get her back. And make sure Miss Hollingsworth stays put this time.*

He strode from the house, locked the door, and swung into the saddle.

Dustin rubbed his chest where Miss Hollingsworth's hand had rested. His heart—pure and beautiful. He stifled a laugh. She didn't know him very well. Not only was he the illegitimate son of a soiled dove, but he'd been a rabble-rouser all his life. Arrested more times than he could count for public drunkenness, fighting, and other such behaviors. Right up until that afternoon nine years ago.

Lord, thank You for leading us from that life. I still don't understand why You brought us here, but maybe it's to get Addie Milroy free of Clarence Roy.

He stopped outside the Gold Spur for the fourth time in two days. Only this time the hitching posts and the saloon's interior were strangely uncrowded. Odd for that time on a Saturday. In his experience, the crowds didn't normally thin for hours.

He peered in the window. Roy wasn't at the table he'd occupied earlier, nor anywhere visible. The soiled doves mostly congregated together at a single table, now that the crowd had thinned. The one who'd pulled the derringer on Miss Hollingsworth sat at a table near the back, keeping company with one of the remaining patrons.

Dustin entered the establishment, and almost immediately the chilling rack of a shotgun stopped him. Cold sweat broke out under his clothes.

"Thought I told you not to come back," the barkeep called.

Lord, I know I'm gonna die, but please, not here and not tonight. "You did, but I have further business with Clarence Roy."

"He ain't takin' visitors right now. Get out, or I'll see to it you leave with a belly full of buckshot."

"Enough, Emmitt." Clarence Roy appeared in a doorway at the back of the room.

Emmitt lowered the gun, though he placed it on the bar within easy reach. Too easy.

"What d'you want?" Roy barked, crossing the room with a pronounced limp. The effects of Dustin driving the table into his legs, perhaps?

Dustin cleared his throat. "I know you were *sleeping* when I said it, but like I promised, I brought you twelve dollars to pay what Addie Milroy owes. And more to buy back Miss Hollingsworth's cameo."

"Sleeping. . ." Roy offered a mirthless chuckle. The smile dribbled off his face, and he shoved Dustin through the doors. "That sweet little girl will hafta pay what she owes all by herself. I made that deal with her—not you. And to restate the terms for the cameo—Pete comes to work for me, and it'll be returned. *Eventually.*"

How easy it would be to take another swing. Just one. Right to the throat. But he wouldn't. He'd promised God and himself—for Jo's sake.

Why, then, were his thoughts straying to Miss Hollingsworth—as if he'd promised *her*? Why was it suddenly important not to disappoint the pretty stranger?

He shook off the thought.

Lord, is there truly no other way? "I want to see Addie for a minute."

"Why would I let you do that?"

"Because I asked. She's not a prisoner, is she?"

"A prisoner? No." Smugness curved his lips. "Just a *working girl.*"

Dustin's muscles trembled with the urge to lash out. "You just remember what Miss Hollingsworth said. Touch that child, and it won't go well for you."

Roy nodded. "Duly noted. Now get off my doorstep. You aren't good for business." He turned to enter the saloon again but stopped. "Oh, and if you do come back, Emmitt'll have cause to unload that shotgun of his in your direction. Consider yourself warned."

The man limped inside.

Lord, what about Addie? Do You really intend for me to leave her here?

What choice did he have? He'd been warned. Step into that saloon, maybe even remain outside, and he could be shot. There was little the town's sheriff could do. Miss Hollingsworth had no proof she'd been drugged. No proof she'd not simply gambled the cameo away. Roy would deny any such accusations. So the cameo was likely lost. And Addie Milroy had willingly entered an arrangement to wash dishes for Roy in exchange for money in advance, which she'd already spent. They were stuck.

He turned toward his horse. "All right, Lord. What do I do?" The last thing he *wanted* to do was tell Miss Hollingsworth he'd failed to rescue Addie.

"Mister?" The quiet voice, young and urgent, drew Dustin's attention to the alley. "You were the one with Pete, right?"

His hackles stood on end. Was this a trap?

"Yes."

"You're Addie's friend?"

"What about her?"

"C'mere." The shadowy woman beckoned.

"Where?"

"Closer. Hurry. I only got a minute before Mr. Roy figures out I'm not inside."

Dustin stepped into the alley, senses primed for danger. *Lord, keep me safe.*

"I'm Edna," the girl whispered. The low-cut bodice and knee-length skirt marked her as a soiled dove.

"Reverend Owens."

"You're a preacher?" Her tone pitched upward.

"Yes, ma'am." One who didn't want to face Clarence Roy's gun. "What is it you know about Addie?"

The girl looked around. "She ain't here."

At the sound of footsteps, she crouched in the shadows. Likewise, Dustin pressed himself against the wall. After a moment, saddle leather creaked and someone rode away.

He strained for any further sound, and when she brushed his arm, he jumped.

Edna cringed. "I'm sorry."

"Forget it. What do you mean, Addie isn't here?"

"After y'all left earlier, Mr. Roy told his nephew, Quinton Bice, to take her to a cabin in the mountains."

Not good. "Where is it?"

"I don't know. I been there once before, but. . ." Her voice dropped. "I couldn't find it if I tried."

What purpose would Roy have for taking her? Not likely she'd be washing dishes at this cabin. Which meant it was likely something far more despicable. "Do you know a general direction?"

She shook her head. "Listen. There's more." Edna checked the alley again before continuing. "Yesterday afternoon Quinton Bice came into the saloon hopping mad. Something about Pete getting him fired."

Miss Hollingsworth hardly seemed the type to elicit someone's termination. Not on purpose, anyway. "And?"

"I heard the two of 'em plotting. I didn't hear details, just that they wanted to get revenge on Pete for messing Bice up."

Had Quinton Bice's firing been the reason Roy drugged Pete and stole from her, or was it something more? "Anything else you can think of?"

"No, but I'll keep listening for things."

Dustin considered. "I'm going to talk to Miss Hollingsworth, see what she can tell me, and I'll contact the sheriff. Be *very* careful."

The girl gave a grave nod, then started down the alley.

"Edna?" He hurried after her. "Which way did Bice go?"

She led him down the alley. "His horse was tied right here." She pointed to the place where he and Miss Hollingsworth had their confrontation with Roy that morning. "And he rode off that direction, straight out of town. From there, I've no idea."

She might not, but the sheriff would surely have a tracker—either in his employ or one he knew of.

"Thank you." He tried to smile, though the thought of leaving Edna, little older than Addie, here to fend for herself didn't set right. "One more question. Did Roy drug Miss Hollingsworth with something?"

She leaned close. "I didn't see him, but I know he keeps ether behind the counter."

So he *had* smelled ether.

"That explains a lot. Thank you. Now get inside."

Edna darted away and eased the door open, checked inside, and slipped out of sight.

Lord God, help us get Edna and Addie out of here.

❧ *Chapter 8* ❧

*T*he moonlit street was dark, devoid of movement other than the occasional swish of Falco's tail.

"I don't like this. I'm going to check on him." Petra turned toward the door.

"You *do* care about my brother, don't you?"

Josephine's question stopped her.

"I'm just curious," she continued. "Dusty said he met you yesterday. It was rather surprising to walk in tonight and find you two. . ."

Oh, Mama would be mortified if she knew how brazenly she'd acted—and with a man of God, no less. Of course, most of what she did as Buckskin Pete Hollingsworth would mortify her mother.

But why did it suddenly shame and humiliate *her*?

"I'm sorry," Josephine whispered. "I didn't mean to embarrass you."

She shrugged. "I'll be honest. I thought a woman named *Pete* wouldn't be easily embarrassed."

Petra shook her head. "Normally I'm not."

Josephine dipped her chin. "Forgive me for making you uncomfortable." From her chair, Josephine patted the settee next to her. "Please. Come sit."

Abandoning thoughts of checking on the reverend, she took the offered seat.

"Would it be too forward of me to ask why you've chosen to be Pete instead of Petra?"

That was somewhat safer territory. "I suppose I don't mind. My father's father was a woodsman in Pennsylvania, so Papa grew up chopping down trees, hunting, tracking, riding, trapping. All sorts of skills. I was the firstborn child for Mama and Papa, and at some point, Papa started teaching me those same things."

Josephine grinned. "How did your mother feel about that?"

"She wasn't as averse as you might expect. In fact, she talked Papa into teaching her to throw knives and tomahawks long before they married. So it was natural that Papa taught me and my three younger brothers all his woodsy skills." They were happy times, wild and free, and she'd built special memories with her family through them, particularly Papa and her brothers.

Petra shook her head. "But when I grew older, Mama tried to cultivate more delicate pursuits in me. After being allowed to romp through the woods, it was stifling to stand in one place near the lake and paint a pastoral scene." She chuckled. "I would rather track the rabbit hopping through the meadow or climb the tree with the bird's nest I painted. And needlepoint? That was excruciating."

"That had to have been a difficult transition for you."

"I tried to be who Mama expected me to be, to act like the other girls my age. Capture the attentions of the young men. A few came calling. Some were even impressed that I enjoyed outdoorsy pursuits. But then I'd prove more knowledgeable or skilled than them, and they didn't return.

When my friends were pairing off with suitors and becoming engaged, I was still alone. So when my great uncle Peter and aunt Letitia scheduled a trip to see the West, they invited me along, and Mama and Papa thought it an excellent idea."

Sadness wound through her, and she itched to pull Papa's book from her saddlebags. "Come to find out, Uncle Peter was dying. This was where he passed, and I couldn't bring myself to leave."

"Oh, I'm so sorry." Josephine laid a warm hand over hers.

She smiled. "I knew I could support myself with the skills Papa taught me, but people wouldn't look twice at a young woman with perfectly coifed hair wearing the latest fashions, much less hire her. I attempted to enter the wood-chopping competition for the Founders' Day Celebration, an event in which I knew I could hold my own. But they wouldn't let a woman participate in that event."

"So how did you register?"

Petra chuckled. "There was a woman in town, Lucinda Braddock, who was scribbling in a book, a very familiar sight to me. Both my parents are journalists and are often jotting notes on articles, so this woman intrigued me. Turns out, she's a dime novelist. When I described my predicament, she gave me a buckskin outfit and all but dared me to enter under an assumed name. I cut off my hair, donned a hat, rubbed dirt on my face, and entered as Buckskin Pete Hollingsworth. And I won." She grinned. "Most everyone took the joke in stride after I revealed I was a woman. So *Pete* stuck around, started getting attention, helped largely by becoming the subject of Lu Braddock's dime novels. And soon enough I was working as a guide, a tracker, whatever jobs I could get."

Josephine laughed, a light, airy sound that could brighten any darkness. "That's incredible. I don't know how you cut your hair, much less the rest of it."

"I was nervous as a cat the first time I stepped out in trousers, and yes, cutting my hair was terrifying." She touched her short hair. "Though I've grown rather fond of the simplicity."

A thrill raced through her at the memory of Reverend Owens's fingers running through her shorn locks.

Oh blast, Petra. Stop. Since when had she grown *this* shameless?

"You're fortunate to have the family you do. They sound wonderful. I hope you've greatly exaggerated the importance they'll place on the cameo."

"Right now, that seems such a distant concern. I'm far more worried about Addie. She's working for a man who preys on women."

Josephine's dark eyes clouded. "Oh yes. I'm very familiar with his type."

Petra shivered at the woman's knowing tone. "May I ask *you* a prying question?"

"That would only be fair."

"Reverend Owens told me about his. . .upbringing."

Josephine stared a moment then chuckled. "In the saloons and brothels?"

Laugher—at such a delicate topic? "Does your response mean it's not true?" Why would *anyone* invent such an awful tale, particularly a man of God?

"Oh, it's quite true." Josephine's features were far more placid and guileless than what Petra would have expected. "Meribel Owens is our mother. She's known as Fair Meri in those places. Last we saw her was about nine years ago in Denver."

"I am so sorry."

"No need to apologize. Both Dusty and I have spent a lot of time praying about our history, and God continues to heal us." She reached for the teacup in front of her, despite it being empty. "Did it frighten you when my brother told you of our roots?"

"Frighten me?" She shook her head. "No. It broke my heart." Her lower lids stung with the memory. "But as I told him, I don't think a person's roots matter as much as their heart. And Reverend Owens has a very kind heart."

This time Josephine's eyes pooled with unshed tears. "I'm glad you can see that." She peeked toward the window, then leaned in. "Don't you dare tell Dusty I shared this, but there was a woman four or five years ago. She and Dusty got close, and I think he hoped to marry her. However, once he told her about our past, she would no longer speak to him. While he's never said so, I suspect he decided that he'd never marry. So I've been praying that God would send a woman who could see the real him. The fact that he's *already* told you our sordid story tells me he's feeling something strong enough to want to scare you off."

Her heart stalled. Reverend Owens might have feelings for *her*? How could that be? They'd known each other for one day. Of course she—a foolish girl, alone and homesick—would quickly grow attached to such a handsome and kind gentleman, but him?

More likely, he was trying to push her away because she was Buckskin Pete. Awkward, unusual, *unfeminine*. But. . .

Lord, I know I haven't really had much to say to You since Uncle Peter died. She swallowed. *But I'm more than a little confused, and—*

At the sound of a key in the lock, she lurched from her seat and hurried toward the door.

Reverend Owens stepped inside. Alone.

"Where's Addie?"

Dark eyes met hers. "Roy's moved her."

No. Lord, please don't let him harm Addie.

Josephine came to her side. "What does that mean, Dusty?"

He hung his hat on a coatrack beside the door. "Roy wouldn't tell me anything. Wouldn't let me pay off Addie's debt. I couldn't buy back the cameo. As I was preparing to leave, one of the young girls who works there—Edna—stopped me in the alley."

"Edna. She's the one who tried to warn me."

"She said that Roy's nephew, Quinton Bice, took Addie to some cabin in the woods on Roy's direction. Edna didn't know where it was, so we'll have to gather a posse and track them down."

"Bice?" Her belly knotted.

"You know him?"

"I had a run-in with someone by that name at the Wells Fargo office yesterday." She recapped the conflict, from Bice calling her out on the street to his rough handling and insults inside the office.

"He got fired when he manhandled you that way?"

"Yeah, the other gent dismissed him on the spot."

Reverend Owens nodded thoughtfully. "Edna says he's Roy's nephew, and he was madder than a cornered rattler about getting fired because of you."

Josephine looped her arm through Petra's. "Sounds to me like it was his own actions that got him fired."

"Yeah. Any rational person would see it that way. But the bigger issue is that Edna overheard those two plotting ways to get revenge on Miss Hollingsworth for his firing. Oh, and I asked her if Roy drugged you. She said she didn't see him do it, but that Roy keeps ether in the saloon. When I found you last night, there was an instant I thought I smelled ether, but I couldn't say for sure."

Her thoughts swirled. He really *had* drugged her. Not that she'd had any doubts, but this was as close to proof as they'd come.

The reverend shrugged. "I figured I'd ride to the sheriff's office and talk to the night deputy, if this town has one."

Petra shook her head. "They don't. But my friend Lucinda Braddock is married to a US Marshal. Lu and Rion live outside of town, but Rion's sister and brother-in-law—a pair of Pinkertons—live just one street over."

A grin sprouted on the reverend's lips. "You've got some powerful friends. But we may still need to talk to the sheriff come morning about finding someone to track Bice and Addie."

"I know who the sheriff hires for tracking."

"You do?" His eyes lit.

"Yeah. Her name is Buckskin Pete Hollingsworth."

By dawn Dustin had slept only about two hours. Based on the whispering and giggles from Jo's room, she and Miss Hollingsworth hadn't slept much either. However, their nighttime chattering had sounded much more pleasant. His sleepless hours were spent churning through the day's happenings—the multiple confrontations with Clarence Roy to visiting with the Pinkerton couple, the Trenamens, and his canceling the first church service in Cambria Springs to search for Addie Milroy. And, of course, the very tantalizing kiss he'd shared with Miss Hollingsworth. He'd alternately pondered the untamed beauty named Buckskin Pete and the softer, sweeter Petra Breaux. Both were beguiling.

And that fact terrified him.

Lord, she couldn't have meant what she said last night.

Only. . .what if she did? In the day and a half he'd known her, Miss Hollingsworth—Petra—had offered Mickey Milroy firm compassion after he'd stolen apples, then bailed him out of his trouble. She'd tried to win enough money to pay a widow's debt, the same widow whom she'd dealt with so lovingly yesterday afternoon. On the ride to town last evening, she'd shared insight into how she'd met Tibby. After a few chance exchanges in town, the man had shown up at her home looking for work. She'd taken the old gent to her neighbor, and by her account, Tibby and the widow Milroy had done each other good. Miss Hollingsworth had a good sense of people.

But of *him?*

Shoving such ponderings aside, he rose and dressed, then stepped into the outer room. Already Miss Hollingsworth and Jo were in the kitchen, and the strong scent of coffee met him. He rounded the corner and poked his head into the room as they laughed. The women turned his way, pleasant greetings on their lips.

"I'm going to the livery to saddle our horses." He pinned his sister with a glance. "Jo, I think you need to come along, in case Bice has harmed Addie in some way."

His sister sobered. "If you think that's best."

"I do."

Miss Hollingsworth eyed them both. "I'll go with you, Reverend."

They reached the end of the street before she spoke.

"I know you'll think me forward for asking, but did something happen to Josephine?"

She'd seemed to take the other news in stride. It would speak a great deal about her if she could handle the next bits of truth. *Lord, please, let her see my heart in this too.*

"When she was twelve, she was. . .attacked."

Her footsteps faltered, but she recovered. "How?"

At the delicate question, Dustin stopped. "A man I thought was my friend offered her a ride in his new buggy. I didn't know about it, or I would've said no." He swallowed hard. "As soon as I realized she was gone, I saddled a horse and went searching, found 'em at his cabin outside of town. I don't know what he used, but he'd drugged her with something. She was hallucinating. Screaming like the hounds of hell were after her." His muscles tensed with the vivid memories. "He had her on the bed and was preparing to. . ."

Miss Hollingsworth clamped her eyes shut. "You stopped him, didn't you?"

"I did." He sucked a breath, his hands shaking. "I fought him off her, knocked him out, but while I was attempting to get Jo's clothes on her so I could get her to a doctor, he woke and pulled a gun on me."

Her green eyes locked on his. "What happened?"

Please, Lord, don't let this scare her away.

"We struggled. He shot me once before I killed him."

Miss Hollingsworth stared, dumbstruck. For far too long.

What was she thinking? He was. . .a murderer. A cold-blooded killer. Nobody she could associate with.

"If you want my help, I'll ride with you. But I'll understand if you don't." He turned.

She caught his hand, tugging hard. "Dustin, look at me."

When he didn't turn, she stepped in front of him, her expression full of compassion and acceptance. "I am so sorry." She slipped into his arms, her own circling his waist. "No one should have to go through the things you and Jo have endured. How have you managed to keep your faith through such circumstances?"

He laughed. "What faith? Jo and I had none until that point. I don't know how, but despite being lung-shot, I got Jo out of there and made it to town before I passed out. When I woke up, we were in the home of a minister, and as we both healed, he shared God with us."

She held him tighter, resting her head against his chest, and the tension leeched out of him.

"It was getting harder to protect Jo in that environment. I knew if we didn't walk away soon, she'd suffer the same fate as our mother. So when the preacher offered us a way out, we said yes—both to leaving that life and, more important, to God. Once I was healthy enough, he sent us to a friend of his in Wyoming Territory. We never looked back."

Then God called him here, just a short distance from where that journey started. Once again, he was dealing with men who had no qualms about taking whatever they wanted from women.

She pulled away, concern etching her features. "Do you think it's wise to drag Jo into this? What if Bice *has* done something to Addie? Will that make her relive all those memories?"

"I prayed about that all night. It may. But you and I have made an enemy out of Roy, and I won't leave her anywhere that he might get to her."

<h1 style="text-align:center;">Chapter 9</h1>

*R*ifle in hand, Pete eased down the alley beside the Gold Spur, Reverend Owens and Josephine on her heels.

"Edna said Bice's horse was waiting there." He motioned to the spot where she'd nearly thrown her knife at Roy the morning before. "And he headed that direction. Straight out of town."

She nodded, whispering as well. "I'll find his trail from here. You two gather the horses and meet me on the edge of town."

Reverend Owens shook his head. "I'm not leaving you alone."

Pete stood tall. "For the length of this alley, you are." She needed to study Bice's horse tracks. Hopefully they'd be clearer in the dust of the alley than outside of town among the grass, rocks, and wildlife.

He opened his mouth to protest but stalked off the way they'd come, Josephine in tow.

Once alone, Pete crouched at the corner of the building, staring at the hoofprints, fixing them in her mind. She kept an eye open for movement, but thankfully nothing and no one moved in the alley. Finally, she heard hoofbeats from the street, hopefully signaling Reverend Owens and Josephine were retreating out of town.

The story the preacher told of how he and Josephine had started over with God had stirred something. She'd longed for a few moments alone to make her own peace with the Creator.

She glanced heavenward. *Lord, I hope You can forgive me. I've been stubborn and angry that You didn't let Uncle Peter live. I'm sorry, Lord. I realized today, listening to Dustin, that I've taken You for granted for far too long. Help me find my way back to You. And if it's not too much trouble, help me get the cameo back. Most important, please help me find Addie—unharmed.*

A weight lifted as she stood. There was so much more she needed to get straight with the Lord, but it was a start, and already she felt the effect. *Once Addie's safe, Lord. I promise.*

Pete started down the alley, careful not to obliterate Bice's tracks before she had a chance to study the stride length, hoof shapes, and distinguishing marks. All would be important in finding Bice and Addie.

"The fact that he's already *told you our sordid story tells me he's feeling something strong enough to want to scare you off."*

Petra shook her head. This was not the time to ponder the validity of Josephine's words.

She forced her attention to the tracks, pausing a moment to make sure she hadn't missed something.

The reverend *had* been rather sharp-tongued when he'd shared about his birth and upbringing. Defensive. And clearly befuddled when she'd not been horrified. Frankly, she was befuddled by her own response. How had she managed to answer so quickly with such grace? But how was it right to hold the man's parentage against him? He had no choice in the matter of who bore him.

"Petra Jayne Breaux, pay attention. A girl's life is at stake, and you're maundering on about unimportant matters."

They *were* important—just not at this instant.

By the time she reached the edge of town, the reverend and his sister were waiting. She took Falco's reins but crouched over the grass, rifle balanced on her knees. Silent minutes ticked by as she shifted positions, searching for the next track. Finally, she found it and eased down the path Bice had taken, each print becoming easier to find as the morning sun mounted higher.

When he'd shared about Jo's attack and his killing the man who'd done it, Reverend Owens had been far more sedate. Penitent, even. Like he'd expected her to reject him immediately for his protecting sweet Josephine. Nor had he tried to keep her from slipping into his arms as he'd done last night. What had changed?

But again. Such thoughts had no place in her current business and would only distract her from her purpose.

As the night's chill burned off and gave way to the heat of midday, she stripped off the coat she'd worn and rolled her sleeves. When she turned to tie the garment behind Falco's saddle, Dustin eyed her with—was it amusement?

A different type of heat crept through her, and she dipped her chin. "What are you smiling at?"

"You." His expression deepened to admiration. "You enjoy this, don't you?"

Bashfulness stole over her. "Very much."

"You're obviously very good at it. Where did a young lady from—where is your home? Pennsylvania?—learn such skills?"

"That's a story better left for another time. Let me concentrate." Petra turned to lash down the jacket, but Josephine also grinned, hers a far more knowing expression.

"What?" She met her new friend's gaze with exasperation.

Jo's melodic giggle filled the air, and she rode around Falco toward her brother. As she drew alongside Petra, she whispered. "He's well on his way to being smitten." Then, facing her brother, "Come along, Dusty. I'll tell you the tale of how beautiful Petra became the very capable Buckskin Pete."

Dusk had just fallen when Miss Hollingsworth gave a silent signal to halt. Dustin drew his roan to a stop, Josephine beside him. Once Bice's trail began to follow a known path, the pretty tracker had ridden her horse, rather than walking as she'd done earlier. But after hours on the trail, it was time to stop.

At least *he* thought it was.

"Are you ready to make camp for the night?" he called softly.

Again, she signaled, but this time only to look back and put a finger to her lips.

Beside him, Jo chuckled.

He bit back his short-tempered reply. "Stay with the horses, please."

Dustin stalked after Miss Hollingsworth, but before he could reach her, she eased around a long line of tall brush, out of sight.

He halted, tension gripping his shoulders. *Lord, what is she doing? As much as Addie needs us, we're all tired enough we should stop to rest. She can't track anything in the dark anyway.*

A moment later, she strode back with renewed purpose. "There's a cabin ahead, a horse in the corral, and lamplight showing from the windows. I suspect it's Bice."

Jo approached with their horses. "You found her?"

His irksome attitude dissolved. "Do you have a plan?" As confident as she'd been throughout the day, he half expected she'd already have a fully formed strategy. She *was* good at what she did. Impressively so.

"We should leave the horses here and go in on foot. Otherwise Bice's mount might nicker and warn of our approach. But we'll have to get up by one of the windows and see from there how we can get her out."

"All right."

Dustin led his horse to a nearby sapling, Jo following close behind. As they tied their mounts, he eyed his rifle waiting in the scabbard. *Lord, just this once?*

After all, he must protect *three* women.

But he'd promised God. He'd not raise a gun against a man again.

Crouched low, they sneaked toward the cabin, and at the nearest window, Miss Hollingsworth peeked in the corner of the windowpane, then ducked back. After an instant, she looked again, this time a bit longer.

She gave an exaggerated nod. "Addie and Bice." She barely breathed the words. "At a table just past the doorway."

Petra motioned him to take a look, and he leaned to peer over the windowsill. Addie sat at a table, shoulders slumped, hands folded, a plate of food in front of her. Untouched. She scowled as the man across from her took a spoonful from her plate and ate it. He appeared to say something around the bite of beans, though the girl folded her arms and looked away.

Dustin ducked out of sight. The girl had obviously listened when Miss Hollingsworth warned her not to eat or drink anything. "What's our plan?"

Again, she peeked through the window, then eased back. "Front and back doors are barred."

"So how can we draw him out?" Josephine asked.

Miss Hollingsworth shrugged. "Plug the chimney? Smoke 'em out?"

Jo craned to see the far end of the house where the chimney stood. "It's pretty tall. How do you think you'd get up there?"

"I'm a good tree climber." Miss Hollingsworth grinned. "I could make it."

He caught her sleeve. "Without being heard?"

She paused and eased into her former position.

Voices rose from inside, stalling their discussion. Both he and Miss Hollingsworth risked another glance.

Bice guided Addie toward the foot of the bed. She sat stiffly, and Dustin's heart seized.

Lord Jesus, no. I can't let him—

As the man tied her wrists to the metal footboard, Dustin reached for Miss Hollingsworth's rifle. This was all too familiar.

Bice stood again, adjusted the gun belt around his hips, then returned to the table where he stacked their supper plates. What on earth? The man slipped them into the cast-iron skillet on the stove and turned toward the back door. He was doing dishes?

Thank You, Lord!

"He's coming out. You two get Addie and meet me at the horses."

Arms full of dishes, Bice stepped out and headed toward the incline away from the cabin. Dustin charged. Before he reached the fella, Bice turned and dropped the stack of dishes. Dustin drove his shoulder hard into the man's midsection, and they both tumbled head over heels. When they settled, Dustin landed two solid punches to Bice's cheek before Bice kicked Dustin off.

The fella rocked to his feet, standing for a split second before he took a staggering step toward the cabin. Dustin also lunged up, tackling Bice again. They hit the ground, Bice grunting, but this time Bice was ready. He landed a sharp elbow to Dustin's temple, knocking him sideways. Then a knee to his belly. Pain lanced through him.

Dustin drove the heel of his palm into Bice's chin as Bice got him in a choke hold. His eyes bulging, Dustin fought to free himself, though the darkness around him grew inky black.

Lord, help!

He struck out, connected. And for a split second, Bice's grip faltered. Dustin raked half a breath before the other man reasserted his hold. His senses faded. His thoughts turned to sludge. Dustin grabbed Bice's wrist with both hands, fighting with everything he could muster.

God, help me!

Suddenly, a sickening *smack* sounded, and Bice screamed, his grip loosening.

Dustin sucked in a loud breath and coughed. Shoving free of Bice's slumped form, he dragged himself away a couple feet. But as he sank face-first into the grass, coughing too hard to catch his breath, someone grabbed him and pulled.

"Let's go, Reverend."

Petra's voice jogged his senses loose. Dragging in another great breath, he pushed himself to his knees. Her hands settled at his hips, and somehow, he got his feet under him.

"Bice—?"

"Go!" She shoved him toward the open cabin door.

Dustin stumbled into the cabin, slowing for an instant. Neither Jo nor Addie were inside, and Petra urged him toward the open front door with a sharp jab to his back.

"Run!"

Feet clumsy, he lunged through the door as a gunshot rang out. For an instant, the constant pressure of her hand faltered but returned. His senses clearing, he drew her in front of him.

They raced toward their horses, his hand settling at the small of her back as he guided her the last thirty paces. Jo and Addie were already mounted, Addie on Falco. At their side, Dustin cupped his hands to help Miss Hollingsworth up behind the girl, but she crumpled into him, her rifle and tomahawk thudding to the ground.

Limp as a rag doll, she folded into the ground, a growing red splotch spreading across her shirt.

❧ Chapter 10 ❧

ust a little longer. You hear me?" Dustin urged, holding Petra all the tighter. She gave no indication the words penetrated her mind.

Could she hear him? She'd been unconscious from moments after she'd pitched into his arms. Throughout the wild nighttime ride along unfamiliar mountain paths, he'd had to fight to keep her on horseback.

By the time Addie recognized the turn to take them to her house—which was nearer than town by several miles, she said—it had been hours, and Petra had been oozing blood for most of it, despite Dustin having plugged the hole with a cloth.

Lord, You've got to keep her alive. Please. His heart aching, Dustin hauled in a breath. *Please, God.*

"Home's straight down this path another half mile," Addie called. "I'll go ahead to roust everybody outta bed." The girl charged down the path, her hoofbeats growing dim as Falco ate up the distance.

Dustin dipped his mouth near Petra's ear. "You hear that? We're almost there. Don't you give up on me."

Still no response. She'd not made a sound in hours.

Jo came alongside. "How is she?"

He shook his head. Not good. *Lord God, You have to do something. Please.*

"Have you told her how you feel about her?"

He raked his gaze from the path to her. "Now's *not* the time to play matchmaker, Jo."

"I know you, Dusty. I can see it written all over you. You can't deny she's special to you." She turned a fierce glare on him. "Tell her how you feel. Give her something to fight for."

With that, she spurred her horse and rode ahead into the silvery moonlight.

He stared after her, thoughts churning. What did he feel for Miss Hollingsworth? Not love. Not yet. Was it?

He dipped his mouth near her ear again. "Miss Hollingsworth. Pete. You listen." His voice shook. "I've never met a woman like you. You're beautiful and smart and skilled. You're compassionate, and you believe in the good in people. No woman like you has ever looked twice at me once they've learned who and what I am. The fact you haven't run scares me to death, but it intrigues me too. I need you to fight. Get well, because I want time to see where that might lead."

She finally moaned, though she'd been so silent for so long, surely it was just a response to the pain she must be feeling. Wasn't it?

Lord, bring her through this, please.

Ahead, the outline of the Milroy family's barn came into view, and he spurred his horse. As he rounded it, he found bright lamplight spilling into the dark yard, both from the house and the lantern Tibby held. Gathered around the white-haired man stood several of the young children, wrapped in quilts and blankets, Bess and Mickey holding the bleary-eyed twins.

"Give her to me," Tibby called as he ran alongside Dustin's roan.

Dustin halted just outside the door, and Tibby handed off the lantern to young Ernie, then reached for Miss Hollingsworth. Once Dustin had passed her down, Tibby disappeared into the house.

Muscles screaming, he eased out of the saddle and stood, gripping the saddle horn for a moment. By the time he turned toward the doorway, Tibby was there, pulling the door closed.

"I need to be in there. To help."

"No, son." The old man pushed him farther into the yard.

"But—" His heart nearly pounded out of his chest. "What am I supposed to do?"

"Wait."

He stared, unable to form a word.

Tibby laid a hand on Dustin's shoulder. "You've done all you can. Let the women handle it. Right now you'll help most by taking care of the horses. Once I get the young'uns settled in the barn, I'll return to help you."

The horses. He nodded. "Yes, sir."

"And pray for our lovely Petra."

A rhythmic rolling sound punctuated by intermittent wooden squeaks entered Petra's consciousness. A rocking chair? She attempted to open her eyes and see, but her body wouldn't cooperate.

After a few minutes, someone spoke. A single unintelligible word, followed by the faltering of the rocker. Who was there? When, a moment later, something cool and damp pressed against her forehead, she startled fully awake. As she inhaled deeply, pain clattered through her.

"Easy now." Tibby, his hand still resting on her forehead, stared down at her. "It'll pass in a moment."

She lay very still, scarcely breathing, until the pain abated, then finally lolled her head toward him again.

"There now." He grinned. "Thank the good Lord above."

Just beyond Tibby, the rocking stopped as Mrs. Milroy leaned forward to peek at her, offering a lopsided smile. "Pete."

Tibby tilted a tin cup to Petra's lips and helped her drink a few sips of cool water before he sat back. "Do you know where you are, child?"

Petra looked at her surroundings and gave a tiny nod. "Addie?"

Mrs. Milroy leaned forward, and the woman's eyes misted. "Good."

Tibby drew Mrs. Milroy's hand from her lap, a sweet smile passing between them as they twined their fingers. "Agnes and I thank you for bringing her home. We're only sorry you were injured in the process."

"Injured." She searched for details among her hazy memories.

"You don't remember?"

She blinked heavily. "Not much."

The stately old gentleman nodded. "We'll make room for someone who can fill in those gaps for you." He assisted Mrs. Milroy across the room, then returned to move her rocking chair. The long dining table came into view, and there at the end, Dustin Owens slept, head on his folded arms.

Despite the growth of beard, the reverend's features were a mix of boyish innocence and exhaustion. Oh, he was a comforting sight, one she could get used to seeing.

Tibby woke Dustin with a gentle shake, and at Tibby's whispered words, the preacher nearly overturned his chair in his haste to get to her.

"You're awake," he whispered as he took her hand.

"You are too." Petra grinned.

His grip tightened. "You took a bullet just beneath your shoulder blade. You'll be laid up for a while. Between the bullet and the surgery to remove it, and the blood you lost, you've got quite a bit of healing to do."

Resting shouldn't be an issue. Her limbs were heavy, and sleep tugged at her mind.

"Do you remember anything from that night?"

"Some." She and Josephine had cut Addie's bonds and started to run for the horses. "You and Bice were struggling."

Dustin nodded. "He had me by the throat, and I was going out. And then you were there. I don't know what you did to him, but it was enough."

A hazy recollection of striking him with the tomahawk surfaced, though she was too week to interrupt.

"You got him off me, and we ran, but he shot you." His brow furrowed, and he shook his head. "We reached the horses before you fell into my arms. I was scared out of my wits. Thought you were going to die."

She shook her head faintly. "Wasn't gonna die."

This time he failed to stifle his laughter. "No? And why not?"

"You kept whispering to me to fight." And she'd clung to every word. "Said you wanted time to explore—"

He laughed, cheeks growing red beneath the scraggly beard. "You heard that, did you?"

"Uh-huh." She squeezed his fingers. "Did you mean it?"

He leaned down and kissed her fingers gently. "Every word. I'm gonna be around a whole lot while you heal so we can get to know each other proper."

✤ Chapter 11 ✤

One month later

Petra grinned as Tibby and the Milroy children sang the last few bars of "Nelly Bly," the wagon rocking with their music. As the song ended, laughter erupted, and the children—all seated in the back of the wagon—clapped.

"Good." Mrs. Milroy gripped Petra's arm, nodding happily.

"More, Tibby!" little Lily called, and her twin, Rose, giggled in agreement.

"Do 'Camptown Races.'"

At Ernie's suggestion, Tibby started singing again, the children joining in quickly. They got especially raucous on the "do-dahs."

Petra was glad for the diversion. She'd worn a dress for church, but donning a corset and petticoats had her feeling uncomfortable, since the corset's boning pressed against her still-tender wound. She had *not* missed the constricting underpinnings, though truth be known, she was anxious to see Dustin's reaction to her proper feminine attire.

Frankly, she was anxious to see Dustin, period. As promised, he'd spent some of every day at the Milroys' house as she'd recuperated. Once she'd grown strong enough, they'd sat outside several hours a day while she'd attempted to whittle—a hobby made difficult at first by her wound. Or he'd taken her on brief walks around the house, just for a change of pace. The reverend had been attentive and sweet, and he'd taken to the Milroy clan and Tibby just as she had. Tibby had seemed to slip into a fatherly role with both Dustin and Jo, and they'd accepted him with open arms.

Still singing, Tibby turned the wagon from the mountain path and headed into town, though he chose the street where the Gold Spur was situated.

"Tibby," she called softly.

He turned, eyebrows arching in a question, though he didn't stop the song.

"Wouldn't it be more appropriate to go another way?" She'd had her fill of saloons and their owners. Addie Milroy had her unfortunate introduction to that world as well. If Petra could, she'd avoid this area of town to keep any more of the Milroy brood from exploring such places.

Tibby didn't respond.

As they neared the Gold Spur, her eyes strayed to the building. But where the large, false-fronted structure had once stood, all she saw were two partial walls and a pile of charred remains. The saloons on either side were also burned—all three destroyed.

Petra gaped. "What happened?"

The strains of "Camptown Races" faded midsentence.

Tibby drew the wagon to a stop. "We've been waiting for the right time to tell you, child. After what happened to you and Addie, Sheriff Downing gathered a posse, including Marshal Braddock and the Trenamens, and went searching for Bice. They tracked him to the Gold Spur, and of course, Clarence Roy tried to protect him. A fight ensued, someone threw a whiskey bottle, which hit a lantern on the wall, and a fire was started." He hesitated. "Roy and Bice both perished."

Her belly dropped. "Was anybody else injured?"

Mrs. Milroy grasped her hand in support.

"No." Tibby started the team again. "Thankfully, everyone else got out safely."

"Thank God," she whispered from behind her hand.

How was she to feel about such news? It was terrible that two men were dead, and she never would have wished such a fate on them. But they were men who'd preyed on her, on Addie, and the Lord only knew how many others. Was this God's justice, His vindication for Clarence Roy drugging her and stealing the—

"Oh!" Petra pulled free of Mrs. Milroy's grasp and looked at the burned shell.

Tibby stopped the wagon again. "What's the matter?"

Lord, please be merciful. "Do you happen to know if there was anything unusual found in Clarence Roy's pockets upon his death?"

"Unusual, child? Like what?"

Her throat constricted. "A piece of women's jewelry. A beautiful blue cameo in a gold setting, with pearls around the edge."

The man stared, seemingly dumbfounded.

"It was a family heirloom, and he stole it from me."

After another instant, Tibby shook his head. "Very little survived that fire, child."

Tears welled as she faced front. *Oh God. I really lost it, didn't I? It's truly gone.*

Tibby flicked the reins, and they rolled toward the pine grove at the edge of town.

He was right, of course. The building was gone, but for two partial walls. Nothing would have survived.

Lord, can You forgive me? Perhaps He could, but Mama? Aunt Letitia? And all her cousins after her? She'd lost Queen Victoria's cameo to a lying thief, and the fire that took Clarence Roy's life was also God's judgment for her wrong actions.

They arrived, the area already full of families gathering for hymns and a sermon. The preacher looked up from the couple he greeted, caught sight of them, and excused himself.

He trotted their way, reaching them as Tibby set the wagon brake.

"Morning." His face lit up as he focused on her, though his expression clouded as she stood, fighting emotion. He lifted her down. "What's wrong? Aren't you well?"

Petra hung her head. "You once told me you thought God had a plan to return the cameo to me."

"Oh." Dustin looked up at Tibby and Mrs. Milroy. "You told her about the fire."

Tibby nodded. "Drove past there on our way here. I didn't realize she'd lost. . .something so important."

"I don't know how to tell Mama and Papa, but once I do, they'll never speak to me again." Even if they did, the rest of the family wouldn't.

He pulled her close, her arms circling his waist under his suit coat. It was all she could do not to sob.

"You've told me and Jo about your close-knit family. Do you honestly believe they'd value a cameo brooch over their beloved daughter?"

"I don't know. That cameo is treasured in our family."

"I think the true answer is that their daughter would be far more important than all the jewels in the queen's treasury. Leastways, if I had a daughter, that's how I'd feel." He gave her a discreet peck on the top of her head. "If you're willing, let's talk more later, but it's nearly time for the service. I've a big announcement today, and I'd appreciate it if you'd pray it goes well."

She dried her tears and smiled. "I will."

"I'll send Jo over to sit with you. You've had a lot of people worried about you. There are several here who've been asking about you, hoping to see you. The Braddocks, the Trenamens, a young cowhand named Bull Simpson, and others."

Petra pulled herself together, and once Mrs. Milroy and the children were out of the wagon, they spread blankets on the ground among the other families and seated themselves. Tibby took up a station between her and Mrs. Milroy, Josephine on her other side. At points where Petra fought to rein in her emotions and focus on Dustin's sermon, Tibby squeezed her hand or Jo rubbed her arm in support. Those touches gave her strength to keep herself in check.

"And in closing," Dustin said, "I've purchased land for a new church building, but there's much work to be done before we'll be ready for services there. With cooler weather coming in a couple months, I'm asking every man for help."

Beside her, Josephine bowed and clasped her hands.

Petra leaned closer to Jo. "What're you doing?"

"Praying," she whispered, then nodded toward her brother.

"Where's the church gonna be, Preacher?" someone called.

Reverend Owens drew a deep breath. "I bought the three buildings that burned."

Petra's eyes widened, then she too bowed her head. *Lord, what in heaven's name is he thinking?*

"You expect us to build a church over the top of three saloons?" one man bellowed.

"Are you daft?" another shouted.

One particularly belligerent man stood. "That's unholy ground, Reverend! And you're a fool if you think such a place is suitable for a church."

"Please." Dustin lifted his hands for silence. "Can we all settle down for a moment so I might explain why—"

"I'm supposin' you used our hard-earned offerings to buy that place?"

It took several moments and the help of several more level-headed men calling for quiet to settle the crowd.

"I knew this would create a stir, but I'd ask you to hear me out," Dustin said. "Particularly about that land being unholy ground. The Bible says that the earth is the Lord's, and the fulness thereof. Doesn't it?"

A murmur rippled through the crowd.

"Just because a piece of ground has been used for unholy purposes— housing a saloon—doesn't mean it's forever tainted and unusable for God's purposes. No. *The earth is the Lord's*, and the fulness thereof."

The tension in the air eased as he continued to speak.

"Recently I was recalling the story of Belshazzar from the book of Daniel." He glanced her way, a tiny smile curving his lips as he recounted the tale of Israel's capture, Belshazzar's wrongful use of the temple serving pieces, and God's goodness in returning the people and the serving pieces back to Jerusalem. "That land may have been used for unholy purposes, but the earth is the Lord's, and the fulness thereof. I think it's only fitting we reclaim that property for God. Is anyone else in agreement?"

Petra's heart grew full, and she stood. "I am."

"That went better than I was expecting."

At his sister's whispered comment, Dustin grinned. "Could've been far worse, Sis. All but two families seemed to understand what I was saying, and one of those has promised to pray about whether they can attend a church built on that plot of land."

She held open the bag they used to carry his Bible, sermon notes, and the offering plate, and he placed the items inside.

Dustin glanced at the Milroy children playing nearby as Tibby, Mrs. Milroy, and Petra talked with a few other families. "Are we okay if I ask our friends to Sunday dinner?"

"Of course. It may not be a fancy meal, but I'll make do."

"Reverend?" A timid voice drew his attention, and he turned to find Edna.

"Morning." He grinned. "How are you, Edna?"

"All right, I guess." She shrugged but didn't meet his eyes. "Can I ask you a question?"

Josephine excused herself, saying she'd speak to the other family and meet him at home.

"Sure. What's on your mind?"

"You told that story there at the end, about the fella using God's dishes for a drunken party?"

"Belshazzar."

She nodded. "If God could take those dishes and make 'em good and clean again, and He can do the same thing with the land the saloon was on. . ." She looked at him for an instant, then dropped her gaze again. "Can He do that with people too? 'Cause I don't want to go back to the life I was living."

Oh, praise God. He'd prayed for such a moment with Edna and the other women displaced after the fires. "Yes. He sent us a Savior, Jesus Christ, *especially* so He could do that for people." He pulled the Bible from its bag and deftly flipped the pages. Though as Edna withdrew a little, he stopped.

She shook her head. "I don't read, Preacher. Never learned."

Dustin snapped the book closed. He should've thought. . . "That's all right. I didn't learn myself until about nine years ago."

Edna looked at him then. "Really?"

"Really. Jo and I didn't have the best start in life. We came out of the same world you've been living in."

"You, Preacher?"

For the next several minutes, they talked, and after praying with her, Dustin offered another reassuring smile. "I know it won't be easy, but if you want a fresh start, I've got friends in Wyoming Territory who'd gladly welcome you in. They helped me and Jo find our way when we left the saloons."

"I might like that. Thank you, Reverend." She scurried over to the Trenamens, who'd opened their home to her after the fire.

When he turned to where the Milroy family had been waiting, their wagon was gone, and only Petra remained. Dustin headed her way, drinking in the fetching sight of her in a dress. He grinned. "You look absolutely stunning."

Pink crept into her cheeks, and she dipped her chin in that bashful way she did sometimes. "Thank you. Josephine's taken the Milroy family to your house already. I told her I'd wait for you."

As they headed home, he shared Edna's desire to start afresh.

"I'll pray for her," Petra said. "Oh, Tibby and Mrs. Milroy said they want to talk to us about something this afternoon."

"All right." He glanced her way. "Any idea what?"

"I'm not sure, but it had a bit of an ominous feel to it."

They turned into his yard, and he escorted her through the door. Inside, Tibby and Mrs. Milroy were seated on the settee, and Jo on one of the other two chairs. The older children had pulled chairs in from the dining room, and the younger ones sat on the floor in groups.

After a moment of pleasantries, Jo stood, offered her chair to Petra, and pinned Dustin with a glance. "Tibby and Mrs. Milroy said they don't want to impose on us for a meal, but they have a bit of news to share."

"Is everything all right?"

Tibby nodded slowly. "Reckon it will be, but it's hard to break the news." He paused, looking at Jo, Petra, and finally him. "I got kin back east. Hadn't written 'em in a long while, but since comin' to work for Mrs. Milroy—Agnes—I been in touch with 'em again. Told 'em about Agnes's condition, and they've spoken to a doctor they know. From what they're sayin', there's treatments that can help with Agnes's speech and movement. They've offered that if she wants to make the journey, they'll pay for passage for all of us."

Dustin's brows arched in surprise. "That's an unexpected surprise."

"They think that you can improve with this treatment?" Petra asked Mrs. Milroy, and the woman nodded.

"She won't ever be like before the apoplexy." Tibby grasped her hand. "But she could improve some—get to where she can speak more words and maybe get some movement back in her hand."

"And you're telling us because you're going to go." Dustin looked at them both in turn.

Mrs. Milroy nodded.

Tibby nodded. "Agnes has indicated she'd like to. We were hoping to leave in a few weeks, but that also depends on Pete and what she needs."

Petra's eyes brimmed with tears, but she smiled bravely. "I'm recovered enough I can move into my own cabin and take care of myself again." She focused directly on Mrs. Milroy. "I want you to go and get better."

"Yes, ma'am," Dustin whispered. "You go and get yourself well. And don't you worry about Miss Hollingsworth. Jo and I will look after her."

They talked a few more minutes, and finally Dustin excused himself to change. Bag in hand, he shut the door then doffed his suit coat and string tie.

Tibby and the Milroy family leaving. While he'd welcome news that Mrs. Milroy was able to improve her present condition, the idea of their home, empty, left a hole in his heart. How much more for Miss Hollingsworth, who'd been their neighbor for as long as she'd lived here in the West.

Lord, it doesn't feel right, them leaving—and Petra living in her cabin by herself.

He'd thought about marriage. A *lot*. And he fully intended to marry Petra Breaux, but as he'd prayed about when to ask her, he'd not felt the timing was right. And he didn't want to allow the Milroy family's move to force him to ask sooner than he should.

When, Lord? I love her, but I keep asking You, and I don't feel like You're answering.

He removed the offering money from the bag and retrieved a clean sock from his drawer. Dustin rolled the paper bills then gathered the coins that people gave. He tucked the money into the sock and checked the bag for anything that might have fallen out. At the bottom, a paper, folded into a thick square lay forgotten. Dustin sat and loosened his top button one-handed, while with the other he unfolded the paper.

Something slid from the folds and clattered onto the floor. Searching between his boots, he didn't immediately see it, so he looked at the paper.

> *Perhaps this can help build the future (of the church—or otherwise).*
>
> *Edna & the Trenamens*

An odd message. Dustin stood and searched for what had sounded like a heavy coin. Not seeing it, he dropped to a knee and peeked under the bed.

"There you are." He reached for it, but something pricked his finger, and he jerked back. What in heaven's name? A quick look showed a tiny drop of blood, which he wiped away. He reached for it again, this time more carefully. Straightening, a bright flash of blue caught his eye.

Brilliant blue agate. With a delicately carved cameo. Surrounded by gold and pearls.

"Oh my stars." He glanced again at the note, then the cameo.

And in a heartbeat, he knew.

Now.

He burst from the bedroom and dashed into the sitting room. All eyes turned on him, but the only pair he sought were the vibrant green of his love.

"Dusty, what is it?" Jo called.

"I, um. . . I've been thinking about something."

"Oh?" Petra stood.

"What if I took some time and escorted you home to Pittsburgh?"

Her pretty features contorted in confusion. "Escorted me home?"

"Would that help any in talking to your family?"

She hung her head. "It's a very sweet offer, Reverend, but I don't know how that would help."

He shrugged. "It was just a thought." He paused a second. "I had a second idea I was gonna ask you about. Would you be willing to help me plan the first event I want to hold in the church?"

His sister stepped into his periphery. "Aren't you getting ahead of yourself? The church won't be built for a couple months yet, at least."

Dustin didn't break eye contact with Petra. "That's all right, Sis. It'll give us time to plan things just right."

Jo folded her arms. "Dustin Samuel Owens, you're making no sense at all. Plan what?"

Petra darted a glance toward Josephine. "I don't want to get in the middle of anything, step on anyone's toes."

"I was thinking to plan our wedding." He dropped to one knee and held out the cameo. "If you'll have me for a husband, that is."

Petra's face blanched, and she stared, mute.

Josephine, on the other hand, squealed, and the passel of Milroy girls seemed to wind up for an eruption of excitement.

"You want to marry *me*?"

"Well, of course I do."

When she still hadn't looked at his hand, he cleared his throat and nodded to his outstretched palm. Her attention strayed to it, then back to his face before her gaze dipped again.

"Oh my." Wide-eyed, she touched the cameo gingerly, then launched herself at him.

Dustin caught her in a bear hug.

"How? Where? Where did it come from?"

"It was in the offering plate with a note signed by Edna and the Trenamens."

She held him so tightly he could scarcely breathe. When, a moment later, she pulled away and reached for his hand again, he cautiously pinned the heirloom to her dress.

"So are you gonna answer my question, Miss Hollingsworth?"

"Question?"

He suppressed a chuckle. "I'll try to overlook the sting of that." Dustin dropped to his knee again and this time took her hand in his. "Miss Hollingsworth, will you be my wife?"

Tears pooled in her eyes. "Yes, Reverend. But I have some questions."

She said yes. *Lord, thank You. I've got so much to learn. Teach me to be a good husband.* "What questions?"

"Well, first, should I keep referring to you as Reverend, or may I call you by your given name?"

Everyone chuckled as he stood. "Dustin. Or Dusty. Whichever you prefer. And how would you prefer I address you?"

"Petra."

"Not Pete?"

She leaned close, that sassy look in her eye, and dropped her voice to a conspiratorial level. "Maybe sometimes Pete."

He laughed. "You had another question?"

"Yes, Dusty. Do we *really* have to wait for the church to be built before we get married?"

Epilogue

Pittsburgh, Pennsylvania
Early spring 1876

Trembling, Petra Owens snuggled closer to her husband as their hired carriage transported them toward the Breaux residence.

"Silly woman." Dusty tucked the blanket snug around her to ward off the lingering winter chill. "You're making yourself sick over nothing. Your family'll love you no matter what."

Cheek against his chest, she glanced at him. "So much has occurred in the almost four years since I left." She'd planned their arrival to coincide with Mama's forty-fifth birthday, but the nearer they got, the more she wondered if that was a wise choice. *Everyone* would be there.

"Yes, and if you'd invited your family for the wedding, all of that would've been in the open."

She sighed. On her request—and against Dusty's better judgment—she'd not told her family of their marriage. Until she'd had time to remold herself as Mrs. Petra Owens, she didn't want her family to come west. One slip by a Cambria Springs resident, and she'd have been forced to tell of her misadventures as Buckskin Pete Hollingsworth.

He touched his lips to hers. "But that stubborn streak is a large part of what attracted me to you."

Her cheeks warmed. "I try to temper it with sweetness."

"Stubborn tempered with sweet equals sass." His voice dripped with mock irritation.

She giggled. "I thought you liked my sassy side, Reverend."

"Lord help me, but I do." He pulled her closer and kissed her again, more soundly this time.

Oh, how she loved this man.

The carriage slowed, and Mama and Papa's grand redbrick home came into view. The three-story empire-style house with its attic belvedere and wide wraparound porch brought a flood of happy memories.

Dusty tensed, shrugging out from under her. "*This* is where they live?" He slid nearer to the window.

"Yes. Mama and Papa dreamed of a large home one day. They finally got it a few years after the war."

He glanced over his shoulder, trepidation in his brown eyes. "I thought you were joshing when you said your cabin would fit inside *any one room* of their house."

"Now wait just a moment. You've been telling me not to worry, my family will love me no matter what. But now you're acting skittish?"

"Yes. They're *your* kin. Your blood. I'm just the son of a har—"

"Dustin Samuel Owens!"

Her husband silenced.

"Those may be the facts of your birth, but that is *not* who you are." She moved closer and cupped his cheek. "You're an amazing man with a wonderful heart, and my family will love you." Staring deep into his beautiful eyes, she kissed him. At first he remained rigid, unresponsive, but he slowly softened until he returned her affection with a toe-curling kiss that left her breathless.

The carriage turned onto the large, arching driveway and drew to a stop near the porch. Various buggies and carriages waited. So the family *had* gathered for Mama's birthday. The driver opened the door, offering her his hand. Grasping her skirts, Petra stepped out as another wave of uneasiness swept her. She settled her hand on her midsection, and Dustin was at her side in a moment.

He touched her forehead. "You sure you're not growing ill?"

She waved away his hand. "I'll be fine. I'm sure it's a combination of the long trip and this reunion."

Not quite the truth. The tiredness had begun a week *before* they'd left Cambria Springs, and she'd started to feel queasy off and on days later. If only Mrs. Milroy still lived down the path so she might ask questions of someone more knowledgeable.

Lord, please let her and her children—and Tibby—be well. I miss them.

But now that she was home, she could pose those delicate questions to her mother to confirm her suspicions.

Once Dustin had paid the man, he picked up their bags, and they ascended to the door. "Ready?" He dropped the bags and knocked immediately.

"Dustin Owens." She sidestepped, bracing a hand against the wall. "You didn't give me a moment to answer." She drew a deep breath in a vain attempt to quiet her nerves.

He shot her a sheepish grin. "If I did, we might both talk ourselves out of knocking."

Almost instantly, the knob turned, and as the door opened, a fist-sized ball thudded onto the doorstep and streaked past Dusty. A blond boy darted after it even as Dusty gave chase and corralled the wayward orb between his boots.

The boy halted, hand poised to grab the ball, but let his gaze travel the length of her husband's body. "Who're you?"

Petra laughed, causing her youngest brother to turn. "He's my husband, Ralph."

Eyes wide, her brother stood for an instant, then launched himself at her. "You're home. You finally came back." The boy turned toward the door. "Mama, Papa, come quick!"

She caught him, and they held each other for a moment before—

"Ralph?" a familiar—if concerned—male voice called from inside, and hurried footsteps pounded their way.

All Petra's senses perked. Trembling, she stood still as her father stepped through the doorway, her mother close on his heels.

"Hello, Papa. Happy birthday, Mama."

Just like Ralph, her parents turned, eyes wide, and both rushed her, pulling her into a bear hug. She couldn't help her tears at finally being once more in their embrace. And if the snuffling she heard was any indication, she wasn't the only one.

"My Petra," Mama whispered. "Oh, thank You, Lord. You brought her home."

"I've missed you both so much."

"Oh darling girl." Papa planted a kiss on her temple. "We've missed you."

Around them, the porch buzzed with excitement as the other family members spilled out into the chilly air.

She pulled free. "I have to introduce you to someone."

As she reached for Dusty's hand, Mama touched the cameo pinned to her dress, a knowing grin on her lips. "Yes, who's your friend?"

She pulled Dusty to her side. "Papa. Mama. Everyone. This is my husband, Reverend Dustin Owens. Dustin, my family."

Dusty gripped her hand a little tighter than usual. "Pleasure."

"Reverend, you say?" Curiosity lit Papa's eyes. "Clara and I knew Petra might lose her heart to a man out west, but we didn't expect a preacher."

"Is that a bad thing, Papa?"

"No, my girl. It's a very good thing." He turned again to Dustin and extended a hand. "I'm Byron Breaux. And my wife, Clara. Welcome to the family, Dustin."

"Thank you, sir." They shook hands.

"Petra?" Mama's cousin Alice touched her arm. "Welcome home. It's good to see you."

"Thank you. I didn't realize how much I missed everyone until now."

Alice drew an adorable girl with dark ringlets and a cherubic face forward.

Her eyes widened. "This can't be little Bertie. Is it?"

"It is. She was barely two when you left, so she doesn't even remember you."

She squatted to the little girl's level. "Hello, Bertie, I'm Petra. I'm one of your cousins." Once or twice removed, but who was counting?

"Hello." Despite Bertie's shy tone, she slipped little arms around Petra's neck.

"Oh, you're sweet." She picked up the child and turned again to Alice. "She's beautiful."

Her brothers, Eddie and Allen, as well as auburn-haired cousin Elizabeth dashed onto the porch from the direction of the carriages. "Mama, may we use your pen and inkwell?"

Mama's brow furrowed. "Of course, but whatever for?"

Fourteen-year-old Elizabeth pinned her gaze on Petra and held out a stack of small books. "I was hoping Buckskin Pete would autograph her dime novels for me."

At the unexpected announcement, Petra lowered Bertie to the porch and took a step back, her stomach souring. Dusty was at her side in an instant.

"Darling, you're absolutely ashen." Mama hurried to her from nearby. "Are you unwell?"

The happy chatter died.

"She hasn't seemed quite herself this last bit," Dusty mumbled.

Someone brought a chair, and her husband guided her into it while someone else wrapped a blanket about her shoulders.

"Petra, what is it?" Mama whispered, stooping beside her.

She couldn't bring herself to meet her mother's eyes. "You know about Buckskin Pete?"

A tiny chuckle bubbled out of Mama, though she stifled it. "Is that why you're upset?" Again, she attempted to stifle a chuckle but failed as she laughed outright. "I'm sorry, darling. I don't mean to laugh, but yes. We know all about Buckskin Pete."

More laughter.

Her cheeks flamed. "How upset are you with me?"

"Upset?" Mama sobered. "Oh dear girl. I think we're all just happy to have you home."

Dustin brushed a strand of her hair behind her ear, and when she glanced his way, his grin said, *Told you.*

"When did you find out?" She'd been so careful not to say anything in her letters home about her life as Buckskin Pete.

"At least a year ago. One of Papa's friends went west to cover a story, and he saw the dime novels, recognized the name, realized they were about you, and brought copies home."

"Gosh, Sis," Allen called. "You were big enough news. You even got a write-up in the local paper, and one of the stores in town started carrying your dime novels."

She covered her mouth. "I'm so embarrassed."

"You made a name by using the skills we taught you," Papa called. "I couldn't be prouder."

"I just wish you had told us yourself." Mama patted her hand.

"I'm sorry, Mama."

"Now, Clara, don't make her feel too guilty. She wasn't the only one keeping secrets."

She raked a gaze to Papa. "I wasn't?"

Mama's brow creased. "She wasn't?"

With a sheepish grin, he limped down the steps, favoring the leg he'd injured during the war. "Follow me, and I'll explain."

"What is this about, Mama?"

"I've no idea." Mama shrugged. "Let's find out."

Dusty helped her up, and as the entire group followed Papa toward the barn, Petra looked around. "Mama, where is Aunt Letitia?"

"She's visiting with a sick friend, but she'll be along shortly."

A moment later, Dusty nodded discreetly toward the group's edge. "Who is that girl?" He barely breathed the question.

Elizabeth walked slightly apart from the rest, head hung low. "Uncle Wallace's daughter, Elizabeth."

"You should go talk to her. She looks upset."

How very astute of him to notice. *Lord, I love this man's heart, always looking for the one in need.*

She extracted her arm from his and navigated through the crowd of relatives. Coming alongside, she bumped her fourteen-year-old cousin's shoulder with her own. "Remind me when we get back to the house, and I'll sign your dime novels."

Elizabeth looked at her with a hopeful little smile. "You're not upset with me?"

She giggled. "No. I'm thankful. Now I won't spend the entire visit fretting over someone finding out about Pete. Everyone already knows."

"I don't know how you did it—living alone out west. Or doing those things in the stories."

"I just did what I loved." Petra looped an arm around Elizabeth's shoulders. "If you could do anything you wanted, any job, what would it be?"

She thought a moment, then turned an adoring look at her father, walking a few paces away. "Become a detective like Papa." She sighed softly. "But they don't let girls be detectives."

A slow smile spread across Petra's face. "Allan Pinkerton does. I have a friend in Cambria Springs—Cassie Trenamen. She works for him."

"Really?" She seemed to ponder that. "I could be a Pinkerton?"

"If you want to be."

Papa stopped the group a little way off from the barn, and taking Petra's hand, drew her to Dusty's side, then silenced the chattering group with a motion. "When you stayed out west, your mother and I were concerned. She did a far better job of placing you in God's hands than I did. Once the dime novels reached us, I struggled even more. I couldn't sleep, I couldn't concentrate. Since I couldn't go west to check on you. . ." He shrugged. "I sent a trusted friend. A groom who used to work for your uncle Peter and aunt Letitia until a couple years ago—Tibault Veilleux."

When Papa stopped speaking, the distant strains of "Oh! Susanna" sounded from somewhere deep in the barn, sung by a familiar, comforting tenor voice.

Petra's jaw dropped, and she looked between her father and her husband.

"Tibby?" Dusty asked, a shocked smile crossing his face.

At Papa's nod, they followed the sound of the familiar singing. As they came upon him, he turned from the saddle he was mending, his expression turning from surprise to joy. After a tearful round of hugs and handshakes, Petra narrowed her eyes at the stately old gentleman.

"Tibby, you were there to spy on me?"

"*Spy* is a rather strong word. I prefer *watch over*. I was told to help you if I could, protect you if I must, but otherwise let you live your life. Of course, it wasn't long before a certain young man came along and captured your attention, then your heart."

"And what about the woman who captured yours?" Dusty winked. "How is Mrs. Milroy?"

"Mrs. Veilleux, you mean." His grin deepened. "I married her last month. She and the children are all doing very well here."

Petra's heart swelled with excitement. "When can we see them?"

Papa wandered up. "How about now? Tibault, take the day off, go get your bride and your children, and let's welcome these two home."

"Yes, sir. Gladly."

As Tibby and Papa walked ahead to the barn's entrance, Dusty waited until they turned out of sight, then drew her to a stop.

She turned, noting the seriousness in his features, and her chest constricted. "What's the matter?"

"You look really happy here."

"I am. It's nice to be home. Nice to be around family, to introduce you to everyone."

He nodded. "How much are you liking it?"

She cocked her head at him. "What are you asking me, Dusty?"

He glanced around the barn, then leaned and peeked at the house in the distance. "I can't provide you this kind of a life on a preacher's pay."

"Dustin Samuel Owens." She spoke the name gently as she slipped into his arms. "You may have tamed my heart, but not so much that I need anything like this to be happy. All I need is you."

Jennifer Uhlarik discovered the western genre as a preteen, when she swiped the only "horse" book she found on her older brother's bookshelf. A new love was born. Across the next ten years, she devoured Louis L'Amour westerns and fell in love with the genre. At the University of Tampa, she began penning her own story of the Old West. Armed with a BA in writing, she has won five writing competitions and was a finalist in two others. In addition to writing, she has held jobs as a private business owner, a schoolteacher, a marketing director, and her favorite—a full-time homemaker. Jennifer is active in American Christian Fiction Writers and is a lifetime member of the Florida Writers Association. She lives near Tampa, Florida, with her husband, teenage son, and four fur children.

PINKERTON NATIONAL DETECTIVE AGENCY

Meet Me at the Fair

by Kathleen Y'Barbo

DEDICATION

To the One and the one,
my heavenly Father and my husband.
Thank you.

And be not conformed to this world: but be
ye transformed by the renewing of your mind,
that ye may prove what is that good,
and acceptable, and perfect, will of God.
ROMANS 12:2 KJV

❧ Chapter 1 ❧

Chicago, Illinois
July 3, 1884

*E*than Butler ought to have been in awe of the number of dignitaries in attendance at the funeral of his employer, Allan Pinkerton. Though he was not a religious man, the founder of the Pinkerton Agency was known to enjoy the spotlight on occasion. Today's standing-room-only event would have pleased him greatly.

The Democratic National Convention would open in less than one week's time, thus the illustrious attendees seated in the first few rows of the service included five of the eight presidential candidates and one vice presidential hopeful as well as a wide array of other highly placed politicians and businessmen.

Today Ethan was doing dual duties, first and foremost as a Pinkerton detective paying his respects, and a distant second as the son of a longtime Pinkerton family friend. For as much as Mr. Pinkerton acknowledged his detective's relationship as middle son of the disgraced financier Patrick Butler, he had long ago forgiven Ethan for it.

Had Father and Ethan's older brother not been otherwise occupied in cells at the New York City Halls of Justice and House of Detention, both of them might be here with him now attempting to distract him with unsavory tales of a select few of those in attendance.

Instead, the redhead seated in the row ahead of him had captured his attention and held it throughout the entirety of the memorial service. Though her auburn curls were modestly tucked up into a black hat adorned with midnight-colored beads and a matching feather, a tendril had escaped to curl along the nape of her neck. Twice now she had swiped at her cheek with the back of her gloved hand, and it did not take a Pinkerton detective to determine that she was quite distressed at the great man's passing.

The man at her side must be her father, or so Ethan hoped, as the white-haired gentleman seemed oblivious to the fact that the glorious creature was seated next to him. Rather, he seemed happy to ignore the sniffling female in favor of keeping up a running dialogue of softly spoken comments with Senator Langford Fulton, a Chicago politician already being mentioned as a candidate for the nation's highest office four years from now.

Another sniffle from the row ahead of him, and Ethan reached into his pocket for his handkerchief. He waited until her companion was once again engaged in conversation to lean forward to tap her on the shoulder.

"Here," he whispered. "I believe you need this more than I do."

She turned just enough for him to see a woman as lovely in profile as he had imagined. Her porcelain skin and the pale pink of her cheeks was partly hidden behind her hat.

"Thank you, but I couldn't, truly," she whispered before turning back to face the current orator, a chief of police from some city whose name he'd missed.

"Allan Pinkerton was looking toward the future even as he realized he had little time left," the speaker said. "Few among us knew that as he lay dying he was working on projects that might have affected not only how the Pinkerton detectives go about their work, but also greatly benefited those of us in law enforcement. Sadly that all went to the grave with him."

"How would he know this?" the woman in front of Ethan said just loud enough for him to hear.

The silver-haired man sent her what appeared to be a warning look before returning his attention to the man at the podium. In response, the redhead swiped at her check again and then abruptly rose to flee the room.

When it appeared her companion did not intend to follow, Ethan set out in pursuit. He found the young woman nearly hidden behind a hedge in the gardens next door. Were it not for the black feather on her hat, he might have walked past.

Then he heard her whimper. The sound was soft and not unlike the mewling of a kitten.

After a moment's indecision, he walked around the hedge. She was even lovelier from this angle, though her blue eyes shimmered with unshed tears.

"Forgive me for interrupting, I couldn't help but notice your distress." Ethan took note of the lone tear that traced a path down her cheek and retrieved his handkerchief. "And your lack of a handkerchief. Please, take mine." At her reluctant look, he added, "It's clean. I promise."

That brought the beginning of a smile as she accepted his offer and then dabbed at her tears. "Thank you," she said. "I am usually not this unprepared."

"I am glad to oblige." He gave a little bow. "Ethan Butler at your service."

Ethan Butler. Elizabeth Caldwell Newton made a mental note to record his name in her notebook. It was a Newton trait to be organized and prepared, and this trait had served her well during her employment with the Pinkerton Agency. Of course, with Mr. Pinkerton's demise, the project of collecting fingerprints for crime-solving purposes was in jeopardy.

The thought of the weeks and months of research they'd conducted being lost forever undid her. Why did the stubborn Scotsman insist on keeping his research mostly in his head rather than on paper?

Worse, why had she agreed to this? The tears rose fresh, and this time she did not worry about hiding them.

"May I?" He nodded toward the place on the stone bench beside her.

"Yes, of course," she said. "Please forgive my manners. I am. . ." She searched for a word and could not find one that fit her swirling mix of emotions. "Overwrought," seemed the best choice.

"Of course."

Mr. Butler settled beside her and stretched out his long legs. Though dressed in the same conservative funeral garb as all the other men, his dark trousers and suit jacket were impeccably tailored, and his vest and cravat were made of a navy silk so deep it almost appeared black.

The tie expertly knotted at his neck had touches of copper, the same color as his eyes. Then there was the quality of the elaborately monogrammed handkerchief she had dampened with her tears.

He looked every bit the prosperous man of commerce, and yet there was something in his demeanor that told Elizabeth this man longed to yank away his tie and toss his hat into the stream that flowed a few feet away. She slid him a sideways glance and noted his tanned skin and the calluses on his hands.

Indeed, this was a man meant for the outdoors and not a fellow intent on spending his life behind a desk. If she had to guess from his accent, she would classify him as a man of the West, more specifically, Texas.

She shook away the thought. Analyzing people was a peculiar habit of hers she had learned from her father, one that Mr. Pinkerton had encouraged even as he secluded her from the other Pinkerton agents so that she might be more available to work with him on his fingerprint project.

Mr. Butler shifted positions and tugged at his collar. "I always forget that July in Chicago is nearly as hot as Houston."

Elizabeth suppressed a smile. The skill of hiding her emotions that she learned early in her Pinkerton career had not diminished with lack of use.

"Were you and Mr. Pinkerton close?"

"Of a sort," she said. "Was he a friend of yours?"

"More of a business associate." Mr. Butler looked away "It's not going to be the same without him, though I'm sure his sons will do a good job of taking over for him."

They would, this she knew. However, their intention was to discontinue a program they considered had less merit than other endeavors. If the fingerprint registry of criminals was ever to be completed, it would be because one of the Pinkerton sons changed his mind.

They lapsed into a companionable silence as Elizabeth gathered her thoughts. Father would demand an explanation for her swift departure from the service, and he would never accept the explanation that she was overwrought.

For as much as her father knew about her, he had no idea she had succumbed to the call of the life of a Pinkerton detective. He had worked hard to provide a life of ease and comfort for her and Mother, and no amount of pleading would have convinced him she was meant for anything else.

Thus, while she could claim a fondness for the gentleman with whom her father had been acquainted, she could never admit he was also her employer. Nor could she claim her emotions were overcome.

Anyone who knew her knew this was impossible. Father would be coming after her as soon as the interminable speeches ended.

While she might manage to escape him here, eventually she would come face-to-face with him at home. Unless she wanted to explain the real reason why she was bereft at the old Scotsman's death, she needed another excuse for her behavior.

Behind her, the sound of conversation drifting on the summer breeze alerted her to the fact that the memorial service was ending. Elizabeth slid another glance at Ethan Butler.

"You seem like a nice man, Mr. Butler, and you've been very kind to lend me your handkerchief." She paused. "I wonder if I might trouble you for a small favor."

He smiled. "Anything."

Elizabeth hesitated only a moment. Father might not believe she would be overcome by emotion, but he certainly wouldn't dare argue that another couldn't feel the same. "My father will be looking for me. I would rather not tell him why I left so abruptly."

"And you would like my help in avoiding this?"

"If you wouldn't mind." She was about to tell him that he only needed to nod as she spun a yarn about being overwarm in the crowded room and needing air. The kind gentleman in the row behind her then came to see to her health. Yes, that would indeed work, for it had been stifling in the room, and she'd been more than grateful for the fresh breeze she'd found in the garden.

"And he is the white-haired man who was seated next to you?"

"Yes," she said as she watched Mr. Butler's attention slide past her to a point on the other side of the hedge. "I do have a plan, but I will need your assistance. I will tell my father that—"

To her surprise, Mr. Butler leaned over to whisper in her ear. "Forgive my behavior," he said, "but he is just on the other side of the hedge, so there isn't time for you to tell me your plan. May I improvise, or do you prefer to take the lead?"

"Oh," she managed, intending to explain that the plan she'd concocted on a moment's notice did not include this.

But she couldn't. Couldn't respond. Couldn't think. Couldn't look away from those copper-colored eyes.

"Please do," finally escaped on a sigh. "And thank you for your help, Mr. Butler."

"I must warn you that my plan involves giving the impression of a familiarity we do not have," he said against her ear. "I will hold you to a promise that you will inform me at once should I owe you an apology."

"I shall at once," she echoed as she felt his arms go gently around her.

"See that you do," he whispered.

He smelled of soap and sunshine, and his eyes crinkled at the edges when he smiled. His lips were soft against hers, a sweet kiss that she longed to savor but knew she could never adequately describe in her journal.

When he moved away to look down at her, she smiled though her insides were strangely mush. "You've stopped," she said.

"I have." There was that smile again. "I wanted to give you a chance to tell me whether you are owed an apology."

"Not yet," she said. "Please, continue."

A few minutes later when Father and the senator peered over the hedge to cause a commotion that would likely garner a bigger headline than the funeral in the society pages tomorrow, Elizabeth had determined three things she would be writing in her notebook.

First, she had never expected that anyone could determine a better plan than she could in a situation involving her father. Second, she would take note of the way in which Mr. Butler caressed her cheek as he kept a respectable distance between them and yet gave an impression of something Father obviously did not deem respectable.

And third, she would regret only one thing, and it wasn't the fact that most of Chicago and a healthy percentage of the men nominated for president watched her disentangle herself from a fellow funeral attendee. Rather, she would regret that when Mr. Butler was finally allowed to escape the garden and go on his way, Elizabeth realized too late that she had never told him her name or how very much she enjoyed her first kiss.

And the ones that followed.

Chapter 2

Pinkerton headquarters, Chicago
May 7, 1885

Though Elizabeth had few complaints, she absolutely hated being called Lizzie. Loathed it, actually. And yet there it was, the awful name bestowed on her in childhood returned to land on her again, this time as part of a Pinkerton assignment.

Of all the identities to be given in her first chance at detective work since Mr. Pinkerton's death, it would have to be this one.

Though the paper in front of her proclaimed her to be Lizzie Nellis, all she could think of was Locked-In Lizzie. She suppressed a shudder at the memory of the awful nanny who thought it great sport to toss Elizabeth into a cupboard in the nursery when child-minding became inconvenient.

And it always seemed to be inconvenient.

To this day, Elizabeth refused to suffer two things: darkened rooms and the name Lizzie.

She stepped inside and shook the remainder of this morning's brief rain shower from her coat then proceeded to her destination. Not once in the eighteen months since she came to work for Mr. Pinkerton at his agency or the ten months since she returned to detective work had she complained about an assignment.

Rather, she had set to the task with the same efficiency that she had learned practically from birth, something that had caught Mr. Pinkerton's attention and gained her a spot working on his fingerprinting project. Always do a job well and without excuse—that was Papa's motto, and Elizabeth's as well.

If only Captain Adams were as easy to work with as Mr. Pinkerton had been. She still missed the old Scotsman, but never so much as at this moment.

Elizabeth mustered her best smile and gave her employer a look she hoped would not betray her feelings. "While I understand you have already made the arrangements, I do wonder if there might be time to make an adjustment."

"An adjustment to what?" Captain Adams eyed her above the wire spectacles that perpetually pinched the end of his nose. "Do you have any idea what it takes to deal with foreign dignitaries? The sultana will not be pleased if there are any adjustments."

"I am merely the hired help, so I assure you the sultana will never know," Elizabeth snapped.

Her grandmother's staff certainly never bothered her with such things. They handled the details seamlessly, without the need to mention anything to Lady Caldwell.

Of course she would never say this to the captain. The slightest mention of who she was and from what lineage she descended would ruin everything. Captain Adams was new and would learn who her parents were eventually, if he had not already been told, but she certainly would not be the one to tell him. Not at the risk of courting favoritism she did not seek.

Favoritism the late Mr. Pinkerton never gave, rest his soul.

So Elizabeth put her smile back in place and continued. "What I mean is, I will see that her staff understands. It's only a minor point, really, but I do have strong preferences in regard to—"

"Miss Newton, please." Captain Adams shook his head as he leaned down from his place beside his desk to sort through the untidy horror that was his filing system. "That is all fine and good, but you'll do none of the sort. We're keeping to the plan."

"Truly, it is but a minor change. What if my cover name has been compromised? Best to change that, don't you think?"

"It hasn't been. I just had the telegram with the hotel reservation sent ten minutes ago, and your train tickets were purchased this morning." He thrust a sheaf of papers toward her. "No changes except what is here. Add these to whatever documents you already have and commit them all to memory."

"Fine," escaped on a frustrated breath. She glanced down at the documents and then politely tucked them away. "If that is all, then I'll be on my way."

"You didn't read them," he said.

"I'm sure everything is in order." She hesitated only a moment. "Other than the new name I will be taking during the course of my time in New Orleans, is there anything else I should know before I leave this office, or shall I entertain myself with these notes later?"

He gave her that half-amused look that he sometimes got during their conversations. She was never quite certain what brought on his reaction, but then she'd never much concerned herself with those trivialities. As long as Captain Adams and the Pinkerton Agency approved of her work, it mattered little how either felt about her personally.

"I could tell you," he said wearily as he sank his thin frame onto the chair behind his desk, "but where would be the fun in that? Besides, I wouldn't want you to miss your train."

Elizabeth glanced at the clock on the mantel. "I have plenty of time. It's only just half past nine."

Again he peered at her over his spectacles. "Not if I answer your question."

"I don't follow." She studied his expression as she'd been trained to study subjects under her scrutiny. "You think I might lodge a protest against whatever you've added to my assignment."

"Not 'might,' Miss Newton. *Would.*" He paused. "You do enjoy a spirited debate."

Had she not assumed the captain was above using sarcasm in the workplace, she might have thought he was inferring something negative from his comment. "I do," she admitted. "Mr. Pinkerton often remarked on it as well."

His smile was slow and a bit unsteady. "Yes, well, I have chosen you specifically for this assignment because you have the unique qualities of excellent detection skills and high society manners. The sultana will like you."

"Thank you. I anticipate that I will get along with her quite well. My research shows she is most likable and quite curious to learn more about our country, hence her visit to the exposition's closing ceremonies."

"However. . ." He continued as if she had not spoken at all. "The sultana alone will know who you are. There is concern that someone on her staff might not be trustworthy, so none of them are to be informed of either your identity or the name of your employer."

"So I have no contacts on the inside?"

"The guards remain, and they know we are involved, but they have no details of how her visit will unfold." He paused. "Unfortunately, the people with whom you have been in contact are no longer in the sultan's employ, and for good reason."

She thought of the eloquently written letters she had received from the sultana's private secretary, Amir, the soft-spoken but watchful elderly fellow with whom she had met here in Chicago. "What happened to them?"

"It's best not to ask," he said. "Suffice it to say that danger sometimes comes from the most unsuspected sources."

"A foundation of my training. . ." She paused to gather her thoughts. "Captain, I assure you that this matter has been handled at the highest priority level since I was given the assignment. Everything is ready for her visit. My preparatory trip to New Orleans in December was sufficient to prepare me for any eventuality. I only ask that I be granted permission to adapt the plan as it unfolds."

"I won't debate you, Miss Newton," he said as he leaned back in his chair and looked up at her. "Nor will I ever tell an agent of mine that he or she has no authority to adapt to a changing situation during the course of an assignment. However, should you feel the need to do something outside the scope of what has been meticulously outlined in those documents, please understand it will not be me or even the Pinkerton brothers who will be demanding an answer as to why."

"No?"

"No." He cut his eyes toward the painting of the United States Capitol that had hung over the fireplace for as long as Elizabeth had been employed here. "The president has a particular interest in seeing that the sultana goes forward with her plan to donate a substantial gift to the Smithsonian Institute. It's his pet project, you know."

She did not, but it mattered little. Nor did it matter that the president had known her long enough not only to bounce her on his knee as a baby but also to call her by that awful nickname. She'd set him straight just as she had anyone else who called her anything but Elizabeth. The story of his reaction and the locket bearing the name Elizabeth that he sent as a gift had become part of family lore as well as a treasured memento.

"Miss Newton?"

She returned her attention to the captain. "Neither the president nor the sultana will be disappointed in me. I assure you of that."

Captain Adams gave her an appraising look. "That is all I ask." He paused. "Just carefully read the documents I've given you and follow orders, diverting from them only out of extreme necessity."

"Yes, sir." She turned on her heel to hurry toward the exit.

"Oh, and Miss Newton?"

"Yes?" She paused to glance back at him.

"I hesitate to mention this, but I will. I have been told that if you are successful in this venture, there will likely be a new project for you as your next assignment."

Her heart rose. "Are the Pinkertons reviving the fingerprinting project?"

"I am not at liberty to say," he said with an oddly wide smile. "But I assure you that you will not be disappointed."

"Well now." Her smile matched his. "Then I will certainly return here having successfully completed this assignment. I will not disappoint."

His expression sobered. "I do not doubt you. However, be aware that when you walk out that door, you will cease to be Elizabeth Newton. From that moment until the sultana is safely gone from New Orleans, you are Lizzie Nellis. Due to the level of security required, I will be your only contact within the agency. If you went missing, even the Pinkerton brothers would not know how to find you. Do you understand?"

Again the name grated on her. This time, however, the smile she offered him was genuine. "I understand completely, and as with all my assignments, I accept the risk involved in completing it. On the other side of that door is Lizzie Nellis, who will keep that name except upon the occasion of extreme necessity."

Another appraising look, and he shrugged. "Why do I have the sneaking suspicion you'll use my words against me someday?"

"I have no idea, sir. Now, if you'll excuse me, I've a train to catch."

Elizabeth made short work of crossing the vestibule and stepping out into the now-sunny Chicago morning. As was her habit, she glanced first to her left and then to her right, taking note of all pedestrians and vehicles. When nothing of suspicion arose beyond the two housewives who appeared to be arguing over the price of some trinket with a traveling salesman, Elizabeth glanced back at the closed door.

"Here is where I leave you, Lizzie Nellis," she said under her breath. "That awful name dies here out of extreme necessity."

Pinkerton Detective Agency, Denver office
May 7, 1885

"Confound it, Captain. I was about to catch him."

Ethan Butler halted his pacing to focus his attention on the view of the Rockies outside the window. He had been assigned to the Denver office of the Pinkerton Agency for less than two years, and yet he felt more at home in this place than anywhere else except Texas.

"Awfully convenient that you're telling me this now." Captain "Red" Dutton rose from his desk to join Ethan at the window.

"Well, it's awfully inconvenient that you're pulling me off the case." He gave his boss a sideways look and then returned his attention to the mountains and the city that unfolded in the valley below them. "He's out there somewhere planning his next move. I can feel it."

And he could. In the same way that some detectives used deductive reasoning or tracking skills, Ethan used his instincts.

And his instincts told him that the perpetrator of more than a half million dollars in jewel thefts in locations stretching from New York to San Francisco—the man the press had named the Diamond Dandy for his ability to travel undetected among each city's elite—was in Denver right now.

If only his instincts would tell him where.

"I don't doubt you," the red-haired captain said as he toyed with one end of his lengthy mustache. "You've never made that claim when you weren't right about it."

"Then let me catch him. There's a ball at the Givens's home tomorrow night. He'll be there." He paused to sneak a covert glance at the captain. "What's a day or two when the next assignment isn't anything more than a glorified errand for a friend?"

Captain Dutton continued to stare out the window. Though he appeared to be ignoring the request, Ethan knew the man well enough to understand that he was weighing his options and considering his response.

Finally, the captain turned to face him. "What does he look like?"

The question took him aback. "The Dandy?" At the captain's nod, Ethan continued. "I don't know exactly, but I'll know him when I see him."

"Any witnesses come forward with descriptions?"

"No," he admitted.

"I don't question much of what you do, Ethan, because although your methods are somewhat unorthodox, you always manage to get the job done. If this were just a glorified errand for a friend, I might be tempted to give you the time you've asked for." His eyes narrowed. "Unfortunately it is not, and I cannot. Not without losing my job in the process."

Captain Dutton left Ethan standing at the window to return to his desk. Even from this distance, he could see the flush of red on his boss's cheeks. While he hadn't yet crossed the line, Ethan was acutely aware he was about to if he didn't change his tack.

He took a deep breath and considered his response carefully. Finally, Ethan decided to let the evidence speak for itself. He retrieved the folded piece of stationery from the Astoria Hotel in New York City from his pocket and followed the captain to place it on the desk in front of him.

The older man looked up sharply. "Where did you get this?"

"It was folded into my morning paper and slipped under my door this morning." He paused. "No one in the boardinghouse saw it delivered or remembers any visitors."

"'The face is next'? What do you make of it?"

"Either my landlady is a jewel thief or the man I've been chasing for months found me first." He paused. "He could be taunting me by letting me know he's ready to show his face."

"Or there's another meaning entirely." Dutton paused. "You were summoned back here to meet with me before he made his move at the Astoria party. Do you think he followed you here?"

"His last note left a pretty obvious clue that he'd be after Mrs. Givens's matched set of blue diamonds. She wore them at the Astoria party, so he would have seen them there. His note said, 'Follow the blue to the G.' It doesn't take a Pinkerton to figure out that one."

"The Dandy does like to scout out the next haul while taking the current one, although he's never been so obvious with his hints or so bold in making contact with one of my detectives." He paused. "All right. I'll allow a delay of one day, but no more than that."

"That's all I need." Ethan snatched up the note and the packet that contained the details of his next assignment and hurried toward the door before Captain Dutton could change his mind.

"That's all you get," Dutton called. "And Butler, study up on what's in that packet. You'll see that your trip to New Orleans is hardly a glorified errand for a friend."

❦ *Chapter 3* ❦

*E*than had never been a fan of partial victories, but at least the Givens's blue diamonds were safe. Between the heavy police presence at the event and the armed guards who surrounded the Givens mansion, the Dandy must have decided not to make the attempt.

No. That couldn't be the reason.

The Dandy had overcome much tighter security than what was in place last night and managed to leave undetected with exactly the prize pieces he wanted. So why now, of all times, did he decide not to take what he had boldly indicated he would?

Ethan sat back against the seat and closed his eyes, allowing the rocking of the train to lull him into something akin to restful slumber. Between the late arrival back at his boardinghouse last night and the early departure for New Orleans this morning, sleep had eluded him.

With the puzzle of the Diamond Dandy still knotted up in his mind, he opened his eyes and reached for the packet that contained his next assignment. Inside was an envelope of documents and a small box. He retrieved the paper on top of the stack and began to read.

Elizabeth Newton, Pinkerton detective, must receive this box post haste. Item in the box is not to be given to anyone but Miss Newton, who is currently on an assignment using the name Lizzie Nellis. Time is of the essence, and this assignment has been specifically given to you. You should know that Miss Newton's father is a close friend of Senator Fulton.

Ethan read that again. "Senator Fulton?"

From what little he could recall, the senator was a longtime legislator from the state of Illinois, a man whose wealth increased each time a train left a station anywhere in the eastern half of the United States. He had been in the papers recently for some project in the capital that the president was favoring. What was that project, and was he for or against it? Ethan couldn't remember at the moment, but the information was easily found.

He did have one other memory connected to the senator involving an auburn-haired stranger and a shared moment in a garden on a warm July afternoon.

That memory he would never forget.

Ethan allowed a brief recollection of the woman whose name he did not know and then reminded himself of the same thing he considered each time thoughts of her invaded his mind: if he was meant to find her again, he would. He was, after all, a Pinkerton detective, so he could have used his skills to track her down.

As much as he would love to see the mysterious woman again, there was something to be said for not ruining what had been a perfect moment. Thus, it was better not to seek out the woman and then discover she did not share his feelings about their kisses in the garden.

Father would say he was practicing the avoidance that he'd been known for since childhood. Ethan would counter that he was listening to his instincts—or his gut, as the captain called it. Those instincts had served him well when he might have otherwise become embroiled in the same financial scandal as his father and brother, and they continued to serve him as a Pinkerton detective.

If only his instincts had told him to avoid a pretty redhead in a Chicago garden. Or, more specifically, avoid kissing her.

Ethan reluctantly returned to the details of the assignment. The remainder of the letter, written in the captain's scrawl, provided basic information about Miss Newton's description and the location of the hotel where the agency had secured a room for her.

"The Centennial," he muttered under his breath. "Impressive for a Pinkerton detective."

Of course, when your father pals around with a senator. . .

Ethan shook his head. Though he was a huge proponent of female Pinkerton agents, he had little patience for any man or woman who was given work due to family connections rather than skill. There was nothing in the dossier to indicate that Miss Newton was one of these. Still, he had been pulled off an active case, which had never happened before.

Not only that, but he was suddenly required to make his delivery to her while she was on assignment. Nothing about this seemed right.

Ethan returned the document to the stack. He reached for the box and opened the hinged lid. There he found a blue and white cameo, the sort that his grandmother favored, nestled in the center of a square of matching blue satin.

Surely there was more. He tapped on the box and tugged at the top, bottom, and sides to try and expose some hidden chamber where an important message might be found. Giving that up, he yanked out all the wrapping that held the box in place. Still nothing.

His temper flared as he snapped the lid shut. So this *was* a glorified errand. Had he not been absolutely certain he would lose his job if he did it, Ethan might have tossed the whole packet out the window.

Instead, he stuffed the packet back into his traveling case and retrieved his notes on the Dandy. Somewhere in all of this, he decided as he opened to the first page, was the clue that would solve the case. All he had to do was find it.

He was still looking for that elusive clue when he arrived in New Orleans several days later. Bypassing the less exclusive lodgings he generally favored when he was in the city, he checked in to the Centennial Hotel and determined to find Miss Newton and deliver her bauble in time to be back to actual detective work before the Dandy struck again.

Elizabeth was, after all, a Pinkerton detective, so she could have used her skills to track Ethan Butler down. Instead, she preferred to keep him right where he was: on a page in her journal that she could revisit whenever she wanted.

Like now, when the endless slide of scenery outside the train's window had somehow given way to boredom she rarely felt. Though she'd brought ample books for her trip and had plenty of paper and ink to attend to the bundle of letters that had as yet gone unanswered, she could focus on none of these worthy endeavors. Even the possible revival of the fingerprinting project failed to hold her interest for long against the seemingly endless hours on the train.

To be sure, she was thrilled to have the possibility of returning to her pet project. But there was something about wanting to hurry up and get to work that made the commute interminable.

Elizabeth turned to the page in her journal where she knew she would find him and relived each moment of their brief encounter. From his offer of a handkerchief to the moment he disappeared around the corner on a warm Chicago afternoon, Mr. Butler made an impression that was best left within the confines of her journal.

Resolutely, she turned the pages until she reached the place where she had begun taking notes about her current assignment. Nothing that would give away the facts of the case, of course, but rather some ideas on how best to proceed written in a way that only she would understand them.

Given that the sultana traveled under extraordinary circumstances, where luxury was paramount and yet so was security, Elizabeth had determined she would carry on the ruse that she too was part of that world. There was no disguising the color of her hair or eyes, so impersonating a woman from the sultana's background was out of the question. Thus, she elected to temporarily become another woman she knew quite well: her grandmother.

Not the aged grandmother of today, but the young woman Lady Caldwell once was. Imperious and always aware of her station as the daughter of a duke, Grandmother was the perfect model of a woman with whom the sultana might associate.

And thus, as she made her final notes on the page, Elizabeth smiled. Though she still grieved the loss of her work with the late Mr. Pinkerton, the detective work she had joined the agency to do had finally become possible.

"Thank you, Petra," she whispered, thinking of her audacious and adventurous cousin who had encouraged her to make her dream of detective work come true all those years ago.

The train's whistle sounded, announcing their next stop and her final destination: New Orleans. Elizabeth tucked away her journal, and along with it went the thoughts that belonged there. A Pinkerton detective on assignment had no time for such frivolities.

She made short work of gathering up her bags and having them sent to her hotel. According to the plan, the sultana would be arriving in exactly one week. Until then, it fell to her to complete the final preparations for her arrival.

Elizabeth looked down at her soot-stained traveling clothes and frowned. First a bath and a change of clothes, for Lady Caldwell would never be seen in public in such soiled attire. But then, Lady Caldwell would have made the journey in the comfort and seclusion of her private railcar.

Her first test of her new persona came as she stood in the vast marble foyer of the Centennial Hotel. Decorated with the latest in decor, scarlet velvet curtains at the windows, an abundance of palm trees in pots, and assorted ferns and greenery on opulently carved stands, the Centennial was indeed the height of luxury in this city.

It was also filled to capacity with guests. Or at least that is what the balding clerk claimed as he studied her from beneath brows that looked like two caterpillars marching across his forehead.

"Lady Caldwell, I fear there has been a terrible mistake. You see," he managed as his eyes widened, "there has been no reservation set for you here, and I just gave the last key to that gentleman freshly arrived from Colorado."

The clerk nodded toward the retreating back and broad shoulders of a dark-haired man who was making his way across the lobby. Something in his walk, in the way he looked as he disappeared up the stairs, seemed vaguely familiar.

Elizabeth returned her attention to the clerk. "And your name, please?"

"H–Harrison, ma'am," he stammered.

"Harrison, there is another room, and I would very much like to sign your book and check in so a bath can be drawn."

He shook his head and pointed to the stairs. "The last room was claimed by that fellow."

That was, of course, impossible. She knew how the agency worked: the hotel would have been paid in advance for her room. The Harrison fellow was merely electing not to mention this. Elizabeth decided to force his hand.

She reached for the guest book and retrieved the pen and ink to sign her name, just as Grandmother would have done. While she had the book within sight, she checked the name of the man who signed in ahead of her.

In place of a name, however, was written, *X*. Beside this, someone had written, "Room 213."

She set down the pen and offered the clerk a smile. "There, I have signed your book. Now, Harrison, when I stay here, it is almost always the Lafayette suite. He was a dear man to my family several generations ago. Positively dear. However, under the circumstances, I am happy to accept other lodgings in your fine establishment without complaint and without mentioning this to your employer."

The poor clerk appeared to study his papers for another moment and then shrugged. "Lady Caldwell, there is nothing that has not already been claimed. I'm terribly sorry."

"Perhaps there is a room reserved for another who has not yet checked in?" she said sweetly. "I am willing to take my leave if he or she arrives to claim it."

Harrison shrugged and his caterpillar eyebrows rose. "I suppose I could check. There might be some sort of, er, well, additional fees involved."

"Do that, please," Elizabeth said sweetly. She retrieved a suitable payment from her reticule and slid it across the desk.

He snatched up the money and quickly hid it in his vest pocket. As expected, he returned to give her the news that there was indeed a guest named Miss Nellis who had not yet claimed the room she had reserved.

"Now, you must understand, should Miss Nellis arrive at any time today, you will be required to give way to her."

She offered her sweetest smile. "You have my word, Harrison. Now do be a dear and have my luggage sent up."

Harrison waved for a porter, and a few minutes later Elizabeth was following her luggage up the stairs to room 212.

Chapter 4

Ethan tucked the box containing the blue cameo into one pocket and the key to his room in the other. As he crossed the room toward the door, a noise outside alerted him to the presence of someone in the hallway. With the Dandy baiting him and possibly following him here, he could take no chances.

Plus, his gut told him there was danger here. What kind, he'd yet to determine.

Turning the knob slowly, Ethan opened the door with his palm resting on his gun. A porter wearing the hotel's uniform and carrying a small trunk on his shoulder held the door to room 212. A swish of skirts and the stack of trunks in the hallway alerted Ethan to the fact that at least one of his new neighbors was female.

The porter turned his attention to Ethan, his eyes diverting quickly to the gun. "Oh sir, I'm sorry to disturb you. I'm just delivering luggage."

"Is there a problem?" a feminine voice called from inside the room.

The porter shifted the trunk and shook his head. "No, Lady Caldwell, everything is fine. Just speaking with a gentleman here in the hallway."

Lady Caldwell. He would remember that name, if only to determine that she was neither a target nor an accomplice in the jewel thefts.

In his time as a detective, Ethan had learned there were no coincidences and that no one was above suspicion. Thus, anyone who checked into his hotel and commandeered the room next to his was a person of interest until proven otherwise.

Ethan closed his door and made his way around the trunks to glance in the open door of room 212. The dark velvet drapes had been drawn against the sun but let in enough light to cast the woman in shadow. In one swift move, Lady Caldwell snapped them open, and sunlight flooded in.

"Oh my, that is bright, but what a lovely view," she said without turning away from the window to face him. "Yes, this will do nicely."

He took note of the woman's slender build and traveling clothes before the porter stepped inside and blocked his view. Something in her voice seemed familiar, but he couldn't quite place it.

"Did you need something, sir?" the porter asked.

"Me? No." Ethan's attention went back to the woman at the window, his view of her still obscured by the porter. "I'm sorry to bother you, ma'am," he called.

Lady Caldwell responded with a regal wave of her gloved hand, her attention solidly transfixed on whatever was happening outside the window. This was obviously his cue to exit.

One more failed attempt at catching a glimpse of her face, and Ethan made his way downstairs to speak with the desk clerk. "I am here to see Miss Lizzie Nellis. Would you please inform her she has a visitor?"

The clerk did not bother to check the book before responding. "I'm sorry, sir. She has not yet arrived."

He leaned toward the man behind the counter. "Humor me and look before you respond, please."

"I don't have to." The man's eyes narrowed. "I just checked for some-one else."

Ethan inched forward. "Who asked about her?"

The clerk leaned away from him. "I—I—I cannot tell you this," he said.

"Of course you can." Ethan hoped his tone would not convey his irritation. "You have admitted Miss Nellis has not yet arrived and that someone else has asked about her very recently. I don't think you under-stand the importance of telling me who this person is." He paused for effect. "You are putting Miss Nellis's safety at risk. And while you're at it, I will need your name."

"My name is Carl Harrison, sir. Since the guest has not yet arrived, it is not my job to concern myself with her safety."

"No, that would be my responsibility," Ethan said evenly.

"Sir, I cannot help you any more than I already have." Harrison's eyes cut to the hallway. "You are going to need to speak to Mr. Thorn."

Ethan found the white-haired gentleman in a well-appointed office directly behind the front desk. The brass nameplate on his desk declared him to be Hannibal J. Thorn III. "Please come in," he said. "I couldn't help overhearing your conversation with my clerk. How can I help you?"

After introducing himself as a Pinkerton detective, Ethan continued. "I can only tell you two things: I am here on Pinkerton business, and it is urgent that I speak with Lizzie Nellis. Your clerk says she is not yet here and that someone asked about her, but he will not give me any more information than that."

"Carl," Mr. Thorn called. "Would you come here and bring the regis-tration book, please?"

The man with whom he had just argued appeared in the doorway with the requested item. He walked past Ethan with a smug look and handed the book to his employer.

"You told this man that someone asked about a guest, Miss Nellis."

Carl nodded, but his eyes cut toward the door. Whatever he was about to say would be a partial truth at best.

"Someone asked about a guest room," he said. "I was able to find a room that was empty for the guest since Miss Nellis has not yet checked in."

Mr. Thorn's expression soured. "So you gave away a room reserved by Miss Nellis to someone else?"

"Not at all. If and when Miss Nellis does arrive, her room will be ready for her." His gaze shifted to Ethan and then flitted back to his boss.

"You may be excused, Carl, and close the door behind you when you leave." Thorn returned his attention to Ethan. "Please, have a seat."

"My clerk is correct, Mr. Butler," Mr. Thorn said after thumbing through the register. "No one with the name of Nellis has stayed here at the Centennial in the past three weeks. Should I continue looking backward, or is this a sufficient answer?"

Ethan let out a long breath and then shook his head. "If you wouldn't mind, please. I understood she would be here now, but maybe that was wrong information. If I missed her, then I can go back to the captain and tell him that. Either way, there are two Pinkerton investigations at stake here, so I want to be certain of the facts."

The manager returned his attention to the book in front of him. After a few minutes, he looked up at Ethan. "No one by that name has checked in to this hotel in the last three months. Is that sufficient for you to be certain?"

Ethan pushed to his feet. "Thank you, sir. It is. Just one more thing. I have an item that needs to go in your safe until I am able to book my return trip to Denver. I'm sure Carl is a nice enough fellow, but I would prefer it if you would do that for me."

"Of course." He rose. "If you'll just give me the item, I'll handle this personally."

"Actually," Ethan said slowly, "I'm going to need to watch the item go into the safe myself. It's protocol so that in case something happens I can verify the transfer of custody of anything that might become evidence."

"Yes, certainly."

Ethan followed Mr. Thorn down a narrow hallway and into a room that the manager accessed with a key attached to his watch chain. "I am the only one with access," he said as he turned the key and opened the door to the room where the massive safe was located. "I am going to have to ask you to turn your back while I open the safe. That is *my* protocol for assuring that no one but me has the combination."

Ethan did as he asked. The sounds of the lock turning and its corresponding clicks filled the room. Then came the sound of a hinge squealing.

"You may turn around, Mr. Butler."

He turned back around and found the door to the safe open. Inside were rows of boxes and bags of all sizes, each with a tag labeling its owner and room number. Retrieving the box from his pocket, Ethan handed it to Mr. Thorn.

"Which room, Mr. Butler?"

"Room 213," he said. He watched the manager complete the information on a blank tag and then attach it to the box.

Mr. Thorn tore off the bottom of the tag and handed it to Ethan. "Is that all you will be placing in the safe?" At Ethan's nod, the manager closed the safe's heavy door and then turned the wheel until the lock clicked into place. "All right then. If there's nothing else I can do for you, shall we call this meeting adjourned?"

Ethan nodded. Now to find a way out of New Orleans and back to Denver so he could get back on the case he never should have been taken off of. The captain wouldn't be happy that the mission could not be completed, but there was nothing to be done about that.

Wherever Lizzie Nellis was, she was not here yet. And that was a problem for another day and possibly another Pinkerton detective.

Elizabeth turned from the window to give the appearance of supervising the porter as he completed the job of delivering her luggage. Still, her hand shook. For a moment, she thought the man from the pages of her journal had somehow appeared in the corridor outside her room.

However unlikely, it was not impossible.

The porter made a swift but quiet exit, closing the door firmly behind him. Silence fell around her as Elizabeth sank to the windowsill and wrapped her arms around her knees.

Mama had often told her that she should remove her nose from the books she preferred to people, because life was passing her by. It wasn't, of course, for part of what she did with those books was record her observations of the life going on around her. However, Mama also warned that someday she might find it difficult to tell the difference in the people who populated her books and the ones who lived and breathed in her world.

Had it come to that? For surely the man in the hall was not that stranger who kissed her beneath the July sun all those months ago. That was impossible.

Or was it?

She sighed. Of course it wasn't possible. The combination of poor sleep on the train and reading her journal to the exclusion of all else had brought this on.

Yes. That was it. Exhaustion was to blame.

If she'd taken the Caldwell railcar, she would have traveled in a luxury more conducive to a good and restful sleep. Her rooms at the Centennial Hotel were nearly as sumptuous as Grandmother's railcar, although there were no servants to assist with her needs as she bathed and donned a clean day dress. Tonight she would sleep well, but first she had work to do.

Elizabeth had just finished pinning up her hair to go out and begin her follow-up investigation of the exhibition site when the most atrocious noise rattled the wall next to her. Rising, she retrieved the hat pin she always kept tucked beneath her collar and went to investigate.

Opening the door just enough to peer outside, she found the corridor empty. The wall next to her shuddered once more. She frowned as she stepped back inside her room.

Whatever was going on next door surely had nothing to do with her at the moment. However, if the rowdy guest continued to cause such a ruckus come bedtime, she would be taking the issue up with the management.

Returning her hat pin to its hiding place, she gathered up her things and stepped out into the hallway. There she saw that the door to room 213 had not been closed completely.

Maybe she should lodge a complaint with the occupant. She had just lifted her hand to knock when the door slammed shut.

"Well, all right then," she said under her breath as she made her way toward the staircase. Just as she rounded the corner to begin her descent, Elizabeth froze.

Him. Her fingers curled around the bannister as Ethan Butler crossed the lobby one floor below her. He couldn't find her here. He just couldn't. Not now. Not after all this time.

And certainly not when the successful completion of her mission meant remaining completely anonymous and, more important, undistracted.

Elizabeth took a step backward and then another until she had a reasonable hope that no one downstairs in the lobby would notice her spying from above. Mr. Butler bypassed the reception desk and headed toward the staircase just as she jumped backward out of sight.

Hurrying to her door, she fumbled with the key, her fingers trembling until it tumbled to the floor. Scooping it up, she managed to jab it into the lock and duck inside as footsteps sounded in the hall.

The footsteps neared and then stalled. Elizabeth held her breath, her heart pounding a furious rhythm as she rested her ear against the heavy wooden door.

The doorknob shook, and she jumped. *What was he doing?*

A moment later, the key slid under the door and landed at her feet. She sank to the carpet. After all of that, she had left the key in the door. "Brilliant," she whispered. "Just brilliant."

Ethan straightened and shook his head. The irresponsibility of some people galled him. In this day and time, what sort of person left a key in the lock in a city like New Orleans?

But then women of quality like Lady Caldwell had help to handle the mundane things of life like locking doors. He cast a glance at the entrance to the room next to his and then shook his head.

Apparently Lady Caldwell needed to choose her help more wisely.

Ethan turned his own doorknob, and it gave way under his fingers. The door had been locked when he left; of this he was completely certain. His palm now on his weapon, he pressed the door fully open.

Though the curtains kept the sunshine at bay, enough light spilled from the hall to allow Ethan to see that the parlor was unoccupied. He reached for the lamp and lit it, then studied the chamber with a detective's eye.

From the multitude of pillows on the four-poster bed near the windows to the heavy rolled-up carpet straight ahead—a victim of a porter's unfortunate accident and not yet removed by housekeeping—everything seemed to be in order.

Still, Ethan had his doubts. And so did his gut.

He did a quick check of the contents of his bags, electing to empty them on the settee rather than take his time. After a thorough search of the room, he was satisfied that anyone who might have entered did not stay long.

Still, he could not completely rule out that someone had been in his room. Maybe this case wasn't just an errand for a friend after all.

❧ Chapter 5 ❧

*E*lizabeth did not slow down until she had crossed St. Charles Street and lost sight of the hotel. Only then did she let out a long breath. Obviously she could not stay at the Centennial while someone who might recognize her was also in residence.

A pity, for the location was ideal.

Her reaction when she thought of Ethan Butler was not, however. So to continue her assignment without distraction, she must seek lodging elsewhere.

This decided, Elizabeth tucked an errant strand of hair back into place and tugged her shawl tighter around her shoulders. Though there was no need for an added layer of warmth against the pleasant spring weather, the well-worn garment helped to disguise her identity.

An added benefit would be to hide herself in case anyone recognized her. Like Ethan Butler. Not that he could possibly know she was here.

He couldn't.

She let out another long breath and willed herself to remain calm. Mr. Butler would neither see her nor recognize her, of this she was certain, for she was very good at what she did.

Elizabeth had been taught that being a female detective often meant she was overlooked by male subjects and not considered worthy of concern. Many times the words they spoke, not caring that she could hear, were the very words that came back to haunt them when they were brought to justice.

Today, however, she had added an extra layer of protection by dressing as a common maidservant rather than a woman of a higher social status. She entered the lavish grounds of the World's Industrial and Cotton Exposition, trailing a step behind a trio of society matrons who were too busy talking to notice her.

"My husband claims there are two structures meant just to hold the cattle and four for the horses," one woman said as she gestured toward the massive building ahead of them. "Now, Mr. Spencer, he does tend to exaggerate, so I am curious whether this time he's telling the truth. Oh my! Would you look at that! Have you ever seen a building so big?"

Her companion gasped. "I cannot wait to see the electric lights. Five thousand of them, or so the newspaper claims. Can you feature it? Oh, and the elevator. I promised Matilda I would see the elevator and report back to her."

"I'll be heading first to see the Liberty Bell," the third woman exclaimed. "Did you know it came all the way from Philadelphia by train with armed guards watching over it?"

"I cannot believe that's true," the first woman said. "My husband believes it's a fake and that the real one is being hidden until the exposition is over."

As the three women debated the authenticity of one of America's treasures, Elizabeth took note of the people surrounding them. Men and women strolled in together, often in costumes of foreign countries. None looked particularly menacing, although a fellow in the garb of a Venetian gondolier did meet her gaze and hold it for a moment too long. Then he had the audacity to wink.

Cheeky Italians. Elizabeth gave him a pointed look then returned her attention to examining her surroundings.

The ease with which she was allowed access to the property troubled her. Though protection officers would surround the sultana, it would be helpful to know there was some scrutiny of those allowed access to the grounds. This was especially important considering the sultana had recently replaced all of her protectors.

With access by street, rail, and river, there were multiple ways for guests to arrive. Just one more complication to consider.

Once she was out of sight of the Italian, she quickly split with the matrons to find a secluded spot in the shadows of the massive exhibition hall. Though the nearby guard's uniform bore no identifying information, she recorded his description in her notebook. She also took note of her surroundings and the meager number of persons strolling the grounds. Though she would never add this to her notes, Elizabeth also continued to look for the memorable Mr. Butler.

"Enough," she said under her breath. She closed her notebook and returned it to her pocket.

Things had changed since Elizabeth visited in December, although many of the exhibits had not yet been set up, and some of the buildings were still under construction. She would need to pay close attention to what had changed.

The docks were bustling with guests coming and going, and the number of vessels lined up was nearly impossible to count. A similar situation existed with the railcars that deposited fairgoers at the gates seemingly in an endless line.

Logistically, this fair was a dream to access and a nightmare to protect. Now that she'd seen it all in person, Elizabeth could be assured of knowing exactly what sort of eventualities to expect.

Though she set off to do her usual tour of the location before determining her plan of action to keep the sultana safe during her visit,

Elizabeth continued to look for Ethan Butler's face in the crowd.

Somewhere between the lush splendor of the gardens surrounding the main esplanade and the door to the massive greenhouse-like exhibition hall, she became aware of someone following her. And it wasn't Mr. Butler.

Taking the usual precautions, she made three quick turns, only to find that the slender dark-haired stranger dressed in the costume of a Venetian gondolier, presumably associated with the Italian exhibit, kept a distant but even pace behind her. She stopped and silently counted to three, then abruptly turned, intending to confront the man. Unfortunately, he was gone.

So was her ability to concentrate.

Until she settled the issue of sharing a roof with Ethan Butler, she would never be able to concentrate on her work. Retracing her steps, Elizabeth walked out of the exhibition toward St. Charles Street and the Centennial Hotel.

Her plan formed as she neared the hotel, and by the time she arrived, she was ready. Hitching the shawl up over her hair, she acted the part of a servant girl from the moment she stepped inside until she reached the stairs.

"You there," someone called.

Not Ethan Butler. She kept walking swiftly across the lobby until she reached the staircase.

"You there," he called again, and this time footsteps echoed behind her on the stairs until a man caught up to her. "For what purpose are you using the main staircase?"

Elizabeth spared him a sideways glance. "To gain access to the second floor," she said without breaking her stride. "Is that not the generally accepted purpose?"

"Oh Lady Caldwell," he said. "I'm terribly sorry. I thought. . ." He shook his head. "Never mind, do carry on."

She might have smiled at the knowledge her disguise had temporarily fooled the man, but she did not want to give him the idea she was pleased at being called out in such a rude manner.

Without offering a response, she continued up the stairs and then turned down the hall toward room 212. Retrieving her key, she inserted it into the lock, only to notice that once again the door to room 213 was ajar.

"Honestly," she said just loud enough for anyone inside the room to hear. "Leaving a door open in a hotel of this size is quite irresponsible. I ought to just let this stay as it is."

She wouldn't however. As a detective and a person sworn to uphold the law, Elizabeth couldn't let the situation remain as is. What if the room's current guest was elderly or infirm? Perhaps he or she was merely forgetful rather than irresponsible?

Letting out a long breath, she tucked her key back into her pocket and stepped over to stand in front of the door. Unlike the last time she found the door ajar, no one hurried to remedy the situation.

Elizabeth knocked lightly, causing the door to slide open another few inches and reveal a darkened room. "Hello? Is anyone there?"

No response. She sighed.

Though the room could very well be empty, she had a duty to make certain there wasn't a person inside who was in peril. Removing her hat pin from its hiding place, she slid the door open with her elbow and put one foot inside the room.

"Hello?" she repeated to the silent room.

Still no response.

Darkness enveloped her, causing Elizabeth to shudder. She shrugged off the feeling and forced herself to assess the situation with a Pinkerton's eye.

The chamber appeared to be a mirror image of her own with a small parlor area near the door containing a settee and at least one chair, possibly two. The shadow of a bed with four posts and mosquito netting could barely be seen against the closed curtains on the opposite wall.

If the rooms were indeed similar, Elizabeth ought to be able to walk straight ahead and reach the windows without any impediment. Once she opened the curtains, she could determine whether the room was empty or contained a person in need of assistance.

With one hand balanced against the wall and the other holding her stickpin just in case, Elizabeth slowly made her way toward the windows. One step became two and then three, and for the first time since checking in to the Centennial Hotel, she wished the rooms were not quite so expansive.

Footsteps rang out at the end of the corridor, and she paused to turn around and look in that direction. Apparently of its own accord, the door had swung back into its previous position, allowing only a sliver of light from the hall to spill into the room.

Elizabeth paused to listen to the footsteps, willing them to come close and claim this room as their own. Of course, she would then have to have an explanation as to why she was trespassing, but that was simply done.

The footsteps stopped. She waited another moment and then returned to her task.

One footstep and then another, Elizabeth shuffled slowly along, Her eyes temporarily blinded by looking at the narrow band of light spilling in from the hallway, she pressed her palm against the wall as she made her way forward.

Just a few more steps until she reached the windows, and then. . .she lurched. Her foot refused to move, but her head slammed forward. Sparks of agony shattered around her. Then silence.

Elizabeth groaned as she grasped for whatever she could reach to try and extricate her foot from its prison. Her fingers found something and tugged at it. Fabric unlike the shawl she was wearing slid over her vision, quickly followed by a crash that sounded very much like glass breaking.

Then came footsteps. Heavy, likely a man.

"Hello," Elizabeth said as she swatted at the fabric. "Who's there?"

The fabric slid away. Lamplight burned her eyes, and she blinked against the pain. When her vision cleared, she was staring at a Colt Navy pistol.

And Ethan Butler.

Her.

Ethan held his pistol steady even as his brain refused to do the same.

Nine months—give or take a few days—separated him from the last time his lips covered hers, and yet he recalled it as if it was yesterday.

This was the second time today he had returned to his room to find suspicious circumstances. He'd just had a discussion with Timothy Parsons, the Centennial's chief of security, who insisted on following him up to his room to investigate.

"Did you get him this time?" Parsons called from the door. "I'll go fetch a policeman unless you want me to stay here and assist."

Ethan's eyes remained on the flame-haired woman wrapped in a tablecloth with her foot caught under the rolled-up carpet and wearing a look that ought to have terrified him. "No need for a policeman, Parsons. I have the situation under control."

"You sure?" he said. "She looks awful mad."

She did, but his concern was less for her anger and more for her ability to charm him. If he had any sense, he'd have her shipped over to the police station and let them handle it.

Though their last encounter had been relatively brief, it had taught him one important lesson. He did not have good sense when it came to this woman.

Still, there was only one answer. "Yes, I'm sure."

"All right then. You're the one who says you already had a prowler in here. If she does it again, I can't be responsible."

"Fair enough."

Parsons lingered just a moment and then walked away, leaving Ethan alone with the beautiful trespasser. Several responses occurred to him, but he kept his mouth shut.

The woman he couldn't manage to forget shifted positions to tug at the tablecloth still draped over her shoulder. "Do you plan to continue aiming that pistol in my direction, or might you consider putting it away now?"

"I'm still deciding."

❧ Chapter 6 ❧

Not true," was Elizabeth's swift response. "If you meant to shoot me, you already would have."

She extricated herself from the white lace tablecloth that had most literally proven to be her downfall and then frowned at the mess she'd made of the hotel's lovely china. "I will, of course, have the cost to replace these added to my account."

The moment the words were out, Elizabeth longed to draw them back in. With that one statement she had given away the fact that she too was a guest at the Centennial. Keeping her expression neutral, she ignored Mr. Butler to continue her assessment of the situation.

Indeed the room was a mirror image of hers. The difference, as she had painfully discovered, was that while her luggage had been neatly put away, Mr. Butler's had been strewn about as if a tornado had taken flight in the room. Worse, he had elected to remove a perfectly lovely carpet from the sitting area and roll it up beside the table.

"Your housekeeper should be fired," she said as she struggled to free her foot from beneath the heavy carpet.

Mr. Butler put away the pistol, then bent down to easily move the carpet off her foot. His gaze scanned the length of her then returned to her face. He straightened up. "Are you hurt?"

"Only my pride," she said as she found her footing and allowed him to help her up. From this vantage point, the room looked as if it had been plundered. "Have you had a robbery?"

"It is possible that someone accessed my room earlier today." His eyes narrowed. "And right now I only have one suspect."

Elizabeth waited for him to offer more. Then she realized what he meant. "You're suggesting that I—? Oh, that's ridiculous."

"Then I suppose you've got a good reason for helping yourself to my hospitality." He paused. "Without me being in the room, that is."

"Of course I have a good reason for being in here. Your door was open."

"So you just decided to walk right in and wander around in the dark instead of closing the door?" He shook his head. "You're going to have to come up with a better story than that, lady."

Elizabeth leaned down to retrieve her scarf from the floor and gave him a direct look as indignation rose. "I was merely being a concerned citizen."

"Explain."

She folded the scarf over her arm. "I don't like your tone, sir."

Mr. Butler let out a long breath. "Explain, *please*."

"Earlier today I encountered the same scenario and assumed the occupant had forgotten to close the door completely. I reached for the knob to close the door, and the person inside closed it before I could. So this time—"

"Did you see who that was?" he interrupted.

"No." She paused. "As I was saying, when I came upon the open door again, I merely called to the occupant or occupants to alert them to the situation. When there was no response, I determined the situation worthy of investigation."

"You determined there was an empty room that you could enter."

"For the purposes of seeing whether the occupant had fallen or was too ill to answer when I called," she snapped. "The room was dark, so I went to the window to open the curtains. Since this room is the mirror image of. . ."

Elizabeth clamped her mouth shut. What was wrong with her? Five minutes in this man's presence and she had already made one mistake in giving away her status as a hotel guest and had almost told him even more.

She considered the possibility that he did not recognize her. That alternative was preferable to believing he had forgotten their kiss under the summer sun.

Either way, somehow in the few minutes since their reunion, a reunion Mr. Butler had yet to recognize, the man of her dreams had become the man of her irritations.

"In any case," she continued, "I was afraid the occupant was ill or injured or had fallen and was unable to respond. I had no idea I would be the one landing on the floor."

Silence fell between them. Perhaps Mr. Butler was considering her claim and would soon apologize. Perhaps he was thinking favorably of their last meeting.

Much as she might prefer the second option under other circumstances, the middle of an important assignment was no place to entertain such thoughts. Thoughts she was having right now.

Best to make a quick escape before either happened.

"So," Elizabeth said as she nodded toward the door, "if you'll excuse me, I'll just be on my way."

She took three steps toward the door before he stepped in front of her. He was taller than she recalled, his dimple deeper and his lashes thicker than she had described them in her journal. Oh, but the way he looked at her, the width of his shoulders and the arch of his brows as amusement showed on his face, these things were exactly as she remembered.

Elizabeth looked away. It was the only remedy for her dangerous thoughts. That and a quick exit. Although she could not return to her room just yet, she could escape the Centennial to find a room elsewhere. She could always send someone for her things later.

"I never knew your name."

She jolted at the statement and said the first thing that came to mind. "No, I do not believe I offered it."

"Are you offering it now?"

This time she braved a quick glance and then darted toward the open door. "No. Now if you'll excuse me, I have pressing business."

Ethan let her go even though he knew he would curse himself for a fool later. She was every bit as pretty as he remembered, and she could still persuade him to do things he shouldn't.

Like let her go even though he had caught her trampling all over a crime scene. Falling over it, to be correct.

His Pinkerton training told him that anyone could be a suspect until ruled out by the evidence.

Ethan surveyed the scene and frowned. He'd caught her here alone, obviously in the middle of something that required breaking the law to do, and this after just reporting a similar situation to hotel management. And he had let her go.

What was wrong with him?

Ethan extinguished the lamp and closed the door firmly behind him, then tested it to be certain the lock held. He caught up with the beautiful trespasser at the reception desk.

"Might I have a word with you in private?"

The desk clerk looked past her to lock eyes with him. "You again?" he sneered. "I suppose you're in need of Mr. Thorn or the security fellow."

"No." Ethan linked arms with the redhead. "Just his office."

He leaned close to her ear. "Come with me, please. It is important."

"Actually, I'm in the middle of something here."

"So am I," he said. "This won't take long."

"Truly." She turned back toward the clerk. "I do not have a minute to spare."

"Have it your way," he said. He turned his attention to the clerk. "Would you mind summoning Mr. Parsons? He's aware of the situation."

Harrison's eyes widened. "I will need more information before I do such a thing."

Ethan slid the woman a sideways look. "Do you want to tell him, or should I?"

"Truly, I don't know what you mean," she said, though he felt her stiffen as she said the words.

"Fine." He returned his attention to Harrison. "Trespassing to start with." Ethan offered her a broad smile. "Have you done anything else you'd like to admit to?"

"I don't understand," the clerk said. "Is this man a friend of yours, Lady Caldwell?"

Lady Caldwell?

Ethan froze. Surely the clerk was mistaken.

"He certainly is no friend of mine," she said.

"Lady Caldwell is correct," he said. "I am no friend of hers. However, I do have much to discuss with her. I'm sure Lady Caldwell will not mind holding that discussion here in the lobby." To punctuate his statement, Ethan returned his attention to the redhead. "Am I right?"

"Though I have absolutely nothing to hide, you are wrong. I do not wish to be party to a scene such as this could become. So, although I am most unhappy with the situation, I will concede to having the conversation in private."

"I thought you might." He led her away from the desk toward Mr. Thorn's office.

"Do you still want to summon Mr. Parsons?" the clerk called.

"Just have Parsons stand by for now," Ethan said as he paused to respond. "He can be called to escort Lady Caldwell to the police station if

I decide to press charges."

"Of all the nerve," said Lady Caldwell, or whoever she was. "I am the one who should lodge a complaint against Mr. Butler's boorish behavior."

Mr. Butler. So she did remember him.

Harrison's thick dark brows rose, and he shook his head. "What crime shall I tell him has been committed?"

"I'll let you know," they said in unison.

Ethan led her to the manager's office door and then stepped back to allow her to go in first. She swept regally past without sparing him so much as a glance and left him in her lavender-scented wake. Lady Caldwell then crossed the small room to throw open the drapes and take up residence behind the desk as if she owned the place.

If he were to depend on her facial expression alone—though a Pinkerton detective never did—he might guess she was bored with the whole thing. Her hands, however, told another story, for she worried with the trim on her sleeve and seemed unable to still her fingers.

Nerves. Yes, she had something to hide. And apparently she did have some skill at hiding things. What Lady Caldwell did not realize was he had plenty of experience in finding what was hiding.

His gut told him she was up to something. What that was, he hadn't decided yet.

He considered the possibility that everything she said and did in Chicago, from the tears in the pew to the please-help-me speech was all designed for one purpose. What that purpose was, he would soon determine, but if he were a betting man, he would put his money on the fact that their being in New Orleans at the same time was not a coincidence.

Pieces of a puzzle began to fit together. This woman had a known association to Senator Langford Fulton, whether through her father—if indeed that is who the older man was—or through some endeavor in which the three of them had partnered.

He could make a case for the argument that the trio had not chosen him at random at Mr. Pinkerton's funeral, but rather had specifically targeted him for some as yet unknown purpose. The female of the group could have been the one chosen to determine his ability to be distracted, a test he had failed miserably. While the senator's identity was certain, the third member of the group—the man he had assumed, and she had claimed, to be her father—was actually an unknown until solid proof could be given.

Could that man be the Dandy? The robberies had begun at approximately the same time, and though the vague descriptions of the thief did not match the stranger, witnesses often remembered wrong. So far his gut refused to weigh in with an answer, so Ethan would have to logic this out.

It took some work, but he pushed thoughts of how she felt in his arms aside to weigh the evidence before him. He gave the woman a sweeping glance, and another thought occurred. The witnesses who had seen the Dandy claimed he was slender and of average height. While he hadn't paid much attention to the stranger, he could say with absolute certainty that Lady Caldwell was both.

Now that was an intriguing thought indeed, especially given the events of this afternoon.

Ethan smiled as he stood between her and the exit. If this was a game, two could play.

❦ *Chapter 7* ❦

*E*lizabeth regarded her opponent with the calculated stare and the mind of a woman highly trained in all aspects of detective work. Her heart, however, refused to cooperate.

Always do a job well and without excuse.

Yes, of course. Focus was all that was required here.

She removed all traces of emotion from her face, but her mind jumped from question to question: Did he recall their encounter at all, or was she merely a kiss tossed away in a Chicago summer garden and forgotten? Had he wondered about her at all? Did he seek to find her and fail?

So many questions, all of them pointless at the moment. Elizabeth stilled her traitorous fingers and forced herself to smile.

The Texan stood in the doorway looking every bit like a man headed for a showdown with a band of outlaws. While he hadn't retrieved his pistol yet, he did look as if he might at any moment.

As she took note of all these things, her attention lingered on those lips. She looked away, momentarily ashamed that she had forgotten the most important rule of detective work: do not allow distractions to deter your investigation.

Oh, but this man was definitely a distraction.

"Let's get on with it, shall we?" She did her best to sound exactly like her grandmother might have in a similar situation. Not that Grandmother would ever find herself in such a situation.

"You go first," Mr. Butler said.

"Me?" She gave him a direct look. "My complaint is simple. I have business to which I need to attend, and yet here I am with you instead."

"That is a fair complaint. I have a similar one." He paused. "But first I must apologize for the way I had to speak to you in front of the clerk. I took extreme measures because I have important questions that only you can answer."

Extreme measures. Her heart lurched. "Your apology is accepted. Now shall we get on with those questions?"

"Yes." His pause was brief but meaningful. Though Mr. Butler intended to give the impression of a man in complete control, she noted the change in his expression. "As we say in Texas, this isn't our first rodeo, Lady Caldwell."

Elizabeth shifted positions behind the desk, her hands firmly remaining out of sight in her lap. It would not be good to show her hand now— both literally and figuratively.

"No, Mr. Butler," she admitted. "It is not. I had hoped you did not remember."

"I have yet to forget." He seemed to be studying her carefully, much as she had been studying him. "Out of all the people at Mr. Pinkerton's funeral, why did you choose me?"

What in the world? She bit back on her response to give the question the consideration it deserved. Mr. Butler was up to something, but she did not yet know what that was.

He closed the distance between them, leaving only the desk to separate them and forcing her to look up at him. "Allan Pinkerton's funeral was well attended. Why choose me?"

"*You* chose *me*, Mr. Butler." Refusing to be intimidated, Elizabeth leaned forward. "You spoke first when you offered your handkerchief, and you followed me outside. I did nothing to encourage either incident."

Her fingers itched to record every nuance of his expression. Whatever scenario Mr. Butler had worked out in his mind, it did not match with her reminder that he was the one to speak first.

"Please correct me if I am wrong," she added because she could not resist. "While I very much appreciate your willingness to offer assistance to me in my distress, any contact between us was initiated by you and you alone, Mr. Butler."

He knew she was right. The truth showed on his face. So, Elizabeth elected to make a bold move and catch him off guard. "You were my first kiss."

Mr. Butler's expression softened. At that moment, she knew she had him where she wanted him. Unfortunately, her mind refused to leave the memory of that kiss long enough to allow her to think clearly.

He sank onto the nearest chair and never looked away from her as he gripped its arms and let out a long breath. "Then I should at least know your real name, don't you think?"

Elizabeth sat back. She hadn't considered this response.

Before she could formulate a response, he continued. "Before you answer, I should tell you that I don't believe for a minute you are Lady Caldwell, and it has nothing to do with the fact that you are dressed as a washerwoman."

She frowned. Washerwoman was not the look she had been attempting, but she could hardly protest at this point. Rather, she stayed on topic and tried to keep the man talking.

In her experience, when a man was talking, he wasn't thinking. "And why not?"

"Because you're too free to give that name to anyone who asks. A person with something to hide usually starts with the name."

Elizabeth controlled her reaction as best she could. Apparently Mr. Butler was acquainted with the rules of Pinkerton detective work.

"Like signing a hotel register with an *X*?" she asked. "What is it you're hiding, Mr. Butler?"

"Or answering a question with a question," he commented easily.

Too easily.

"So it appears we are at an impasse," she said. "Maybe we should leave this line of questioning and move on. You mentioned there was another attempt at accessing your room today. Would you share what you know about that?"

He shook his head. "We are not at an impasse. You're evading the question, but for now I will allow it. Just know we will be revisiting it very soon."

She offered a smile. "If you wish, though my answer will likely be the same."

"Are you in the habit of kissing strangers?" he asked. "Because I am not."

So much for keeping the man talking. Elizabeth felt a flush climb into her cheeks and determined to change the subject. "What do you think the intruder was after?"

"Another question with a question. Diversionary tactics." He shifted positions to cross his arms over his chest. "I have no idea."

"And yet unless it was a case of mistaken identity, the intruder was after something. Would you like to talk through some scenarios?" At his surprised expression, she gathered her shawl closer and continued. "In my experience, it can be helpful."

"Lady Caldwell, do you happen to have Pinkerton detective training?"

Her eyes widened, and Ethan knew he had her. "I thought so. Would your name happen to be Lizzie?"

"Absolutely not," she snapped.

Ethan shook his head. "No, sorry. That is the name you were given by the agency for your current assignment. That was Lizzie Nellis, and you are. . .let me think. . .Elizabeth," he said triumphantly as the name occurred to him.

No response.

"Yes. That's it," he continued. "Elizabeth Newton, Pinkerton detective from Chicago. You are a family friend of Senator Langford Fulton and, according to my dossier, also of our current president."

Was that a flinch he saw? Brief as it was, if he had seen a reaction, the beauty was now back to an unreadable expression. The only solution was to continue.

"Your father, Wallace Newton, is a well-respected attorney who, it is rumored, was a close friend of Mr. Pinkerton and also the source of many rules of detective work that we all now follow. Congratulations, Miss Newton. You possess an impressive Christmas card list."

Miss Newton—and his gut told him this was indeed her—remained stoic. "Why would you say these things?"

"Because they're true." He shrugged and affected a neutral expression when what he really wanted to do was shout with relief that he'd finally completed this assignment and could move on to one that was much more important.

"Why would a Pinkerton agent come to me with these allegations?"

Of course she would deduce this. He'd said too much, but his pride at letting it slip would not allow him to so easily admit it. "Why would you think I am a Pinkerton agent?"

"Because it is true."

"It is," he said, "and I know this because my current assignment is to find you."

She rose abruptly and moved to one side of the desk. Her eyes looked past him, presumably to the door. "That is preposterous," she said in a dismissive tone.

Textbook Pinkerton behavior, he noted. *Never allow yourself to be blocked from an exit when the situation may not end well. Don't let your opponent know he has rattled you.*

Now that he thought of it, he had seen her do the very same thing upstairs when he allowed her to exit his room. He might applaud her technique if he hadn't been too busy trying to keep her from bolting.

"I know you're surprised to hear this, Miss Newton, but my reason for being here is simple. I have been assigned to deliver a piece of jewelry to you. I have no idea why or from whom, just that the captain pulled me from an important case to make this delivery."

Her expression softened even as her fingers curled around the ornately carved edge of the desk. "What kind of jewelry?"

"One of those pins like my grandmother wears." He paused to think of what it was called. "A cameo," he finally recalled. "Kind of a blue background color with the image of a face carved in white."

Face. Why did that word catch in his mind as something important? His gut told him to think. To recall where he had last seen that word. To understand why that meant something.

The face is next.

Ethan's thoughts jolted in a completely different direction. The Dandy. Could this bauble that was meant to be delivered to a Pinkerton detective have something to do with the jewel thief's next crime?

"The Victoria cameo."

It took a moment, but he returned his attention to Miss Newton. "Excuse me?"

She shrugged. "Many years ago Queen Victoria gave my ancestor a cameo that is as you described, a lovely blue with a white face on it. Since a cameo is always borrowed and never owned—or something like that— it is passed down to the next family member at a time determined by the current wearer."

"So the emergency that pulled me off an important case was because someone in your family decided it was time?"

She met his gaze and gave an almost imperceptible nod. "Yes, and that someone would be my cousin, Petra, unless there has been a transfer since I last spoke with her that I am unaware of."

That was possibly the craziest thing he'd heard all day.

"Well, all right then." He nodded toward the room where the safe was kept. "Let's get Cousin Petra's bauble out of the safe so I can consider this mission completed and I can catch the train back to Denver and do some actual Pinkerton work. And I can let you do the same," he added as he recalled her occupation as a fellow detective.

He stepped out into the hall and motioned toward the clerk, who appeared to be flirting with a dark-haired young lady who seemed to reciprocate his attention. Ethan waited for the man to see him and then gave up and called out, "Harrison, get me Mr. Thorn. I need my box from the safe."

Without sparing him a glance, Harrison shrugged. "I can let him know when he returns."

"And when would that be?"

The clerk looked at him, his expression less than pleasant. "Mr. Thorn does not keep me apprised of his schedule."

Ethan's attention went from the clerk to the pretty lady he'd been entertaining. "Interesting. I thought you might be important enough to be told."

The expression on the lady's face was almost as funny as the one on Harrison's. Ethan left the odious man scrambling to recover and stepped back into the manager's office.

"It looks like we're going to have to wait until the manager returns."

Elizabeth now leaned against the desk, her attention seemingly focused on something outside the window. He crossed the room until he could see what she appeared to be watching.

Across the street at the entrance to the fairgrounds, a group of tourists from Arabia were gathered. Most were chatting in an animated fashion, their colorful clothing a brilliant contrast to the gathering storm clouds in the sky above. In contrast to the others, however, one man did not join the group in the conversations.

It was this man that Miss Newton must be watching, or so he assumed. "What do you think he's doing?" Ethan moved as close as the desk between them would allow.

She spared him a brief glance. "My guess is he's security."

He would have guessed the same. "So why the interest?"

This time Miss Newton's attention remained on Ethan. "I'm sure as a fellow Pinkerton you understand there are things I cannot tell you."

"I do," he said.

"Then I cannot tell you." She gave one last look to the man across the street and then offered a polite smile. "If you'll excuse me, I've got things to do. I very much appreciate you coming all this way to deliver the cameo. Perhaps you could just leave it in the safe, and I will retrieve it when I am able."

She stepped into a streak of sunlight, and his breath caught. Miss Newton was every bit as beautiful as he recalled, even more. And then she moved past him, leaving the scent of lavender in the air and an empty room.

❧ Chapter 8 ❧

*E*than let Miss Newton go, secure in the knowledge he could follow her if he wished. When she ascended the stairs to disappear inside her room, he did the same.

This time there were no surprises awaiting him, no unlocked door or closed curtains. He stepped over the rolled-up carpet and went to look out the window. The colorful group had moved on, all traces of them replaced by the usual drab-looking dark-suited businessmen and a few smaller groups of ladies in their daytime finery.

He turned his back to the window and thought of the woman on the other side of the wall. Even dressed as a washerwoman she was much more beautiful than any well-dressed female he had ever encountered.

What was it about the feisty redhead? A few minutes in a garden with her had marked Elizabeth Newton in his heart and seared her into his mind.

Irritated with himself, Ethan snatched up his notes on the jewelry thief case and tried to make sense of what he saw on the page. If there was a link between the Dandy's last warning and the cameo Ethan had been sent to deliver, he could not find it.

"Look again," he muttered under his breath. "There are no coincidences." His mind was elsewhere, unfortunately, and after he realized the document he had been holding for the past five minutes was upside down, he gave up.

If he couldn't do detective work, maybe he could at least make himself useful in something that required only his muscles. Since the hour was late and the porters had yet to come and collect the carpet they'd ruined and then rolled up in his room, Ethan decided he would take the carpet to them.

Hoisting the heavy roll onto his shoulder, he stepped out into the hallway. Rather than take the main stairs down to the lobby, he headed in the opposite direction to descend the narrower stairway meant for the employees.

Halfway down, the staircase turned, and he nearly collided with the man he'd seen watching from across the street.

In the moment that it took for Ethan to react, the other man merely stood very still. "Who are you and what do you want?" Ethan demanded as he thought of the attention Miss Newton had given to this man when he'd been standing across the street.

The stranger stood still for a split second, and then he winked. A moment later, he fled down the staircase. Casting off the weight of the rug, Ethan gave chase, but the man was too quick for him.

By the time Ethan reached the bottom of the stairs, the hallway was empty. He went from room to room, first looking in the supply closet and then the laundry and finally the kitchen, but found only hotel employees everywhere he searched.

Footsteps on the stairs alerted him to someone approaching. He went to investigate and found a porter inspecting the rolled-up carpet Ethan had dropped.

"From room 213," he told the porter. "Got interrupted bringing it down. I'd appreciate it if you'd finish the job for me while I attend to other business."

He left the porter shaking his head and emerged into the busy hotel lobby. Harrison no longer stood behind the counter, and the dark-haired young lady was also gone. Outside the skies had turned from gray to a deep purple, the indication of a balmy New Orleans night ahead.

He thought of checking to see if the manager had returned, but a flash of green on the staircase caught his attention. Ethan turned to see Miss Newton making her way downstairs. Gone was the milkmaid attire, and in its place was a dress that would look more at home in a ballroom than a hotel lobby.

Before she could spot him, Ethan stepped behind a massive potted palm tree. By the time he left his hiding place, she was leaving through the front doors. He caught up with her just in time to escort her across the street.

She fixed him with a look that ought to have stopped him in his tracks. Instead, he merely offered his broadest smile.

"Where are we going on this fine evening, Miss Newton?"

Elizabeth should have been surprised, but she was not. The idea that the man on the other side of the wall might be monitoring her comings and goings, especially now, was to be expected. In fact, his arrival at her side might actually be a case of excellent timing.

A woman alone was always considered more of an oddity than a woman in the company of a man, especially at the sort of event to which she had been invited this evening.

"Did you bring me the cameo?" she asked.

"I have not yet seen the Centennial's manager, so no, I did not."

"All right. Then we are attending a reception," she said. "I had hoped you might be dressed in something more proper, but we do not have enough time to allow you to change your suit."

Oh, but his smile was dazzling. "You know, it's the strangest thing. When I packed for this assignment, I wasn't informed of the need for formal wear. Unfortunately, this is the best I've got."

Elizabeth pretended to be disappointed when, in fact, she was certain the man would look absolutely wonderful in whatever he wore. "Then we will have to make the best of it," she said, affecting a shrug. "I suppose I should tell you what we're doing this evening."

"Yes, please," he said as they fell in step with the crowd of late arrivals heading toward the fairgrounds. "But first I would like to know why you've had this change of heart. Less than an hour ago you didn't want to tell me anything, and now you're going to allow me to be part of the fun?"

"Fun?" She gave him a sideways glance as he guided her around a puddle. "Hardly. I am working here. You are merely along as my companion. If you wish, that is."

Their gazes collided. "I do," he said. "And I don't mind that you're not telling me the real reason you're attending this party. However, I do need to be briefed on any possible security threats."

Elizabeth hesitated. Up ahead a bell clanged.

"Professional courtesy," Mr. Butler added. "I would do the same if the roles were reversed. One Pinkerton detective does not allow another to go into a situation without discussing the dangers. Just the basics will be fine."

The truth, and she knew it. "All right," she said. "The basics it is. How much do you know about the exposition?"

He glanced around and then returned his attention to Elizabeth. "That it is big, crowded, and, I would guess, a security nightmare with multiple street entrances that appear to be loosely guarded at best."

"Correct, all of this," she said. "But there is also a train that deposits guests inside as well as more entrances along the river."

"Dockside entrances?"

She nodded. "Anyone with a vessel worthy of traversing the river can slip into the exhibition without having to leave the dock."

"Interesting."

Not the word she had used when she first learned of this wrinkle in her plan for the sultana's safety. "The event planners had hoped making access to the exhibition would encourage more people to attend. No one considered the fact that once all of the entrances were open, there was absolutely no control of who entered and exited."

"I don't suppose they figured they would need to worry about that," Mr. Butler offered as they bypassed the last of the St. Charles Street gates and kept walking. "So where exactly is tonight's event being held?"

She pointed toward the river up ahead. "The first part of the evening is a reception and early supper aboard a steamboat on the river, and then a ball will follow in the Palm Court of the Horticultural Hall."

"And to whom do we owe the honor of this invitation?"

It was a good question, and she was not completely sure of the answer. Her invitation, slipped under her door while she was away today, seemed legitimate, although the fact she'd had almost no time to prepare for the event was a bit unsettling.

"Senator Fulton," she told him. "It is a reception to honor those involved in the Illinois exhibit."

Mr. Butler stopped short. "How did he know you were here?"

"He is a senator. I'm sure he has his ways."

"All right. Well my dossier said you were here as Lizzie Nellis." He shook his head. "Why the change of name? Do you have something to hide?"

Only the fact that the name Lizzie brings back awful memories. "It was a choice that seemed wise given my assignment. And speaking of my assignment, how much do you know?"

"Nothing beyond your name and the history I gave you. My job was to find you and then get back to work in Denver."

"I see."

They continued walking in silence until the river loomed ahead. Finally, Mr. Butler leaned toward her. "Tell me about this cameo that is so important to your family."

"The Victoria cameo," she said with a wistful smile. "It all began with my great-aunt." She told him the story of Great-Aunt Letitia's encounter with Queen Victoria and how the cameo had come to be passed down to subsequent generations. "And so when the current wearer believes it is time to pass it on, she sees that it goes to the next recipient."

"And there's no rhyme or reason as to who that will be or when it should happen?"

"Nothing logical," she said. "It is more of a feeling that it is time and a knowledge of where it should go next."

"So your cousin just got the feeling and the knowledge, and here we are?"

"I suppose you could say that," she said. "Although hiring you to find me while I was on an assignment does seem a little bit much." She paused. "And somewhat strange."

"How so?"

"My family has no idea that I am a Pinkerton detective."

❧ Chapter 9 ❧

*N*othing about this situation seemed right. Between the agent in disguise agreeing to attend a party where she was known, to an explanation of handing down a queen's pin, it all defied logic. Attending this party, however, had the added distinction of also defying good sense and more than one rule of Pinkerton detective work.

And now this.

Ethan slid her another look. "Even your father?"

She sighed. "Especially not my father, although I hope that if he someday finds out, he will at least be pleased that I was a good enough detective to hide this from him."

He chuckled. "More likely he will wonder how his detective skills got so rusty."

"Hey," she said in a good-natured tone. "Are you accusing me of not being good at what I do?"

"I would never do that, ma'am," he said in his thickest Texas accent and then added a grin. Sobering, he continued. "I'm curious why you're keeping this a secret from them."

"Because I'm a grown woman and free to make my own decisions, which should include not concerning myself with my parents' opinions?" she asked.

"Well," he said slowly, "I was thinking that, but I would not have asked. Now that you have, I'll agree. You're a grown woman and free to make your own decisions, so why are you hiding this?"

"Since you know who my father is, you can probably guess part of the answer. I was not raised to be a Pinkerton detective, because that is my father's legacy, not mine. And if you were to meet my mother and, more so, my maternal grandmother, the real Lady Caldwell, you would know that they all expected I would turn out to paint pretty pictures on teacups and practice the fine art of managing my society engagements while my very wealthy husband attends to business matters and provides me with a suitably large home and staff. However, none of them asked me if that was what I wanted."

"Is it?"

She paused. "Someday, perhaps. What about you?"

"Me?" He shook his head. "I never much cared for painting pretty pictures on teacups. I kept breaking the saucers."

He made her laugh, and that was enough for Ethan to join her.

"It's different for men," she continued. "I'm sure your father did not object to your following him into his line of work if you chose to do so."

He thought of the last time he'd seen Patrick Butler. It was just a few weeks before his parole hearing when his father, now a reformed man, begged just one thing of Ethan. Father's parole was denied, as was his brother's, likely because half the parole board had been victims of their scams. The next day Ethan did as his father requested and took steps to become a good man, a man who could look himself in the mirror and be proud of what he did. He joined the Pinkertons.

"Then you would be wrong, Miss Newton."

She looked as if she was waiting for him to laugh or to give some indication that he was joking. When he did neither, her expression fell. "Oh. I see."

"He's quite proud of me," Ethan said, returning his attention to the crowd around them. "I would wager a guess that if you gave your father the chance, he would be proud of you too. Now, Lady Caldwell, I've met her, and she's quite difficult."

This time he did grin, and she followed suit. "Do not judge me by my disguises, Mr. Butler. I can be quite congenial when given the chance."

"Then I do hope I am around when you are given the chance," he said.

"You were," she said with a sly smile. "In a garden. I believe it was July."

"The sun was out, and I had forgotten that Chicago in July could be almost as hot as Houston." Ethan returned the smile. "But I never forgot you."

She looked past him. "Nor I you, Mr. Butler."

"Ethan." He linked arms with her.

"Ethan," she repeated softly. "Only if you'll call me Elizabeth."

"As often as I am allowed, and I would like it to be frequently," he said, knowing the statement was probably more than she expected from him. For it was more than he'd expected to admit.

They continued to walk together toward the river, but it took all he had not to stop right there and kiss her again. Instead, he allowed the fact that they were here together through the strangest of coincidences—though he did not believe in coincidences—and had a night of dinner and dancing ahead to be enough.

She paused her steps, taking Ethan by surprise. "I would like that very much," she said. "But you should know how very unlike me this is."

"I was about to say the same," he said as he lifted her hand to his lips.

Her smile was an invitation to speak more, but the crowd milling around them gave him pause. Even as he allowed his growing feelings for Elizabeth to flood his heart, Ethan kept watch. Few gave them much notice, but that held no consequence. Any operative with decent training could shadow a man without being noticed.

And right now, when he would rather give Elizabeth Newton all of his attention, Ethan knew the danger level would increase unless he got his mind back on his surroundings.

His gut told him they were fine, at least for now. Still, his Pinkerton training refused to allow him to relax his guard, even as they were escorted aboard the brightly lit riverboat a few minutes later.

The senator waited at the end of the gangplank, a welcoming committee of one, but flanked by at least a dozen men who looked capable of causing harm to anyone who looked at the senator the wrong way.

The senator's delight at seeing Miss Newton was echoed in the embrace he offered. "Elizabeth," he said joyfully, "how wonderful to see you here."

"I am very happy to accept the offer of your hospitality."

"As I am happy to offer it." He shifted his attention to Ethan. "And who is your companion?"

Without waiting for Miss Newton to answer for him, Ethan squared his shoulders and stuck out his hand to the senator. "Ethan Butler, Senator Fulton. Very pleased to meet you."

"As am I." The senator released his grip and returned his attention to Miss Newton. "Please, enjoy yourselves this evening."

Elizabeth swept past, and he followed in her wake, all the while feeling the eyes of the silver-haired legislator on him. All through the meal, which featured multiple courses representing many of the countries in attendance at the exhibition and at the dinner, Ethan continued to feel the older man's scrutiny.

That did not bother him, but the search for faces that might belong to the man he chased in the stairwell occupied him as well as any other potential threats and kept him from enjoying the lovely lady seated beside him.

Finally, the group was ushered toward the Horticultural Hall. There a jazz band, orchestra, and dance floor awaited along with electric lights for illumination and a fountain that filled the center of the room.

Senator Fulton and his guests were joined by New Orleans dignitaries and businessmen and their heavily bejeweled wives. The illustrious locals gathered at the entrance and formed a receiving line as the senator's party entered the hall. Near the head of the line was Hannibal J. Thorn III.

When he spied Ethan, Thorn's eyes widened, and he practically leaped toward him. "I have men out looking for you," he announced. "We must speak now. It is of the highest importance." He paused to glance around, then returned his attention to Ethan. "Regarding your box in the hotel safe."

"Then this will also concern my companion." Ethan glanced at Elizabeth. "Lady Caldwell, a moment of your time, please?"

Elizabeth gladly left her place in line to join Ethan and the hotel manager. Just walking beside the handsome Texan put a lift in her step, though she knew she must dampen her enthusiasm until her assignment in New Orleans was complete.

As much as she might enjoy the company of this man, she could not forget that the safety of the sultana rested on how well Elizabeth did her job. Thus, as she followed the men to a secluded corner of the hall, she took mental notes of the building that would eventually be transferred to her journal.

The more information she had, the better she could plan the events surrounding the sultana's arrival. Oddly, she still had not received an actual date for her arrival. Just one more thing to add to her notes tonight when she returned to her room.

Ethan glanced back to see that she was still close behind, and she offered a smile. Just like that, concerns of her assignment fled, only to return a moment later along with a warning.

This man was a distraction.

And yet she had never failed to control the distractions around her on previous assignments. Surely this one would be the same.

Then she realized that both Ethan and the manager were staring at her as if waiting for her to react. "I'm sorry. What did I miss?"

"I'm so very sorry," Mr. Thorn said as he wrung his hands and lifted his eyes to the electric lights overhead, and presumably the heavens above. "There you are!"

Elizabeth turned at the sound of a familiar voice. Too familiar.

"Papa?" She shook her head. "What are you doing here?"

And how did you know I was in New Orleans? went unspoken.

Her father grinned as he moved toward her through the lush greenery surrounding them. "Can't a father surprise his daughter?" he said before enveloping her in an embrace.

Looking over Papa's shoulder, she spied Ethan watching closely. When the embrace ended, her father turned her around to walk with her back toward the entrance to the hall.

"Where are you taking me?" Elizabeth craned her neck to look around. "Is Mama here?"

"No, of course not," he said with a dismissive wave. "She and your grandmother are too busy preparing for their trip to Europe next month to travel all this way. I fail to understand how women can spend two months planning and packing for a journey that involves buying clothing to send back home. It does baffle me. Just get a good local tailor and be done with it, I say."

Relief flooded Elizabeth along with a healthy dose of amusement. Papa had not been born with the wealth he now enjoyed, so there were still remnants of his prior frugal life, clothing chief among them. Tonight he'd worn the same serviceable suit Mama had purchased for him some ten years ago. She knew it was ten years by the number of anniversary parties to which he had worn it.

"I've not yet spoken to the senator, so I thought it prudent to arrive in front of him with my second favorite date—your mother, of course, being my first." Papa grinned down at her. "I am terribly sorry I missed dinner, but I understand it was delicious."

"Papa," she said, stopping short. "How did you know I would be here?"

"Len told me."

She looked past her father to where the senator stood watching. "All right then. How did Senator Fulton know?"

Her father opened his mouth to speak and then closed it again. Finally, he shrugged. "You would have to ask him."

"And yet you were planning this visit all along?" Elizabeth shook her head. "A trip from Philadelphia takes time. And planning. What are you two up to? Have you been having me followed?"

"Bette, my baby girl," he told her, invoking the childhood name he rarely used. "I adore you. Len is like an uncle to you. Why would you believe such a thing?"

She frowned. "Because it is true. Admit it."

Papa smiled that smile that made his eyes crinkle at the corners. "I admit nothing. Now let's go find your uncle Len and see what sort of a welcome I get from him. I certainly hope he doesn't intend to quiz me on why I am here like my precious daughter has."

"I doubt you've had him trailed, so I would expect a rather warm greeting." She paused, her irritation gathering. "Why did you not expect I would guess I was being followed? While you're answering questions, I have one more. Did you not think I would figure this out eventually, given the fact that I am a—"

Good sense finally caught up with her words. Elizabeth snapped her lips together.

✺ Chapter 10 ✺

A Pinkerton detective?" Papa's gaze searched Elizabeth's face. "Did you not think I would figure this out eventually?

"A fair question," she mumbled under his intense scrutiny.

"For both of us," he admitted. "And even though I am the one with the background in detective work, I have to confess it was the combined team of your mother and grandmother who first proposed the idea."

"That I was a Pinkerton detective, or that you should deliver the news that the family knows?"

He appeared sheepish, a rare expression for Wallace Newton. "Perhaps both."

"Consider the news delivered then," she said. "I shouldn't admit this, but I am in the middle of an assignment, so I hope you will understand if I ask you to excuse me so that I may continue my work."

"About that assignment," he said as he looked away.

"Yes?" A feeling of dread came over her. Surely her father hadn't gone poking his nose so far into her affairs that he had actually inserted himself into her investigation. "Papa," she said slowly, "what kind of terrible thing have you done?"

"Done?" He shrugged. "I don't know what you mean. I haven't actually done anything terrible. I merely. . ."

Favoritism. Of course. Just when she thought she had earned her place at the Pinkerton Agency, the truth was exposed.

"I see," she said when his words trailed away. "You created a fake assignment and hired me to complete it. There is no sultana, is there?"

"Elizabeth, please. Of course there is a sultana, and she is a wonderful woman and a dear friend of your grandmother, so this is no fake assignment. She also plans to make a substantial donation to the Smithsonian Institute in the name of her family as a measure of her gratitude for our country's friendship with hers. The donation will be presented at the closing ceremonies.

"So at least that much is true," she said. "What else is fact, and what is fiction?"

"The fact is, she is very concerned with her safety when she visits the exhibition, especially now that there has been unrest in her country and most of the palace insiders have been banished for treasonous behavior. She is most grateful that you have seen to the necessary precautions." He paused to smile. "I assured her the Pinkerton Agency had put their best man—or rather, woman—on the job. I sent a telegram to your captain this morning to let him know you have discharged your duties in an admirable fashion. He responded with thanks on behalf of the sultan that he had only just received."

She looked up into her father's eyes, now swimming with tears just as hers were. "Thank you, Papa," she said slowly. "I hope you'll forgive me for keeping this from you."

"I am so very proud of you." He shrugged. "There's nothing to forgive. However, I do hope that you will forgive us old meddlers for working out a rather complicated way of letting you know it is fine by your family that you've chosen to become a Pinkerton detective. More than fine."

"Even Grandmother Caldwell?"

"Especially your grandmother. In fact," he said as he leaned conspiratorially toward her, "Lady Caldwell admitted to me that she once toyed with the idea of doing some sleuthing of her own as a girl of your age. She's quite pleased that you actually did it, although you absolutely cannot tell this to your mother."

Relief flooded her. Elizabeth chuckled as she swiped at her tears with the back of her hand. "You could have just told me you were fine with all of this, you know."

Uncle Len stepped up behind Papa. "Where would the fun be in that?" He glanced at Papa. "Has she forgiven us yet?"

"Mostly," he said as he gave his friend what Elizabeth swore was a warning look.

Her chuckle became laughter. "Are you two hiding something else?"

The senator frowned. "Wallace, is that the fellow over there?"

She turned to follow the direction of the older men's gazes and saw Ethan waiting at the edge of the fountains. He gave her a curt nod but made no move to walk toward them.

"How about we table this conversation, Senator?" Papa said to his best friend. "It looks like these two young people have some business to discuss." He nodded toward Ethan. "Go speak with the detective."

Elizabeth lifted one brow. "What makes you think he is a detective, Papa?"

Her father's expression quickly went neutral. Before he could speak, Senator Fulton clasped his hand on Papa's shoulder.

"If you'll excuse us, Elizabeth, I need to borrow your father for a few minutes." The senator nodded in the opposite direction from where Ethan stood. "I've got a constituent I'd like you to meet. He's looking for advice on a legal issue he's got with making a donation of items in his exhibit, and you're just the man to give it to him." He returned his attention to Elizabeth. "Enjoy your evening, my dear."

She watched the two old friends walk away secure in the knowledge that their plotting extended well beyond whatever her father might have just confessed. Finally, she turned toward Ethan, who seemed to be studying the fountain and its splashing water intently.

"You look upset," she told him when she reached his side.

He glanced down at her, his fingers clutching the brass rail. For a moment, he appeared to be choosing his words. Then he shook his head almost imperceptibly.

"The cameo has been stolen."

"Oh no," she managed as the breath went out of her. "Are you certain?"

"Hannibal J. Thorn III of the Centennial Hotel is," he snapped, and then he shook his head. "Sorry. Look, I need to go back to the hotel and see what I can do about finding this thing. You stay here and enjoy the party, and I will let you know what I find."

"*This thing* is a family heirloom," she said, "so if you're going, I am going with you."

"It's my case, Elizabeth," he said as his eyes narrowed, "and it is my fault that it's gone."

"No, Ethan," she said firmly. "It is the hotel's fault that the cameo is gone. As to this being your case, that is just too bad. There are two Pinkerton detectives on the assignment now."

"You've got your own assignment," he said. "How can you do both?"

"Apparently my assignment is mostly over." She linked arms with him and allowed him to lead her toward the exit. "And no, I will not explain that answer right now. We have bigger things to concern ourselves with. Do you have any idea what else was taken?"

"Just the cameo," Ethan said through his clenched teeth as he scanned the crowd on their way out the door. "And just as promised."

"You know who did this."

A statement, not a question. This woman was good at reading faces, a bit of information he'd be wise to remember in the future.

"Yes, I am fairly certain I do," he said.

He paused to look down at her. Even in the harsh glare of the electric lights, the sight of the redhead caught his breath. Words failed him.

"What?" she asked. "Do you see your suspect?"

No. My future. He shook off the thought. "It is possible that the perpetrator in the theft case I was working before I was ordered to play errand boy has found me here in New Orleans. In light of the fact that you're now personally involved, I would like to interview you to see if anything you know matches up with previous victims. Now, however, is not the time."

"Agreed." She paused. "And as a Pinkerton detective, I would like to see your notes from the other thefts in case I might provide some insight."

"I don't generally share my case notes with anyone other than my captain," he told her.

"And I do not generally find myself a victim of jewelry theft, but here we are. As we are under the same employ, I cannot imagine what the problem would be in making that information available to a fellow Pinkerton detective, but please do consult with your captain first."

"I plan to," he said as he tried to contain a smile.

It was easy to see how a woman this pretty had managed to convince Allan Pinkerton to hire her. Her combination of beauty and brains was disarming.

"I would wish to do the same if the roles were reversed," she continued. "In the meantime, I would very much like to speak to Mr. Thorn." She turned to search the crowd. "Where is he?"

"Right where we left him in the receiving line," Ethan said, recalling the heated conversation he and Mr. Thorn had just had. "I insisted on taking him back to the hotel to investigate and examine the safe myself, but he refused."

She returned her attention to Ethan. "He has no right to refuse. A crime has been committed, and he is blocking the investigation."

"I said something to that effect and added that he ought to be brought down to the police station for questioning."

"What happened?"

"The chief of police was standing next to him in the receiving line and did not agree."

Elizabeth looked away as if considering the statement. "I see. So they're either in on it together or. . ."

The lady Pinkerton went still, her expression unreadable as her fingers drummed against the brass rail that surrounded this portion of the hall.

"Or what?" he offered.

"I know you think you know who took that cameo, but I'm not sure you and I are on the trail of the same person." She shook her head and set off in the direction of the entrance to the hall. "Or persons," followed in her wake as Ethan hurried to catch up.

Ethan followed her through the crowd, dodging ladies in tiaras and gentlemen arguing politics, until she returned to the receiving line. Though he expected her to take the hotel manager—or possibly the police chief—to task, instead she bypassed both of them and went directly to the event's host.

Though the senator seemed pleased to see his friend's daughter, she did not seem pleased with the senator. "A word, please," she said, her tone polite but threaded with steel. "And with Papa as well, if you might be so kind as to locate him."

"Of course," he said. He made his apologies to a pair of delegates from Brazil. "I think he is still meeting with my associate, but I will go and check. Why don't you meet us over by the fountain?" His gaze landed on Ethan. "Will you be joining us, Mr. Butler?"

"I will."

The Senator's grin was unexpected. "This may take awhile, so please enjoy yourselves." As if on cue, the orchestra began to play. "Go on. Dance with her, Mr. Butler." And then to Elizabeth, he said, "I look forward to our conversation."

Before Ethan could respond, the politician was gone.

"You shouldn't," he heard her say under her breath after the senator had gone.

"Shouldn't dance with you?"

"What?" Elizabeth looked up at Ethan. "No. Actually, I think the dance floor is a very good place for you to tell me all of the facts you know in regard to my stolen cameo. I will want to record them in my journal, but that might draw unwanted attention."

He chuckled as he led her toward the sound of the music. "On the dance floor, yes it might. And for the record, usually when I ask a lady to dance, she just accepts without explanation."

Elizabeth grinned. "Well then, Ethan. I accept without explanation."

He whirled her into his arms and held her close as the music rose around them. "Too late, Elizabeth. You've already explained, but I'll dance with you anyway."

"You know this is a serious situation," she told him as she allowed him to lead her across the dance floor. "The cameo is a family heirloom. It cannot be replaced."

She felt so good in his arms. So right. In that moment, he knew he would do anything for Elizabeth Newton.

"It will be found," he told her. "What is it you think your father and the senator know about the theft?"

She shook her head. "It's a hunch, so I'd rather not waste time talking about it until I know for certain. You've said you think you know who the thief is. Tell me what you can without asking permission from your captain." Elizabeth paused. "Unless you've decided I did this, in which case, I would like to know how you reached that deduction."

Ethan stopped short, and the dancers nearby had to dodge to get around them. "How did you know I suspected you?"

"I know things," she said as she gently guided him back into dancing. "It's hard to explain except that I just follow the trail of logic. My logic tells me you've suspected me of something nefarious ever since you found me in your hotel room." He opened his mouth to respond, but she shook her head. "Not that I blame you," she added.

"Yes, there was a time when I thought you were up to something, and possibly your father and the senator too."

Her brows lifted. "All three of us? Interesting."

"It started with you. I rarely find innocent people trespassing in hotel rooms—or anywhere else for that matter."

"Agreed," she said sweetly. "What changed your mind about me?"

"I know things too," he admitted. "It didn't take long for me to know you were telling the truth."

"Which, by default, then, let my father and the senator off the hook."

"Yes," he said as they danced beneath the glass ceiling.

"I wouldn't count them out so quickly," she told him.

Once again, he almost stopped but caught himself. "Why?"

"The short version of a rather long and complicated story is that I am here in New Orleans thanks to the two of them and their meddling. Now that I know about the cameo, I suspect you are as well. What I don't know is whether they also planned this theft, which I suppose wouldn't actually be a theft if my father has it in his possession."

"Not true," Ethan said. "My instructions were to see that the cameo was delivered to you and no one else. I think your theory is wrong. Someone else has the cameo."

"Since you cannot tell me more than that without permission, for the sake of argument, if my father has the cameo in his possession, is he in big trouble?" she said with a grin.

"For the sake of argument, yes."

"Now that is interesting, especially when his best friend, who is facing an election year, might be involved."

"Don't get too excited about all that," he said. "My theory doesn't involve either of them."

"Then I look forward to hearing your theory when you're able to tell me about it. Just one question: Is the person here tonight? Your suspect, that is."

"It's possible, and that's all I can say." He paused. "Now about that dancing."

"We have been," she said, obviously confused.

He gathered her closer. "We have been detectives discussing a

Pinkerton matter, Elizabeth. Now it's time to forget about our jobs and just dance. May I improvise, or do you prefer to take the lead?" He held his breath, wondering whether she would remember the conversation that led to the most memorable kiss, or rather kisses, of his life.

"Please do take the lead," she said against his ear in a voice just above a whisper.

"I must warn you that my plan might involve giving the impression of a familiarity we do not yet have," he said just as he had back in the garden in Chicago. "I will hold you to a promise that you will inform me at once should I owe you an apology."

"I shall at once," she echoed as she rested her head on his shoulder.

"See that you do," he whispered against the lavender scent of her hair.

And though he wanted a kiss, he settled for a dance. And then another.

❧ *Chapter 11* ❧

Elizabeth could have danced all night. Such was the danger of spending even a few minutes in Ethan Butler's arms. Leaning against his shoulder, she felt drowsy with the comfort of his arms and yet oddly aware of every move, every sound around her.

Finally, the song ended, and he paused to hold her against him. "Elizabeth, I know this is poor timing, but if I don't tell you this right now, I may not have the chance for a while."

She forced herself to stand still when she desperately wanted to stop talking and return to dancing once more. "All right."

"I told you I know things, and this I know: I lost you once, and I don't want to lose you again." The music started again, but Ethan remained in place as the other dancers fell into step.

"I know things too, remember?" she managed as she determined she would not ruin the moment with tears.

"And?"

Elizabeth reached to cup her hand on his jaw and felt it tense beneath her fingers. "What kind of Pinkerton detectives would we be if we couldn't find each other?"

"That is an excellent point." He pulled her back into his arms and danced with her until the music finally stopped and the orchestra temporarily tucked away their instruments.

Papa and the senator had been watching for a while now. A part of her was furious at the both of them, of course, for their meddling was unconscionable. It was also very sweet, and Papa had been quite understanding regarding her hidden career as a Pinkerton detective, so she couldn't possibly stay mad at them for long.

How long she would let the pair squirm before she told them this, was another subject entirely.

Elizabeth's gaze scanned the room, taking note of every face to determine whether a potential suspect might be there. Ethan's admission that he, indeed, might be watching hadn't bothered her until this moment.

One more danger of spending time in the handsome Pinkerton detective's arms.

She shook off the thought and made her way to the private alcove where Papa and the senator were waiting. Before she could say anything, Ethan stepped in front of her.

"I have questions," he told them. "Is there a place where we can speak privately? It would also be helpful if Mr. Thorn, the police chief, and whoever else is in on this theft were to be present."

Senator Fulton's face went slack, and then he shook his head. "I will not be spoken to like this," he sputtered. "Do you know who I am?"

"I do, sir, and with all due respect and with your position in the Senate aside, right now you are a suspect in the theft of a cameo that was to be delivered as part of a Pinkerton detective's assignment."

"An assignment her father and I concocted so as to right a wrong committed by two stubborn. . ." His words trailed away as Papa placed his hand on his best friend's shoulder.

"I hadn't mentioned that part," her father said.

"Oh."

Papa stepped forward to give Ethan his full attention. "Detective Butler, may I speak with you in private?"

Ethan glanced down at her and then back at Papa. "No, sir. Anything you want to say to me can be said in front of my fellow Pinkerton detective, Miss Newton."

Her heart swelled. No one said no to Wallace Newton, and yet Ethan Butler just had. And he'd tamed the senator too.

"Fair enough," Papa said. "The chief has nothing to do with this, so leave him out of it. Thorn will produce the cameo. I just have to say the word."

"Papa!" Elizabeth said before she could stop herself. "It is one thing to create some sort of investigation where there is none and quite another to falsely report a crime. You know this."

Her father turned his attention to her. "I do, and I did no such thing. Butler's the only one who was told."

"And why was that, sir?" Ethan asked.

"Because your captain told me you were to return to Denver as soon as the delivery was made."

"I don't understand," Elizabeth said. "What's wrong with him going back to headquarters?"

"Oh for goodness' sake, Wallace," Senator Fulton said. "Just tell them. These two are so slow to catch on that I cannot believe they're both Pinkerton agents."

"Elizabeth," Papa said to her. "It had to be abundantly obvious to anyone who saw you in the garden in Chicago that you and this fellow were meant for each other. I decided when you didn't do anything about finding him that I would."

"Papa!" she managed, though her heart raced and the words she wanted to say lodged in her throat. "And to think I was under the impression you planned all of this as a way to show confidence in me as a Pinkerton detective."

"I have confidence in you, or I would never have recommended you as the one responsible for seeing to the sultana's safety, especially after her staff was exposed as traitors. That was not a favor granted, my dear. You earned that assignment."

"I'll echo that," the senator said. "I had to go straight to the top to get the okay, and even then I had to vouch for my belief you were the only one the agency should choose. Just so you know, your captain insisted on complete anonymity for anyone who took that assignment well before he was told it was you, and that requirement did not change just because a couple of old men with some pull might have wanted to know where you were and what you were doing while you were down here."

"I appreciate all you both have done, but I wish you hadn't gone to my superiors at the agency. In the past I have received assignments based on merit, and it troubles me that I got this one because my papa and his friend arranged it."

Her eyes stung as embarrassment and anger collided. "Further," she continued, "I cannot believe you would orchestrate all of this to play matchmaker. Did you think for a moment that it might be prudent to ask me or, for that matter, to consult Ethan? He might very well have avoided finding me because he wasn't interested."

"I assure you that is not the reason," Ethan interjected as he reached for her hand and clasped it in his.

Had he not, she would have fled.

"I already know the reason," Papa told him. "That's why the senator and I decided to take action. Not that I blame you, but if you've got it in your head that I wouldn't allow a match between you and my daughter just because of who your father is, then you would be wrong. I of all people have no room to judge a man for who he was or, for that matter, for who his family might be."

"Papa," she said again. "Just stop. You're not helping."

"No," Ethan said. "I disagree. Explain, please."

Her father gave him a direct look. "I know who your father is, and I know what he did. He was my friend, although not a close one. Many of us trusted him, and a few of us lost a sum of money when he scampered away without paying us. However, I am not one of the ones pointing a finger. He and your brother got what they deserved, possibly a little more than they deserved, considering the men they stole from had plenty left afterward."

Ethan cringed but said nothing. Rather, he held her fingers tight and remained motionless, his back straight and his expression unreadable.

"I'm no better than anyone else, and at one time I was worse than most." Papa looked down at her, sadness etching his features. "You've always been proud of who I am and wanted to be just like me. Well, Bette, my baby girl, you may want to be like the person I am, but you would never want to be who I was." He shook his head and then returned his attention to Ethan. "And that is why you are both here."

"What's he talking about, Ethan?"

"He's talking about my family history," Ethan said through clenched teeth. "I would have told you first, but we didn't exactly get that far. However, my father and brother are in prison. Have been for three years. They swindled a lot of people, and your father's right. They deserved what they got." He gave her a sideways look. "I'm not like them."

"No," she said. "You're not. Remember, I know things."

Senator Fulton pressed his palm against Papa's shoulder. "I'll go get Thorn."

"And I will come with you," Ethan said as he squeezed Elizabeth's hand. "With your permission, that is."

Elizabeth smiled, barely, and then managed a nod.

"But first," Ethan said, "I would like to address this situation directly with you, Mr. Newton. I appreciate what you've said and the lengths to which you've gone to bring Miss Newton and me together. If you are amenable, I would like to speak with you further in regard to my intentions."

Papa grinned. "I would like that very much."

"Good," Ethan continued. "Then I will have that conversation with you at a date and time of my choosing and after consulting with your daughter. Do you have a problem with that?"

"None whatsoever," her father said.

Ethan gave Papa a curt nod and then turned to Elizabeth. "Do you have a problem with that?"

"None whatsoever," she said with a broad grin.

He lifted her fingers to his lips and then released her hand to turn away. When the two men had disappeared into the crowd outside the alcove, she stepped into Papa's open arms and listened while he told her a tale of his past—of the time before he changed his life and married Mama. When he was done, she smiled and said, "I love you, Papa."

And she still did. Oh, but she was also swiftly falling in love with Ethan Butler.

Ethan returned with Mr. Thorn in tow. There he found Elizabeth swiping at tears and her father doing the same.

"Something in my eye." Wallace shrugged. "This oversized greenhouse is bad for the health, I'm certain of it. I see you've got Thorn with you. The plan has changed," he told the hotel manager.

"After the senator explained the situation, Mr. Thorn agreed to open the safe for us," Ethan said.

"I suggest we do that quickly," Mr. Thorn said. "So as not to alert my wife to the fact I have gone. While the senator is charming and has promised to keep her occupied on the dance floor, my wife is not easily fooled. Please, if you will follow me."

"So the cameo was in the safe the whole time?" Elizabeth asked him as they accompanied the hotel manager back to the Centennial Hotel.

Mr. Thorn had the good sense to put on a guilty look as he led them into his office. "I'm terribly sorry about that," he told them. "Had I not agreed to help your father, Miss Newton, I wouldn't have had to misrepresent myself. A grievous error on my part."

"Grievous error is just the beginning," Ethan snapped. "Just open the safe. Please," he added grudgingly.

"Yes, absolutely." He nodded to the room where the safe was kept and then headed in that direction. "I'll just go and do that."

The sound of wheels turning and clanking filled the room, followed by the protest of hinges that needed oiling. A moment later, a loud clang filled the air as the safe shut once more.

Thorn returned to the office holding the familiar box in his open palm. "There you are, Miss Butler. I believe this belongs to you."

She accepted the box. "Thank you."

"Yes, well, I believe that ends our deal, Wallace, and ends any association I might have with the Pinkerton Detective Agency. So if you'll excuse me, I will get back to my wife."

"Wait just a minute," Ethan said. "Elizabeth, open the box, please. This man has misled us once today. I will believe the cameo is there when I see it."

Chapter 12

$\mathscr{E}$lizabeth opened the box and smiled. Nestled inside was the familiar cameo that she had last seen on Petra. "Yes, this is it," she told them. She turned the box around so everyone could see.

"It is indeed," Papa said, slapping Mr. Thorn on the shoulder. "I do appreciate what you've done for the senator and me. We won't forget."

"Neither will I," Ethan said. "And before you go, maybe you can explain how that box got all smudged. It was perfectly clean when I saw you put it in that safe."

"Smudged?" The hotel manager's brows rose. "There's no possible way a box could have gotten dirty while it was safely in. . ." He leaned forward and took a closer look at the item in question. "Well, how about that? I have no explanation for it, but there's something there."

Turning the box back around, Elizabeth studied the imperfection in the lining. "Not just something, and certainly not a smudge." She looked up at the manager. "That's a fingerprint. Are you the only person who has access to this safe?"

"I am." His expression fell. "Well, that is, I was. But that couldn't possibly be. . ." The hotel manager shook his head. "I was at a very important meeting with the mayor and city leaders today. Perhaps you saw in the newspapers that we are giving a rather generous gift to the Smithsonian folks on behalf of the city."

"Unfortunately, no," Elizabeth said. "But do go on."

"Well, the city inspector of safes paid us a call to do his yearly inspection and certification per the new ordinance, and I could hardly leave my meeting before the photographs were taken."

"Hardly," she echoed.

"So?" Ethan said in a terse tone.

"So I gave a trusted employee the combination and the key." He nodded to the door. "You see, when I am out of the building for an extended time, I lock the door to the safe room as an added layer of security."

"I've not seen you do that, sir, so I will have to rely on your word," Ethan snapped. "But finish your story."

"Well," he said, flustered. "That is the whole of my story. When I returned from the meeting, my employee returned the key to me and, just to be sure, I checked the safe, and all was well."

Ethan shifted positions. "The box was there?"

"It was, as was everything else that we are currently holding for safekeeping."

"You're certain?" Elizabeth said.

"Completely." His look of offense was unmistakable. "I did a thorough check, as I said."

"Yes," Ethan said. "But I'm sure you'll understand if I don't take you at your word."

"As I said before, that was a favor for a friend," he pleaded. "Do not judge me by that."

"He's right," Papa said. "It wouldn't be fair to judge him by an obligation I requested of him."

"With all due respect, sir," Ethan said tersely, "I judge him by the fact that he accepted that obligation." He turned his attention to Mr. Thorn. "Were you paid for that?"

His eyes widened, and a red flush climbed higher in his cheeks. "Just a nominal amount," he said. "But there are few for whom I would do this."

"I will need a list of those names, sir." Ethan looked at Elizabeth. "Do you have any more questions for our suspect?"

"Suspect?" Mr. Thorn shook his head. "Now see here."

"Thorn," Papa said evenly, "the man is doing his job." He paused. "As is my daughter. You can see for yourself that the box was tampered with after we put it in your safe. I will take responsibility for you leaving to rejoin Helen now if you will swear to these Pinkerton detectives that you will present them with that list in the morning."

"As well as a list of all your employees," Ethan added. "For now the name of the man you gave the combination and the key to will suffice."

"That would be my clerk, Carl Harrison."

"Harrison?" Ethan shook his head. "Why not Parsons? He's your chief of security."

"He was," Mr. Thorn said. "Unfortunately, we are without a chief of security at this moment."

"Why?" Ethan demanded.

"Parsons resigned without explanation." He shrugged. "He didn't even bother to pick up his pay envelope."

"And you didn't find that odd?"

"Until this moment, no." His gaze swept the room and then returned to Ethan. "This is a big hotel, and I employ a great number of people. He could be in jail, besotted with some woman who convinced him to leave town, or lying dead in his bed right now. If I wondered about every abrupt departure, I would have no time to do my job properly."

Elizabeth frowned. "That sounds rather callous, sir."

"Then so be it," he said. "It is, unfortunately, the truth. People disappear in New Orleans all the time, and not all of them for suspicious reasons."

Elizabeth's fingers itched for the journal she had foolishly left in her room when she departed for the event this evening. "So you called upon Mr. Harrison to open the safe for the city investigator. Why Mr. Harrison when, as you say, you employ a large number of people?"

Mr. Thorn gave Papa a look before returning his attention to Elizabeth. "Because he's the only one of my employees who came to me with a letter of recommendation from your father and Senator Fulton."

"I never gave any such recommendation," Papa said. "Who is this man?"

Mr. Thorn's expression soured. "I'll go get him." A moment later, he returned. "Apparently he is gone for the evening. Some family emergency, but I will speak with him when he returns in the morning."

He wouldn't return, of this Elizabeth was certain. With Mr. Parsons gone and the fussy clerk absent when he should be here, things were shaping up to produce not only a longer list of suspects but also the possibility of collusion.

"Where is this letter?" Ethan demanded. "Mr. Newton can easily determine whether he wrote it."

Mr. Thorn went over to a cabinet and sorted through a stack of papers until he found what he was looking for. He brought the letter to Papa, who looked it over. "That's not my handwriting, and I've never heard of this fellow. Thorn, you've been duped."

"It appears I have," he said. "I offer sincere apologies to all of you. I thought I was helping a friend. I should have investigated further."

Papa placed his hand on Mr. Thorn's shoulder. "No harm done here." He glanced over at Ethan. "At least none that cannot be remedied."

"You're excused to go back to the party," Ethan told him. "But we will be needing your office for a little longer."

The hotel manager nodded and swiftly made his escape. Ethan closed the door behind him.

He moved closer and pointed to the back of the box. "Is that something sticking out of the lining?"

She turned the box around and took note of what looked like a slip of paper tucked between the box and the lining. "I think so, Ethan. I'll hold the box steady, and you see if you can remove it."

A swift tug and the paper came out. He unfolded the scrap of paper. Instantly his eyes narrowed as a look of rage rose. "Mr. Newton, I would like an explanation, please."

He handed the paper to Papa, who shook his head. "I have no idea."

"What does it say?" Elizabeth demanded.

"'The face is back. Next is DC for the Smith raisin.'" Papa paused. "I did not write that, and neither did the senator. You have my word on it."

Ethan shook his head. "And I suppose you didn't write the note that alerted me to your intention to steal the cameo either? The one that was planted in my boardinghouse in Denver?"

"I absolutely did not. I know nothing of any notes. That was never part of the plan." Papa handed the note to Ethan. Like the others, this message had been printed in small and precise letters on an unremarkable piece of plain white stationery.

"Whoever duped him knew what Papa and the senator had planned," she said. "There is no other explanation for any of this."

"Agreed. How they knew is the question. Mr. Newton, did you or the senator have anyone outside the two of you handle any part of the assignment you paid for?"

Papa shook his head. "No. We planned it together, and then I handled the details."

"But you had to have spoken to someone within the organization. Who was that?"

"Allan Pinkerton's sons, of course. Who else would I speak to?" Her father's look of annoyance was swiftly replaced with a smile. "You know, I think I'll head back over to the party and snoop around over there. If I see something of interest to this investigation, I will let you know."

His kiss grazed Elizabeth's cheek. "I never meant all this trouble to happen," he told her.

"I know, Papa," she said to his retreating back.

Then they were alone. She sank onto the nearest chair and placed the cameo on Mr. Thorn's desk. "What a night."

"And it isn't over yet," Ethan said. He made his way around the desk to take his place in Mr. Thorn's leather chair. "What are your thoughts so far?"

She couldn't help laughing. "I have far too many thoughts to make good sense of any of them right now. I need my journal and a good night's sleep, then maybe I can answer that question."

"Fair enough. Should we discuss what happened at the party first or table that for another day?"

"If you're talking about how my father and his best friend conspired to bring us together by creating one Pinkerton assignment and apparently disrupting a second one, then could we not? At least not just yet? And maybe not until whatever it is we appear to be working on together comes to a conclusion?"

Ethan grinned. "Absolutely. So, moving on. You called the smudge on that box a fingerprint. I've heard the agency was working on something in regard to those. Would I be wrong in assuming you know more about that project than I do?"

"I don't suppose it would hurt to say it now," Elizabeth began, "but yes, Mr. Pinkerton and I were working on a project—a fingerprinting project—when he died. Most of the information died with him because he refused to allow me to take notes and I never saw him take them."

"But you were part of the project."

"I was." She paused. "The basis of the theory is that we all have a unique fingerprint that could potentially be used to identify us. If we were to collect the fingerprints of criminals, then we might be able to match up a print to a person and get a conviction." She paused to once again study the print. "Or that was the theory anyway."

"It's a good theory."

She leaned back in the chair and regarded Ethan with an appraising look, stifling a yawn. "You're thinking of an application for this theory, aren't you?"

"I am." He rose and came around the desk to stand beside her. "But it is late, and neither of us has what we need to discuss our assignments."

At her questioning look, he continued. "Your journal and my permission from my captain."

"Yes, I think that is wise," she agreed.

Ethan helped her to her feet but made no move toward the door. "Elizabeth," he said slowly, his gaze meeting hers, "did you know what your father and the senator planned?"

"Of course not," she said, indignant. "Had I even a hint of an idea, I would have put a stop to it immediately."

"I believe you." His lips turned up in the beginnings of a smile. "Then I am glad you didn't have even the hint of an idea."

He stood close. Too close. Yet not close enough.

"So am I," she managed.

"Elizabeth," he said again, his voice soft, "I said I know things, but right now I cannot tell whether you want me to kiss you or not."

She smiled. "Just as much as I did in that garden in Chicago. And every day since."

And so he did.

Then he kissed her again.

"Though I could continue," he finally told her, "I should not."

She held tight to his arm lest her legs give way. "Definitely not. So we will part here and meet again tomorrow then?"

He shook his head. "I'll see that you get safely to your room."

Rather than argue, she merely nodded and followed him through the lobby—casting a quick glance to confirm Harrison's continued absence—and up the stairs to stop in front of rooms 212 and 213.

"This party we attended tonight, when did you get your invitation?" he asked.

"It was under my door this afternoon. I thought it was odd that I'd been found out by the senator, but then he does have a way of doing things like this." She paused. "When did you get yours?"

"I don't think I did."

"I'm sure you did. Otherwise there wouldn't have been much match-making going on tonight."

"I suppose." He paused. "One more question," he asked as she unlocked her door. "Who was the Arab man standing across the street earlier? The one who captured your attention enough to cause you to stare for quite a while?"

"Amir," she told him. "Or at least I think that was him. He was my contact on this assignment, until he was fired, that is."

"Fired for what?"

She looked up into his eyes. "Treason, though I cannot believe it's true. My guess is he knew I would believe his innocence so he was likely coming to ask for my help."

"That doesn't explain why he ran from me."

"Ran from you?"

"He was in the stairwell earlier. I guess he thought I was after him, so he ran. I lost him but found Cinderella headed for the ball, and here we are."

She smiled. "Yes, here we are. Amir is a good man. I cannot imagine he would be involved in whatever case you were working before this one. It's just not possible."

"Anything's possible," Ethan said. He leaned down to press his lips to her forehead. "Just look at us."

❧ *Chapter 13* ❧

*E*than waited until he heard her lock turn before leaving the hotel and finding the nearest telegraph office. He summoned the telegraph clerk from his sleep to send a telegram to the captain.

He then returned to his own room and, not long after, his pillow. Though exhausted, his eyes refused to shut until he attempted to sort all the pieces of the puzzle and fit them together.

He rose and found his notes, then carried them into bed with him to read until he fell asleep. The next morning when he awoke, he gathered them all up and began again. He also found a telegram and a note had been slipped under his door. When he leaned down to pick them up, he noticed something white beneath the table beside the door.

The invitation.

That explained how he had missed being invited. Likely he'd walked right over it several times. He tossed the invitation on the table and read the telegram first and then the note, which was from Elizabeth.

Armed with the captain's permission to include Elizabeth on the hunt for the Dandy, he tucked the telegram into his packet of notes and case files and went in search of his fellow Pinkerton detective.

He found her holding court at a table in the hotel café. The man to her right was easily recognizable as the fellow who'd bested him in the race to the bottom of the stairs. The other was a woman whose regal beauty was visible even from a distance.

"There he is." She smiled as he joined them. "Ethan Butler, may I present. . ." She looked at the woman. "I'm sorry, I don't know how I should introduce a sultana to a commoner."

The dark-haired woman's eyes twinkled. "Just Noor is fine. No need to stand on circumstance and formality here. After all, I am the reason you are here. Had your father not requested you to act as security for me, you might be doing something much more fun."

"Noor, it is." Elizabeth waited while Ethan greeted the sultana.

"And you've met Amir," she said.

"I have." He shook hands with him. "He's quite fast."

"Terribly sorry about that," he said. "In order to keep Miss Newton safe, I needed to determine with whom she was keeping company."

"So you were watching after Elizabeth, who was watching after Noor?"

"I was preparing for her arrival," Elizabeth corrected. "But as it turns out, she changed her mind and won't be appearing at the exhibition after all—upon my advice."

Noor smiled but said nothing. Ethan turned to Amir and lifted a brow. "So all of this is the reason for you breaking into my room?"

Amir had the good sense to show remorse. "It was necessary and ordered by the sultana herself."

"It was," Noor said. "As was the use of locals to aid Miss Newton, although I have now understood that Amir declined to let her know."

He ducked his head. "I did not want to bring any unnecessary danger to her. At first I even thought to disguise myself." He looked at Elizabeth.

"It worked too. Perhaps you recall a Venetian gondolier who paid you a bit of unwarranted attention?"

"That was you?"

"It was."

"And these locals," Ethan said carefully. "Would they be named Parsons and Harrison?"

Noor and Amir exchanged conversation in a language Ethan did not understand. Then the lady shook her head. "Parsons, yes. But Harrison? Neither of us knows him."

"The hotel clerk," Elizabeth offered. "Perhaps he used another name?"

"No," she said. "Because your mother and I are old friends, and by virtue of that, your father is a confidant, we chose not to use anyone other than Mr. Parsons at the hotel."

Elizabeth frowned. "Then who was the other local?"

"Actually," Ethan said carefully, "I think the more important question is who is Harrison, and is he the one we should be investigating?"

She grinned. "That's easily determined. Well, the part about whether he has anything to do with the cameo being removed and then returned to the safe is. I'll just see if his prints are on the safe. If Mr. Thorn is correct, there should only be three sets on there: his, the safe inspector's, and Mr. Harrison's."

"Do you believe there is a safe inspector?"

She shook her head. "Not for a minute, actually. So, we're down to two prints. If either of them match the print on the cameo box, then we have our thief."

"And may also have caught the man I've been chasing."

"Your previous assignment?" Elizabeth asked.

He nodded and patted the pouch under his arm. "Permission granted. Welcome to my team."

"Our team," she corrected.

"Our team," he said.

Noor rose, and Amir bobbed to his feet. Ethan did the same. "I will allow you two your team discussion in private. Amir and I have a train to catch." She turned to Elizabeth. "Will I see you at the Smithsonian reception in Washington, DC? It would not be the same if you weren't there."

While the women conversed, a thought struck hard, and the pieces of the puzzle fell into place. Ethan kept silent until Noor and Amir were gone.

"I have the answer to the riddle in the note. 'Next is DC for the Smith raisin.' Raisin as in sultana and DC as in our nation's capital." He shook his head. "Don't you see? The answer is going to be found at the Smithsonian reception the sultana is attending in the capital."

Elizabeth rose to make her way toward Ethan and embrace him. "You are brilliant."

He shrugged. "I just know things. Now, while I arrange train tickets, why don't you go take care of the fingerprints?"

"I have a better idea," she said. "Come with me, and I'll show you how to lift a fingerprint. Then we'll leave a note for my father letting him know we'll be using his Pullman car. It's much safer than traveling any other way."

"Are you telling me that to convince me or to practice for when you have to convince your father?"

She shrugged. "Perhaps a little of both."

"I just see one problem with that idea," he said. "It wouldn't be proper for the two of us to travel unaccompanied."

"That is not a worry," she told him. "I've invited Noor and her entourage to join us. Have I mentioned she travels with a sizable entourage?"

"Define sizable."

She shook her head. "Trust me. You'd rather I didn't."

✿

Three weeks later
Washington, DC

Where was Ethan? Elizabeth took a deep breath and entered the ballroom alone.

The ballroom had been decorated in an around-the-world theme with Chinese lanterns giving way to embroidered tapestries from across Europe and lush plants from south of the equator.

Guests had been asked to dress as if they were from one of the many countries represented at the exhibition. Elizabeth had chosen a dress with Spanish influence, knowing the lace mantilla would help to obscure her features should she need to hide from a potential suspect.

And they had their suspect.

After weeks of study and telegrams that flew back and forth from Denver, New York, and Chicago, they had managed to lift fingerprints from each of the safes that had been robbed by the Dandy. All of them pointed to the man they knew only as Clay Harrison.

Scanning the crowd, she saw a few familiar faces from Chicago but no sign of her escort. The orchestra finished a slow tune and switched to a waltz. Someone tapped her on the shoulder.

She turned around to see a handsome bullfighter smiling back at her. "May I have this dance, *señorita?*"

He led her to the dance floor where they moved easily among the dancers. "You look breathtaking," he whispered, leaning closer.

"Thank you," she said, "but keep your focus where it belongs."

"Harrison?" he said. "We've been following him for the past five minutes." He nodded toward a man in an Arab's garb dancing with a woman wearing a Japanese kimono.

"I've seen that woman," she told him. "In New Orleans."

"So have I," he said. "But I don't remember anything in our combined notes that would indicate he had a partner. So I asked Amir." He gave her a sheepish grin. "That's why I was late."

"And what did Amir say?"

"Remember how they told us the sultan had used two locals to help you. . .without telling you they were helping?"

"I do."

"But we never did find out who the second local was." He nodded toward the couple. "Meet Mrs. Amir. They met while training for the sultan's security forces. A match made in training, as it were."

"His wife?" She grinned. "Oh, that's brilliant. But she wasn't on the railcar with us."

"No, too risky. She's been trailing Harrison, so she had to remain apart from her husband until Harrison was caught."

"So the sultan was already looking for the same thief that you were looking for?"

"Apparently the Dandy had taken quite a haul from the sultan's safe while the entourage was staying in Philadelphia. It was kept very quiet, which is why the theft did not show up in my notes." He paused. "Unfortunately, while Harrison is connected to the Dandy, he has an alibi for the past two thefts. You see, he was confirmed by numerous unimpeachable witnesses, including me, as being in New Orleans."

"So he isn't our man?" Elizabeth asked.

"No, but he knows who our man is. So, are you ready to take down the Dandy's right-hand man?"

She grinned. "I am."

At his signal, Elizabeth twirled away from Ethan and into the arms of the man who was about to be arrested. Though the surprise change of partners gave him pause, he smiled down at Elizabeth, obviously unable to see her face well enough to identify her through the mantilla.

When the music ended, she lifted the heavy lace from her face to reveal her identity and the fact that the Victoria cameo was pinned at her throat. "Hello, Mr. Harrison, or whoever you are."

His eyes went wide, but he made no move to run. Nor did he attempt to speak. Finally, he shook his head. "It wasn't me."

Ethan grasped the man's wrist and pulled it behind his back. "Don't make a scene."

That was enough to subdue the man. A moment later, Amir arrived to escort his wife out and take the prisoner away. The entire operation went so smoothly that none of the dancers or the guests milling around the dance floor realized it had happened.

"Come with me," Ethan said as he led Elizabeth out of the ballroom. "If Harrison is telling the truth—"

"Which is doubtful," she interjected.

"Yes," he admitted. "But if he is, then I am willing to bet I know where the Dandy will be about now."

She grinned. "Stealing from the sultana?"

At his nod, she hurried to follow. Sure enough, the door to her chambers was unlocked. The security guard left to keep watch had been knocked in the head and lay unconscious. Ethan drew his gun and motioned for Elizabeth to cover him as he turned the knob.

Before he could make another move, the door flew open and Timothy Parsons slammed into him. A fortune in diamonds landed on the floor, and so did Parsons.

Acting quickly, Elizabeth aimed her gun at the former chief of security's head while Ethan held him down. "Don't move, Dandy," she told him.

"I don't know what you're talking about," he said. "I was hired by the sultana to keep her jewels safe."

"By taking off with them? I don't think so." Ethan yanked the man's tie from around his neck and made short work of binding his hands behind his back and shoving him into the suite.

A few minutes later, two of Amir's men arrived along with a half dozen local policemen.

After sorting out what happened with the lawmen, Ethan allowed them to take the thief away to join his accomplice in jail.

"Now what?" Elizabeth asked.

Ethan grinned. "I say we let them sit in a jail cell for a while then see if they're ready to talk. In the meantime, there is dancing to be done. Shall we?"

"I would like that very much," she said.

Arm in arm, they strolled back to the ballroom where a waltz was just starting.

"Elizabeth," he said as they stepped back onto the dance floor. "There's just one more thing that needs to be done to wrap up this evening."

"What's that?"

He grinned. "You'll see."

The music stopped and clapping rose among the guests. A moment later, the sultana appeared on the stage accompanied by her husband.

"As you know, we are here to celebrate my wife's gift to your country's new museum, the Smithsonian. We shall get on with that in a moment. First, however, I wish to introduce you to two very honored and special guests. Mr. Butler and Miss Newton, would you join me here, please?"

Elizabeth shook her head. "This was not part of the plan."

Ethan grinned. "Not part of your plan, but definitely part of mine." He led her to the stage and then shook hands with the sultan. "Thank you," he told them. "I will make this brief so that the focus can return to the real purpose of the evening."

"Ethan," she whispered. "What are you doing?"

"Forgive my behavior," he whispered against her ear, "but your father, mother, and grandmother are right over there. They're lovely people, by the way." His voice became husky with emotion. "I must warn you that my plan involves giving the impression of a familiarity we do not have. I will hold you to a promise that you will inform me at once should I owe you an apology."

The familiar words, once spoken in a Chicago garden on a July afternoon, brought tears to her eyes.

"I shall at once," she managed as she felt his arms go gently around her.

"See that you do," he whispered. Then he raised his voice. "I have spoken to this lady's father and received permission to announce my intentions here tonight. Miss Butler, I would like very much to court you properly. When we are not teaming up to solve crimes, that is."

He smelled of soap and sunshine, and his eyes crinkled at the edges when he smiled. His lips were soft against hers, a sweet kiss that she longed to savor but knew she could never adequately describe in her journal. Just like they were on that afternoon in Chicago.

When he moved away to look down at her, she smiled though her insides were strangely mush. "You've stopped," she said.

"I have." There was that smile again. "I wanted to give you a chance to tell me whether you are in agreement, and whether you are owed an apology."

"Yes, I am in agreement. As to the apology? Not yet," she said. "Please continue."

And so he did.

Bent History and Fun Facts

*A*s a writer of historical novels, I love incorporating actual history into my plots. As with most books, the research behind the story generally involves much more information than would ever actually appear in the story. In truth, I could easily spend all my time researching and not get any writing done at all!

Of all the cities in the world, New Orleans is one of my favorites. The history of the Crescent City, a melting pot of cultures before most of the cities in our country were even in existence, is rich with true stories and, to a writer, the possibilities of fictional stories. As I type this, the city has just celebrated its three-hundredth anniversary.

Because I am a history nerd, I love sharing some of that mountain of research I collected with my readers. The following are just a few of the facts I uncovered during the writing of this novel. I hope these tidbits of history will cause you to go searching for the rest of the story.

Here are just a few of the interesting things I've discovered during the writing of *Meet Me at the Fair*, and a few historical facts I may have "bent" to fit the story:

Allan Pinkerton founded the Pinkerton Agency prior to the Civil War and was known to employ both male and female detectives. My research did not turn up any official details of Allan Pinkerton's funeral—if indeed he had one—only that he died on July 1, 1884, and was buried in Chicago's Graceland Cemetery. I am left to surmise that a man of his stature would have been memorialized in some way, but I had to bend the facts a little to write a scene that took place at a service for him.

The 1884 Democratic Convention took place in downtown Chicago. It opened on July 8, 1884, one week after Mr. Pinkerton's death, so I surmised that if some of the VIPs were already in the city, they would have likely attended a service for Mr. Pinkerton. While I do not mention any of the actual attendees in this novel, the convention's nominee, Grover Cleveland, did go on to become the twenty-second president on November 4, 1884.

After Mr. Pinkerton's death, his sons, Robert and William, took over the running of the agency. Allan Pinkerton was indeed working on a way to compile a registry of fingerprints for use in detective work. His research on collecting the prints of criminals and the database that he began formed the basis, many years later, for the science of fingerprinting that we know today.

The 1884 World's Fair, officially known as the 1884 Cotton Exchange and Exposition, was officially opened to the public two weeks behind schedule on December 16, 1884, with a telegram from President Chester A. Arthur. Exhibits varied from those representing thirty-eight states to those representing twenty-seven foreign countries and three republics.

The largest of the buildings, the grand exhibition hall, was a historical wonder in that it was the biggest building under one roof in the United

States at the time. Inside the halls and out on the grounds, electric lights, electric streetcars, and an elevator were some of the curiosities on display, along with a 5,640-pound silver ingot on display in the Mexico pavilion exhibit. The Liberty Bell even made an appearance.

The Horticultural Building, where the fictional ball was set, hosted rare plants from all over the world in an environment that was very much like an opulent and very grand greenhouse. A reporter from *Frank Leslie's Illustrated Newspaper* wrote in the January 17, 1885, issue that the Hall "beckons like a great glowworm amongst the shadows of the soft Southern night." An interesting image, to say the least!

The Smithsonian Institution, named after its British founder, James Smithson, was established in 1846 and signed into existence by President James Polk. Many of the exhibits at the 1884 World's Fair featured items that went on to be purchased by the Smithsonian. The Smithsonian shipped so many things from the New Orleans site back to their museum that they were given a special low shipping rate by rail.

The fictional Centennial Hotel is loosely based on another New Orleans institution, the beautiful Monteleone Hotel, still in existence and hosting guests today. However, I have bent the facts a bit to create a location near the site of the exhibition on St. Charles Avenue that did not exist then and does not now. Oh, but it would be amazing if it had— except for those awful heavy curtains that block out the daylight. Fun fact: the exhibition actually commissioned a hotel to be built in anticipation of guests that would arrive at the site. Unfortunately, that hotel was so poorly built that it fell apart before it ever opened.

The cameo has a long history, but the pin became popular in the late eighteenth century due to the influence of Empress Josephine of France and even more so in the early nineteenth century thanks to Queen Victoria. Ancient cameos were made of gemstones, while more modern versions can be made of shell or glass. Ironically, the award medal for the 1884 New Orleans Cotton Centennial, cast from bronze by the P. L. Krider Company of Philadelphia, featured Lady Liberty and Columbia and looks very much like a cameo.

Bestselling author **Kathleen Y'Barbo** is a multiple Carol Award and RITA nominee of more than eighty novels with almost two million copies in print in the United States and abroad. She has been nominated for a Career Achievement Award as well as a Reader's Choice Award and is the winner of the 2014 Inspirational Romance of the Year by *Romantic Times* magazine. Kathleen is a paralegal, a proud military wife, and a tenth-generation Texan, who recently moved back to cheer on her beloved Texas Aggies. Connect with her through social media at www.kathleenybarbo.com.

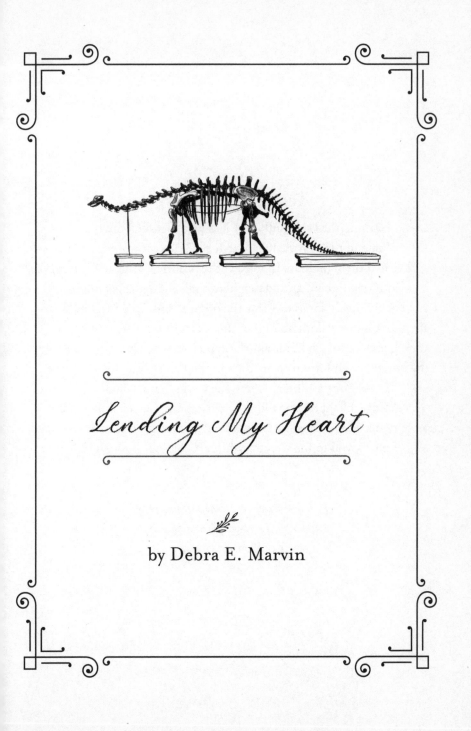

Lending My Heart

by Debra E. Marvin

Acknowledgments

Nothing thrills an author of historical fiction more than walking in their characters' footsteps. And so it was for me as I visited the Children's Library at the historic Carnegie Library in Pittsburgh's Oakland neighborhood and—thanks to the current children's librarian—saw the original sink used by children of the sooty, industrial Pittsburgh of this story. But my greatest appreciation goes to research librarian Marilyn Holt, who patiently answered my questions. I'd love to spend days in the Pennsylvania Room of the Carnegie Library where she works, but having a knowledgeable librarian willing to correspond via email had to do! Lastly, thank you to Susanne Dietze for dreaming up this collection, and thank you to the Creator who carried us all through it!

Two are better than one; because they have a good reward for their labour.
Ecclesiastes 4:9

❧ *Prologue* ❧

Squirrel Hill, Pittsburgh
January 28, 1895

Dearest Cousin Elizabeth,

The cameo has arrived, and it's lovelier than I've imagined all these years, having seen it once as a child of four. I admit I'm a bit in awe of its history. Being once in the possession—the very hands of— Queen Victoria is one thing, but the fact that it has become our own true family treasure makes it a treasure beyond compare.

Roberta Hart sat back in the delicate chair by her bedroom's desk. If only she were longing for the love of a lifetime. If only that were possible. As a girl, she'd dreamed of possessing this very impressive jeweled cameo. But facing it now, long after learning of her father's arrangement with his business partner, made the romance of this legendary piece bittersweet.

Your love story confirms the legacy the queen gave our family, and I can only hope to one day pass it on having been blessed by our heavenly Father with a sweet tale of my own.

Affectionately,
Bertie

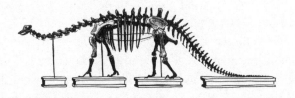

❧ *Chapter 1* ❧

Oakland neighborhood, Pittsburgh
October 29, 1895

*R*ussell Smart once despised his name. Now he despised wasting time.

Inside his makeshift office, the clock's evidence clicked away like a disapproving matron's tongue. Filling the position of children's librarian for the impressive Carnegie Library had been today's order of business.

And so far he'd failed.

A letter of introduction from Andrew Carnegie himself promised that Mr. Russell Smart, lately of Dunfermline, Scotland, bore the innate skill of finding the right man for every job.

Without delay.

After all, administration was like breathing to him. If everyone was as effective as he, there'd be little need for prodding those around him like a glorified sheepherder. People would be treated fairly and kindly and with opportunity for all.

He rose from his straight-backed, bottom-numbing chair, stretched, and pushed the door open far enough to peer out. "Mrs. Oates, ma'am. Will ye send in the last applicant?"

According to his list, that would be the eminently qualified Mr. Bertie Hart, whom the staff had consistently put off as the last interview of the day. Hart's volunteer experience with the library, his English literature degree, and the names of impressive personal references proved his suitability. With such giants of industry on his side, why wasn't this Mr. Hart already employed?

"Mr. Smart?"

Russell glanced up from scanning Hart's application.

And froze.

She asked again.

"Yes. I'm Russell Smart."

Snickering whispers conferred in the hallway.

"And I'm Roberta Hart."

Needing the applicant's crisp handwriting to help clear his confusion, he read the name again. "You've a message from Mr. Hart then?"

"No. I am Mr. Hart—I mean Miss Hart, that is."

Annoyance and warmth edged up Russell's ears. Beyond the door, Mrs. Oates shushed witnesses who sneaked away, amused at the expense of the new, unwelcomed administrator brought in without warning.

He wasn't here to make friends, but this?

"Very well. Come in, Miss Hart," he bid, circling her to close the door. Weary from the day's disappointing interviews, he was unable to stop studying her.

With her back straight and chin up, her bold stare ended his gawking. "Shall we get on with it, sir? I'm sure you'd like to finish so you can make your decision."

Her businesslike manner brought him back on task, yet all the words he read and reread blurred into *You've been duped.*

Or, as the lads in the orphanage would taunt, "Ye're not so verra smart."

"I'm sorry for the confusion," she announced without an ounce of sincerity.

Russell waved her to the empty chair, sat, and took a slow sip of his cold tea. "Not so much confusion as misdirection. Is your name Bertie or Roberta?"

"It's both. My friends call me Bertie, and as I know everyone here—"

"Except me. I would have appreciated knowing this before."

"I apologize again, but as I'm now here, and you have met all the other applicants. . ."

And, Russell concluded, it was all going as she'd planned. That would change. He casually checked his pocket watch to remind her just who was in charge.

She took a deep breath and glanced away, with a wee bit of regret in the way she bit her lip. "Would you have canceled the interview if you'd known I was a woman?"

Likely so. "I can't say."

Doubt sent one elegant brow high. "But you'll agree I am qualified." She leaned forward and tapped one perfectly manicured nail on the proof lying between them on his desk. "I have experience in all aspects of library work, and I volunteer at one of the Minersville schools three days a week, while not one of your candidates has actually worked with children."

True. Proving that, unlike Russell, she had the eyes and ears of the staff on her side.

"You will not find one valid reason against my taking this position. My references will convince you of my good character."

Having an English degree did not automatically make one a librarian any more than having rouged lips made one kissable.

He drained his cup. "May I offer you some water?"

She shook her head. "You may offer me the job so I can tell you what I know I can accomplish."

The problem with Miss Hart's qualifications were her unfair advantages, borne out by her pushy, highbrow manner. The upper class were notorious for volunteer work—when it did not interfere with their social life.

"How does your family feel about you taking employment, Miss Hart?"

The subtle shift in her gaze answered for her. "I fail to see the relevance of your question."

No. She wouldn't. "The man I hire will be someone for whom this position becomes an integral part of his life. There will be times when he is called upon to work unexpected hours."

Surprise—too obvious to be genuine—widened her eyes. "He will?"

"Yes. It is a job, Miss Hart. It is not afternoon tea."

She placed her hand on the desk. When they both noticed her fingers were shaking, she withdrew it and cleared her throat. "What I mean is, you clearly intended to hire a man."

"Of course I did! Especially when no women applied."

Her mouth betrayed a hint of amusement. "What do you think I am?"

"A fraud, I'm afraid."

Her efforts to stifle a response resembled a rattling lid on a heating kettle. She whisked her beaded purse off her lap and stood. "I'm sorry you feel that way."

Russell rose to face her. "And I'm sorry you thought you could waltz in here and find me amused by your trickery. I find it disrespectful."

"Trickery, is it? Do women not work in. . .wherever it is you come from?"

"Scotland, Miss Hart." He leaned forward, resting one palm flat on his desk. "And I can assure you they work quite hard."

"Just not in libraries."

"On the contrary. In libraries, engineering, medicine and law, as well as factories. When they're not taking care of their homes."

"Then you should have no problem with my application."

Shadows bobbed behind the door's frosted glass. They wanted him to give her a chance. Would they do the same for him?

"Please sit down, Miss Hart, so we may start over."

If Mr. Carnegie heard of this—and this society lass would likely raise a stink—Russell would have to explain himself. He took a deep breath. "I admit to. . .feeling bamboozled. Obviously, you have support here among the staff. That is more important than your. . ." What dare he say that wouldn't show his disregard? "Your esteemed references."

She sat but wouldn't meet his eyes. So far she'd refrained from employing tears. *So far*. But there was clearly a pout.

"Your application shows much promise. In fact, I found it the most qualified of the lot."

Intrigued, she turned, and this time honest surprise showed in her eyes. "Really?"

Those eyes were smoky brown like her hair, lushly lashed and thoroughly disconcerting, just like the rest of her.

"Oh aye."

A flashing smile only enhanced her beauty.

"Then hire me."

Hold on, lass. That smile was not going to be the breaking of him, but the pressure he inflicted on his new fountain pen was disastrous. Black ooze leaked from the barrel and along his fingertips to mar her application. He set it down and sought to wipe his fingers on a handkerchief. Ruined. "I need someone who will be here for a number of years and who will train others as future libraries open. I need someone. . .like me. If you'd been a man with a family, I'd have offered you the job by now."

Any trace of a smile vanished. Miss Bertie Hart leaned forward as if shocked he hadn't bent to her will. "I am qualified, and I intend to have this position," she warned. "I promise you I will show up as scheduled with Mr. Bolton, and accomplish much. You ask anyone here, and they will tell you how hard I've worked for this."

"I get that impression."

No doubt expecting further argument, she searched his desk for her next words, her eyes blinking rapidly. "I understand you've been brought in because Mr. Carnegie trusts your judgment."

"Yes. That's true."

She sprang up, regarded the slow inky destruction of her application, and stormed for the door. "Well, I don't."

"Wait. Miss Hart."

She did, but only when her gloved hand clutched the doorknob. "You will hear more from my—" Her pretty mouth bit back an all too obvious threat. "From me, when I am capable of understanding your reasoning."

She wasn't alone. Knowing nothing sensible or kind would come out of his mouth, he watched trouble blow out the door.

Miss Bertie Hart's heels pounded the floor all the way to the stairwell. After the door shut, he heard a loud, frustrated growl.

Elbows on his desk, Russell's forehead sank to his open palms.

That's when he remembered the ink.

❧ *Chapter 2* ❦

*N*ever, never, ever had she been so humiliated.

Bertie Hart shut her bedroom door with more than necessary force. The carriage ride home hadn't been long enough to cool the flush across her cheeks over that. . .that poor excuse for an interview with that poor excuse for an administrator. Even if he did have the most charming accent. She was not one to second-guess Mr. Andrew Carnegie, but Mr. I'm So Smart's arrival out of nowhere, and his confident idea he knew better than everyone else had destroyed her door to freedom.

His coldhearted rebuttal had left her no option but to go over his head.

The fleeting urge to beg had shifted to such anger, she'd almost threatened to sic Father on him like a terrier in a three-piece suit. Not that Father supported her foolhardy notions.

How embarrassing!

If he'd been the least bit sympathetic, she might have welled up with tears. She'd barely achieved a dignified exit.

Bertie dropped to sit on the edge of her high bed and unlace her stylish new boots.

Women of her social standing volunteered when it didn't interfere with their family's needs. Her parents had hoped that attending the nearby Pennsylvania College for Women would satisfy her appetite for a broader education yet convince her of the blessings of a favorable marriage.

Marriage! She unhooked and rolled off her stockings, then wiggled her toes in the plush Oriental wool rug.

Mother—dead set against this—would be pleased the embarrassing ploy had failed.

While Father had feigned interest, she knew he considered it charitable work. After all, she'd marry as he'd arranged—and marry soon despite his current displeasure with Henry Kendall III, his business partner's son. Henry had had the "harebrained notion" to forgo their investment firm in favor of journalism. If it wasn't Henry's tawdry headline stories, it was his blatant attacks on the better families. His own people. *Her people.* Henry seemed determined to point out every social injustice visited upon the poor, while he conveniently lived off his fortune. He taunted the very men whose companies and banking interests provided much-needed jobs for the working class.

She'd expected too much today. Being qualified wasn't enough.

Her collegiate classmates understood. They weren't all against marriage by any means, but many longed for opportunities their mothers never had.

Her throat felt thick with emotion. She wouldn't cry, and she wouldn't give up.

A light knock turned her attention to the door, and she wiped her face. "Come in."

"Miss Bertie?" Their ladies' maid slipped in far enough to face her. "Mrs. Hart would like to speak with you in her room."

"Thanks, Cecile."

Cecile dropped a curtsy, and after her retreat, Bertie sighed with an allowable amount of self-pity. The wintry weather could account for her pink cheeks and watery eyes. She padded quietly down the hall, hoping Mother wouldn't notice her bare feet, and knocked at the big double doors before entering. Twilight fell around Mother's chair by the window. The massive bed in the open bedroom beyond looked just as royal to the grown-up Bertie as it had to the child. Father's room, a woody cave smelling of pipe smoke, leather polish, and old dogs, was half this size, but of course he was gone all day managing the Hart family fortune, just as she would be if she'd been born Robert as hoped.

"Did you forget Aunt Aurelius is coming for dinner?" Mother asked, not looking up from her embroidery.

She sighed on the inside. Yes, she had. "I've not had a very good day. May I beg off with a headache and make a plan to meet her for lunch this week instead?"

"And break her heart? Absolutely not! She's just now well enough to go out after that awful ocean crossing. I do believe your father thought she wouldn't survive."

Bertie did adore her outspoken aunt, but if the old girl intended to discuss the lingering lack of an engagement ring, it would be a tedious night indeed. Bertie was twenty-three and still holding off the arrangement made fifteen years ago between the Hart and Kendall families. So far it remained a well-known, if not officially announced, type of company merger.

With a growing headache, it was best to get on with the tedium of dressing for dinner. "Very well," she offered on her way out the door.

"Oh, and she's bringing that boy with her."

Bertie leaned her head back in. "What boy?"

"Armstrong's ward. Have you forgotten their little charity case?"

"Apparently. That was years ago. Isn't he off in boarding school or something?"

"Hardly. To honor Armstrong's wishes, she must at least see the young man established on his own." Mother rose to examine her hair in the mirror. "Oh, and wear that new sea-foam dress."

"Rather ostentatious for a family meal. I don't know how I let you talk me into it."

"Nonsense! If it doesn't suit you, I will have them redo the sleeves. You and Henry will soon have more dinner invitations than you can manage."

"Very well." A young guest might just restrict discussion of delayed engagements and Father's tirades against European bankers.

Tomorrow she'd call on Mr. Bolton, the overworked supervising manager of the library and museums, and plead her case. Surely he'd have some pull with Russell Smart.

"Go on then, and get ready. Your father is likely pacing the drawing room carpet to threads. Insists he must speak with you. No doubt it's the corporate board. See if you can calm him."

Bertie obeyed, hoping Cecile was waiting to assist her. There was no avoiding a family meal, and a visit from Aunt Aurelius was just what she needed.

Twenty minutes later she thanked Cecile and examined herself before the cheval mirror. She ran a hand over the fitted bodice and waist of her new sea-green dress, wondering if things would have gone better at her interview had she worn a soft, feminine design instead of aiming for sensible and mature. These bodice pleats and the swaths of delicate lace across her shoulders were quite flattering. And horribly uncomfortable.

Or maybe the discomfort came from anticipation of Father's upcoming lecture. One last check of her red-rimmed eyes and she was soon in the drawing room.

"Very nice, Roberta," Father pronounced before kissing her cheek.

Even nicer would be praise for her efforts and accomplishments. What was the point of a lovely coif if her brain deserved no regard?

"Before your aunt arrives, I must ask you why Henry's parents believe you'll be bored by marriage. You must be more careful what you say in their presence, as you know they are also quite unhappy with the delay."

You don't say. She was especially careful in her conversation, which was why she dreaded dinner events at the Kendall home. If anyone was bored with marriage, it was the frosty Mrs. Kendall. "I don't recall such a statement, but as I expect to work even after I marry, I won't have time to be bored."

Father harrumphed. "Your mother has never been bored. You will learn to keep busy as well." He fingered his thick brush of a graying mustache before leaning close. At such proximity his eyes were distorted by the round lenses of his eyeglasses. "There will be an engagement announcement at Christmas and a wedding date for the spring."

Unable to control the rolling of her eyes, she turned her back. Would he never see her as an accomplished adult unless she performed her duty for the company?

"Roberta? Pay attention. Mr. Kendall and I are about to undertake the most important step in our expansion, and until Henry joins the board as my son-in-law, the board and the bank lack confidence in our company's future."

She'd love to say she didn't care. But it would be a childish reaction.

Mother arrived in time to end the discussion and take her accustomed spot alongside Father. Cecile trailed behind, looking like she'd just been the target of a tongue-lashing. Before Bertie could protest, Cecile pinned the cameo onto the new dress's neckline.

"What are you—"

"I'm sorry, miss."

Of course she was. Bertie turned to the culprit. "Mother!"

"Not now, dear."

No. Not now, for she'd planned this right to the minute.

Hartfield's butler, Gordon, opened the door. "Mrs. Aurelius Armstrong, sir. And her. . ."

Aurelius sailed through the door like an ocean liner in stiff plum taffeta. "And my ward, Mr. Russell Smart."

Bertie sat hard on the conveniently placed arm of the davenport.

"Roberta!" hissed Mother.

Bertie stood and stepped forward with practiced ease. "Aunt Aurelius! How I have missed you." But leave it up to the old eccentric to bring her Scottish orphan to America in time to ruin Bertie's life. Couldn't she have brought a little terrier instead?

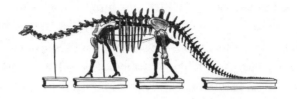

❧ Chapter 3 ❧

Aunt Aurelius's hug was as warm and loving as Bertie remembered, and she gave in to the lengthy squeeze. Unfortunately, Aurelius Armstrong, her father's pigheaded sister, was the one person who might understand and sympathize with today's disappointment. But how could she tell her?

The niceties continued until, forced smile in place, Bertie had to face her foe. There'd been no need to pinch her cheeks for color. Already her racing heart flooded dampness under her corset.

"Miss Hart. It is a pleasure to see you again."

"What's this?" asked Father.

Bertie's grip on the back of the overstuffed wing chair tightened. "I— We—"

"I met Miss Hart at the library today, sir, though I didn't realize at the time who she was. Mr. Carnegie placed me here to ensure we become the best in the nation and serve all Pittsburgh children equally."

Mother's half-closed lids suggested she wasn't impressed. "Yes,

Aurelius did mention something about that."

Half-hidden annoyance deepened the line between Father's brows. "You didn't tell us you got the position, Roberta."

"I didn't." A glance caught Mr. Smart wiping his brow with a neatly folded handkerchief. Good! At least she wasn't suffering alone.

Aunt Aurelius waved her fleshy hand dominated by a massive emerald. "I've waited too long to see my favorite niece as a woman on the verge of marriage, and you've talked nothing else all week, Russell."

Bertie couldn't hide her surprise, nor keep from inspecting his face. "Marriage?"

"Most certainly not!" he countered. "My work at the library takes up all my thoughts."

"What a coincidence." Bertie turned her back for a proper good sneer, her frustration returning.

Aunt Aurelius leaned toward her brother. "Our Russell's finding the position challenging. Not everyone appreciates his. . .his practicality."

"Mrs. Armstrong. Ma'am. Please."

Bertie glanced over her shoulder. Two spots of color below Russell Smart's gray eyes contradicted his self-possessed manner.

He cleared his throat. "I admit it's difficult to come into a position where everyone knows one another while I try to. . .improve on their system."

"Russell likes things done a certain way. Don't we all?" Aunt Aurelius laughed and took his arm, pulling him close and eliciting a warm smile from him. "But as I keep reminding him, he wouldn't be here if he wasn't eminently qualified. Perfect timing, as I was ready to come home and be with family. Scotland's too lonely for me without my dear Armstrong."

In Bertie's estimation, perfect timing would have meant a week's delay by storms. "Well," she began, "the specific qualifications are really only part of being a children's librarian. You must be able to work with people and value their opinions."

Mr. Smart tipped his head as though his hearing was poor or he wasn't ready to believe her capable of intelligent conversation. "I'm glad you're willing to see things my way."

"Your way?"

"Roberta," Father interrupted. "Take Russell to see the best view of the gardens while I see to our drinks. Young man, what may I get you?"

"Water will suit me, sir."

Bertie studied her hands, twirling her amethyst ring around her finger. Anything but look at Russell Smart. He just wasn't going to back down and admit he'd been too hasty in dismissing her. To think he was the boy her aunt had talked about all those years ago. Little Rusty this and Little Rusty that. Having little interest in Little Rusty, to her he'd remained a scamp with scraped knees and ragged clothes.

Now she vaguely recalled mention of some ancient university in Edinburgh and some tour of Italy with Uncle Armstrong.

She wasn't doubting Russell's intelligence, just his willingness to see things her way.

Rather than follow her, he chatted with Father in the corner. Investments? Mergers? Father never wasted time pinning down a man's opinions. The Scotsman couldn't be much older than she, so what made him so experienced? And why did he put her so much on the defense?

She watched him examine the display of Byron Breaux's natural history collection. By the color, she recognized *Fort Pitt: Early Pittsburgh and Environs as Experienced by George Washington, the French and First Americans* when he flipped it open to peruse. Something caught his interest. Apparently investment banking didn't fascinate him as Father might have hoped.

She really did need to try and be decent.

Mother and Aunt Aurelius attempted to drag her into the latest family gossip, but she was saved by their persnickety butler's reappearance.

"Dinner, ma'am."

Father offered Aunt Aurelius his arm. With chins high, they looked much like brother and sister as they led the way to the dining room. Mr. Smart offered to escort Mother.

Goodness. Mother might even be smiling as she looked up at the well-built Scot. "What charming manners, young man. Aurelius, you've done a fine job with him."

Bertie cringed. It's not like they'd found him in a cave and taught him to walk upright, for goodness' sake! Though the details of how he'd come to be in their care escaped memory. And she wouldn't ask.

She didn't care.

Charming manners? Hardly.

All right. You weren't exactly composed.

But he'd judged her frivolous. A spoiled child!

Perhaps because you acted like one?

He was their guest, and she'd make an effort for her aunt's sake. Complaining now would prove him right. Was she supposed to be sorry that her family was wealthy? She closed her eyes.

Yes. Sometimes she was.

Mr. Smart helped Mother with her chair, then, usurping their footman, he came to Bertie's side. Did Aunt Aurelius not employ enough servants?

"May I?"

She nodded and stared up at him, finding her irritation failing.

She'd no sooner taken her first sip of consommé when Aunt Aurelius cleared her throat.

And so it begins.

"Roberta dear, I'm so pleased to see that Victoria cameo on you. It is stunning!"

"As a matter of fact—"

"Aurelius," interrupted Mother, "as she is promised to Henry—you met Henry years ago—she has yet to wear it. After asking my cousin Elizabeth for it, I'm horrified to admit to her than I'd yet to see it on Roberta. Great-Grandmother Letitia would be so disappointed."

Oh, the drama. Bertie rubbed her forehead and silently petitioned help from Father.

"The whole thing is hooey," he said, turning toward their guest. "Mrs. Hart's grandmother received a cameo brooch as a gift from Queen

Victoria, and then came the fanciful notion it brought the wearer true love and happy marriage. Well, Alice didn't need it to find me, did you dear?"

Bertie wanted to crawl under her napkin. It was almost a year since its arrival. The cameo itself was a stunning piece of jewelry and family history, one that Mother had repeatedly hinted at claiming from her cousin merely to pressure Bertie. Now it was not just a lovely pin, but a sticking point between them.

Father sat back, smiling at the notion. "But we've already taken care of Bertie's future."

Bertie dared not glance at Mr. Smart. For all her actions to prove herself a modern woman, he was learning the medieval practice of uniting two wealthy families still lingered in contemporary American society.

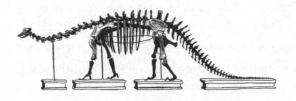

Chapter 4

After a poor night's sleep, Russell had been one of the first on the streetcar this chilly dawn. But after listening to Mr. Hart describe all that Pittsburgh had to offer, he'd looked beyond the belching smokestacks and found greater interest in the river, the countless bridges and the broad hillsides surrounding it. While industry kept the sky tinged gray and the rivers filled with barges, he sensed excitement in many he met. Steel was building the country, and Pittsburgh was the center. But Andrew Carnegie was also building culture. He'd donated more money to promote art and science and literacy than Russell could comprehend. And here he was working in the complex of buildings housing the grandest of the Carnegie libraries, its music hall and museums for art and natural history. A venture to fulfill Carnegie's philanthropic dream to bring knowledge, culture, and new opportunities to all.

Today would be a better day, and if Miss Hart happened to show up, their forced evening together had been a satisfactory if not relaxing chance to start over.

He'd begun to pity Roberta. Last night her mother had taken him aside to thank him for discouraging "that foolish idea." He'd thought the same during that dreadful interview but now had to credit Roberta's efforts.

The children's library needed someone to stay on one or two years until it was operating smoothly. The evening's dinner conversation proved Miss Hart wouldn't be available long. According to her father, her one responsibility was marrying his business partner's son as planned.

Besides, she couldn't understand what it meant to be a child in need of opportunity.

But he could.

He might never know children's literature as well as she, but he knew what it was like to be a child without a book or a warm, quiet place to read. He was here because of what he could accomplish, and he would work hard to learn the rest. That made him the best man for the job.

After arriving at an empty office, he composed a letter to Mr. Carnegie then headed out to find his supervisor. The poor fellow had enough on his hands with the grand opening. Russell traveled the corridors, exhibit halls, and wide marble stairs before finding Mr. Bolton standing well under a dinosaur's gaping skeletal jaw.

"Russell? How can I help you?"

"I've come to a decision."

"Have you?"

He took a bolstering breath. "I have, sir. I myself will stay on in the position of children's librarian, assured I can be a help to you as well. Will you agree it's best for all concerned?"

Bolton's bushy brows made perfect arches under the disarray that was his thinning white hair. "Except Miss Hart."

Apparently, everyone else knew the situation. Russell sighed. "She's free to continue to volunteer. I don't believe she is used to being told what to do."

"Don't be so sure." Mr. Bolton's smile returned with a choppy laugh. "They did take advantage of you, I'm afraid. I think you've made a good decision, but I'm glad I don't have to tell her. Lovely girl. Smart. I mean she's smart. Oh, and persistent. Don't judge her too harshly."

Russell hadn't meant to amuse the man with his opinion of Miss Hart. "Right. But it's highly unlikely she'd see this through. Her parents seem most adamant she focus on marriage instead."

Bolton tilted his head. "And you know this, how?"

"I was at Hartfield last night for supper."

"Really?" Mr. Bolton removed his round-framed glasses to look him over. "Then she wasn't as upset as I expected."

"Oh, she didn't invite me, sir. I'm . . . Mrs. Armstrong, my . . ." How he hated this part. "My benefactress is her aunt."

"Practically family. How convenient."

"Believe me, sir, she wasn't pleased to see me, but she is too well-bred to berate me publicly." Russell held his gaze, hoping to hold off any more references to relationships, family or otherwise.

Bolton released another of his unusual chuckles. "Very well," he continued, reaching for a handshake. "Congratulations on filling the position."

"I've written to advise Mr. Carnegie I'll be staying on longer than expected, but I still plan to administer the other library openings. I don't mind working the extra hours."

His supervisor looked off down the hall. Following his gaze, Russell found no one there. Did he doubt Russell could manage it? Was he concerned over Carnegie's reaction?

"I suggest, Russell, that you learn the names of our many wealthy patrons. It's best not to upset them."

"You're speaking of Mr. Hart in particular?"

Bolton considered this. "Not likely. He's shown no real support in his daughter's desire to work here. Like most investors, he and his partner, Mr. Kendall, are busy with their dogfight against J. P. Morgan's bailout of the government. They are still recovering from the financial depression of '93."

"I know little of it, sir."

"Just as well. I find our work here comforting, while the wealthy face constant worry."

He couldn't resist peering up at the series of neck bones arching high above them. He really must take more time to examine these fascinating creatures. "With the interviews completed, I'll begin my letters of introduction to the publishers right away."

"Good. Good." Bolton wiped his glasses with a handkerchief and replaced them on his thin nose. "I hope we don't lose Miss Hart's assistance. She's created her own lists of books sorted by age of the reader, and I've signed off on her suggested layout of the children's tables and nooks."

"Wasn't that best left up to the new director?"

Bolton's professionalism covered most of his reaction. "Your appointment was a surprise."

"I realize that, sir. But I hope the staff soon sees that I will be a benefit here."

Bolton enthusiastically agreed. "I know you will make my job easier. That's why Carnegie is. . .well, Carnegie. He sees things as a whole, an organization working as a machine. A sum of its parts. I suspect you are like him in that way, which is why we're glad to have you here."

"Thank you, sir. I will let you get back to your work."

So it was true. Bolton had all but hired Miss Hart when the unknown Mr. Smart had been sent in with little warning. After yesterday's humiliation, the manager's appreciation was affirming.

With plenty to do, Russell turned the corner at his usual pace and collided with the redheaded beauty who distributed mail and messages throughout the extensive building.

"Oh! Mr. Smart." Her hand remained on his sleeve. "What a lucky day. I was looking for you."

"Really?" How odd. He glanced at the armful of mail she held against her chest.

"Some of us are going out this evening, and I'd hoped you'd join us at a little piano saloon downtown. What do you say?"

She stood close enough that he stepped back. His gaze traveled across the powdery finish of her cheeks and fell to her painted red lips. He looked away. Her job was to be pleasant and helpful. And, yes, congeniality would be essential to his growth as an employee. He had to make the effort. Just not today.

"I don't think so, Miss. . ."

"Miss Springer, silly. Don't tell me you forgot my name already."

"I'm sorry. Yes. I've been so busy."

"Which is exactly why you need a break." She leaned closer as though they were sharing a secret. "I'll stop by your office later and give you the address. Or better yet, you can come with me so I know you won't get lost." She reached up and straightened his tie.

He stepped back as if stung.

Cheeky lass! These American girls were so. . .modern. After the effort to make conversation last night, the idea of dinner with more people he barely knew made his head throb.

And it would be noisy. And Miss Springer would want to dance. Cling to him. . .

"I have to go. Not with you." He raised a hand. "I mean, to my office." Disappointment filled her eyes and filled his chest with remorse. "Thank you for thinking of me." Before that led to obligations, he made his escape.

She called to him as he got to the end of the hall and waved coyly when he turned. He couldn't help but smile. She was rather attractive, and he would have to venture out sometime. She was certainly friendlier than Miss Hart, gave herself no airs, and was apparently unspoken for.

He opened the stairwell door leading to the wide hallway crossing the basement and took a deep breath of relief.

Then held it. Miss Hart?

All else disappeared, but he continued toward her and his makeshift office as if it wasn't unusual to have visitors. As if she'd been the last thing on his mind. If he could avoid falling victim to those eyes, he might manage his way through telling her his decision.

You're in charge, Russell. "Have you been waiting long?"

"Please give me five minutes of your time. It is for the good of the library, and I think you should listen."

Oh, do you? "Then, please, come in." Out of habit, he straightened his cuffs, smoothed his lapels and tie, and pictured his benefactor's confident posture and poise. That's when Miss Hart's perfume caused an urgent tickling of his nose. He retrieved his handkerchief in time to cover two monstrously jolting sneezes. "Excuse me. I'm sorry. Please take a seat."

A moment's discomposure crossed her face. "No, thank you. It's best I say what I need to say and then leave. I know you're a busy man."

He wiped his nose again then affected a smile. "First, let me thank you for your hospitality." When her expression remained fixed, he studied the empty teacup he'd left on his desk. "How can I help you?"

"You can tell me you've chosen me as the children's library director, that's how."

It was good they'd both remained standing. That would help. She'd leave with that much more ease. "I appreciate your enthusiasm."

"You know I'm the most qualified."

Unfortunately, yes. But better to keep this light. Go for something witty. "Did you wait outside the door and interview all the applicants as they left?"

By the look on her face, he'd been anything but amusing. "No, but I know these things."

"Then mind reading is another of your many skills? Or was Mrs. Oakes involved?"

"Of course not. She's a wonderful secretary, and she would never do something so unprofessional."

He smiled like this wasn't getting worse. He'd relived yesterday's disastrous interview a hundred times. "As a matter of fact, this will save me the trouble of writing a letter. I—" He was at once stifled by the anticipation and longing on her face. Vulnerability like that weakened his resolve. *Don't be a coward now.* "I've come to a decision."

"Me?" Her uncharacteristic transparency tore through him with equally uncharacteristic remorse. Deep remorse. But it had to be done. Miss Hart had to deal with disappointment at some point in her life. "No. Me."

❧ *Chapter 5* ❧

*I*t was all Roberta could do to speak and smile as she passed others in the hallways. Actual employees.

Russell I'm So Smart had done it. Wiped out years of planning, effort, and prayers. Well, she would not let it happen.

Bertie knocked on Mr. Bolton's door. No response. Laughter at the far end of the hallway drew her to where three gentlemen stood in a circle, silencing when they saw her.

Mr. Bolton met her halfway with his usual brisk pace and an unusual tightness about his mouth. "Miss Hart. How nice to see you. We have a big day ahead."

"You are always so kind." The shuffling of feet and throat clearing among the others suggested they already knew what the Scotsman had done. "I won't keep you long." She turned as Mr. Bolton came alongside, and they walked beyond earshot. She could wait no longer. "I thought he was here just long enough to interfere with my hiring. Isn't he some *wunderkind* needed elsewhere lest the world flounder on its own?"

"I gather your interview with Mr. Smart yesterday did not go as you'd hoped. Forgive me, Miss Hart, but how Mr. Carnegie administers his philanthropy is not for me to say. I know you're disappointed, but—"

"Disappointed? I'm, I'm. . ." What was she? Angry? Disappointed and fighting tears.

And horrified. She covered her mouth. She'd just come running like a spoiled child. She turned away. Her hands fisted just thinking of the smile on Smart's face. He'd enjoyed telling her.

He was a brute.

Well, a brute with long lashes, but he hadn't needed to be so smug.

"Mr. Smart is accomplished at what he does, Miss Hart. But Carnegie won't let him sit here ordering children's books for too long, because, I agree, he's likely too valuable to the corporation."

Valuable? "So what are you saying?"

"I'm saying he spoke to me. His reluctance to hire you had to do with. . . Well, as a woman of your social class, he doubted your availability for long-term employment."

She gritted her teeth. Ooh! He must have liked tossing that around.

"I suppose he thought you'd have your father or Mr. Heinz sort things for you. Uncle H as you call him?"

Bertie's face reddened. "Like what I've done here."

Mr. Bolton politely looked down.

"I don't know if I can work with him. Volunteer, I mean. Henry expected this—you know Henry Kendall. He says the city's central board of education is looking for someone to address the reading needs of children. The teachers and schoolmasters have enough to do, while I have the advantage of. . .more time." The benefit of her station. Despite its short tether. A paid position with the city was one Father might better approve of, but— Irritation throbbed in her temple. "But I've come to feel at home here."

"Miss Hart. You will have to decide, but if you learn to work with Mr. Smart, you will benefit from some of his experience and methods. That way, when he leaves—and he will—you'll have much to offer us or the city fathers. Surely you see that Mr. Smart felt he was making the best decision." He wiped his glasses. "You and he were the only two with the fire to fill this role. While he excels in the organizational side of business, you have the passion to fuel children's interest in their futures by a love of reading. I don't want to lose that." Bolton's small smile seemed aimed at drawing her out. "You don't think Russell Smart will be found on the library floor with a child on his lap, do you?"

He was right, of course. And despite her foolish decision to run to him to complain, she was mature enough to see his wisdom. What she accomplished now would change the course of her future.

"Thank you, Mr. Bolton. I'll continue to volunteer and work with Mr. Smart because those children need me, and I need to do this."

"I'm glad to hear it."

"I think it's best I stay out of his way today, but I'll make up for it tomorrow. May we keep this conversation to ourselves?"

"Eleven a.m." Russell snapped his pocket watch closed with a wee bit of self-congratulation. Two days now since Miss Hart's boasts of her reliability. Her words were proving to be of little value.

He fought the desire to gloat, but his head ached with frustration. How dare she march into his office to belittle his decision then prove herself as indifferent to business structure as he'd feared. Even more foolish was he to watch for her all morning.

The frantic activity and noises echoing throughout the marbled halls felt empty without her.

He'd carefully packed a lunch pail to enjoy outdoors and now felt some comfort in seeing busy bee employees prepare the landscaping for Tuesday's grand opening. The sidewalks were clear of fallen leaves, but his thoughts were in chaos, leaving him too unsettled to enjoy his buttered bun and cheese.

Her dismissal of his knowledge and experience irked him as much as his schoolmates' judgment of his penniless beginnings. It had taken years to shake off the effects, language, and attitude of being poor and orphaned, but he'd vowed not to turn judgment on the wealthy. He clearly hadn't succeeded.

Thankfully, his coworkers here were mostly working class, settled and accepting in their place *between*. Despite his love for Mrs. Armstrong, she'd slipped easily back into Pittsburgh society. Upon their arrival, he'd insisted on renting a small room while she took a suite at the Hotel Monongahela.

She treated him with complete respect, still doting on him as the young boy he'd been, but her brother's family—the Harts—clearly hadn't forgotten his origin.

The cure would be holding on to his dignity. He'd fought hard enough for it.

For dear Mrs. Armstrong's sake, he'd find Miss Hart and make peace. There would be family events he could not avoid, and he wouldn't let hard feelings linger.

The necessary but inconvenient waxing of his office floor this afternoon left him unable to accomplish much else today. This was a chance to visit the school where she claimed to volunteer. There he'd speak with the schoolmaster about the woman who had, so far, shown none of the laudable skills paraded on her application.

Heading to the Minersville neighborhood, Russell was on the streetcar before he could change his mind. He imagined her surrounded by wee lasses gazing up in admiration as she read a fairy tale. *And they lived happily ever after.* Fine, if you were a prince finding your princess.

For him it was the pleasure of a job well done, one that would honor the Creator.

Rain speeded his walk to the school's front doors, where he brushed off water drops and rattled the large knocker. He stepped back when facing the stern woman who let him in but soon recognized weariness rather than hostility.

"I'm Mr. Russell Smart, and I'd like to speak with the schoolmaster." She studied him warily.

Most had little trouble understanding him, as he made it a point to speak slowly and carefully.

Her comparatively heavy accent answered, "Do you have an appointment?"

How broad this land of opportunity. One could travel two hours in Scotland and hear different dialects, but how was one to learn to recognize such regional differences in a country that took weeks to cross?

"No, ma'am. I don't."

This wasn't an orphanage, but he felt the same false cheeriness.

A rustle of taffeta took his gaze down the corridor.

Roberta Hart glanced over her shoulder, her body turned toward a crying young lad alongside her on a bench. She waved and rose. "Wait, Miss Mudd."

The woman frowned at Russell. "Do you want to see the headmaster or not, sir?"

"It's all right. Mr. Smart is a friend of mine."

"If you say so," Miss Mudd replied indifferently.

Surprised at such a friendly introduction, Russell's more immediate concern was the distraught boy left alone on the bench.

"I'll be right back, Thomas," Miss Hart assured him. Then she stopped in front of Russell. "What are you doing here?"

She bore a heavyheartedness he hadn't expected. She looked like she could use a friend. He shook his head, embarrassed that he'd gone to this much trouble. "I'm not sure. But is there something I can do?" He imagined reaching for her hand.

She closed her eyes, her shoulders slumping as she leaned against the wall. "Mr. Pettybridge sent me a note by messenger this morning, after receiving some news. Thomas"—she nodded toward the boy—"came in, not knowing his father had been killed in an accident at the plant."

"Steel?"

"Not Carnegie's, if that matters. An independent foundry." She glanced over her shoulder and nudged Russell farther away. "An older brother is home with his mother, but Thomas refuses to leave." She rubbed the back of her neck. "I've been with him since. I should have sent a note around to his mother. There's no telephone here."

"I'm sorry too. For the lad. As you're a volunteer, I can't exactly make demands."

"Believe me, I wanted to be there as I'd promised, but Thomas begged me to stay." She raised those brown eyes to him. "I'll make it up to you tomorrow."

Her sincerity and the stricken look on her face emptied him of any frustration. So much so, he longed to comfort her instead. "Nonsense. You are far from owing me."

Roberta Hart was confident and skilled, yet he found himself overwhelmed by the desire to take her sadness, to offer her his shoulder. To be someone she turned to in need. Clearly a thought he must banish.

"He's right down here, sir."

Approaching footsteps and Roberta's glance led him to a harried, older man.

"I'm Mr. Pettybridge. I understand you were looking for me?"

"Yes, I was." But now he regretted it. That said. . . "If we might have a word in private. In a few moments?"

The gentleman slumped. "Now is best, I'm afraid."

Russell glanced at Miss Hart. "I'll be right back and at your disposal. Please wait for me."

He followed Mr. Pettybridge's ill-fitting suit down the narrow hall, passing a single-file line of ragamuffin boys. Remnants of dirt around one redhead's ears showed the extent of his washing. Grimy skies and streets as play yards and mothers barely able to keep up with both laundry and cooking—that was the way of it. That was the world Russell had known, one that grew bleaker upon his mother's and sister's deaths.

Until Mr. Armstrong. With his help, Russell Smart had discovered books and decided that keeping his hands clean and his mind busy would keep him out of the workhouse.

Pettybridge turned a corner and pointed to an open office door.

"Thank you for seeing me, sir," Russell said after settling in the wee, crowded room. "I'd come to ask about Miss Hart. I imagine you know she volunteers at the library?"

"Of course. Here she runs a special reading program for our boys and girls."

"Girls? Here?"

"In the other half of the building. The children seem to learn better when separated. Fewer distractions."

Oh aye. Right enough. "I'm the new director of the children's library." He glanced over his shoulder, unused to claiming the title. "Your name was on her list of references, so I feel I'm within my rights to ask." Justified, but he felt rather foolish now. "Do you find her work satisfactory? Is she reliable?"

"More than satisfactory. The children love reading with her. We'll be sorry to lose her, though we've never been able to pay her for what she does."

"Are your female staff all single?"

Pettybridge edged back. "Oh no. Some are married. Why?"

"Simple curiosity." He rose. "Thank you for your time." Pausing by the door, he fished for more. "But Miss Hart is not likely to stay on after she marries."

"I have no idea. But we are happy to have her for as long as she will."

Stabbed with contrition, Russell made an effort at a pleasant nod as he excused himself. Any pride in his administration skills faded away. While he might be the best man for the job of children's library director, Roberta Hart was the best woman for any job, and her attitude at the interview came from desperation to serve. He'd immediately judged her, yet it was young Thomas who had the right idea, begging her to stay.

She outranked Russell in what was important. She had heart.

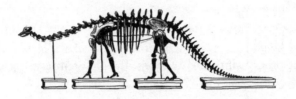

❧ Chapter 6 ❧

The absolute last man Bertie expected to appreciate today was Russell Smart.

But he'd returned from Mr. Pettybridge's office, reassured Thomas that he'd see him home, and promised he and Miss Hart would do what they could for Thomas's mother.

All well and good until Thomas cowered, shaking his head. "No, sir. I can't."

Russell went down on one knee, his hand on the boy's shoulder. "Miss Hart? Would you say Thomas here has no reason to trust me other than the fact you and I are friends?"

"Yes, that sounds right."

Russell continued in the same tender tone, his accent more noticeable. "Then, lad, I hope you will trust me enough to tell me why you don't care to go home."

Thomas didn't answer. Just as he'd refused Bertie.

Russell diverted his gaze to the end of the hall, or to a distant memory. "Have you ever seen your mum cry? Cry hard?"

Searching Russell's face, fat tears pooled in Thomas's eyes until the shaking of his head set one loose.

"It's not easy when someone you love dies. Nor when someone you love is hurting and you can't help. Do ye know what I mean?"

Thomas wiped a dirty sleeve across his face, catching the wet dribble under his nose.

Russell rose, keeping a gentle hand on the boy's back. "Let's take a walk."

The boy, with Bertie nodding encouragement, slipped off the bench, and his holey, oversized boots—one lacking a lace—clumped to the floor. Russell's level-headed prompting was just what Thomas needed.

"My da—my father—died when I was no taller than you."

Now curious, Thomas looked up at him. "Did you cry, sir?"

"Oh, that I did. Quite a bit. There's no shame in it."

"But Mama? She'll be. . ."

"Sad and frightened, I suspect. And, well, you'll want her to take care of you. But because she'll be so sad, you're afraid she can't. If I were you, I'd want things to stay the way they were."

Sniffing loudly, Thomas used his sleeve again as a handkerchief. "What if she won't stop crying?"

"Ah, but she will. Mind you, it will come and go."

Bertie heard little more. They'd gone out of earshot, but Russell's voice remained a reassuring hum as he squatted down to Thomas's level, dabbing at the boy's face with his own square of white cotton. She'd heard enough to understand Thomas feared going home. More to the point, he feared seeing his mother's pain.

They turned back. "What do you think, Miss Hart?" Russell asked, drawing her in. "Will Thomas's mum feel worse if he cries in front of her?"

Bertie fumbled with the ruffles at her neck and had to clear her throat at the rising lump. "I think she'd feel worse if he didn't." She reached for Thomas. "She doesn't expect you to be all grown up."

"Then can I go home now?"

Russell met her eyes with such relief she wanted to clutch his arm as well.

Now she stood holding Thomas's dirty hand and waiting for the carriage Russell had gone off to procure. She could call him Russell in her head, she supposed. Practically a cousin and all.

It was then Thomas gave in to his first wracking sob. She squatted down and held him, caring little for the state of her shirtwaist and the fox trim of her coat. All that mattered was he'd be home and back with his family, and she would find a way to help.

Had Mr. MacCormack been part of a union, and if so, what was their role now? Could the family stay where they were without his income?

"Bertie?"

She recognized that voice and ardently wished it wasn't so. "Henry? Whatever are you doing here?"

"I heard what happened." He leaned close and squeezed her arm.

Her job? Her humiliation? "This is not a good time to talk," she warned, gesturing toward the lad.

"Oh my dear, no. It's the perfect time to talk. How long have I been warning you something like this would happen?"

Swirls of unease wrapped her chest. "I have no idea. Really. If you must go on, then at least wait until I am home this evening. Please."

"I'm talking about the factory. This is just the story I need." He glanced at Thomas. "This is the MacCormack boy?"

"Yes, but—" She looked up at the carriage's approach and started toward it.

"You're leaving?"

What did he expect? The boy was in no condition to remain. "We are taking Thomas home. You and I will speak later. We can't put it off. I'm tired of the farce each time Father brings up the agreement."

"No wonder, given what he and my father are promising just to please the board."

"This is not the place."

But Henry stepped in front of her, bending his head down to gain the boy's attention. "Thomas? I'm Mr. Kendall from the newspaper. We need to let everyone know what accidents like this do to families. You do want to help, don't you?"

Appalled, Bertie shoved Henry's shoulder. It did little but startle him. "What can you be thinking?"

"What's going on here?" demanded Russell, bounding out of the still-moving carriage.

Henry positioned himself as though they were two rams ready to battle. "And who are you?"

Russell scowled, establishing himself at her side.

She felt the boy tug at her sleeve. Seeing her own apprehension in his face, she pulled him closer.

"I'm Russell Smart from the Carnegie Library. I work with Miss Hart, and we've come to help the lad."

"Well, aren't you the hero." Henry dropped a possessive arm over her shoulder. "Miss Hart knows very well who I am, and I can assure you, neither of us have to answer to you."

"Stop it, Henry!" She shrugged off his arm. "We are leaving. You're making things worse."

"I have a deadline. This story is going to be front-page news, and that's what I need." Henry moved to slow her. "Success is the only thing that will change our future, and you know it."

Russell's forearm went across Henry's chest.

She gasped.

"That will be enough. You won't be bothering the lad now, and if you're a friend of Miss Hart's, ye'll respect her wishes. If you care to make yourself useful, get down to the site of the accident. There's your story." Russell dropped his arm but not his threatening glare.

Henry's silence reflected affront at such impudence, rather than fear. "Do you have any idea who I am?"

"Can't say I do." Then adding, "Nor do I care," Russell gestured to the carriage's open door and pressed his way past a flabbergasted

Henry, blocking further interference.

"Roberta! You know why I'm doing this."

She did. Henry's idealized desire to see rights wronged and protect the working poor was admirable. But lately he seemed to treat the same people he claimed to care for as little more than characters in a story. Henry's rebellion had doubled in the months since the start of their fathers' well-known fight with J. P. Morgan over his infusion of gold into the national treasury, an act which they believed put the United States under control of European interests.

"You'll be hearing from me later," Henry called. "Whatever your name is."

"Smart."

"Of course it is."

She stepped up into the carriage, keeping Thomas close. Once seated, she put her arm around him, shuddering at how Henry's threat echoed her own during her interview.

"Where to, sir?" called the driver.

"Thomas?"

The boy dropped his head. "I don't want you to see it."

"Nonsense." Russell handed her a second clean handkerchief, mimicking a much-needed wipe of the boy's nose. "You've nothing to be ashamed of. Miss Hart and I care only that you get home, and then we'll see to helping your mum."

"All right. Trent Street, sir. Off Webster."

Russell relayed the address to the driver and then feigned interest beyond the coach's window so Thomas could regain his young dignity. Russell closed the door soundly. "We'll have you home soon, Thomas." He sat opposite. "I've brought these," he added with his earlier gentleness, gesturing to a bundle of cut flowers. "Let's give them to your mum, eh? It won't change things, but it will be a reminder that she has friends and a caring son."

"What will happen to my pa, miss?"

Bertie met Russell's eyes, noting how dark the soft gray had become.

He answered for her. "I don't know. But I'll find out. That's not your worry. You just think about how much he cared for you all and worked hard to provide."

Thomas nodded, his lower lip quivering.

Bertie couldn't have spoken, for fear of falling apart. If it was up to her to get Thomas home and see to things like this, would she be able? Proud as she was of her abilities, right now it was all she could do to move her limbs.

Freed from the inspection of his schoolmates, Thomas released a morning's worth of tears. His pain wrapped around her until her ribs ached. She caressed his back in an effort to reassure him.

She couldn't face the questions Russell must have. How, when the truth appalled her, could she explain that Henry and she were promised to one another like medieval royalty? What they privately called "the agreement," referred to in the same tone as others said "the gallows." Worse, they'd allowed their parents to believe nothing had changed lest they be pressured to consider others. Bertie had no desire to become the newest marriageable commodity in the finer East Coast communities, and Henry had no desire to be an investor.

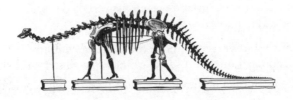

❧ *Chapter 7* ❧

*T*he silence in the carriage grew, causing her to hope they soon arrived at Thomas's home.

Russell Smart might be her aunt's ward, but he didn't quite hide his disdain for the ways of her parents' society. How could she tell him the embarrassing truth?

The light coming in silhouetted Russell's face, and she couldn't look away. He really was striking. Perfect nose. Perfect mouth. And now that he wasn't glaring at her, she could see the gentleness of eyes framed by annoyingly long blond lashes. She continued to stare until his gaze shifted to hers with enough questioning that she had to look away.

She'd awakened this morning full of thoughts of him. Enough so that she'd taken the cameo brooch out of its box and placed it at her throat. The mirror confirmed how lovely it would look on the neckline of her shirtwaist. Perfect. Like it was meant to be worn there. Today.

He straightened his tie and the stiff round collar. "I'd like to apologize, Miss Hart. And ask that you consider an offer of employment. To assist me. I can't do more at the moment, but I would be a fool not to take advantage of your experience with. . ." He glanced at Thomas. "Choosing the right books for the children we will be serving."

"How many hours?"

"Similar to the average number you currently volunteer. I studied the sign-in sheets and—"

"Russ—Mr. Smart. Did you come to the school to offer me this job? Or to seek out the schoolmaster and inquire of my worthiness?" She hated the whiny pitch in her voice, but she had to know for sure.

As expected, consideration crossed his artless face. "Honestly? I came to prove to myself that I was right about you." He looked at her straight on now.

His honesty begged study.

"But I was wrong."

She had no answer for that. Thankfully, the slowing of the carriage reminded her there were more important things to see to.

Thomas sat up and looked out the window. "There it is, sir. Down the street where all those people are."

A street too narrow for the coach.

Russell gave him a reassuring smile, one that soothed her as well. She could work alongside him.

Yes. Most definitely.

He stepped out first and offered a hand. She'd left her gloves behind in the confusion, and found the warmth of his skin pleasant, however fleeting. She'd seen but not visited neighborhoods like this, crowded and deep in sooty shadows. Once they were near Thomas's tenement, Thomas's brother Andrew came forward, and Mr. Smart introduced himself. It had been a long time since Bertie had to offer sympathy to a stranger, and it had certainly not been in the case of a tragic accident. Any sense of self-assurance ebbed away. Was it because Russell had relieved her of the need? For all she'd considered him far too businesslike, he was the one making his way through the crowd with his hand on Thomas's back, while she was satisfied to follow at his side.

"We'd have to work together," he whispered, apparently still thinking of his offer. "Closely. Could you do it?"

She studied his face. Lord forgive her and help her. "Yes. I'll most definitely try."

He was far more relaxed here among the working poor than he'd been at Hartfield's broad dining table. Was that because of her treatment of him earlier or because of his earlier life? She'd been condescending from the first and just shy of antagonistic toward his cool politeness. Her face warmed with shame.

By the time they'd climbed three stories, offered their condolences to Mrs. MacCormack, and considered the family's needs, it was past time for her to be home. Last week she'd been eager to attend tonight's event. Now it lacked importance.

The driver had waited, chatting with the neighborhood children, and stood at attention when she and Russell came into view.

"Next we'll get the lady home. Hartfield." He glanced her way.

"Beacon Street," she clarified. "Corner of Murdoch."

The driver nodded. "Heard of Hartfield, miss. I'll get you right home."

Once the cab was under way, Russell confided that he would learn more of what could be done to help.

Bertie could offer nothing but silent appreciation and felt a bone-deep exhaustion as the long ride out to Beacon Street continued. When the coach rattled up the hilly circular drive that flattened out before their wide, welcoming porch, Russell hurried to exit and assist her as she stepped down.

But he wasn't looking at her. Last night he'd arrived in the dark. Now he scanned Hartfield's three stories of stonework, balconies, stone columns, and gables before meeting her eyes as she thanked him for all he'd done.

"I'm so glad you were there." It was true. How she longed for his respect. She'd work for it, and then?

"What we did was but a wee part of a day that has forever changed that family."

The truth of it made her chest ache. "Yes."

He smiled gently, but the sadness remained. "If there was ever a chance they could leave such poverty behind, it's gone."

Bertie stepped back, unable to acknowledge his words, or maybe it was what he hadn't said. She'd never known what poverty like that meant, and never would.

Russell climbed in and closed the door. She watched the carriage go down the hill and disappear up Murdoch.

What could she do? She couldn't help them all. She worked to improve lives by encouraging a love of books and learning, but Thomas was only one of thousands of children. This afternoon it all felt like too much. A landslide of misfortune.

Was that how Uncle Armstrong felt when he'd chosen one inquisitive, stalwart orphan? Had he done all he could for just one child, knowing he could do so little for them all?

But by doing so, look what this one would accomplish.

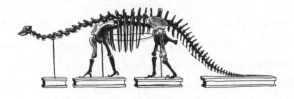

❧ Chapter 8 ❧

As late afternoon light slanted through his office windows, Russell surveyed the two crates of used books on his desk.

Having accomplished so little here, yet feeling more settled than he had since his first day, Russell had gathered donated books stored in the basement. New books would wear with age and dirty fingers in their own good time but would first come off the Carnegie's shelves with uncreased spines, spotless paper, and the promising scent of pages ready for discovery. Though he appreciated the donors' generosity, the library would stock only new books. These would go to Pettybridge's school.

"George? I'm ready to go."

Employee George Smith, a most genial fellow, would make pleasant company on the way. Russell hoped to catch Mr. Pettybridge at his job, for the schoolmaster had told him he lived in the annex. Both carrying a crate of used books, Russell and George traveled by train and streetcar to find, as expected, the schoolmaster pleased to see them when Russell knocked on his window. A moment later he welcomed them inside.

"I would prefer to offer new books," Russell explained, setting them down, "but until then. . ."

Pettybridge waved off the apology. "We are most happy to accept these, Mr. Smart. They are finer than any we have, and Miss Hart will enjoy having new stories to read aloud as long as we keep them here. I'm afraid the children are not allowed to take them home."

The idea warmed his heart. He'd like to see her, listen to her himself. Now that Roberta had accepted his offer, they would work together and become friends who could put the discomfort of their first meeting behind them.

Only she mustn't learn of this, lest it become more than he'd intended—a charitable act not meant to draw attention. "She doesn't need to know who donated them, eh?" After Pettybridge nodded, Russell stared at George, hoping he too understood he was to keep this quiet. "Isn't that best, Mr. Smith?"

George pondered this before nodding.

"Very well then. We'll be on our way. I'm glad to have caught you."

Pettybridge checked his pocket watch. "And how is young Thomas faring at home?"

How did any child feel with the loss of a parent? Fearful. Broken-hearted. "I don't know, but I will visit them soon."

"Miss Hart is a wonder. The way she took care of him."

"Yes, well. . ." Best not to think of that. Which, of course, worked just the opposite. "I expect you will have difficulty replacing her."

Pettybridge stopped unloading the books. "She's leaving?"

"I mean when she marries."

"Oh. Did I miss an announcement?" He shrugged. "Not that it's my business how they live over there in Squirrel Hill."

A most curious urge to explain—brag—his connection to the family surprised Russell. He should be glad the schoolmaster didn't take him for a toff.

Pettybridge sat and leaned back, folding his hands over his paunch. "Though wealth like that comes and goes in their kind of business. I don't envy them at all."

Russell considered this. "While we know that desk work will always be there in the morning. Which is why we must go."

Pettybridge rose to shake their hands. "Thank you again, Mr. Smart. Mr. Smith. Please continue to keep us in mind. We don't turn away old books."

George seemed pleased with his part, but there was a change in him as they waited for the streetcar. He cleared his throat with a hint of unease.

A glance confirmed it.

"I regret what happened the other day with Miss Hart. You not knowing and all." George met Russell's gaze. "I should have spoken up. She's a favorite of ours, and, well. . ."

"You will all be pleased to learn I've realized the benefit of her experience. Can you keep it to yourself until then?"

He turned to study Russell. "Then you've hired her after all?"

"A few hours a week." And those hours paid out of his own pocket. With Mrs. Armstrong convinced her niece and Henry Kendall would announce the long-planned engagement at Christmas, the situation wouldn't last long. "And that will be the end of any discussion."

Instead, George chatted about the public's fascination with *their* dinosaurs, as the staff had begun to call them. Soon enough, George bid him a good evening as they parted for their walks home.

Russell wouldn't talk about the staff—with staff—and certainly not about Miss Hart. Not with anyone. Not the way her face, her smile, and her teasing laughter was always with him. The way she'd stood up to him. The way she'd comforted Thomas. The way she'd gratefully accepted his offer. Was it possible she looked forward to working with him?

He'd hired her because she was the perfect choice for director's assistant. It was that simple.

The silly grin tugging at his mouth told him it was anything but simple.

He glanced at his watch. Five o'clock. That meant twelve, plus three.

Fifteen hours until he saw her again.

"Oh no!" He'd forgotten that fancy reception tonight. Thursday had arrived so quickly, and the day had kept him at sixes and sevens.

Russell arrived at his room in a rush. Just time enough to shave and dress for this evening's reception held downtown to honor the library staff's efforts in the grand opening and thank those of Pittsburgh society most involved in the establishment of the library's museums of art and history. He'd found out yesterday he was expected to attend despite his minimal days as employee. He'd go, make a polite circulation, then leave as quickly as possible.

An hour and a half later he stood in a ballroom thick with cigar smoke and heavy perfumes. The Monongahela's gilded ceilings watched over enough sparkling jewelry to rival its chandeliers. Any chance of early escape was thwarted when a Mr. and Mrs. Oosterling, clearly wealthy benefactors, deposited their giggling daughter at his side, gave her a wink, and paraded away.

Abandoned as such, he could hardly turn his back on the lass and disappear. "Have you lived in Pittsburgh all of your life, Miss Oosterling?" was all he could manage.

"How kind of you to ask."

Really?

Just as well she didn't have high expectations for snappy conversation. He might even appreciate nervous chatter on her part, but she remained quiet, twisting her hands and stealing glances.

"I've just arrived in your city—your country for all that. Perhaps you could tell me what I must see here. Places you like to visit?"

She turned suddenly. "Will you say that again? And my name. It's just that. . .the way you talk. That accent."

"I apologize if you find me difficult to understand."

"Oh no! I could listen to it for hours." She made little twists of her body like a wee lass with a ruffly new frock.

Rather endearing, and monstrously embarrassing. At least he wasn't the only one here completely uncomfortable. "I am glad to hear it."

"And I'd love to join you, Mr. Smart. Father would be happy to let us use the carriage to see the city. He forbids me to use public transportation." She giggled. "Though I know I'd be safe with you at my side."

What had he missed? "Pleasant as that sounds, I'm afraid—"

"Saturday then?" Her gaze shifted past him, and the sparkle in her eyes faded.

"Miss Oosterling. How nice to see you." Roberta Hart breezily came to a stop. "Oh, and Mr. Smart. What a surprise." Her attention shifted immediately back to the lass at his side. "The last time we spoke, you had just returned from Europe."

"Had I?"

Roberta waited, and when it seemed Miss Oosterling couldn't think of more to say, Roberta bestowed upon him a furtive grin.

"Miss Hart," ventured Russell. "I should have realized you'd be here."

"Yes, Father insisted we come. After today it was the last thing I felt like doing." She returned her attention to Miss Oosterling. "You've met our Mr. Smart, then? Oh, and how is your sister? Hilda. So close to the wedding."

Roberta might not be pleased to be here, but he admired her ease at conversation. With such natural grace and beauty, her vivacity made her the only woman in the room for him and left him unequal to the task of focusing elsewhere.

"Frantic, I'm afraid," Miss Oosterling replied. "Father says he will not go through this again."

Miss Hart acted taken aback. "Surely he's teasing. Pittsburgh does love its big weddings."

"Well, of course, I'll marry, but he's hoping for something small and intimate. Fifty or a hundred guests. After four daughters, he's lost his insistence on the perfect match and perfect wedding."

Roberta's eyes darted to Russell. "Then you are free to marry the man of your choice."

He took a step back. That wide arched exit was calling him.

"My older sisters are quite displeased about it," Miss Oosterling proclaimed, gaining momentum. "My parents have given up on me after taking so long to find the right match for Hilda." She covered her mouth. "I shouldn't have said that. Your father must be happy to have just the one daughter, though they must both be disappointed with the lack of sons."

Roberta's response faltered. "We do share that burden, don't we?" Though she laughed, something had changed.

"Excuse me, ladies. I see someone I must speak with. It was my pleasure to meet you, Miss Oosterling."

"Oh dear. Please don't go."

Russell felt his face redden at her display of such disappointment. Like a wee lass pulled from the candy shop window. "I'm afraid I must." He searched Roberta's face for help and found her biting her lip against a mischievous grin.

"But what about our engagement?"

He sucked in his breath and then coughed. "What's that, lass?"

"Saturday. When would you like to get started?"

Russell coughed again into his handkerchief, his eyes watering. "I'm afraid I must decline. Things are busy at the library, and the weekends will be quite full."

"Nonsense, Mr. Smart," purred Miss Hart, eyeing him with none of Miss Oosterling's innocence. "You must take some time for yourself. A relaxing day with a new friend."

She knew exactly what she was doing. But why? "You of all people know how much work I have to do."

"And with my help you will get it done. Oh, by the way, I don't come in on Fridays." She turned to Miss Oosterling. "You know, Mr. Smart and I are practically cousins." Those beautiful brown eyes opened wide. "Oh! Perhaps the two of you could join me for lunch someday."

The gangly debutante squealed. "And you must bring Mr. Kendall, Bertie dear. Oh, wouldn't that be fun?"

Of course the lass would think so. Anything that sounded like an *engagement*. Apparently, Miss Oosterling was under no obligation to bring home a man of means.

Both women waited on his reaction. He must escape before they brought in reinforcements.

"And now I really must go." He bowed his head. "I'm sorry, Miss Oosterling, but I'm unable to make plans for Saturday. Or Sunday. Or next week. Enjoy your evening." Russell walked away much faster than was proper, but American women could be so. . .so forward. So canny. Mrs. Armstrong had a cheeky sense of humor, but he blamed it on her years in Dunfermline.

Miss Oosterling's desperation was frightening enough, but Miss Hart practically had them an item. At this rate, his name would be on the social page by next week. Engaged. If Roberta had any idea how he felt about her, she wouldn't tease so.

Then her teasing was a good sign. It meant she didn't know that he longed for every moment of her company as much as he dreaded the way she turned his mind to mince.

✥ Chapter 9 ✥

*R*ussell waited at the coat clerk's desk, eager to leave before another bombardment, but it was not to be.

Mr. Oosterling, a man with an impressive waxed mustache, stopped Russell and bent his ear for a good twenty minutes with no mention of the single daughter.

While Russell knew he must cultivate support for the library with those capable of financial donations, he struggled to pay attention as Roberta flitted around the room, charming everyone she met.

"Have you met Miss Hart?" Mr. Oosterling asked. "That's Mayor McKenna she's talking to. I can introduce you."

"I know Miss Hart. She. . ." What? She's my cousin? She's my assistant? *She's made a mess of everything I'm working for because, like Mr. Darcy, I have fought my feelings for her since the first moment we met?* It had happened far too fast for him to admit. "We work together at the library."

"Quite right. Wait. You are Hart's nephew. Of course you know her."

"Not a nephew, sir. I am merely Mrs. Armstrong's ward."

"I suppose you know old Hart's dealings against Morgan?"

Thankfully not. "No. I have just arrived last week, and I'm more than busy with the library."

"Then forget my ramblings. I'll stick to that lovely Miss Hart. She's always carrying on about books for children. But the little rascals don't appreciate them. What they don't steal, they leave dirty and torn."

"And reading them in between, aye?"

"Of course. I'm not so much a cynic as I sound. But they need clean clothes and food as well. Books are rather a luxury, don't you think?"

Already fighting a headache, Russell breathed in slowly. "No. I have to disagree. They are doorways, sir. They are the greatest opportunity. I myself am here because. . .because of Mr. Carnegie's fierce determination to provide books for the poor."

"Yes, yes, of course."

Russell's time with young Thomas and the visit to his home had stirred up old memories. Mr. Oosterling's dismissive attitude annoyed him, as his patience ebbed away. Carnegie might be the richest man in the world, but many born to wealth still considered him an upstart. "I will see that as many of Pittsburgh's children as possible have the opportunity to read, sir. They will be your future employees and, if I succeed, your future competition." He waved for his coat and hat.

Mr. Oosterling's eyes narrowed, but he offered a tip of his head as he walked away. That might just be the much-needed end to romance with his remaining single daughter.

Russell was just shrugging into his coat when Roberta approached. "I'm sorry."

"For what?"

"You can't have forgotten already." She shifted her attention toward the giggling women in the corner.

But he preferred to study her. "Oh. Your encouragement of Miss Oosterling?" Pleased at her endearing show of regret, he added, "You weren't helpful to my cause."

"And that would be bachelorhood? You could do much worse. Miss Oosterling is a lovely girl. Quite wealthy. She's not usually that. . .shall we say, chatty? I'm afraid she's simply over the moon for you."

"I should find that a compliment, but I neither have time nor the inclination to court. I wasn't minimizing the work I have to do." Standing by her side, he watched others in the room rather than look at her now. It would be difficult enough to hide his feelings while she worked with him.

"And I will help, Mr. Smart. I expect you like things not only done right but done well. I'm glad to see you, although I begged to stay home. After what poor Thomas and his family went through."

"Forgive me, but staying home wouldn't have changed a thing, other than worrying your friends and admirers. Although I'm not much for socializing tonight either."

"No matter the situation, I have all confidence in you, dear cousin."

That brought him around to face her again. "Please don't use that term. I feel it's disloyal to my benefactor. As much as I have to thank them for, I never once presumed to be family."

"I apologize. I won't do it again."

"No?" Once captivated by her eyes, he found he couldn't look away. "I was beginning to think that you found enjoyment in. . ." *Irritating* was the right word, but. . . "Keeping me on the defense."

She dropped her gaze. "You must think me a bother."

Endlessly fascinating as well. This compelling need to be near her was a problem. "I wouldn't say that." In fact he wished for more time together. More lighthearted conversation. "I don't see the famous brooch tonight."

"No, and you won't. That was the only time I've worn it. Oh dear. Here she comes. Run, and I'll cover for you."

Fifty feet off, through an increasing crowd, Miss Oosterling was in pursuit. "I'm in your debt, Roberta."

Her surprise at his familiarity brought instant regret. "I'm sorry."

"Don't be." The brightness in her eyes and smile said as much. "I think it only right when we are not at work. And there's that *almost* cousins thing. With our new friendship, I'd like you to use my name."

"Roberta is a bonny one."

Her eyes went a bit dreamy. Like the way he felt right now, staring at her mouth.

Then she flinched. "Run, if you value your enviable freedom."

He did, just in time to step out into the November night.

Freedom? For that, he'd pray someone would come into his life, capable of usurping the unavailable woman who reigned over his thoughts. That would be freedom.

Thank goodness he would have a few days before he saw her again.

"Smart, is that you?"

Could he ignore that, rather than waste one breath on Henry Kendall *the Third*? "Yes, but just leaving."

"A moment is all. I know I acted abomi–abomda—terribly today. Bertie will soon forgive me because she's so much more, well, decent than I. You might have noticed."

"She is protective of the lad."

"That's her. And too good for me. Now that I've heard about you being part of the family, you might know about our. . . The agreement."

The pause gave him time to worry where Kendall was going with this. "I was at the Harts' home Tuesday night, so I gathered there's an expectation of marriage." It dawned on him that Henry Kendall might not be fully sober.

"Well, it's a long story. Did she get the job, by the way?"

He shook his head, hoping that would suffice.

"That's too bad. You will keep an eye on her though. She's determined to get herself employed. I approve, of course. I want her to be happy, but it causes no end of remarks from the old tyrant."

Russell glanced around. "Mr. Hart?"

"No, no. Her mother. Though mine is chiseled from the same bloodless stone."

"I'll see that she doesn't overextend herself. If I can. I'm not sure I have much sway with her."

Kendall snorted. "No, no one does."

"But once you two marry?"

Henry Kendall scratched at his scalp. "Bertie and I were put in a gilded cage as children. And we're both fighting to get out."

"I'm sorry to hear it."

"Yes, because she'll need looking after if they lose this injunction case and the company folds. If Hart or my father approach you about investments, you'd be smart—" He laughed at his idea of a joke. "You'd best tell them to— Well, you wouldn't be so rude." Henry straightened himself. "Chin up, old man. It's not you chained to an anchor and expected to make it float. Now, point me in the direction of my dear Bertie, will you?"

Russell obliged. If Henry and Roberta succeeded in defying their parents, what would be the real cost?

❧ Chapter 10 ❧

Bertie twisted her amethyst ring, enjoying its sparkle on a bright and refreshing Sunday morning. Little pieces of dancing light were just barely visible on the back of the pew before her.

During the opening prayer, their pastor sounded unusually chipper. Or was it her? Somewhere between that contentious interview and the teasing at Thursday night's reception, she'd gone from resenting Russell Smart to admiring him. More than that. She held him in high esteem. No, like poor Miss Oosterling, she was over the moon.

Caught by the sight of the signature plum ensemble, Bertie realized that Aunt Aurelius had slipped in late to sit next to her parents. Was Russell here or sitting elsewhere?

"You, my children are each a masterpiece," their minister declared, his voice rising over the assembled. "Don't see yourselves as you were, but know that, despite your daily failings, He who has begun a good work in you will complete it. You are already accepted and loved with an unceasing love. You will grow as you accept it. Forgive others, but don't forget to forgive yourselves."

She knew this in theory, but after her embarrassing reaction to the unexpected change in plans wrought by Russell, she'd acted just as entitled as the society girls she'd come to pity. She and Henry wanted different lives than those of their parents. No more arranged marriages and lack of options. Of course, neither of them was in a hurry to strike out on their own and leave their nicely feathered nests.

Yes, the minister was right. She failed every day.

"You are not the mistakes you've made," he continued. "You are measured by the fact that you are a child of God. In Christ, you've been given a seat at the Father's table. He welcomes you whether you feel worthy or not."

Auntie's head dropped forward; a snort jerked it back up. When she glanced around, Bertie gave her a knowing look before risking one more survey of the sanctuary. This time she found Russell watching. He acknowledged her before returning his attention to the pulpit.

At least she'd see him at supper. Father elbowed her. "Sit still."

"In Proverbs eleven, we are admonished that 'when pride cometh, then cometh shame: but with the lowly is wisdom.' Friends, don't make the mistake of thinking pride is simply being puffed up with a high opinion of yourself. Many are those who take pride in their refusal to change. It can be as simple as refusing to accept your own value." He scanned the congregation's faces. "That will be my prayer for this week. Now, turn to hymn number 127, 'When I Survey the Wondrous Cross.'"

Once dismissed by the benediction, Bertie, already impatient, was slowed by her family and then by those wanting to greet her and chat. *Wait for me, Russell.*

Before she reached the massive double doors, she saw him leaving. Father turned to face her. "Go wait with your mother."

"Wait up, Smart!" Mr. Hart waved from the church's top step.

Russell had planned on taking a nap, then examining his wardrobe to determine what he must purchase or order from the tailor. Now that he'd been in Pittsburgh a full week, he had a better idea of what was needed for his new position. He would not be taking meals at the Hart mansion until he and Roberta came to a more comfortable place in their friendship.

When seeing her doesn't cause my pulse to stumble.

Her father gestured for them to move farther down the sidewalk and out of view, then nudged him out of the wind. "We appreciate your help with Roberta. I hope she's learned her lesson."

Not again. "I'm sorry sir, but—"

Hart rolled on. "I blame Henry for her ideas, as he's determined to defy his father and imagine himself champion of the common man, regardless of what it does to his own future."

"Actually sir, before you continue, I myself believe she's vastly qualified. Did she not tell you I've offered her a paid position? Assisting me."

Hart's mouth tightened, and he exhaled sharply through his nostrils. "Oh. I see. Well, that explains much. As I intend to enjoy my day, I will not bring it up at dinner. You need not worry."

Which meant Russell was still welcome. "Thank you, sir, but I won't be joining you today, though I do appreciate what Mrs. Armstrong called an open invitation."

"The ladies will be disappointed." Mr. Hart shrugged deeper into the comfort of his woolen scarf. "You've met Henry Kendall, I believe?"

Russell nodded.

"When you are a father, you will realize your children continue to need a guiding hand. Even at Roberta's age. Once they are formally engaged, we will be placing Henry on the board. The bank sees that as a promise of future stability, and that's very important now. Very important. You will be doing us all a favor by encouraging her to that end. I'm afraid this job, as it were, leaves her open to gossip. I will not allow her to risk her good name, as happens when single women work in the company of men. They must announce an engagement before she accepts a paycheck."

"I don't think it's my place to tell her such a thing."

"But you'll find a way." Mr. Hart glanced around and waved to a friend. "I'll see you at the grand opening, I suppose? Tuesday, I believe?" he asked, already stepping away.

"Yes, sir." But Russell wasn't done. "Wait. Mr. Hart. Have you considered placing Roberta on the board? She's your daughter and extremely competent. Encouraging her input in the company strikes me as the best way to gain Henry's interest as well."

"Is that why you've kept her coming around? For her bright mind?"

If he hesitated now or looked away. . . "Of course, sir. She would have been made children's director had I not interfered, and I daresay she'd have done a grand job of it."

Mr. Hart's harsher study of him made Russell regret his enthusiasm.

Roberta deserved his accolades, but clearly Mr. Hart found Russell's sudden devotion suspect. "I have met Mr. Kendall—Henry—and I expect there will be an announcement soon." Just maybe not the one the Harts wanted to hear. "They make a handsome couple."

If he wasn't mistaken, the lines around the man's mouth softened.

"That's our hope, Russell. As Aurelius's ward, it will be your hope as well. Now, I must be on my way. The wife will be waiting."

Mr. Hart had become one of the biggest investors in the East by seeing through people. He was right to worry. Russell hadn't fooled him at all.

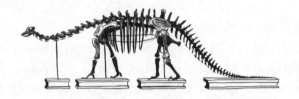

❧ *Chapter 11* ❧

Bertie arrived at the library early on Monday, determined to make up for the time she'd lost last week. Between her bout of self-pity and poor Thomas's heartbreak, she'd not spent an hour on her correspondence with publishers. And yet Russell had trusted her enough to offer a paid position.

She wasn't surprised to see a light on in his office as she entered the otherwise dark and silent hall. Practically tiptoeing, she paused when she saw him half sitting on his desktop, a sketchbook on his lap. He hadn't heard her, and she didn't rush to change that.

When she'd studied him long enough, she stepped forward. "Mr. Smart?"

He startled, sending the sketchpad to the floor as he stood. She appreciated his good manners, but she'd enjoyed seeing him caught up in his thoughts, completely relaxed.

"I didn't mean to disturb you."

"No. I'm just thinking. About tables. How best to allow the children to sit and read while keeping an open feeling. I'm sure you've thought of this, Miss Hart. Honestly, I know you have. If you care to share your drawings, I'd be sure you received due credit. But tell me, will they get up to mischief if we can't keep an eye on them?"

He'd sketched out the largest area of the children's library, something she'd already discussed with Mr. Bolton. She needn't remind Russell of their awkward start by telling him that. He so plainly wanted to make this right.

Bertie leaned closer to study his drawing. The large windows would be so inviting when many families lived in rooms with little or no daylight. "I think that's up to the child, not the dividers."

A sound of amusement drew her to meet his eyes. They seemed more blue than gray today.

But it wouldn't do to stare. "There will be a sink for them to wash their hands. Right along that wall." She pointed to it. "It's in a small closet. Have you noticed?"

"No, but it's a grand idea."

She'd been too casual with him Thursday night, teasing about romance of all things. Friend or almost-family, perhaps, but inappropriate for a man who'd given her a second chance at what she'd wanted. To succeed, she'd have to work just as hard at a sterling reputation as at her accomplishments. Seeing Miss Oosterling fumble over herself for Russell's attention had brought out a competitiveness that proved she was more like Father than she'd imagined.

Russell wasn't interested in Miss Oosterling, and certainly not in her, the heiress Roberta Hart who was talked about on the society page of the *Pittsburgh Gazette*.

After Father's lecture in the drawing room last night, Russell's disinterest was for the best.

She'd once longed to prove Russell wrong.

But it was she who'd been wrong. So wrong. His compassion and that analytical mind were just what Mr. Bolton needed to manage a library that was more museum, gallery, and music hall than the name implied.

Russell was. . .wonderful really, and completely inappropriate in Father's eyes. Father liked him, of course, but not as a son-in-law.

At age eight she'd been told she would marry Henry Kendall. It sounded grown-up at the time, and after all, Henry was great fun.

If Russell Smart had remained as prickly as she'd first found him, she wouldn't be fighting these feelings. Father's lightly veiled remarks about Little Rusty's dubious beginnings had the opposite effect he'd intended. She'd met others who'd been wards of a wealthy benefactor, and they'd taken utmost advantage of it, sometimes at a detriment to their elders.

"I'm glad to see you," he said.

Just how much, she longed to ask. "I imagine you have work for me."

"Yes. I'd like you to look over my list of publishers and tell me what small companies I've overlooked. I do have some contacts in London and Edinburgh, but sadly the Dunfermline Library where I worked only had a few shelves of children's books."

"That's where you met Mr. Carnegie."

"Yes."

She studied him, considering his days as a student at some gothic university where his eagerness to learn, to excel, would be apparent. As a child, she'd imagined him some poor Dickensian waif. And then promptly forgot his existence.

"I guess I should get started."

He was fussing with his collar and tie again. Why was he suddenly uncomfortable? Was he regretting his offer?

"Mr. Smart?" called a child's voice. "You around? Hey. Where's Mr. Smart?"

They turned at the plaintive request, and she followed Russell out and along the narrow hallway. Mrs. Oates had just arrived and appeared confused by the young visitor.

"I'm Mr. Smart. What is it?"

"Andrew MacCormack sent me. Thomas is in jail, sir. They've arrested him."

Bertie gasped. "Arrested?" She clutched Russell's sleeve.

"Yes, miss. You gotta come and help."

Russell wasted no time donning his stylish coat. "There's no need for Miss Hart—"

"I'm coming. I can't stay here and wonder."

He showed no interest in arguing. "Then hurry." He turned back to the boy now collapsed in the nearest chair. "How did you get here?"

"My pa delivers bread, but I had to run from Center Avenue."

All that way? Shaken anew by the gravity of it, she rushed to button up the fur coat she had yet to remove. It was bitterly cold today, and she'd fretted over the short walk from the carriage.

The carriage! Yes! "I'll meet you at the Forbes Street door. My carriage is waiting just down the way."

Russell's brows questioned her as if it was the most peculiar notion. Was it? Thoughtless then. She'd just assumed poor Sawyer must have a way to stay warm through hours in the cold, waiting until she was ready to return home.

She hurried on but was no farther ahead of the others when the boy's chatter and their footfalls echoed on the marbled floor. Just as she turned, the boy stumbled, and Russell lifted him up into his arms. "You're an excellent friend."

"You can help him, can't you, mister?"

Under the brim of his flat tweed hat, Russell's face was sober. "I'll certainly try. What is your name, young man?"

"Billy."

Oh, how she desired a more confident promise. But he was right. What could they do?

Outside, Sawyer's resilience to the weather relieved her. He was dressed warmly and waiting with the carriage and, noticing her, went to the small brazier where the men assembled around its fire and retrieved the heated brick he would place in the tin box at her feet, thereby adding a small amount of warmth for their journey.

"The city jail, Sawyer. And it's urgent."

Once seated, she wrapped a blanket around the young boy, who recuperated enough to sit forward, leaning his wind-chapped face against the glass. Bertie studied his bare calves, pink with the November weather. His too-large wool cap overwhelmed his head, and his boots were perilously thin in the sole, which she'd observed when Russell carried him to the carriage. Billy glanced at her, and rather than pull him to her side as she had Thomas, she tried to encourage him with a smile.

"I might as well give this to you now," Russell said, interrupting her thoughts. "Sign it when you are ready."

She took the envelope. *The Esteemed Miss Roberta Hart.* She hid a smile, but he had anything but amusement on his face when she looked up at him across the carriage's interior.

She broke the seal and removed a paper with one short paragraph detailing the position, the hours, and the pay. The second sheet requested a signature as agreement when returned to Mr. Bolton's secretary.

The hours were fewer than she'd hoped for.

The hourly wage? She sat back against the smocked leather seat, her hat tipping as it struck the fine interior wall. She'd managed to find out the weekly pay of two or three people working in the building. Was this a mistake? Surely it was lower than that of a streetcar conductor, but she had a college degree and experience.

Russell didn't look away, and she didn't bother hiding her feelings. "I am not above discussing money in this case. How can this be correct?" She handed it to him. He didn't take it. He'd seen it. Of course he had.

"The position was not in the budget, Miss Hart. That was the best we could do."

"You're serious."

"Quite. You either take the job as offered, or you don't. I hope you do."

"But. . ." She shook her head, letting further words linger on her tongue before swallowing them. It felt like a snub and reminded her that this was business to him. Business took negotiation.

"I'll just say I don't believe this is fair."

"Of course it's not. But if you think life is fair, then I wonder what exactly keeps you going back to that school." His gaze shifted to the boy's back.

She stared hard at him. "You know what I mean."

"I do. And I will remind you that the men we employ are supporting families. Rent, food, clothing. Public transportation." His eyes scanned the elegant interior of the carriage. One of two Hart family carriages.

Bertie looked down at her lap, the fur at her cuffs. What must he really think of her?

It was everything about her life that she both took for granted and often despised at such moments. With no brothers, she'd always felt guilty for being a daughter and not the heir Father must have wanted. From the moment of her birth, she'd disappointed him. It wasn't about to change.

If she was to take Sunday's sermon to heart, she must remember that what she made of today was more important than who she'd been. She would be true to herself and win Russell's respect in turn.

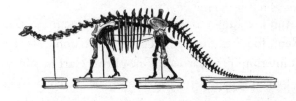

Chapter 12

W ee Billy stayed in the carriage, fear being stronger than curiosity now that they were outside the jail. Russell stepped out onto the street and turned to offer Roberta a hand. They could work together. He would put aside his traitorous feelings for her and learn to meet her glance with nothing more than a working friendship. She might be an heiress, but that didn't define her, much as he'd fought his label all these years.

"We must hurry," she warned him, as if she wasn't already rushing to keep up.

He leaned closer to reassure her. "It will be all right." He'd see to it for her sake as well as Thomas's.

Once inside, he went straight to the uniformed man behind the front desk. "We've come out of concern for Thomas MacCormack, a young boy from up near Webster Street. Could we speak with him and to someone in charge about his release?" He was half surprised Roberta hadn't spoken up first.

"Not so fast, sir." The officer behind the desk stood, glancing over his shoulder and nodding to someone out of sight. "Jarvie? Take these fine folks down to cell eight. I think that's where the young weasel is. Whether he's released is not up to me or you, sir."

With this accomplished, Russell looked straight into Roberta's eyes. "Stay here."

"No, I must talk to him."

"And you will. But not in there. Trust me."

"But he'll want to see me."

He took her by the shoulders. "And so will every other man along the way. No, Roberta."

Her shoulders relaxed, and she nodded. Reasonable, after all? Had he finally managed to gain her trust?

Farther inside the jail, he knew he'd been right to insist. In the corner of a large cell housing men of all ages—petty thieves or murderers?— Thomas huddled at the end of a long bench. "Thomas?"

There was no response until one of the rough-looking men shook the lad's arm. "You're in for it now, boy."

Alive again with hope, Thomas rushed to stick his arms through the bars. Russell did likewise, relieved to offer some comfort through their awkward hug.

"That's enough," warned the guard. "Step back."

They reluctantly parted, and Russell bent to speak privately. "Did you do what they say? Did you steal the food?"

Thomas's eyes filled with tears. "But they took it from me before I could get it home."

"I'm afraid that doesn't change what happened. Listen to me. I can't guarantee anything, Thomas, but I'm going to try and help. Do you understand?"

"Yes, sir."

Risking a glance at the guard, Russell reached through and squeezed Thomas's shoulder. "Chin up, eh?"

He left, thanking the guard in the hope it would benefit Thomas's care. "Whom do I speak with to have him released?"

"Talk to the front desk."

Roberta wasn't in the foyer, but he caught sight of her elaborate hat through the window. She paced the sidewalk while her coachman watched from where he stood by the horses. "Miss Hart!" She rushed to him, and he offered a reassuring smile. He covered her hand where she'd placed it on his sleeve. "He is well but frightened."

A muffled cry matched the pain in her eyes.

"Let me see what I can do. Come back inside. It may take awhile."

It did.

An hour later, Russell had signed responsibility for the boy, paid a fee, and arranged to make amends with the grocer.

Thomas burst through the inner door, arms spread as he rushed across the lobby to where Russell and Roberta stood side by side. His impact might have bowled them over had they not been watching.

"Oh Thomas. I'm so glad to see you." Roberta attempted to scoop him up.

"Not as glad as I am to see you, miss!"

Roberta exchanged glances with Russell, then lingered in her gaze. "Thank you, Mr. Smart. I'd never have been able to do this alone."

"I'm not so sure. You're hardly the type to give up."

She laughed as Russell rubbed the boy's shaggy head. "Your friend Billy is outside waiting. Shall we go?"

Thomas whooped as they exited, running ahead and ignorant of the icy wind.

"We'll get them food on the way home," Russell suggested. He couldn't stop smiling, so relieved was he at their success.

Roberta nodded. "I'll purchase it."

"No, no. No need."

"Please allow me. You've done the work of seeing him released."

He sighed. Arguing with her was pointless. At least she'd temporarily forgotten about that low hourly wage. Billy and Thomas's chatter sounded like enthusiastic appreciation for what they must perceive as an adventure. Consoled now, Roberta never looked more beautiful despite the cold and wind and the two lads clinging to her. But it was Russell she watched.

He imagined pulling her close to share the moment.

"Bertie?"

Henry Kendall invaded Russell's runaway thoughts.

"What are you doing here?" Roberta's pleasure faded to surprise as she accepted a kiss on her cheek.

Russell disliked the jolt of irritation it caused him.

"I was in their neighborhood and heard about it. Which one is he?"

Shrinking with guilt, Thomas gave himself away.

"Aren't you the lucky boy?"

Russell lunged forward, his hands clenching for want of twisting Kendall's lapels. "Think what you're saying." Lucky? To have lost a father and be so frightened for your mother that you thought stealing food the way to help?

Kendall had the sense to backpedal. "I meant he's lucky to have such friends as you and Bertie, though I'm tiring of your interference, Smart. I've tried to be courteous."

"If you have a problem with me, we can discuss it later."

"Henry!" Roberta pleaded, watching Thomas's growing anxiety. "Listen to him."

Instead, Kendall stepped closer to the lad. "All I want is to hear your side of things before I speak to the officer."

Furious, Roberta tugged Kendall's arm to turn him away.

Russell's jaw ached from biting back his anger. *One more move like that. . .*

"All right," Kendall relented. "No more questions. Wait. One more. Can I bring the photographer to your house, Thomas?"

Russell's hand tightened on Thomas's shoulder. The boy searched his face. Russell gave a warning shake of his head.

But Thomas stepped forward. "How much will you pay me?"

Surprised enough to be amused, Russell began to lead him away. "Not enough to warrant upsetting your mother," he said. "Now leave the MacCormacks alone, Mr. Kendall."

"How old were you when you were taken out of the poorhouse, Smart?"

Russell stopped in his tracks and took a very slow breath. "Leave it be. Let us go."

"Us is it? You and Roberta?"

"Yes. We are friends," she declared. "Something to do with respect, Henry. Have you forgotten?"

Thomas reached for her hand. "Leave us alone, mister. And leave my mama alone. Go bother those men at the factory," he warned, an echo of Russell's suggestion yesterday.

"Wait. I'm. . . I don't know why I. . ." The desperation on Kendall's face was real as he kept pace at Roberta's side. "I have to succeed here, Bertie. You know it's the only way I'll escape them. I'm doing this for you as much as for me."

"Not like this, you're not. There has to be another way."

"All I know is that they will have to sink or swim without us, because we're not giving in." Henry Kendall's words didn't match his countenance. He looked like a man defeated.

"Excuse us, Mr. Smart," Roberta said, her eyes pleading his indulgence. "I'll meet you at the carriage. Please take Thomas along."

Ignoring Kendall's apology, Russell walked away with Thomas and Billy at his side.

Behind them Roberta and her beau exchanged sharp words. He tried not to watch but glanced back and found her hurrying to join them. Without comment, she took Thomas's free hand. Not wanting to be left out, Billy did the same with Russell.

His chest felt encased in a vise. Sweat moistened his back. He was ten years old again, hungry and humiliated. But now he could do something about it, and his grip tightened on Billy's hand. The deaths of his own mother and sister had left him feeling alone in a vast ocean. Life teemed around him, yet he belonged to no one.

These past days—these moments with Roberta—made him reconsider how much he'd remained in that loneliness. He never blamed the Armstrongs. They'd been so very good to him, kind and supportive, but he'd filled his emptiness with accomplishments in his mother's memory.

Now he wanted more. His heart had awakened for a woman who, if she returned that affection, would be going against the wishes and financial stability of two families. He owed Mrs. Armstrong better.

He didn't have a chance.

Feeling her attention on him, Russell noticed unshed tears in her eyes.

But she was smiling. "Thank you."

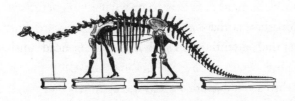

~ Chapter 13 ~

*R*ussell could ask for nothing more. She appreciated him. That would have to be enough.

Under Roberta's direction, the carriage stopped at the market where it soon became clear her shopping experience did not include groceries. An understanding of what went into the making of meals? No again. Even the lads had better insight and patiently explained their way through the produce section.

Russell had paid attention during those early years before boarding school when he'd enjoyed the comfort of the Armstrongs' kitchen and made clumsy attempts at the small tasks given him by their cook.

Roberta shrugged it all off, cheerily loading him down with package after package. "I will learn, Russell. I promise. Just see if I don't."

A strange promise, but her enthusiasm lessened the ache in his arms as he, Thomas, and Billy carried her accumulating purchases. By the time they reached the last shop, he'd had to reach for his money clip. She might know what she'd pay for a tea with her friends at the hotel, the cost of a bundle of flowers, or a new hat, but Miss Bertie Hart's domestic skills were minimal.

What did it matter? Other than what his benefactress called pin money, Roberta's father—and, no doubt, her future husband—used accountants to deal with things such as shopkeeper bills.

With noses against the glass, Thomas and Billy chattered over the sights out the carriage windows and the abundance of meals that would result from the bounty.

Once they'd arrived, Thomas burst through the door, bouquet in hand. Mrs. MacCormack steadied herself on his older brother Andrew's arm, before pulling Thomas against her. At the sight of their many purchases, she began to weep.

Russell handed her a handkerchief. "I will see that you have help, ma'am," he promised, but they were words worth little if not backed up by action. "And my prayers. Miss Hart is responsible for the food, and therefore deserving of your appreciation."

"You've both done enough, you have. We can't rightly be taking your charity, but it's welcome today, so it is. You must let me do your sewing for you, sir."

She glanced at Roberta, and Russell wondered at her reluctance to extend the offer, until he realized what the housewife knew in one glance. Roberta had a ladies' maid to see to such things.

Roberta took the woman's hardworking hand in her own. "I too shall keep you in my prayers. And I believe that though you've suffered an irreplaceable loss, God will see you through. You have friends, and as I've come to know Thomas, I hope you will consider me a friend as well." She glanced at Russell. "And you have a champion in Mr. Smart. There's no better place to be than under his concern."

Russell's throat thickened.

"Remember me, sir. When you've married. I'm a hard worker. Anything." Mrs. MacCormack's pleading gaze traveled from his face to Roberta's. "You won't regret it, miss."

"I. . .I will keep that in mind," Roberta replied.

Did the woman think them more than friends?

He searched the tabletop for a scrap of paper and instead found one of the books he'd just delivered to the Minersville school—a book that wasn't supposed to leave their tiny library. He glanced at Thomas, who clearly knew he'd been found out. "Would you have a pencil and paper, lad?" He glanced at Mrs. MacCormack. The matter of the book would be taken care of another time. "I'll give you the address of where I'm staying, ma'am. You send one of the lads over if you need me."

Andrew reached up to a shelf, took down an old cigar box, and provided the requested items. Russell was finished when a knock came at the door. Before an invitation, the door opened, and Billy entered. His interest remained fixed on the wealth of food yet to be stored.

Russell, with his own wame suitably filled, hadn't thought of the starving boy sitting in the carriage beside a crate of crisp, fragrant apples.

"Good thing you returned, lad. We forgot to give you a few. May I, Mrs. MacCormack?" Russell asked, handing three apples to the thin boy, then adding two coins from his pocket. "Good work today, Billy."

"We should be going," Bertie added, her voice uncharacteristically fragile.

She was right.

They made their way to the door, leaving Mrs. MacCormack to a new round of tears.

Andrew followed them out. "Do you get to see those dinosaurs, sir?"

Russell felt a loosening in his shoulders at the young man's curiosity. "Oh aye, we can hardly miss them. Ye'd think they walked there on their own for the excitement they bring."

Andrew's eyes grew wide. "I've read everything I could about them. I hope to see them after the opening. I've been trying to save up for a new book my teacher told me about." The words faded away, much as the chance of it happening.

"But now you have other concerns."

He nodded, the change in his face dramatic.

Russell realized his mistake. For one brief moment, Andrew Mac-Cormack had forgotten he was now the man of the family. "That's why we have this grand new library." Russell paused before the carriage. "Bide awhile, will you, Andrew? While I help Miss Hart?" The boy waited as Russell gave Roberta a hand up into the carriage. He closed the door just shy of latched. Andrew hadn't moved. "How well do you do in school, lad?"

"Very well, sir. I want to be a scientist someday."

"Oh. That does take a lot of study."

"I've collected a box of bird and mouse skeletons."

"Well, now, if you think you'll keep up with your studies, I'll see that you get to see those dinosaurs. Nothing you need worry about now. I have an idea that might be beneficial. Now go back and see to your mum."

Bertie watched the conversation outside the carriage, smiling when Russell shook young Andrew's hand.

Her Russell, said her heart, for hadn't she just fiercely defended him against Henry's remarks? *"In one honest word for those boys, he's shown more empathy than you've manufactured under your byline."*

"It's all well and good for your family to say they've helped the downcast, but you know as well as I do, they'll never accept him as anything but a poor orphan off the streets."

Henry had to be wrong.

Outside, Russell called up to Sawyer. "Hotel Bihlman on Forbes, please. I believe it's on your way."

Henry considered himself a champion against injustice—and at one time she would have agreed. He was eloquent on the rights of the poor but lacked deep compassion for them. His ingrained sense of importance and entitlement still shone through. His eagerness to point out the failings of the upper class sprang from the need to injure his father and break free of obligation, not from genuine concern for the less fortunate.

Bertie examined the fur-trimmed muff at her side. She'd long fought shame for such privilege in a town built on dirty factories, and Henry had understood that. Or so she thought.

The door opened, and Russell joined her inside.

"Thank you for the use of your carriage, Miss Hart."

Kind as he'd meant them, Russell's words proved his estimation of the vast space between them. It had to change. What mattered was who they were here and now. His early life meant little when faced with the man he was now. And the woman she longed to be.

He had the manners of a gentleman. But imagining him at her side under Mother and Father's scrutiny? "I hope you and Aunt Aurelius will consider the carriage available for your use. This one often sits unused." Even as she said it, she knew it unlikely, given his disdain for the trappings of wealth.

When Thomas had walked between them, she'd dared to think of what could be. Russell Smart stirred feelings she'd never known nor expected.

Would Father ever accept him as more than his sister's ward? For that matter, would Russell accept her family or continue to keep himself apart? Did she truly care for him, or did he symbolize for her the kind of person she wanted to be? He appeared comfortable inhabiting a world between the wealthy and the very poor. He lived simply. Could she learn to do so as well?

Henry was a dear friend, but the ruse must end, and their parents must hear and accept the truth. Let Henry find another heiress.

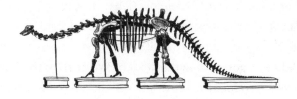

❧ *Chapter 14* ❧

$\mathcal{T}$he coach moved south from the Minersville neighborhood. Bertie watched Russell's feet shift nervously, his hands rubbing his knees.

"I'm sorry, Miss Hart. I should not presume to be here with you. Alone. I've not considered your reputation."

"Oh well." She laughed, more to cover her disappointment that he'd reverted to such formality. "Neither have I. Because I'm quite relaxed in your company."

"We must stop the driver," he declared, standing.

"No, Russell. Please. That's ridiculous. Please. Our family connection—"

"You know this would not be acceptable to your father."

Bertie studied his face and found him quite serious. She'd not thought a thing of it. "I do know I'm tired of worrying about what others think. What you've done today, this week, for those children. No one would dare suggest our time alone was an indiscretion."

"Your family. The Kendalls. That corporate board. They would thank me not to mar your good name. The library likewise." Despite his words, he sat, for the risk of being seen was no worse now than it would be closer to home. "I must take care, as I hope to stay here in Pittsburgh for a few years at least."

"You do?"

"We did some good today, though it pains me so to think of that poor widow. There are so many in need, and we can't feed them all."

"But we will feed their minds." She edged forward, wishing she could reach out and quiet the fingers that tapped nervously on the bench alongside his leg. "You and I will bring change with books." She felt tears sting her eyes. "We will bring them new hope. We will take books to the streets and read to them, welcome them into the library, have reading fairs and meetings with authors. Show them globes and encyclopedias. And we will make a difference."

Russell returned her smile. "I see I will have to reexamine our budget."

"Yes, you must. I'm even more convinced now." Crowds of worn-down people filling the sidewalks on these narrow streets made her doubly conscious of how comfortably she lived.

A rut in the road tossed them both side to side, but with no more than an awkward smile, they traveled on in silence. How could she comprehend a life like Thomas's? Like Russell's had been?

A tear set loose down her cheek.

He removed a handkerchief from his pocket and handed it to her.

She wiped her eyes. "Russell, you must understand that Henry and I will never marry. Our families will soon be told. Believe me. I. . ." She had to look away. He'd gone motionless, staring at her. Did he fear her words as much as she feared keeping them inside? "I admire you so much. In a way I've never known."

His entire body shifted away, cutting her off. After a deep breath, he said, "Please say no more. We will work together and become friends, just as we should, given your family's role in. . .in my life."

"Is that all, Russell? Friends? I can hardly breathe for how I feel."

He closed his eyes and shook his head. "It's been a taxing day. You will feel better after some rest. We have much to accomplish before the opening."

Bertie covered her mouth. He knew what she meant, and he was purposely stalling her. "I don't think rest is the cure." She rose and, holding on, took two quick steps to cross and sit at his side. "Russell. You're not listening to me."

He turned aside; at least he didn't rise to escape, though his breathing was as uneven as hers. "Roberta. If we are to work together, I can't be seen to show favoritism. Because of your family."

Of course it was. It always was. Her family name, her family wealth—it ruled over every aspect of her life. She couldn't say more without risking too much. Was he so ignorant of what had changed between them?

Russell's subtle shift away could be considered cowardly if it didn't shame her and break her heart.

She returned to her seat across from him. "Forgive me."

"You've had a difficult day. Please don't apologize. I was glad to help the MacCormacks, but don't make me more than I am. I am not and never can be your equal. Please, however, consider me your most devoted friend, on whom you may call anytime."

"Then be that friend and more. I call on you now to see beyond this foolish debutante. I am a woman with a woman's heart, and I will not choose a future like my mother's."

"Then you know the ramifications, if. . . I beg you, Miss Hart. It's best we speak of it no more lest we face awkward days ahead."

"No more calling me Roberta either?"

He didn't answer.

For a moment, she thought she'd be sick to her stomach. "Are you judging me on something beyond my control? An accident of birth that made you poor and made me. . .something I never wanted?"

"Yes. I'm judging correctly. Nothing changes where I've come from, and I will not conveniently forget it."

But saying it proved he'd been thinking of her, of possibilities. Pondering their future.

"You do care, don't you?"

What sounded like a laugh bore no resemblance to the disappointment in his eyes. "How could I not? You are cherished by my benefactress, and you will be an important part of our work at the library. You've just admitted all we can accomplish for the children." Yet the tight smile on his face failed to fool her. "Henry insists that you are quite the best of the lot. I wouldn't count him out, Roberta. You expect me to believe he could walk away from a future with you?"

Perhaps she was too spent to make sense of this. They'd only known each other a week, and here she was selfishly pressuring him to divulge a secret affection. She should instead be relieved he didn't and would not have to endure the firestorm if Father suspected her feelings.

Shame rolled through her with such force it left another wave of nausea.

Russell sat back, keeping his gaze out the window. "Whatever is going on with the company, do you really believe you and Henry will turn your backs on your family?"

She wanted to argue the point, but she'd always been a coward. All her bluster last week wasn't fooling him. She'd been mired in family expectation far too long.

The coach stopped, and she glanced out. They were only blocks from the library.

Russell gathered his hat from beside him as though they'd finished a casual conversation on the changing skyline of Pittsburgh. "There is much to do tomorrow. I hope you rest well." His hand was on the latch, but it opened for him, as the conscientious driver had hopped down to assist.

"Russell. Wait."

He paused, near her, ready to step out. But what words could make him understand?

"I must go," he said softly, glancing about. "Together we will make a grand success of the library, but. . ."

She wanted to shake him for what was coming.

"There's absolutely no place in our lives for more."

Her ability to breathe was lost. He'd taken all the air out of her, and all her hope. She watched him take a deep breath and let it out slowly. If only she could do the same.

He stepped down, glanced at the coachman, and then back at her. "Please be on time tomorrow, Miss Hart. It's our big day."

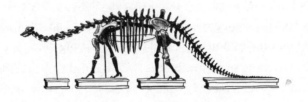

❧ *Chapter 15* ❧

*T*uesday, grand opening day, had finally arrived. Russell stared at the long wall of books before him.

Regrets had danced around him through the restless night. That didn't mean he'd been wrong, but the words with Roberta left him exhausted this morning.

As a boy, soon after his arrival at the orphanage, he'd seen a lass in leg braces who insisted that she'd one day walk straight if she endured the current pain. Whether she'd been right or not, Russell didn't know. He'd run away soon after, certain he'd find a new home faster on his own.

And it had worked.

Recognizing the friendly man's carriage by watching it come and go, Russell followed Mr. Armstrong down the street three days in a row. And he'd prayed—earnestly, as his mother had taught him—that the man would help him.

He often thought of that brave lass and the power of such optimism, but he'd learned well enough that honest evaluation was better than false dreams.

His words, his practical—if harsh—solution for Miss Hart's confusion, had frustrated her, but she'd be better for it when she realized he was right. He knew without a doubt that she believed her heart full with the hope of him—perfectly impractical—as were his feelings for her, something he'd never believed possible. His fanciful thoughts, a sudden bout of entertaining such possibilities, would only bring heartbreak. He'd been warned to remember his place. Even if Roberta was not already entangled in that marriage agreement, Mr. Hart wouldn't accept him as an equal for his daughter.

Russell rubbed his face. Somehow he'd given too much away. She'd guessed his feelings.

The Armstrongs had given him every opportunity, a solid security, and measured affection. But they hadn't made him their son nor given him leave to call them Mother and Father. The wall was there. Invisible. Sometimes he went months without bumping into it.

The wall went to university with him, and although he mixed in well enough, he always watched his classmates, wondering when they'd see him for who he'd been. Inevitably, they did.

Around him, the once quiet building was suddenly full of activity as he shook himself from his dismal thoughts.

He must reassure the other employees that yesterday's sudden departure with Miss Hart had simply been a mission of compassion. If he could act as if heartbreaking sentiments hadn't filled that carriage, his adored Miss Hart—the heart of the children's library—would follow his lead. She wanted this job. He'd given it to her. If she was so set on employment, she'd have to learn that, unlike the women in her social set with their volunteer activities and social awareness, employees came to work whether they felt like it or not. Whether their hearts ached or not.

Roberta seemed not to know that Kendall-Hart Investments was on precarious financial footing. If the Harts lost their money, Roberta needed a prospect among her peers. For that, Russell must ensure that her name remained above reproach.

Right now he had a meeting to attend.

But by ten in the morning, there was no sign of her, and it became difficult to ignore the not-quite-whispered whispers regarding her absence. How much worse it would be if they weren't so filled with anticipation for the grand opening.

Today of all days.

Where did he go so wrong? Hiring her because of his feelings for her? Deciding to take the position himself rather than give it to her?

He'd never expected Roberta Hart's surprising admission. Her words were like sunlight falling on the hope he'd hidden in his heart. But it was the words he hadn't allowed her to say that left him most unsettled.

He could never encourage her to give up the life her parents wanted for her. She'd never shame her parents, and he'd never be able to face them, nor Mrs. Armstrong, if they knew how he felt.

He'd never expected heartache to be an actual physical pain.

Reliving their conversation with different endings wasn't getting him anywhere. He went off to look for Mr. Bolton, expecting to find him near the hall of dinosaurs. If Russell wasn't needed here, he had plenty to do to keep the promises he'd made to himself yesterday at the MacCormacks'.

Roberta and Henry would marry because they'd grown up knowing it was their duty.

His was to stay out of the way.

Stepping out of the stairwell into an ants' nest of a large noisy room, Bertie knew she'd made a mistake.

"Bertie? What are you doing here?"

As the rattling clicks of typewriter keys slowed, Henry's surprise turned to a wide grin. Ten other men's faces mirrored his.

She tried to acknowledge a few of them with polite nods as she made her way to him. "I need a moment. Can you break away?"

His face somber, he quickly rose, ushering her past desks and the comments directed their way.

While the day was just dawning, she'd asked Celeste to fix her hair in a style more appropriate for the evening, as there'd be no time for fussing later. She hadn't fooled anyone by dressing in dreary colors or styles meant to show maturity. So, for confidence she'd chosen her favorite dress. She would no longer allow old conventions to keep her from being herself. She and Russell were the future of a new society where a person's heart was more important than their financial portfolio.

Her morning meeting with the city council had been a success. Now she must get Henry's promise that tomorrow night's dinner with their parents would also go as she planned.

He led her into a windowed room where a glass door offered private conversation. "You look upset."

"And you're far too blunt."

"So?"

"You must come to the house tomorrow, before supper. Wednesday is Father's night home. I can't do this anymore. They have to be told."

"I admire your courage. However. . ."

She studied him, a curl of unease moving up her back.

"My father forced me to look over the board's statement regarding this latest delay with the bank. It's true, the company is in trouble. More than we could have guessed." Gesturing as if he could hold back her anger, Henry dipped his head. "Please let me explain what I've decided."

Every muscle tightened, right up past her jaw. She didn't want to hear it. "No. You can't change your mind now."

"I have no choice. I don't have the stuff to make a go of it on my own. You see my desk. I thought I'd shoot to the top of the heap, and we could walk away from it all by now. Blue blood is thin blood, Bertie. And I don't relish a cold walk-up apartment, any more than you can depend on your cooking skills."

"You don't have to do it alone."

"That's just it, I'm afraid. I've met someone. She wouldn't have me either, were I to break off on my own. Face it, Bertie. I wasn't meant to be poor."

Bertie rubbed her forehead and took a much-needed seat on the nearest chair. *Not now, Henry. Not when we've worked so hard to fight their control.* Henry was giving in.

"I will do this without dragging you back in. I promise. I'm telling Father I will join the board and devote myself to the company. That's what they want. A confirmation that Kendall-Hart Investments will go on."

"And the expectation of our marriage? That stinking agreement we've been tied to all these years?"

"I'm breaking it." He shook her shoulder, his eyes again full of possibility. "We're breaking it. Just as planned. But a suitable marriage will bring its own financial benefits, and a bit more security. Don't you see?"

"So, what do we tell them?"

"We tell them the truth. And we insist on allowing ourselves to marry for love. You will succeed, Bertie. You're the strong one."

"Oh Henry. Do you really think you can do it?"

That confident smile returned. "Yes." He rested his hands on his hips. "And by the way, I quite admire Russell."

She sat back to peer up at him. "You hardly know him." Her face heated before she could deny it. "He's not interested."

"Right. Not interested in putting his feelings for you ahead of your security." Henry stood. "I envy that."

"What are you talking about?"

"He's no fool, Bertie. He has little to offer."

"Then he's wrong." She rose and pushed past him, circling the room, holding her forehead. "You'll still come tomorrow? Shouldn't your parents come as well?"

"First, I'll convince my father, and then we'll work on yours." He reached for her hand, then stopped. Too many sets of eyes were watching. "Go home, Bertie."

"Will you be at the opening tonight?"

"Depends on how my meeting with Father goes." Henry opened the conference room door and headed for the stairwell. "Freedom is in sight, my dear, and as your oldest friend, I will see you get it."

"Good, because I've just accepted a position with the city. Under the conditions that they pay me properly as an employee and not a volunteer."

"Bravo. You are on your way, my brave girl. I always was getting the better half of the deal."

"Hardly."

"Now all you need is to learn to boil water, and you can have both tea and an egg at each meal."

She poked at his arm to fight off a sudden sadness. In a way, they'd been partners for years. "I will always love you, Henry. And I expect to be godmother to your first daughter."

"I'll see to it."

Bertie longed to hug him. "And just who is this woman who's stolen your heart? I have countless stories to tell."

"Give me until next week so I can be sure I'm not making this all up in my head. Now go." But when she turned, he grabbed her arm. "Our new futures start today."

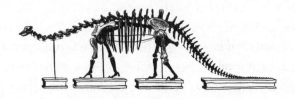

❧ *Chapter 16* ❧

"A re you almost ready?" called Father up the stairs.

Wishing she hadn't sent Cecile off so quickly, Bertie checked herself in the mirror. Not because of how her new dress hung, but for confirmation she could do what she set out to do. After carrying on so to work at the library, how could she announce her news and face Mr. Bolton?

And Russell.

But the opportunity to work for the city had come at the perfect time. She'd lead a committee to assess and then improve educational opportunities. They'd expand relations between libraries and schools and build up the number of textbooks in the classrooms. And it paid more than the library job. Not that it mattered. She'd have worked for free to be with Russell if he returned her affection, but she couldn't face him day after day and expect her heart to heal.

Tonight, with Henry's news, the door was opening to a real future. She'd prayed for this. Just who was she, and where did she belong? Now she would find out.

She couldn't change her birth any more than Russell could, but if he could look at her as plain old Bertie Hart—with no expectations brought on by her family—then they might have a chance.

Aunt Aurelius had arrived early for dinner and would be going to the opening in their larger carriage. But Father had whisked his sister into his study and closed the doors. Before Mother had sent Bertie to her room, she'd heard both sharp words and Russell's name.

Yet they'd been pleasant company during dinner. Father even complimented Bertie on her new position but was quick to add he found it difficult to understand. "I guess business and negotiation is in your blood, after all."

Now it was time to go to the grand opening, and she couldn't put it off any longer. Bertie descended the foyer's wide circular stairs, pausing halfway when her mother stuck her head out from the drawing room.

Mother's hand went to her throat. "It's true then. You're wearing the cameo."

"I've had it eleven months now. Time is running out."

For once, Mother didn't have an answer, but offered a slight nod and a bittersweet smile.

Bertie had been promised into marriage long before the Victoria cameo arrived. But now she wore it as a reminder to follow her heart. She wanted her parents' blessing on this, but it was up to Russell now. He cared for her, she knew it, but he had to be confident they could have a future together. A simple life, carried out like so many others'. Not in poverty and not in wealth. She didn't long to manage a household on her own, but she could learn. She would start by making her own living and learning how to budget, and—she laughed to herself—someday learn her way around a kitchen.

Until children came along.

Her face pulsed beet red as Father and Aunt Aurelius entered the foyer.

"This should be quite the evening," he announced.

That was what she was afraid of.

"You're sure Russell will meet us there?" Mother asked.

That was an interesting change. "He is one of the directors now."

Aunt Aurelius grinned. "That he is. And gaining respect. He'll be an important part of the Carnegie empire someday."

Bertie nodded, wishing the heat on her face would cool.

Father and their butler assisted with their fur coats, ushering them all out to the carriage. The ride to the library took forever.

On the very last street corner, Bertie caught sight of her favorite newsboy. She waved out the window. In him, she saw Russell's drive to better himself. She would soon ask Auntie more about him. Could Father see what a wonderful man Russell was, and approve?

Yet even Russell had his preconceptions. Until he saw her as his equal, he would allow her birthright to keep them apart.

They alighted from the carriage in front of the broad marbled steps of the building's grand entry. While the library and music hall were awe-inspiring, many people were eager to see Carnegie's dinosaur.

Father escorted Mother, smiling at those watching and then looking back to where Aunt Aurelius and Bertie followed. Spectators whispered and pointed from behind policemen. Most couldn't afford a tenth of her dressmaker bill because of the need to feed their families. They might judge her, but they didn't know her. She would no longer struggle with guilt. She was blessed to have the opportunity of a secure life, and she made every effort to help others. It was why she'd fought so hard to be part of the children's library, and now this new position with the city would allow her to impact even more children.

As much as she admired Russell, she knew better than to think him perfect. But under his slightly bristly exterior was a heart full of compassion that could learn to appreciate her family's eccentricities, much like he adored Aunt Aurelius.

She would no longer judge herself. *From glory to glory, He's changing me.*

The invited guests made their way to the grand new music hall for the opening ceremony. Inside its rounded cavernous walls and balconied seats, well-heeled devotees of art and music, history, and literature gathered to send the institution into a future few had imagined only thirty years earlier when steel went off to war. The boom in rail lines and bridges changed Pittsburgh forever.

From her place near the front, Bertie searched the music hall seats for Russell, just as she had during church on Sunday. But if he was in the massive, circular auditorium, she couldn't find him.

She studied the circular ceiling's intricate molding and chandelier. She'd seen nothing like it outside of Europe.

At eight o'clock, the audience quieted. From the first notes of Weber's *Jubilee*, the music hall's ability to magnify beauty was clear. "There's Governor Hastings," Father whispered.

Yes, but the orchestra's magnificence left her breathless. After the invocation, speakers, including Mr. Carnegie, extoled the treasure they had in their midst. The choir's performance of "Hallelujah" from Beethoven's *Mount of Olives* covered her skin with gooseflesh.

It was a moment she felt she'd never forget.

Afterward she spoke with friends and associates as she, Mother, and Aunt Aurelius toured the building. Her hands continued to tremble. Bertie had purposely avoided most of the art and natural history displays so she could see them through the eyes of others today. Her father's peers, even some down from New York, gathered to see Carnegie's dream for Pittsburgh, and eighty feet of dinosaur skeleton. The dinosaur named *Diplodocus carnegii* honored their founder's time and money invested in seeing it retrieved and prepared to be on display.

But who could focus on splendid artwork when Father had hurried off with Henry's parents?

She dragged Aunt Aurelius aside. "I'm worried about Russell. Where is he?"

"I have no idea," she replied, frowning. "I did see him stepping out of Kaufmann's Department Store on my way here, but I know he's coming."

"How odd," Mother added. "We do like him so."

Yes, as a ward of the family. But how about as a son-in-law?

It was girlish to get so far ahead of herself, yet in a week's time her heart had turned from frustration to admiration with such speed, she'd be embarrassed to admit it.

With the crowd dispersing after the emotional ceremonies, the Harts gathered in the large foyer. Mr. Raymond, her newest employer, approached her parents and Auntie. Bertie recognized the unspoken question in his eyes.

"Mr. Raymond. How lovely to see you. I've given my parents the news."

He sighed with relief. "Good. Then we are likewise free to make the announcement?"

"If you could give me a few days to tell my friends here at the library, I'd appreciate it."

"Of course."

Strange how his gaze kept drifting to her unusually quiet aunt, and his cheeks now bore a boyish pink.

Father hadn't missed it either, but she'd never known Mr. Raymond to be part of her parents' social circle. "You've met my aunt, sir?"

"Yes, many years ago, when we were young and I thought I could change the world."

"Chester Raymond. Haven't you done so yet? I daresay hiring Roberta proves you have!" Auntie's eyes twinkled above a flush deeper than her already rouged cheeks as she fidgeted with her chunky jeweled necklace.

"I'm sorry to hear of Armstrong's passing," he replied. "I had no idea you were visiting."

"Actually, I'm staying on in Pittsburgh."

Yes, there was definitely more to this story.

But she wouldn't hear it now.

Just behind her, Mother's chatting ended midsentence, causing Bertie to turn at whatever had surprised her.

Russell stood in the middle of the doorway, focused on Bertie. Before she could respond, he moved toward their party with two tidy, well-dressed boys at his side. There could hardly be a handsomer or more well-dressed man in the room. If Miss Oosterling was here, she'd likely faint to the floor.

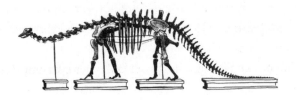

❧ *Chapter 17* ❧

*T*homas, careless of protocol, ran forward and threw his arms around Bertie's waist. "Miss Hart. Look at us."

"Thomas?" She stepped back to look his brother over as well. "Andrew. My goodness." They were adorable, but she knew enough not to say so. Andrew was a young man, the man of his family now.

"Mr. Smart took us to the top floor at the department store, and we could see the whole city!" Thomas announced.

Bertie locked gazes with Russell. "And now a visit to the most wonderful place in Pittsburgh."

Russell stood across from her. "Mrs. MacCormack allowed me their company. Her sister is there now, and this will give them time to talk." He nodded and bowed to her parents. "Good evening, sir. Mrs. Hart. These are my guests, Master Andrew MacCormack, and his brother, Master Thomas."

Aunt Aurelius made further introductions. "Mr. Raymond, this is my ward, Mr. Russell Smart."

"From Edinburgh. Yes, I've heard of him already. He reached to shake Russell's hand. "My pleasure to finally meet you, young man."

Aurelius took Russell's hand, patting it affectionately. "The day Russell came to live with us was the most joyous of our marriage. Armstrong would be so proud of him."

Surely no one could miss the dampness in her eyes, but Russell stared at her. "Thank you, ma'am." He cleared his throat and smoothed his tie and lapels, his glance sweeping back to Bertie. "I promised to show these two around. There's a surprise in store tonight." He turned to Bertie's mother. "I hope you forgive our disappearing so soon, ma'am," he said.

The boys froze in their perusal of the room, eyes and mouths wide as they exchanged delighted glances. "A surprise? What is it, sir?"

"Have patience." He turned back to Bertie, glancing at Auntie and Mr. Raymond, who'd quietly stepped aside in quiet conversation. "The young gentlemen here have asked if you might join us, Miss Hart."

Bertie glanced at her father. He was frowning but gave the slightest nod. She returned it, wondering when she would stop turning to him for his permission. After all, she rarely obeyed. "I'd be glad to, Mr. Smart. Very much so."

She took Thomas's hand and placed her other on Russell's arm. Andrew walked a step behind, already chatting with excitement.

"Wait up, Roberta."

Couldn't Father let her have this one night to enjoy? She appealed to Russell. "Shall we go on?"

But he wasn't moving.

"Roberta. I need to speak with Russell. This shouldn't take long."

No doubt. But she wouldn't allow it. "No, absolutely not. What can't you say in front of me?"

Father sighed. "Very well. You'll find out soon enough."

Her shoulders dropped as all the possibilities spun like a top in her chest.

Russell's eyes closed in resignation before they reopened with resolve and a lift of his chin.

She placed her gloved hand on Thomas's back. This was her world after all, standing between someone like Tiberius Hart and a boy from the Minersville neighborhood. This was where she wanted to be, with Russell at her side.

"It has come to my attention, as I was speaking to Mr. Thompson—"

"The finance officer?" she asked.

"Yes. You can't be surprised that I would look into things here and. . ." He refocused on Russell.

"Me," supplied Russell. "As I'd be working closely with your daughter."

"That's right."

"Father, how could you?"

"When you have children of your own, you'll understand."

"That doesn't give you the right— But I'm—" *No longer going to work here.* But what if Father blurted it out? She hadn't even told Russell. She'd begged for the job then threw it aside. Proving once again his earliest assessment.

"Roberta? Let me finish. Russell is a rather modern young man, you know. He told me that he didn't understand why you, as my daughter and only heir, had to be married to serve on the board. Quite capable, he called you. He understands that the board only wants to see where the future of the company might lie."

She bit back further replies. She must catch her breath, or this far-too-snug corset would make a fool of her when she slumped to the marble floor.

"Now, Russell," continued Father in his usual imperious manner, "I've learned this so-called assistant director position was not part of the business plan. But you insisted it be added."

"I did."

Father's hands settled on his hips. "So you could work with my daughter?"

Russell glanced her way, smiling. "Indeed. After taking the position myself, I realized that I was wrong not to give it to her. I was too quick to judge."

"And?"

"And so I offered her a position. No one can deny her knowledge. And no one could have a more caring heart, nor fight harder for the children of Pittsburgh."

"Please. Not here." Bertie wanted to drag Father away, but both men ignored her, eyes locked on one another.

"And your opinion of her? Personal interest?"

Bertie turned away, wishing the boys had run ahead.

"I must be honest sir. She's. . .hard to describe."

And holding her breath.

"She's a rare woman."

Father thumped Russell's back. "I'm glad you noticed. You know, when I first met you, I thought you too ambitious to think of anyone but yourself. Aurelius bragged of your accomplishments at university. And, handpicked by Carnegie? That's quite impressive."

Russell barely blinked.

Bertie grabbed her father's arm. "Enough, Father. These boys are eager to go."

He turned to her, calm as could be.

She wanted to shout, rip off her long evening gloves, and flail him about the head until he was out the door!

"I need to ask about your pay, Bertie. Be patient."

Well, this would be the end indeed. "This is not the place."

"Miss Hart," Thomas cried out. "You're squeezing my fingers!"

"Oh. Sorry."

Father had no mercy. "Do you know why your pay is so low?"

She stepped squarely in front of him, so she could shout in a whisper, begging him to quit this foolishness. "Because the assistant director position was not in the budget. I could continue to volunteer. I'm afraid it was the recognition I wanted."

"Well, money means something. Look at these boys."

Mother's hand on her shoulder brought her back to her senses. "I'm quite aware."

"And are you also aware that Russell is paying your salary out of his until the board approves your position?"

"What?" She stared at Russell, not that he was looking at anything but the marble floor.

"Well," Father added. "That doesn't matter now, does it, Roberta?"

That was it then. The night ruined. Her head dropped just as Russell's came up.

"What do you mean, sir?" Receiving only raised brows as Father's answer, he turned to Bertie. "What is he talking about?"

But she couldn't utter a word. She'd complained to him about her pay, and here he was covering it out of his own wages. And now she was leaving him without the help she'd promised.

Russell tried again. "Sir?"

Father's gaze singled her out. "I think you owe Russell an explanation. Though," he added, "I'm curious if you've yet to actually work an hour under his supervision."

Aunt Aurelius tittered. Anyone not already staring turned their way.

With a nervous chuckle, Russell shook his head. "Not that I recall."

Both he and Father watched her in anticipation. She breathed in, preparing to explain herself.

"Wait," Russell said. "I know. It's my fault. I owe you an apology."

"No, that's not it. I'm going to resign."

Russell froze long enough to be noticed before he tipped forward, his eyes widening. "Because of—" He didn't finish, but his hand went to his chest before he glanced at Father, and then Mother.

This was getting worse by the second.

"Can we go now?" Thomas tugged at her hand.

But Russell. His face. His eyes. . . "No. Please don't leave on my account, Roberta."

"You don't understand. I've accepted another position." Bertie nodded toward her aunt and Mr. Raymond. "I'll be working as an adviser for the board of education."

Russell stepped closer, disregarding the family crowding around them.

His eyes were full of disappointment. "When were you going to tell me?"

Her fingers twisted together against her bodice. "Tonight?"

Thomas gave a firm pull on Bertie's hand. "Mr. Smart, when can we go see the dinosaurs?"

Father waved them on. "Go on, and enjoy the evening. All of you. Roberta, I'm very proud of you, and I trust your decisions." He reached for Russell's hand. "And thank you, Russell. I'm proud to have you here as part of our family."

Bertie gasped.

Mother nudged her, looking at Russell. "We'd like to see you at the house more often. Certainly for dinners."

Pleased—well, shocked—as she was, she also knew tomorrow was not at all good for dinner guests. Henry expected to bring his parents for their long-delayed meeting. "But not tomorrow!"

They all studied her.

"Thank you, ma'am, I believe I'm available at your request." Russell chuckled. "Just not tomorrow." He bowed to Mother and then offered his elbow to Bertie. "Miss Hart. Shall we begin?"

Yes. Absolutely. "You're not going anywhere without me now." At that, the boys hurried them on. Her parents' strange behavior had put thoughts of the previously mentioned surprise out of her mind. Not so the MacCormack brothers. Still chattering about the upcoming surprise, they practically dragged her and Russell through the crowds. "Isn't it funny?" Thomas asked. "Hart and Smart. You could put them together and be Miss Hart Smart."

She eyed Russell. Or *Mrs.* Hart Smart. . .

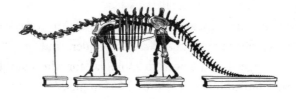

Chapter 18

There was so much here she wanted to see, but not right now. "I think we'll need to return, Mr. Smart. On a much quieter day."

His hand slipped over hers. "I don't understand what just happened back there, but do you suppose we could go for a walk the next time you come to work? Or should I say, come to resign?"

She wanted to lean against his arm for comfort. "I made such a fuss, and now here I am resigning. Are you still convinced there's too much between us?"

"There is, but it's all for the good. Do you suppose we might find ourselves—"

Thomas pulled on his arm. "Come on. Look at that!"

He waved them on. "Go on, lads. But walk, eh? No running!"

Bertie flinched as Thomas raced past a bejeweled matron. Spying a place along the rail, she and Russell took it and stared up at the fossil bones, then managed to stare at each other.

"I've been trying so hard to prove I was no longer that boy. But I failed."

"No, Russell. Don't say that."

"I mean, I am that boy, and I'm not ashamed. I'm today's version of him, and I'm satisfied with that. Tell me you understand."

"I do. I no longer feel the need to apologize for who I am. Especially to myself." She studied his face. "I think my parents. . ."

"I do too. I don't know how it happened, but. . ." He smiled.

"You've settled in, lad?"

They both turned at the question, as much for the kindness in it as the light resemblance to Russell's accent.

Russell stood at attention. "Mr. Carnegie. Sir. Yes. Thank you. It's an honor to be part of this."

"I'm pleased you're here."

The man's white hair and beard emphasized the cheery blue eyes that settled on her.

"This is Miss Roberta Hart."

"Of course. I know your father."

"She has been volunteering in the library and has now taken a new role with the city's schools."

"That's quite a lot on your plate, Miss Hart. In fact. . ." His brows furrowed. "I've heard about that, and I applaud the new committee. Your name is hard to forget."

"I—I don't understand," she stammered.

"Miss Hart. With a heart for the children. I applaud your efforts, both of you. And wish you well."

"Did you see that other one, mister?" Thomas asked, tugging on the sleeve of the wealthiest man in the world.

His eyes sparkled above a broad grin. "They're fascinating, I agree. Why don't you show me your favorite, young man."

"Be patient, Thomas," admonished Bertie.

Mr. Carnegie looked down at the boy. "That was my brother's name."

"And I'm Andrew. We were named after someone famous."

Mr. Carnegie chuckled and waved them forward. Thomas barely controlled his pace, chattering as Andrew and Mr. Carnegie, cane and hat in hand, followed.

Bertie wondered what else could happen tonight. As the crowd noise grew, she moved closer to Russell. "What's the surprise you mentioned? Was that it?"

"No, I had no idea he'd even recognize me. The surprise is for Andrew. Mr. Bolton is willing to take him on here as a page."

"Paid to work here?"

Russell's face brightened even more. "Yes. He'll like that, no?"

"Oh, that's wonderful, Russell."

He offered his arm. "Let's go tell him, and rescue Mr. Carnegie in the process."

Curious to see how much sweeter the evening could be, Bertie accepted Aunt Aurelius and Russell's offer to join them in their hired carriage. After dropping the exhausted MacCormack boys at their home, Aunt Aurelius showed similar signs as her head lolled softly in her hand, her pearled tiara tapping against the carriage's window with each rocking movement.

"I'm truly pleased for you, Roberta," Russell said, just above a whisper. "The city board has made a wise choice."

"I hope so. I'll really have to prove myself." She huffed at his skeptical smile. "It's true! Just to prove it's not a mistake to hire a woman. You'd agree?"

"Let's not delve into that. I admitted I was wrong."

She grinned. "I'm not sure I recall. Maybe I need to hear it again."

Russell laughed. "I do apologize for making assumptions. It does no one any good." He leaned forward. "You forgive me?"

"Of course. I am guilty of the same. I took your well-founded misgivings as an affront."

"You'd worked so hard, and I had no idea. And your pay? The truth is, we couldn't pay you what you're really worth to us."

"To us?"

He glanced at her aunt. "Maybe it's best we don't work together. In the end."

"And here I thought you were beginning to tolerate, even enjoy, my company, Mr. Smart."

He chuckled, looking down as he shook his head.

"I will be making a better income. I insisted on it."

He slowly raised his head to meet her gaze. "Oh, I'm sure you did."

This was it then. She had to know. "Henry planned on telling his parents tomorrow that he has decided to leave the newspaper and join the company full time. But not as my husband."

"I'm sorry he's had to do something he'd fought against."

"He's met someone, and well, let's just say he could hardly approach her father on a junior reporter's salary."

"He will be much more able to help the less fortunate. That counts for something."

"Yes. It does. I have the feeling my parents heard the news as well." Her chest felt full of buzzing bees. Like she'd eaten too much divinity. Bertie reached out, her white gloves almost glowing in the dark interior. When his hand met hers, she had to try. "Sit with me?"

He shook his head. "I might sneeze and wake her."

"I've stopped wearing that fragrance. Hadn't you noticed?" She waved him closer. He crossed to join her but kept a respectable distance. "My parents' marriage was arranged for them, but that ended with me. It's over, Russell." She heard him take a deep breath.

He cleared his throat. "I expect suitors will line up when this news is out."

"In that case, I need your help. Your administrative help."

"You want me to interview them?"

"That's not what I had in mind."

❧ Chapter 19 ❧

She couldn't just kiss him, could she? He already thought she was pushy, far too modern, and at times, irresponsible. "Russell. You are good at knowing how people work together. Where each person will make the best fit in any group of employees. And in partnerships." She moved closer. The Victoria cameo shifted against her throat where she'd pinned it on a ribbon.

She was a rule breaker, much like her cousins who'd worn this cameo before her. Great-Aunt Letitia's niece Clara had chased down ruthless criminals to protect her family. Elizabeth had become a Pinkerton agent! And Petra. . . Heavens! Petra, who'd managed to be known as Buckskin Pete, was a rawhide-wearing, tomahawk-tossing wonder of the West and worthy of being written into dime novels. It was a miracle the cameo made it to Bertie's neck after all her family's adventures.

Yes, she too was a rule breaker. Russell Smart, with all his conservative ways was not. What would she have to do to get him to even ask to court her?

She had an idea that involved staring at his mouth.

He leaned in with intent. "This, Roberta, is why it's best we don't work together at the library."

The scent of his soap and the thrill of having him this close made it hard to breathe.

As she reached to touch his face, he caught her hand and kissed the back of her glove. The sky opened, and in the pale glow of a rare show of moonlight, she placed her free hand against his cheek.

She had never kissed anyone before. Not since, well, Henry had suggested it before their Christmas pageant. At age ten she'd found it hard to believe anyone would do such a thing, but maybe by the time they were old. . .

That said, she lifted her face to his and shut her eyes. A mistake, aiming in the dark, but after a breathy, nervous laugh from each, Russell's mouth found hers and the attempt seemed to be working.

It was working quite well indeed.

Before she knew it, she'd slipped her hand on his neck and shifted closer to him. His mouth left hers, trailing light touches across her cheek. He wasn't quitting already, was he?

No.

"Roberta?" he whispered near her ear. "Are you sure?"

Goose bumps danced up her neck. "Yes." Whatever it was. Yes.

He pulled back enough to look at her, but he was little more than a dark shadow and eyes reflecting moonlight. He kissed her again, his fingers tracing the line of her jaw. The softness of his touch matched the tenderness of his mouth, and she once again breathed in the scent of his shaving soap.

It was delightful, and she wanted to do it again. She did.

This time aware of every hint of a whisker and. . .his quick intake of breath.

"Roberta!" cried Aunt Aurelius. "Your reputation!"

Russell scrambled back so fast, he landed on Auntie's feet. Her howling was part discomfort, part laughter. "When your father hears of this, he'll insist you two become engaged."

Bertie struggled to catch her breath. Aunt Aurelius's amusement filled the carriage's interior and shook it.

"It's not funny. I can't believe you did that," Russell complained, crawling up to regain a seat. "Did you hear everything we said?"

Bertie couldn't help but giggle.

Russell straightened his tie. "Mr. Hart will say we hardly know each other."

Her aunt's laughter was contagious. "Enough to kiss, though? Russell Smart, I never took you for a rogue."

Bertie's mouth flew open. "He's a perfect gentleman. It's my fault. I wanted him to kiss me. Please, Auntie. Don't make things worse."

"Worse? Your parents already know you and Henry will remain nothing more than friends. How do you explain the way your father acted tonight? He's tired of fighting your independent spirit, young lady, and Russell is the perfect match for you."

Russell appeared stunned. "But ma'am, I can't ask Roberta to leave her parents for what I can offer."

"Love? That's not enough?"

"No. Not on my wage."

Bertie stopped looking from one to the other. "Wait. I'll be working too, Russell. Don't forget."

He sat back hard. "This is—"

"Don't be so hasty, Russell," Aunt Aurelius warned. "Whether it's in the home or away, it will be a partnership. I believe the scriptures say two are better than one, because they have good reward for their labor."

Russell looked from Aunt Aurelius back to Bertie. He then reached behind and pulled his new top hat out to examine. Ruined.

"I'd like a chance, Russell. I think it makes perfect sense, but if you don't, this will go no further than the doors of this carriage." With her fingers on the cameo at her throat, Bertie stared hard at her aunt. "Isn't that right, Aunt?"

Her aunt took Russell's hand. "Have you never wondered what will become of Armstrong's money when I'm gone? Why I've come home? Do you think you'd have nothing to show for all the years of happiness you brought us?"

"What I've done for you? I don't understand."

"No, you wouldn't." She turned to face Bertie. "A fair portion of your uncle Armstrong's money is already in trust for Russell. I feared he wouldn't accept it. What's left when I'm gone will also go to him. More than enough to live comfortably. And he's already a treasured employee of Carnegie Corporation. Handpicked. Now, can you tell him why he should not feel fit to provide a home for a wife?"

Russell took hold of Aunt Aurelius's shoulder. "Ma'am. Consider what you're saying."

"You deny it?"

He wasn't going to answer.

The silence ran on.

Bertie held her breath until he moved, crossing again to sit at her side.

"No, I can't deny it. Roberta Hart, may I ask your father for the privilege to court you? Quietly. I mean quietly court. I promise to speak clearly on this subject." Grinning, he studied her for a moment. "I have too long put you far above me because of my early life. But as your pastor reminded us, we are not constrained by our pasts. We are valued, not only for what we are now, but also because we are beloved of Christ. As such, I intend to do my best to be your equal, your partner."

When she couldn't speak, he turned to Aunt Aurelius. "You allowed me to see a marriage of respect, affection, and partnership, ma'am. Thank you."

"I miss him so. Despite our difficult start."

Bertie studied her aunt's face. "I can't believe it. You were always laughing."

"Because we were friends first. Like you and Henry. But I was in love with someone else. Someone completely inappropriate for my father's approval."

"Mr. Raymond?"

Aunt Aurelius sighed. "Was it so obvious?"

"You were flirting like a debutante, and he had eyes for no one but you."

"I have no regrets, Bertie, and I could not think of a better man for my favorite niece than my very own Russell."

"Thank you, ma'am," Russell replied, his voice scratchy with emotion.

"Now, can you at least sit closer together? We'll be there in two blocks!"

Bertie delighted in the warmth of his hand holding hers. She fingered the Victoria cameo, knowing its appearance on her today would someday be a lovely story to share with their children.

Author's Note

While I would have loved to spend another few months researching this setting, the truth is that fact will always be fictionalized in a story such as this. I've used as many true references to the Pittsburgh of November 1895 as I could find, and created the rest. Any errors in authenticity are mine and not the library's! I also recommend the University of Pittsburgh's history website, Historic Pittsburgh (historicpittsburgh.org), for its wealth of maps, directories, photos, and every manner of document. Truly an author's dream resource, short of a time machine! As for Mr. Carnegie, a true rags-to-riches story of America, Pittsburgh hasn't forgotten his mark on the city, including the Homestead Riots. Carnegie went on to be a legendary philanthropist and worked tirelessly in his later years to prevent war in Europe. But he's just one part of a complex city's history.

During my recent visit, I fell in love with both the smoky, Gilded Age Pittsburgh and its vital modern version. Visit, and you'll see why for yourself!

DEBRA E. MARVIN tries not to run too far from real life, but the imagination born out of being an only child has a powerful draw. Besides, the voices in her head tend to agree with all the sensible things she says. She is a member of American Christian Fiction Writers and Sisters in Crime, and she serves on the board of Bridges Ministry in Seneca Falls, New York. She is published with Barbour Publishing, WhiteFire Publishing, Forget Me Not Romances, and Journey Fiction, and has been a judge for the Grace Awards for many years. Debra works as a program assistant at Cornell University and enjoys her family and grandchildren, obsessively buying fabric, watching British programming, and traveling with her childhood friends. Learn more at http://debraemarvin.com/.

Epilogue

by Susanne Dietze

The Breaux House, Pittsburgh
1898

Byron Breaux!" Clara Breaux fisted her hands on her hips in mock horror. "If you track mud into my clean house again, you'll be the one with the mop."

"Yes, ma'am. We'll be good." He winked at his wife before letting the screen door slam behind him. "Who's ready for baseball?"

A chorus of children's squeals carried inside from the wide green yard. Through the window, Clara watched as a horde of children clamored to play, gathering around her husband. He'd never allowed the limp he sustained in the Civil War to keep him from engaging with the children, although she knew his old wound caused him pain. No one would ever guess he suffered still, the way he smiled at the young ones, from the littlest of the brood, like her niece Elizabeth Butler's boys Evan, Joe, and Solomon, to bigger girls and boys like her grandson Tibby Owens. Then again, even grown men like Tibby's married brother, Sam, jogged to join the game, as did Elizabeth's husband Ethan, Clara's son-in-law Dustin Owens, Clara's brother Wallace, and one of the newest members of the family, Russell Smart, husband to cousin Bertie. A few of Clara's daughters-in-law hurried to play too. Every face was smiling, and everyone seemed to be enjoying the summer sunshine and each other's company.

Her heart was full. *Thank You for my family, Lord.*

Smiling, she rejoined the group of ladies gathered in the parlor. "I think they'll do more sliding and jumping out there than playing actual ball."

"I hope that means my boys will sleep well tonight," Elizabeth said with a chuckle. "They have more stamina than I do."

"This little one has plenty of stamina too." Bertie tucked the corner of the white crocheted blanket over her newborn daughter, Victoria Mary Smart, as the child slept in the arms of her great-aunt Letitia. "You wouldn't believe it right now, as soundly as she's sleeping."

Taking a seat, Petra adjusted the rustling silk of her skirt and grinned. "Oh, we'd believe it. My four never wanted to sleep."

"We sleep now, Mama." Seventeen-year-old Letty looked up from the baby's sweet face.

"Some of us even snore," Letty's twenty-one-year-old sister, Mollie Jo, joked. "Not you, Letty. I meant the boys."

And perhaps Bertie's Aunt Aurelius, who napped in a nearby chair, breathing heavily.

Clara kissed Mollie Jo's blond curls. "You girls were as pretty as baby Victoria is."

"She is a pretty one, isn't she?" Aunt Letitia smiled down at the newest member of the family, and her fingers smoothed the dark fuzz atop the baby's head.

She might be over eighty, but Auntie's health and spirits were as vibrant as ever. Clara patted her dear aunt—her closest friend—on the shoulder, grateful they could all be together again for a family reunion. They seldom had opportunity to share fellowship now that family members were spread to Colorado, Chicago and, soon, Washington DC, where Bertie and Russell would oversee the Carnegie Library.

Perhaps Bertie was thinking the same thing. Her beautiful brown eyes misted as she gazed at each woman in turn, no doubt wondering how long it would be before they were together again.

Mollie Jo glanced at the blue agate cameo pinned to Bertie's blouse before returning her devoted gaze to the baby. "I wonder if this little one will wear the cameo someday."

"Or if someone else will receive it first," Elizabeth mused.

Letty's brows rose. "Like who?"

"I have an idea." Bertie's gaze fixed on Mollie Jo. "Someone I love. Someone whom I think God wishes me to give it to. You, Mollie Jo."

For a minute, the only sounds were the baby's snuffling snores and the whooping in the yard.

Mollie Jo's lips parted. "Me?"

"If it's all right with your mother."

Petra nodded. "I think it's time."

Mollie Jo's hand flew to her chest. "Really?"

Clara twirled one of Mollie Jo's blond curls around her finger. "When Aunt Letitia gave me the cameo, she said it was a symbol of her support and love, once I'd come of age."

"And when I received it from Queen Victoria, she said the cameo often accompanies adventure." Aunt Letitia's gaze was on baby Victoria, but she was clearly seeing something else, something from the past, like her early days with Uncle Peter. "It was true for me."

"Me too." Elizabeth smiled. "The cameo has certainly seen its share of adventure. Hasn't it, *Buckskin Pete*?"

Petra's cheeks flamed, and her eyes narrowed playfully. "I'll have you know, I haven't been called Pete in a very long time."

The room erupted with laughter.

With steady fingers, Bertie unpinned the cameo from her blouse. "I know you've heard the story, but Queen Victoria said one never *owns* a cameo. One wears it," she said, pinning it near Mollie's collarbone. "One enjoys it, but one is merely a custodian of it, preserving it and protecting it for those who come after."

Mollie Jo's fingers covered the cameo. "Are you sure I should— I mean, thank you."

The previous caretakers of the cameo shared conspiratorial smiles.

Clara pulled Letty close, breathing in her sweet soapy smell. "It might come your way next."

"It might," Letty agreed. "If God wants it to."

Clara looked at each of her relatives in turn. Letitia. Petra and her girls. Elizabeth. Bertie and Aunt Aurelius and baby Victoria. And from outside, the shouts and laughter of everyone else Clara loved carried through the windows.

God bless our family and the adventures You bestow.

She could never have asked for a greater gift than this.